Downfall

Dr. Mohsen El-Guindy

Copyright @2021 by Dr. Mohsen El-Guindy

This publication contains the opinions and ideas of its author. It is intended to provide helpful and informative material on the subjects addressed in the publication. The author and publisher specifically disclaim all responsibility for any liability, loss or risk, personal or otherwise, which is incurred as a consequence, directly or indirectly, of the use and application of any of the contents of this book.

WORKBOOK PRESS LLC
187 E Warm Springs Rd,
Suite B285, Las Vegas, NV 89119, USA

Website: https://workbookpress.com/
Hotline: 1-888-818-4856
Email: admin@workbookpress.com

Ordering Information:
Quantity sales. Special discounts are available on quantity purchases by corporations, associations, and others.
For details, contact the publisher at the address above.

Library of Congress Control Number:
ISBN-13:   978-1-956017-39-7 (Paperback Version)

                 978-1-956017-40-3 (Digital Version)

REV. DATE: 20/08/2021

DOWNFALL
DR. MOHSEN EL-GUINDY
WORKBOOK PRESS
RECOMMENDED

CHAPTER 1

Operation Bright Star is a series of biennial combined and joint training exercises led by American and Egyptian forces.

Omar Abdel Aziz, the deputy commander of the Egyptian Special Forces, participated with his battalion in Bright Star 1994 and 1996.

It was in Bright Star 1996 that Omar knew Colonel Kenny Walker, commander of the American Special Forces. The operations of this Bright Star included landing on the Egyptian coast, air operations, and surface-to-surface engagements, rescue, and data sharing. Omar was watching the operations of his troops from a Gazelle light observation helicopter, while Walker, with twelve soldiers on board in a UH-60 Black Hawk helicopter, was practicing rescues.

The two choppers were only five hundred metres apart, and Omar could see Walker's helicopter plainly. Just before the soldiers were to descend to a mock-up of a downed helicopter and rescue soldiers pretending to be injured, Walker's helicopter plunged into quicksand. The chopper burned up and began to sink slowly into the sand. Omar quickly instructed his pilot to descend the chopper as close to Walker's helicopter wreck as it could. Omar tied a rope around his waist and hung down from the chopper. Omar could see the pilot crushed and dead against the instrument panel. The soldiers had been burned to death and thrown out of the chopper. Walker, still strapped in his seat, was also thrown out of the chopper. He suffered burns on his hands and buttocks and had his pants burned off. His left wrist and left collarbone were broken, and he lost two upper teeth.

Walker was nearly unconscious and the quicksand began to swallow the blackened corpses and the chopper wreck. Hanging by a rope, Omar attempted to free Walker by trying to unbuckle his seat belt, but he was unable to. With a sharp blade, Omar freed Walker by cutting his seat belt, then wrapped Walker with the rest of the rope and with an enormous effort pulled him out of the seat. The chopper flew for twenty minutes to reach the airbase, during which it took all of Omar's strength to keep Walker and himself from falling. In the airbase, Walker received first aid and then was transported to an Egyptian military hospital to take care of his burns and broken bones.

As an appreciation for his heroic action in saving Colonel Kenny Walker's life in Bright Star 1996, Omar's special force department received in 1997 an official invitation letter from the United States Department of Defense, inviting Omar to visit the United States Military Academy at West Point and the Naval Academy at Annapolis, Maryland. Colonel Kenny Walker was appointed by his department to keep company with Omar during his stay in America. Walker was the same age as Omar and the son of a general; the army was in his bloodstream.

Walker lived in Maryland in an elegant house. He willingly offered to let Omar stay in his house during his short visit to America. At first, Omar insisted on living alone in a motel in order not to interfere in Walker's private life, but at Walker's insistence, Omar had to accept the generous offer. Omar was to live in the guest room located on the first floor; Walker and his wife occupied the second floor. Omar stayed in America for one month, during which his friendship with Walker became firm and close.

When Omar first arrived in America, Walker welcomed him warmly at the airport and then drove him directly to his house. After a light knock on the door, Jennifer Jones opened the door to see Omar and Walker standing on the doorstep. She smiled at Walker, then shook hands with Omar, and led him to the guest room. The room was large and comfortable and attached to a sizable bathroom. When Omar thanked Jennifer for her kindness, she smiled, saying that she would be happy to host a friend who had saved the life of the man she truly loved.

Jennifer was a tall, slender woman, with long black hair and wide blue eyes. Her white skin, perfect body, and soft musical voice enhanced her beauty more. She was an independent American woman working as an executive manager in a company that developed computer systems. Omar realized that Walker had good taste in women. Jennifer was certainly a good match for Walker. Omar thought that Jennifer and Walker were newly married since no kids were around.

At lunchtime, Jennifer prepared a wonderful table with baked ham, rice, fried potatoes, salad, and a bottle of good red wine. According to Islamic law, liquor and pork were prohibited, and accordingly Omar abstained from eating ham or drinking wine. He did not even touch the rice, fearing it might have been cooked with pork butter. Omar only ate salad.

Jennifer was annoyed to see that her effort in preparing a good meal for Omar was in vain. Disappointment showed on her face. Omar noticed Jennifer's upset and was utterly embarrassed.

"You don't like American food, I suppose?" Jennifer asked politely, not wanting to hurt Omar's feelings.

Omar explained, "Sorry, Jennifer, but pork and wine are prohibited in Islam. In the Holy Koran, it is the divine will of Allah that pig should not be eaten and wine should not be touched."

Jennifer commented, "In the United States, we have inspection and governmental seals on pork to make it safe for people to eat. The pork we have here on the table is not raw meat; it was cured before I cooked it for you. I am afraid I don't understand why Islam is against pork."

"Pork is often referred to as 'cured'. If pork has to be cured before we eat it, then we should not take the chance of eating it. You are what you eat, so why not eat the best? Do not allow this diseased meat to be brought into your home."

Omar's words were like a slap on the face to Jennifer. She'd done her best to prepare the best meal she could for him, yet he rejected her food without any logical reason. She did not want to embarrass Walker by arguing more with Omar, but she just couldn't stop herself.

"I am not a religious woman, and I don't base facts on religion. Science is what we must rely on. There is nothing wrong with the hog. The pig was made for human consumption. All parts of it, including its by-products have been a primary food for Americans. Veterinarians, public health officials, and the agricultural department say that thorough and slow cooking removes any danger found in pork. Additional cooking of pork purchased in the summer or processed pork products makes the pork safe for eating."

"Since you rely only on science in your judgements, I will add to your information some facts about pork. The swine eats until it is sick and has to lie down, but as soon as it finds a vacancy in its stomach, it eats more food. It does not matter what kind of food it may be; the swine eats anything. The swine's life is very short because it eats itself to death, and death soon takes its life away."

"So what," Jennifer said. "There is nothing wrong with that."

"The pig is a mass of worms. Each mouthful you eat is a mass of small worms the naked eye cannot detect. Worms thrive in the hog. When these worms are digested into your system, they cause a high birth rate of hundreds of new worms, which travel the bloodstream of your system and lodge in your muscles. These worms even enter your brain, lungs, or your spinal fluid. They cause muscular aches, fever, and many other symptoms of sickness. The worm has an amazing ability to go undetected in your system for many years. Thorough and slow cooking of pork does not remove the danger of worms found in all pork. Inspection and governmental seals on pork do not remove such danger. In the Bible, Moses forbade the children of Israel from eating the swine: 'Thou shall not eat the swine, nor touch its carcass.' Strict Orthodox Jews do not eat pork, so their food is good for Muslims and our food is good for them."

Omar added, "Pork is not forbidden to Muslims only. The Jews and the Christians are also forbidden from eating pork. Here is a quote from the Old Testament to that effect: 'And the swine, because it divideth the hoof, yet cheweth not the cud, it is unclean unto you: Ye shall not eat of their flesh, nor touch their dead carcass.' That's from Deuteronomy 14:8. Many Christians believe that this verse was directed only to the Jews. But Jesus himself said during the Sermon on the Mount, 'Think not that I have come to destroy the Law, or the Prophets. I have not come to destroy, but to fulfil.'

Omar's justification for swine forbiddance seemed convincing to Jennifer; however, her fighting spirit pushed her to ask him more about what else was forbidden in Islam. Jennifer pointed at the bottle of red wine and said, "And why does Islam forbid wine too?"

"Islam prohibits intoxicants because of the potential effect they have on the human intellect, the human faculty of reasoning, and the human conscious. Numerous diseases have been attributed to alcohol, like dyspeptic trouble, peptic ulceration, cancer of the stomach, pancreatitis, cirrhosis of the liver, vitamin deficiency, and coronary heart disease. It is a shameful retreat from reality and an irresponsible insult to the human mind to be entangled in the tight strands of intoxication or cornered in the vicious whirl of alcohol. Islam banned alcohol fourteen centuries ago among people whose love for alcohol was second to none. Islam has declared alcohol to be the root of all evil, and no power on earth can change that designation."

"I heard that Islam forbids gambling too."

"Yes, it does. Gambling is an old evil. Gambling is denounced in the Hindu code, the Koran, and the Talmudic law. Aristotle denounced gamblers."

Jennifer glanced at Walker, who was listening to the conversation while voraciously eating a large portion of pork. She then turned her head to Omar and said ironically, "It is evident, then, that nearly all the dishes on my table are unlawful to you. In this house, we drink wine and eat pork. Walker and his friends gather here twice a week to play poker with good money. You Muslims are living a dry life devoid of enjoyments."

"Muslims live on earth only to serve Allah. Their road to this is by applying the Koranic instructions in their daily lives. The spreading of virtue among people is something worth living for. All the pleasures Muslims are deprived from while living their mortal lives on earth will be given to them more splendidly in heaven. In heaven, they will eat the desirable meat and drink the agreeable wine."

Jennifer continued her debate with Omar. "What was Allah's purpose of giving life, then? What's the purpose of this whole existence if we don't enjoy the amenities of life to the fullest? Have you ever heard about the American dream? It is achieving wealth and power in all fields. The Americans made their dream come true, and this is how America became the strongest nation in the world."

"Man's deeds in the hereafter are not judged by materialistic gains. Allah created the heavens and the earth, and created life and death for the purpose of testing human beings. The time and place of our births, the environments that surround us, the mental capabilities we have, and the opportunities that come our way are predestined for us. But Allah gave man the freedom to choose between right and wrong. This granted freedom is the very essence of the grand scheme of things, without which the whole existence becomes meaningless. If Allah had so wanted, He could have made all men follow the right path. But that would have meant that man was not given any freedom to choose. And without this freedom, the human soul could not have been tested. Reward or punishment would then have become meaningless. It was Allah's abounding mercy to give eternal life to man in the kingdom of heaven. With His absolute wisdom, Allah decided to make this eternal life conditional to man's behaviour in a temporary life subjected to Allah's laws relating to life and death. Those who cleanse their minds, bodies, and souls in the life of this world and follow the laws of their creator shall deserve the bliss of the eternal life in the kingdom of Allah. Those who ignore the call of their creator and live lives of arrogance, turning a deaf ear to the commands and interdictions of their creator, shall be put to a painful chastisement. Thus Allah is testing man on earth by giving him free will to choose between good and evil. The purpose is to select cleansed souls for paradise."

Jennifer looked at Omar for a long while and then said, "How could a nice-looking man like you abstain so easily from the pleasures of life?" She gave Walker a quick glance and then continued. "Most people are carried away by the thrills of life."

Omar replied, "For the sake of trial, Allah has sanctioned man's freedom on earth, and at the same time, He provided him with considerable liberty to choose between good and evil. Allah has prepared the paradise for those who volunteer to fear Allah, even on occasions when fearing is not seemingly warranted; those who despite wielding full authority surrender all their authority to Allah. They believe that it is Allah who provided them with sustenance — and not because of their skills or capabilities. They have the power to rule over others, but they live in modesty and humility. They spend their wealth in Allah's way and give without asking for anything in return. They have the power to be unfair to others, but they restrain themselves from hurting others for fear of Allah's punishment. When they are hit by calamities, they remain steadfast and are thankful when living in contentment and ease. They believe that the present life is a test after which every individual will be accountable to Allah for his deeds. These are the winners of paradise."

Walker, who hadn't uttered a word since the beginning of lunch, laughed happily at seeing Jennifer struggling with Omar to prove her point. He knew her like the back of his hand. Jennifer was a typical free independent American woman. She was proud of her American heritage. Like most Americans, she knew nothing about other cultures except her own. He even doubted whether she had ever heard about how Muslims think or look at life from its different angles.

Walker joined the Gulf War in 1991, and participated in two Bright Star war games performed in Egypt. Before going to Egypt, he was given special courses about Muslims and Islamic traditions. Yes, Muslims are different people. Their aim in life is to please Allah by abiding by his laws. They believe that this materialistic world is perishable and that what counts are the good deeds they have been ordered to do for themselves, for their families, and for others. To them, Allah is always there, looming on their horizon. They strive to seek his consent and forgiveness in the Day of Judgement. This is why good Muslims live their lives in strict straightforwardness. The free American life that he and Jennifer were living, a life of comfort and pleasure they both thought was most perfect, a strict Muslim like Omar could see as a big failure. Because Muslims combine materialism with spiritualism while crossing the road of life to the hereafter, they believe that money and power are not important goals in life. Allah's blessing to Muslims in the form of money or power is but a tool for enabling them to construct the world and inhabit the earth as their sacred Book told them, not to tyrannize or oppress others. This blessing is also a test. Would they use their money properly as Allah has ordered them to or would they use it to cause injustice and rise over others?

Muslims could easily fight and sacrifice themselves for a noble cause like defending their homeland against the enemy or defending their religion. They call this fight "jihad", which means fighting in the cause of Allah. In these wars, they seek martyrdom because the reward is to enter heaven and be close to the Almighty. It is false to say that Islam teaches its followers to resign meekly and passively to their fate of destiny. Rather, Islam challenges the believer to fight against wrongness and oppression and to strive for the establishment of righteousness and justice. In jihad, Muslims stand equal, rich and poor; both strive to die in the cause of Allah. Although Islam teaches its followers to be merciful and incline towards forgiveness even in time of war, it never teaches them to turn the other cheek. The concept of jihad is one of the highest concepts in Islam.

The term has at times been translated as "holy war"; however, this translation is incomplete, for jihad also means "struggling". It is a concept that places much emphasis on the struggle of oneself against the temptations of Satan by living righteously.

The Koran instructed that Islam was the last of religions, and that it was not only sent to the Arabs but also to the world at large. Muslims were ordered to spread Islam to the whole world. It was a divine message; it was jihad, so they fought in the cause of Allah to deliver His last message to the people until Islam reached the four corners of the world.

Muslims make themselves subservient to Allah with their own free will; they choose to remain constrained within the divinely ordained restrictions, despite enjoying the freedom to remain unrestricted.

Omar was one of those good Muslims; he spoke the words of Allah and applied them in his life. He was a wonderful soldier but also a man of Allah. Walker would never forget what Omar did for him. He still remembered the steely grasp of Omar holding him tight lest he should fall. Although he was nearly unconscious, he was aware all the time of the strong arm holding him firmly, the other holding the rope. He was like a helpless baby, unable to move or think. To him, that arm was like a navel string attaching a baby to life. In that critical instant of total desperation and helplessness, he had a tremendous love and gratefulness towards Omar. He suddenly realized the true meaning of devotion and loyalty – the meaning of love and giving without expecting anything in return. He was sure that Omar did that not because of courage but because he was urged on by his religion to help others, no matter what their religion or race.

After the end of the Bright Star war games and his return home, he never stopped writing to Omar, and Omar always answered back. Over the past few months, they grew to understand each other better and their friendship grew stronger.

Walker poured himself a glass of good red wine and frowned at the thought of forgetting to tell Jennifer about some Islamic traditions that might have helped her to cope with Omar. He should have told her that Islam forbids wine, pork, gambling, and something else that might extremely offend Omar: fornication. Oh God! What would happen if Omar knew that Jennifer was not his wife but his girlfriend? She had been living with him for five years now! Based on the Islamic ethics, Walker was committing adultery with Jennifer all those years. According to Islam, Walker had been committing four grievous sins in his house: pork, wine, gambling, and fornication. Omar was right to insist from the beginning that he should live alone in a motel. He should not have persuaded Omar to accept staying with him in his house!

After lunch, Jennifer collected the dishes and cleaned the table. Walker helped wash the dishes and started a conversation with her. "Don't talk deeply with Omar about the odds between his world and ours; let him fit easily into our life without feeling any difference."

"My father was a teacher. My attitudes came from him. He taught me from the earliest age to think for myself, pointing out that there are always other sides to the story. He taught me that before accepting any fact, I have to research it. There are many times in my life when I wished he had not taught me these things and that I could innocently accept information like others and just go on and be happy."

"Sometimes thinking, discernment, and intellect are more of a curse than a gift," Walker commented, laughing.

Jennifer continued seriously. "Perhaps by sharing the little I perceive and have learned with others, my thoughts might find their way to someone about to make a major mistake in our world and perhaps change his mind."

"I hope you are not bothered by Omar's confrontations." Walker said hopefully.

Jennifer said, teasing him, "Your friend looks strong and is very good-looking. He is also polite and highly knowledgeable. I have many questions in my mind about Islamic heritage, and I want to hear some answers from your friend. Don't worry, Walker. I'd like to have a person like Omar under my roof for a while."

CHAPTER 2

Walker was able to get a permit for Omar to visit the United States Naval Academy. In the academy, they visited the Armel-Leftwich Visitor Centre. They went on a walking tour and saw exhibits on midshipmen life and the Freedom 7 space capsule.

Omar and Walker were also granted permission to visit the USS *Abraham Lincoln*. Aboard the fantastic carrier, Omar and Walker, along with three thousand sailors, attended a show. The navy had brought singers and comedians to entertain the sailors. The show was thrilling. At the end of the show, all the entertainers gathered on the stage and sang "God Bless America". They then spent some time taking pictures and signing autographs with the crew before they prepared to depart the carrier.

A week later, Omar and Walker travelled to New York to visit the United States Military Academy at West Point.

Omar invested his days properly in America. To stay in shape, he alternated his mornings by exercising and bodybuilding in a well-equipped gymnasium and running for an hour at dawn in the empty parks.

Omar spent his evenings with Walker and Jennifer after their return from work. As time passed, Omar was able to understand the nature of Walker's life with Jennifer. Walker spent most of his time playing poker with three of his closest friends. They were heavy drinkers and heavy smokers. When drunk and the bet was high, they produced lots of noise and shouting. Omar hated such poker games and usually withdrew to his room or to the living room to watch TV.

In order not to leave Omar alone, Jennifer frequently joined him. She was always dressed in very short skirts, revealing her thighs and long legs, and open blouses, revealing a good part of her breasts. Nudity seemed to be everywhere in American society.

Timidity is one of the primary values of Islam. In a mixed gathering, both the Muslim men and women should wear clothing that adequately covers their private parts. Any garments that were revealing or that might arouse sexual thoughts in the minds of any members of the opposite sex in any way should be avoided.

When Jennifer sat close to Omar wearing clothes revealing a large part of her body, Omar's face would become redder than usual and he would listen to her with a blush. He never looked straight into her eyes but rather lowered his gaze to keep his mind clear of sexual thoughts.

To Jennifer, Omar was a peculiar human specimen – a man coming from backwardness and unable to cope with modern civilization. A man stuck in old traditions, hampering his intellect to adapt to the free world, but his beauty and strength, piety, and abstention from the temptations of life intrigued her tremendously. She was curious to show this perplexing puzzle who refrained from her food and dumbfounded her with excuses that he was nothing but a crushed remainder coming from decayed ages. She became curious about him, and her curiosity led her to search his room while he and Walker were visiting the Military Academy at West Point.

The moment she entered his room, she was faced by a strong odour of musk. This was the perfume he wore when praying. On a chair near his bed were a prayer mat and a chaplet. The Koran was carefully placed on the bedside table. It was not exactly a bedroom but a sanctuary where he took refuge away from the temptations of life. She even opened his cupboard and breathed the pleasant fragrance emanating from his suits; musk mingled with the scent of him.

Jennifer found herself comparing Walker and Omar. They were very different. Walker was living his life to the fullest, while Omar was living like a hermit, abiding by Islamic laws. Walker drank and smoked, while Omar prayed five times a day, and before each prayer, he performed ablution by cleansing himself with pure water. Although she loved Walker and they now lived together, she knew that on his endless military missions, he was cheating on her whenever he got the chance. However, these capricious relationships did not bother her so much because Walker always returned to her. No strong commitment was there to join them together forever. Since she'd graduated from the university, she'd lived for short periods with other men, and Walker had lived with other women. This was simpler, no obligations and no permanent ties.

While sitting with Omar watching TV, Jennifer addressed him, saying, "How do you feel about American TV programs?"

Omar said, frowning, "I feel like a stranger in America. I am in a world that is completely different from mine. What you people think is good, to us it is bad. What you think is liberal, to us it is wrong and unlawful. What you think is a modern lifestyle, to us it is backwardness and dangerous. To me, from the outside, America seems like a ripe apple, but on the inside, there are worms eating its pulp and kernel."

Jennifer said, "Explain more, please."

"I've been watching the TV for a while, and I was amazed at what I saw. It was as if I were watching a grievous comedy. Apostasy has become blatant, having no fear of exposure. Plain falsehood is being peddled. Moral depravity is sold on TV under the name of art and openness. Perversion prevails arrogantly and openly day and night. Violence, sexual images, and sex outside marriage are characteristics of today's American lifestyle. By watching television, children often learn that sex is casual, that it has no negative consequences, and that it's cool to have sex. Homosexuals are enormously extending in your community, thus threatening the country's morals. The normal creation of God has been changed by giving lesbians and homosexuals the right to live together and even marry each other and work in the army."

"We are a nation of freedom of choice, just as the Christian religion teaches that God allows us to make choices for ourselves," Jennifer responded. "I know of many young people who are virgins, university age and older, because that is a life of choice they have made for themselves. I know many families that are stable, loving, and caring, where the man loves his wife and cherishes her and the wife loves and cherishes the man. They raise their children in love and stay married to each other without other partners. I know many businesspeople who are honest, who take care of their customers and would never cheat anyone. I know many people who have never taken a drug, never had a drink of liquor or smoked a cigarette, or gambled. I know people who regularly give to the poor, work for the poor, help take care of the sick, help the homeless, mentor fatherless young people, and on and on. There are millions of very decent, very good people here in America, of every religion. Also in the Christian religion, we are taught that God will spare a nation if there is only one true good person residing there. I think we have more than one. What else don't you like in America?" Jennifer concluded earnestly.

"I don't like the way the priests preach their followers. I saw them preaching in a theatrical way, far from veneration. The priests with long hair spreading over their shoulders, casually dressed, were preaching with shallow words and singing and dancing with a jazz band in the background. It was not a dignified preaching but rather a musical show. I think that instead of guiding people, they lead them astray. The audience, however, seemed to believe them and looked impressed!"

Jennifer said, "The priests with long hair that you described are preachers, or pastors, or maybe ministers. These pastors are either of a Protestant denomination or they are their own creation. Many such churches exist across America. One man's philosophy becomes the whole teaching of the church. There is also a movement in Christianity called 'charismatic'. The charismatic Christians are very much involved with music during worship, especially with what they call Christian rock. I think people gravitate towards these church groups because they want an audience for their music. They change the lyrics to ideas about God, and all of a sudden, they are great Christians. Most churches are social clubs, and people want to have a good time at their social clubs."

"You have churches led by lesbian preachers," Omar said. "There are marriages performed in many churches between homosexuals of both sexes. Homosexual couples are allowed to adopt children in most states. Teenagers who are homosexual can bring homosexual partners to school dances."

"There is no discrimination allowed by the US government concerning homosexuals. The thought here is that homosexuals are not hurting anyone. They do not teach homosexuality to others, and they do not prey on young people. They are not paedophiles, as some Catholic priests are. Most are law-abiding, tax-paying, solid members of society, with only this difference in their sexual persuasion. Does Islam disallow homosexuality?"

"Islam and in fact virtually every other religion have condemned homosexuality as an evil act and abomination."

Jennifer said in a low voice as if whispering to herself, "The pendulum swims back and forth, and if now America is too far a certain way, the pendulum will swing back as people change their minds and their ways. Finally, the pendulum will stop in the middle ground – who knows when? Or perhaps America will be only a brief flash in the timeline of the universe, such as the fabled Atlantis – too much, too soon."

"Jennifer, could we meet halfway?" Omar asked hopefully.

Jennifer smiled at him and said, "We have already met halfway. Openly discussing these things, desiring to stretch a bridge between two cultures, is a halfway point, I think. But now will one of us throw the other off this bridge?"

CHAPTER 3

As it looked to Jennifer, Omar was lonesome and fearing coping with American society. She knew many girls who could easily tame this beautiful and traditional man. Maybe if she introduced Omar to one of them, he might remove this false mask of piety and show his true feelings towards women. A woman was the only creature who could easily make a man's virility flow like a running river.

While sitting before the TV one day, Jennifer looked straight in Omar's eyes and said, "I have a friend named Christine. She is decent and beautiful. I can introduce you to her if you like. You are a very attractive man, and she will be happy to give you company."

A blush spread over Omar's face, and he said quickly, "No, thanks. I am okay."

Jennifer said, trying to persuade him, "Man feels a longing for someone to share his joys and to keep him company in loneliness."

"In Islam, there is no sex outside marriage."

Jennifer said, annoyed, "Why should two people marry one another if the commitment is just as if the two were married? If two people love each other, then their bond is their love and commitment."

"Marriage is no longer sacred when women sleep with men without commitment. Woman's most intimate secret places have been violated.

A woman's purity, the most beautiful thing in her, has long since vanished. In Western societies, women are like a piece of paper torn into shreds by her numerous lovers. Each took away a piece of her purity. The scrap that is left does not entice man to marry. Sex without marriage is a clear injustice to women. Our religion considers sex without marriage fornication."

"Your thoughts about life are rather old-fashioned," she replied. "I don't think marriage is so important in our modern lives."

Omar said, "Allah has created men and women as company for one another so that they can procreate and live in peace and tranquility. This implies that women should be chosen based on high morals and religious devotion, not merely based on their attractiveness or wealth. In Islam, the thing to be treasured most is the devoted wife who causes pleasure when seen, obeys orders instantly, and takes full care of herself and her husband's property when he is away."

"What you are saying is purely ideal, but reality is different. Marriage is always sacred to women, but how could you have a happy marriage in such a restless world! Women and men now prefer to live together in an easy life without commitment."

"Women in Islam get all the rights women hope to get. She is the queen of the family, half the society, has the right to marry, divorce, work, inherit, keep her family name after marriage, work as a judge or a minister, fight battles with men," Omar said, hoping to end the discussion.

Jennifer shouted disapprovingly, "This is the part where you will have to forgive me for being blunt, and you may become irritated or even angry! You have to be patient with me when you do not like what I am saying. We learn that Muslim women are treated so horribly by their husbands and brothers. In Islam, women are stoned to death if they have sexual relations outside of marriage, while the married men, if they had private affairs with another women, would go unpunished."

"Jennifer, I am afraid you have the wrong idea about Muslim women!"

Jennifer said, "Women in Islam mean nothing to Muslim men. They are less than the dirt under a snake's belly."

"Give me a chance to explain the truth, please," said Omar.

"In my earlier personal experiences, I have encountered Middle Eastern men in clubs whose behaviour was just disgusting," she said. "They were lecherous, gross, and just nasty; I hated them. Now take a break and remind yourself that you asked for honesty and promised toleration. Don't be mad at me, Omar. You asked for this."

"Understanding a certain religion from the attitude of some of its nominal followers is misleading," said Omar. "Many people confuse culture with religion, many others do not know what their religious books are saying, and many others do not even care. We should distinguish between real Islamic belief and varied Muslim practices influenced by culture and social customs.

"Islam as a religion has nothing to do with the deviations you have just mentioned. Would I judge Christianity according to the behaviour of Christian homosexuals, priests sexually abusing children, and women in churches preaching Christianity through dancing and singing, buying God's consent by passing a collection bucket, lesbian preachers, open sex in the movies by Christian actors and actresses, Christian drunkards and gamblers, Christian men and women living together without marriage, pregnant girls seeking abortion and thus killing a soul without right? Christianity and Islam do not allow any of these abnormalities. Christianity is a great religion, and it has been mentioned in the Koran.

"Now let me clarify some of the misconceptions you raised about Muslim women. Muslim women have the right to inheritance. They have the right to run their own trades and businesses. They have the full right to ownership, property, and disposal over their wealth, to which the husband has no right. They have the right to education and a right to refuse marriage as long as this refusal is according to reasonable and justifiable grounds.

"A woman is allowed those divine rights whether her husband approves or not; otherwise, she will sue him in court and may divorce him because by depriving her from her Islamic rights, the court will consider him a sinner.

"Islam teaches that the woman is not inherently inferior to man; rather that man and woman are of a similar nature. They both are equal in intellectual and spiritual capacity. Furthermore, they are equally responsible for their deeds before Allah.

"In Islam, a woman has a primary role to play in the constitution and running of the family. Such is the importance of the role of motherhood that Prophet Muhammad informed us that paradise lies under the feet of the mother. In other words, one must respect, honour, and be good to one's mother. If you visit a Muslim home, it will become very noticeable how the entire family pivots around her, and it is extremely rare in Muslim countries to hear of a mother or father being farmed off to a nursing home when elderly.

"Islam places great emphasis on the role of the Muslim woman as a wife and particularly as a mother. Muslims are often of the opinion that the best position of the woman is in the home with her children and family. However, the Muslim woman is not prohibited from leaving her home to pursue education, a career, or other worthwhile goals that profit not only her but society as well.

"A husband is commanded by the Koran to treat his wife with equity, respect her feelings, and show kindness and consideration. He not only should avoid hurting her but also should bear with her if she ever does something disagreeable, so long as this clemency does not spoil her and she does not habitually behave out of bounds.

"The prophet said, 'Fear Allah, fear Allah in the matter of women. They are weak partners, a trust from Allah with you, and they are made by the divine word permissible for you.

"He also said, 'Whoever of you whose wife behaves in a disagreeable manner and he responds by kindness and patience, Allah will give him rewards as much as Job will be given for his patience.'

"The relationship of the Muslim husband to his wife is not that of master to slave. Rather, the entire responsibility of economic support is placed on the shoulders of the husband alone. The Muslim husband is responsible for the protection, happiness, and maintenance of his wife. He is responsible for the cost of her food, clothes, and accommodation. He cannot demand of his wife that she also become economically productive to support the family, although she is able to do this if she desires.

"One of the main duties of the wife is to contribute to the success and blissfulness of the marriage. The wife must be faithful, trustworthy, and honest. She must not allow any other person to have access to that which is exclusively the husband's right. She must not receive or entertain strange males in the house without his knowledge. She should not be alone with a strange male. She should not accept gifts from other men without her husband's approval. This is meant to avoid jealousy, suspicion, and gossip. The husband's possessions are her trust. She may not dispose of his belongings without his permission.

"A wife should make herself sexually attractive to her husband and be responsive to his advances. The wife must not refuse her husband sexually, as this can lead to marital problems and, worse still, tempt the man into adultery. The angels curse women who refuse their husbands, for this is one of the wife's most important roles.

"The purpose of obedience in the relationship is to keep the family unit running as smoothly as possible. The man has been given the right to be obeyed because he is the leader, not because he is superior. Obedience does not mean blind obedience; it is subject to conditions.

"The wife must accept her husband's leadership, but men should not consider their position one of power and women's as subservience or submission. The office of leadership is not founded for the man. It is allocated to him, and he is appointed to it because he is better qualified for the position. The man, as part of the family unit, is bound by the rule of the office. He is answerable to Allah at all times, so he is not given free reign to rule as he pleases. His leadership is not unquestionable. If he does something unethical, the wife is entitled to tell her husband that his behaviour is unacceptable in Islam. The rights and obligations of each of the sexes are complementary. These rights and obligations are set out to give the marital relationship the best chance of success and survival. It is Allah who knows what is best for His creation. If we have true faith, we will accept Allah's law so that we can prosper in this life and in the next.

"We are often asked why Muslim women are covered. The attire of a Muslim woman is that of modesty, where her figure is not apparent for outsiders and her head is covered with a scarf. In the present days, when rape is a common occurrence in the West, she finds modest clothing to be a protection from unwarranted advances by the opposite sex.

"In the Koran, the sin of adultery is mentioned alongside polytheism and murder, illustrating its seriousness. Islam has not only forbidden adultery and fornication but has accompanied this prohibition with legislation that seals the avenues to them. Anything that is a precursor of fornication is itself a minor form of fornication. The prophet said: "The eyes commit fornication, and their fornication is the look.""

Jennifer looked at Omar and said appreciatively, "Who are you —a sea of knowledge?"

Smiling, Omar answered, "I am just a Muslim looking at the universe with Allah's eye."

CHAPTER 4

Jennifer became addicted to Omar's conversations. She was quivering with emotions to know exactly what sort of structure Omar was composed of. Such a preserved and upright attitude overwhelmed her. She saw him as handsome and robust, yet he unbelievably abstained from the temptations of life surrounding him. He was obedient only to the world of his own religion. He has planned his life in a way that would benefit his body and soul.

In the mornings, Omar was working out either in the gym or by running for an hour. During the hours of the day, he performed his five prayers without fatigue. He was a man who respected his body, purified his soul, and enlightened his mind. On his prayer mat, he sat in the attitude of meditation, irradiating serenity, goodness, and selflessness. His mind was a book memorizing the words of Allah and the tradition of Prophet Mohamed – words matching reason and intellect. He preserved his body for a wife who could share with him the life of justice and truth.

Omar answered all Jennifer's questions with logic and understanding. It was true that his answers were based on Islamic laws, yet they were honest and made sense to her. Somehow she felt that his pure soul that had not committed sins before could ask God and be heard. God was looking over him because he was confronting the world of sins and falsehood. A man like that, willing to lay down his life for his beliefs, would certainly win the kingdom of heaven, and all doors would be opened for him.

Omar's personality penetrated into Jennifer's soul to the extent of feeling that he was the only one who could lead her to the shore of safety, the shore of freedom. But what kind of freedom was she seeking when she was already a free, independent woman? She wanted the freedom of being a virtuous woman. She wanted to claim her right to be a mother of the many children that could fill the beautiful house she'd bought. Hers was the generation that degraded America, and she would not continue to take part in it. Omar's sincere words made her wish the ground would open up and swallow her. She must change her life for the better.

Yes, the words of Omar about the role of women in Islam penetrated deep into her heart. It made her think deeply about her life. She was highly educated and well off. She had everything she needed. But what was she truly doing with her life right now? Earning money and satisfying her physical needs! Something deep inside her was missing. What was it, exactly, to feel whole? She was living an unlawful life with a man who would shout at her face if she ever raised the subject of marriage again. So many times, she had tried to convince Walker to accept marriage as a better lifestyle, but he always refused. Because she loved Walker and did not want to lose him, she reluctantly refrained from raising the subject of marriage again. But now she felt stronger than she did previously. Now she felt that her body was so precious that it should be offered only to the man who deserved it — a man who would accept the responsibility of a home, a wife, and a family. There was something else more important. She needed forgiveness, and this could be achieved by being lawfully attached to a man by marriage. She also needed guidance, and Omar guided her to the true role decreed for women by God, the role of a good mother – a role she knew perfectly well as a woman, but she had just let it fade away.

The many conversations Jennifer had with Omar about marriage made her feel that she sinned terribly against the laws of God, so a peace and a reckoning must be made with God before there could be healing. Living in a peaceful home with a lawful husband would make her wish come true. Omar awakened her to the fact that her role in life was not yet fulfilled, had not even started. She wanted to experience motherhood and carry her own baby in her arms. Every woman must have a baby. No woman could realize her full potential until she had given birth. Omar made her feel that she was living an abortive life.

What was wrong with her as a woman not to live as God wished her to be? She came from a good family. She graduated from the university and got a good job. She worked hard to buy her house, and she furnished it with good furniture.

The several men before Walker had lived in her house with her. All they wanted was sex and to live with her without commitment. At that time, she didn't mind. But Walker was different. He was her classmate in high school. He'd always impressed her with his jokes and amicable discussions. Their friendship had quickly turned into a quiet love that made the years of high school go quickly. Walker then joined the United States Military Academy at West Point in New York, while she joined the school of business administration at Maryland University. They did not see each other for years until they reunited at a party. They renewed their relationship and agreed to live together in her house.

Walker was the man she truly loved. They could live together as man and wife. He could be the father of her children. She'd wanted to open the subject of marriage with Walker again, but she feared he might reject her offer as he had several times before.

Early one morning, Omar surprisingly found Jennifer wearing her training suit and waiting for him at the entrance of the house. She said she wanted to share his morning run with him. They ran for half an hour, and on their way back, she suggested that they sit in a quiet park. They came to a vacant bench and sat. The air was cold and refreshing, and the leaves of the trees were dancing with the morning breeze. Omar knew that Jennifer had questions to ask or something important to say.

Jennifer commenced the talk: "Omar, there is a secret I want to share with you, but please be understanding and don't be angry with me," Jennifer said hesitantly, with signs of embarrassment covering her face.

"How could I be angry with you? I haven't seen anything from you but kindness and generosity," Omar said, smiling.

"Walker and I live together under the same roof without marriage. It is a liberal way of life that is now common in our society. I hope you will understand."

"What? You mean you and Walker are not married!" Omar shouted with shock.

He kept silent for a moment to digest what he had just heard. He then said, "I am truly sorry for you, Jennifer. You are just a nice woman, and you can do with your life better than that. It is your right to live a decent life of purity and giving, the life of motherhood. Don't waste your life running after the illusion of modern lifestyles, for they are the road to perdition."

Jennifer swallowed the lump of tears that had formed in her throat and said with apparent sadness showing in her eyes, "Omar, I consider you more than a brother. You are my saviour. I want to relieve my soul by telling you another secret tormenting my conscious for over two months now. I am pregnant."

Omar was overwhelmingly distracted. Confusion and embarrassment showed on his face.

"I don't know what to say, Jennifer, except that if your will to reform is sincere, Allah will enable you to change your life to what He thinks is best for you. No matter how great the sins of human beings may be, Allah can forgive them if you turn back to Him in sincere repentance."

Jennifer pleaded desperately, "You mean God will forgive me?"

Omar recited to her a Koranic verse: "Say, 'O my servants who have transgressed against themselves do not despair of Allah's mercy; surely Allah forgives sins altogether; verily, He is the All-Forgiving, the All-Compassionate.' That is from Az-Zumar, verse fifty-three."

Jennifer and Omar kept silent for several moments. Omar then pleaded tenderly, "Jennifer would you allow me to stay in a motel for the rest of my days in America? Please try to understand. We Muslims are not allowed to stay close to wine, gambling and … and …" Omar held his tongue; he just couldn't continue.

"I perfectly understand, Omar. If this is your will, it's okay with me. You have been a sweet soul, filled with the strength of gentleness and love. You have made my house a much more beautiful place simply by being in it."

"I will pack today if you don't mind," he said, trying hard not to offend her.

She couldn't utter a word but nodded approvingly with tears in her eyes.

CHAPTER 5

Although Omar looked gloomy when Walker was taking him by car to a nearby motel, it did not cross Walker's mind that Omar knew about the nature of his relationship with Jennifer. Omar's sudden decision to move out was not quite a surprise to Walker because he knew that the general atmosphere in Jennifer's house was not healthy for a strict Muslim like Omar. Wine and gambling were forbidden in Islam, and Walker and his friends were sunk almost every night in such enjoyments, which Muslims considered sins!

After a clamorous poker game and a good amount of whiskey swallowed, Walker went to bed. Jennifer was deeply asleep. Walker felt horny; his hand began to search for the intimate places of her body. Jennifer woke up terrified, as if a serpent had bitten her. She left the bed and sat on a nearby chair. Walker was astonished. He sat in bed and said with annoyance, "What's wrong with you, Jennifer? Are you okay?"

"I'm fine. It's just that I don't want you to touch me anymore."

Walker stared at her in disbelief. "What's gotten into you?"

"I needed to give my soul a rest, that's all."

"I'm afraid I don't quite understand. What's that supposed to mean?"

Now was the time to put a stop to this. Jennifer had made up her mind, and there was no way to dissuade her. She was ready now. She wanted Walker to be her husband, and she wanted to be the one who gave him children. She wanted a family of her own, where love would never hurt and only heal.

"You are the only man I have ever truly loved. I want you to marry me," she said quietly, without a shred of doubt in her voice.

A shocking lump rose in Walker's throat. "What sort of a damn fool do you take me for? I told you many times before that I don't want to settle for marriage."

"Marriage is the perfection of what love is aimed at. Marriage is love personified. One should believe in marriage as the immortality of the soul."

"Goddamn, Jennifer, you and your goddamn madness. I am in love with you. No sin in that."

"Are you willing to live like that? I want to walk with my head held high and look the whole world in the face. I need a man who can keep me firmly in hand."

"You are stubborn and pig-headed. I've had enough of this idiocy."

"You must fathom the purpose of your existence. You know what we are doing, Walker? We are committing fornication. God will punish us for our sins."

"Ah, now I understand. It's Omar, right? Because of that fanatic Muslim who thinks he is master of the earth, you are ruining our life together. What did he do to your head?"

"Omar is always such a perfect gentleman. He is more human than you will ever know. He is my conscience. He knows my soul. He lifts me up when I am sinking and helps me to float again. His words to me were like that green you see in the heart of a white rose. His presence in my house was a benediction. It was an act of God. He brought the ultimate truth to my door. It seems we were destined to meet. It was far more than mere fate that brought us together, something almost spiritual. I have at last arrived at peace with myself."

"I am not as good as you are with flowery speeches and pretty words, but hear me carefully, Jennifer. I want to live free like a bird. This was my condition before I came to live with you here, and that is final."

Jennifer saw the determination written across his face. Anger flamed within her, sparked by his unfairness and raw belligerence.

"I don't want to be a thorn in your side, Walker. You are a cruel man and deaf to reason. You are better off without me."

"And why can't I stay with you?" Walker said fuming.

"Because women are not supposed to flirt with men who are not their husbands. You have the strength to kill the truth but not to face it."

"Please, Jennifer, try to understand. I love you too much to hurt you."

"I've made up my mind, and there is nothing to dissuade me. There is no middle way. Either we live as a married couple or you pack your things first thing in the morning and leave."

Jennifer rose from the chair and headed to the door. She said while opening it, "I will spend the night in another room." She then turned to face Walker and added with great sorrow, "Having an illegitimate baby isn't wrong. I'm with a child on the way."

Jennifer left the room and closed the door behind her. Walker was unable to say a word as he stared shocked at the closed door.

Ten days had passed since Walker left Jennifer. He lived in his old apartment, which was only two blocks away from Jennifer's house. He thought he could get over her and find himself another woman, but it was much harder than he ever would have expected. Jennifer was like a drug, an addiction. Her love seemed to permeate his very marrow. He yearned for her with every breath and heartbeat. Walker buried his sorrow in poker, wine, and work, but nothing helped. Life suddenly had no meaning.

It was amazing, however, that Walker didn't avow his sorrows to Omar. He felt somehow that Omar was not all to blame. Jennifer was the one asking Omar all the time. During the long hours he spent on poker, Jennifer only had Omar to talk to. Her incessant questions about the view of Islam in the different American aspects of life pushed Omar to explain as comprehensively as he could. At first, her provocative questions were destined to attack, and not to understand, but his calm explanations, supported by the words of God and the prophet of Islam, subdued her heart, making her believe every word he uttered. And when Omar came to the point of marriage, Jennifer opened her mind completely to him, as if she were waiting for words confirming what she embraced in her heart. Her persistent questions opened the floodgates of Omar's knowledge of Islamic principles, which would certainly contradict with the modern American lifestyle. His words touched a sensitive cord in her heart. He made her realize that she was living a sinful life with him. He had had several quarrels before with Jennifer about the nature of their life together. She wanted him as a husband, as a father to her children, but he wanted her only as a lover. Then came Omar to establish this fixed idea in her mind, thus ruining their relationship. He didn't think that this could ever happen to him and Jennifer. Oh, shit. He should not have invited Omar to live with him and Jennifer in the first place. But still, he must face Omar to rebuke him and makes him mind his own business.

According to Omar's schedule in America, he was supposed to visit the aircraft carrier USS *Hornet*, docked at Brooklyn Naval Shipyard in New York. Omar shared a room with Walker in a hotel for the night, and in the morning, they were aboard the *Hornet*. The Hornet had a military history. In 1945, it launched predawn strikes on Tokyo.

It was a beautiful day full of beautiful scenes and amazing discoveries. The legendary Cab Calloway Orchestra was there playing sweet melodies, and the guests enjoyed three large dance floors, a cash bar, and scrumptious food. Dining and dancing were held in the enclosed heated hanger deck of the vessel.

The night before leaving for Maryland, Omar was in the hotel room, performing his evening prayers. Walker was downstairs in the bar, drinking a few glasses of whiskey. He had to face Omar but with a strong sedative repressing his nervousness. When Walker entered the room, Omar was sitting in a chair reading a book. Walker sat on a chair opposite him and started the reproach.

"Omar, what have you done to Jennifer? You ruined her mind with your fanatic ideas. I have been a devoted friend to you, and you now knife me in the back. Is this a way to repay friendship?"

"What do you mean by ruining her mind with my fanatic ideas?" Omar asked, surprised.

"She refused to sleep with me and kicked me out of the house."

"So what! You are not her husband, and you don't own the house," Omar said simply.

Walker shouted angrily, "The matter is not that simple, you idiot! She loves me, and I love her too. We have been living together for years."

"God in heaven, have you no common, ordinary decency, Walker?" Omar said, amazed.

"This is an American lifestyle that you cannot understand. In America, we live the lives we choose, not fettered lives as you Muslims do."

"So you prefer to live an ugly life without assuming the responsibility of a husband and a father."

"God rot you to hell, Omar. I lived with her the life she desired. There was no compulsion in our relationship. It was smooth like running water until you appeared in our life."

"Do you know that she is carrying your child, Walker?" Omar said angrily.

"She told me that she was pregnant," Walker said, as if reproaching himself for disappointing Jennifer.

"You know how I see you, Walker? As a coward leaving behind a woman carrying his child after he disgraced her. The minute I set foot in your country, I was confronted with immoral behaviours. American parents live with their illegitimate children. How many illegitimate children have you sired, Walker?" Omar asked ironically.

"Put a brake on your tongue. You love playing God, don't you, Omar?"

"I have been raised to believe that men and women do not enter into sexual relationships unless they have already been legally joined together under the sight of God and men. You think your relationship with Jennifer, which is void of any commitments, is equal to that of a valid marriage? The commitment between man and woman in marriage must be socially and legally recognized so that a clear line of distinction can be drawn between an actual long-term commitment to share one's life with another individual and a one-night stand. Legal and social protection can be granted to the rights, status, respect and honour of both the individuals who are a party to this commitment and also of those potential individuals who are born as a result of this commitment."

Walker clenched his fist and shook it towards Omar's face. "Are you a blue blood and we're something a dog pulled off the road? You are a devil from hell. You and I are not cut from the same mould. We are worlds apart."

"We are cut from the same mould, Walker. We all came from Adam, and Adam was created from dust. Man has been given the choice to do good or bad deeds according to his free will, and that is why in the hereafter, he will be rewarded for his good deeds or punished for his bad deeds. You will reap what you have sown, Walker. The Koran gives the glad tiding of forgiveness for all sins if the sinner is truly repentant and sincerely resolves to correct his behaviour. The Koran has specifically mentioned three crimes, including fornication, which can doom the sinner to the everlasting torture of hellfire, except in the case where the sinner sincerely repents his doings and corrects his behaviour. If the sinner is true in his repentance and sincere in his efforts for correction, then the Koran not only promises forgiveness but also the conversion of these sins into good deeds. God demands responsibility for your actions. I am now trying to hold you to them."

Walker knew that his anger was in fact a reflection of his sorrow for abandoning Jennifer. His sadness was so overwhelming that he had no more to say. He kept looking at Omar with petrified tears in his eyes.

Omar felt sorry for him. "I mean no harm. We are not on opposite sides," Omar said consolingly. "You know," he added suddenly, as if he'd remembered something important, "Jennifer is the best thing that ever happened to you. Go to her and ask her forgiveness. Heal the wounds of her heart by proposing to her. It is not a big deal. What would be so wrong in asking a woman to marry you, and as long as she says yes, then that's it."

"She was a lovely dream that walked into my life," Walker murmured as if he were talking to himself. "She was the only woman I really loved. Oh, God, she is carrying my child. I pray it isn't too late to put things right."

"Tomorrow we will be back to Maryland. Don't worry; everything is going to be all right," Omar said, giving Walker an encouraging pat on the shoulder.

Walker took Omar's advice and knocked at Jennifer's door. She opened it to see him standing in the doorway smiling. He looked very handsome in his military uniform. Jennifer's eyes lit up when she saw him. Her heart was flooded with joy.

Walker got down on one knee, stretched his hand out with a long-awaited ring, and popped the question. "Jennifer, will you marry me?"

Jennifer looked at him with happy eyes and an expression of adoration. She found herself enjoying him.

Walker stood up when she stretched her hands to him. She wrapped her arms around his neck and pulled his mouth down to hers. "I thought you'd never ask."

She then leaned back, looked into his eyes, and said, "Took you long enough to spit it out. Was Omar behind this?"

"He gave me a hard time, but I came to you of my own free will. Oh, God, I missed you like hell. I've got no home. My home is with you," he said with a shaking voice.

"I missed you too. I want you here, to give the place a bit of life."

"Well, I didn't hear your answer yet."

"Marrying you has been the dream of my life. Of course I will marry you, sweetheart."

"Can you do it in fifteen days? I wonder what your parents will think when we tell them we're getting married in fifteen days."

Jennifer only laughed, too happy to think of anything that may be difficult.

Walker was on a mission in Florida. Since it was Tuesday night when he got home, he and Jennifer decided the next Sunday would be just too soon. However, she was sure she could be ready by the following Sunday. There seemed to be an infinite number of things to do and plans to be made. It was hard to imagine getting the license and blood tests, selecting announcements and mailing them out, notifying those who would be in the wedding party, arranging for bouquets and church decorations, and planning a reception, including a wedding cake, all in eleven days.

Jennifer chose a beautifully decorated church with seats for over 120 guests in a comfortable and delightful setting. The church had the beauty and warmth of antique glass windows, bright and clean pastel walls, hardwood-padded pews, high gloss finished wood floors, a beautiful wood altar, and preparation room for the bride.

Jennifer wanted to make her wedding personal and unique. It was to be a small, intimate wedding. The only guests would be family members and friends who had loved them during their lives. She would not go by the book in terms of finding a partner to walk with down the aisle. Traditionally, the bride's father walked her down the aisle. But this important task would go to Omar. She wanted Omar to share in her pride and happiness. Omar would wear an elegant military suit rather than a tuxedo. She certainly did not want to hurt her father's feelings or leave him out. There were plenty of special duties to be done at a wedding. Making everyone included in some way was the main goal. It did not matter who did what, so long as she was satisfied with the arrangements. She would have her father do some other important thing such as making the first toast at the reception, which would be held at Jennifer's house.

Jennifer selected the junior ushers, the ring bearers, the flower girls, and candle lighters.

It took days for Jennifer to select the perfect gown that would reflect her personality, taste, and style — the wedding gown that would dazzle Walker.

Jennifer had her own special song written and recorded on a CD. The song would be played at their wedding when walking down the aisle and several times during the reception.

The days went quickly. Walker and Jennifer got their marriage license from the clerk at the courthouse. The invitations were mailed and the acceptances returned.

Jennifer ordered the cake from a local bakery. She wanted a bride and soldier groom for the top.

Jennifer's mother jumped right in by helping to get the house ready for the reception.

At the appointed date, the church was full of many loving friends and relatives. The pastor was waiting for the groom and the bride.

It was a beautiful sight. The ushers assisted in seating family members and friends. Ring bearers looked charming in white suits with short pants. Flower girls made an adorable addition to the wedding party. They were dressed as miniature brides in beautiful white flowing gowns. Each was carrying a basket of flowers.

In a heavily beaded and embroidered ivory strapless bodice and ruffled silk organza skirt, Jennifer looked stunningly beautiful.

Jennifer looked completely calm at first, until it was her turn to go down the aisle with Omar. Her heart started beating fast and hard, but she was smiling incessantly, looking around, looking at Walker. *That's my man,* she thought, so proud and confident.

Walking down the aisle with Jennifer in his elegant military suit was a shining moment in Jennifer's wedding and Omar's life. At that moment, he felt that he was attached eternally to Jennifer and Walker. His relationship with them was everlasting. God loved those who constructed the world, and marriage was a construction blessed by Allah. Omar was extremely happy. He prayed silently to his Lord to make this marriage successful and to forgive the past. He prayed that the offspring would be righteous and good to their parents.

The flower girls sprinkled fresh flowers along the pathway before the bride and Omar. This meant the bride would enjoy a rosy life. All eyes were on Jennifer. Her guests stood up to honour her as she proceeded down the aisle with Omar. When she reached the end of the aisle, she honoured her father by handing him a flower, thus symbolizing his importance to her. Omar hugged Walker and handed Jennifer over to him. Walker's face broke out into a large smile. He would never forget the wonderful smile on Jennifer's face. There was his beautiful bride in her elegant wedding dress. Jennifer would soon be his wife, not just his girlfriend.

Jennifer and Walker joined hands and turned to face the pastor.

"Walker, do you take this woman to be your wedded wife?"

"Yes," Walker said.

"Jennifer, do you take this man to be your wedded husband?"

"Yes," Jennifer said.

"I now pronounce you man and wife. Walker, you may kiss the bride."

That kiss was the sweetest kiss that Walker had ever experienced.

Now the marriage was official. Walker and Jennifer lit the unity candle that Jennifer had made from the dried flower petals that she had been saving from all the flowers Walker had given her from the time they first met until after his return to Maryland.

Jennifer and Walker stood in the arched door of the old stone church to take pictures.

Walker looked proud and happy. Jennifer looked calm with her gorgeous flowers. She'd made her bouquet from hand-picked silk flowers and satin ribbon. The arch was decorated with silk greenery and white flowers.

When they finally got back to the house for the reception, the customary cake-cutting ceremony took place and all except Omar were served cocktails. The cocktail was a blend of red grapefruit juice and Citron vodka, garnished with lemon zest sugar and a candied fruit slice.

Jennifer and Walker took pictures upstairs, and then Jennifer's father began the toasts, followed by Walker's father before the dinner buffet.

Walker and Jennifer danced to music that she'd recorded on mixtapes, with songs from the forties through the nineties. Everyone had a great time dancing, even the pastor.

The crowd was varied, but everyone flowed in the essence of marital love – beautiful moments to be treasured.

With tears of gratitude in Jennifer's eyes, she and Walker bid Omar farewell. They flew to Miami to spend their honeymoon in South Beach.

Omar returned to Egypt to find on his desk instructions commanding him to join the United Nations peacekeeping force in Kosovo. The purpose of the mission was to deter renewed hostility and threats against Kosovo by Yugoslav and Serb forces.

Because of the daily engagements between the military forces of the Federal Republic of Yugoslavia and the Kosovo Liberation Army, Kosovo was facing a grave humanitarian crisis. Ethnic tensions were at their highest, and the death toll had reached a historic high. Nearly one million people had fled Kosovo as refugees.

CHAPTER 6

In his early forties, John Rosh, a Republican senator, was easily elected to Congress. He was a natural candidate; he spoke well in public, and his grasp of issue was logic and clear; he was a part of a practicing Republic family who had lived in New York for generations; and he charmed the voters as he charmed everyone else. He came from a wealthy family owning huge enterprises, including diversified assets such as in the oil and drug industries as well as in farm machinery. John W. Rosh was considered one of the three richest billionaires in the United States of America and probably in the entire world. His wife, Amanda Rosh, was his cousin, thus close to him in kinship and wealth. Although the position of the president of the United States of America was most appealing to any Republican or Democratic senator, John W. Rosh, due to his wealth, was not much interested in becoming president. His interest was mainly concentrated in running his huge enterprises and serving his state in Congress. However, eight months earlier, the Republican Party was able to convince him, with difficulty, to run for the presidency.

Senator Rosh had to plan for his presidential campaign. Religious leaders in America had a lot of power; they spoke loudly, organized voters, and collected a lot of money. Senator Rosh had to win the votes of the Christian coalition, whose power was rising enormously in the country. The votes of the influential Jewish lobby in America's political and economical life must also be won.

Senator Rosh appointed Mary Mackenzie, his daughter's best friend, as the head of his election campaign. Mary was an experienced political reporter with *Time* magazine and was a well-known aggressive TV interviewer.

Mary advised Senator Rosh to satisfy the strong Jewish lobby by visiting Israel. But before doing that, he had to pay the obligatory dues, speaking at the American Israel Public Affairs Committee and visiting the Simon Wiesenthal Center in Los Angeles, where, after touring the sobering Holocaust exhibit, he incongruously signed the guest book "God bless this world". In order to gain the votes of the Jews who work insidiously behind the scenes, Senator Rosh accepted the view of the fundamental Christians, who believe that the Jews are biblically ordained to live in the Holy Land.

In 1998, Senator John Rosh took his first and only trip to the Holy Land. During a helicopter tour guided by none other than the prime minister of Israel, Rosh was astonished to discover how tiny Israel was compared to its Arab neighbours. The Israeli prime minister commented that this situation must be corrected, saying that a step could be taken in this direction by adding the West Bank, which belonged to the Palestinians, to Israel. Senator Rosh frowned but nodded as if approving.

Senator Rosh later described the visit as one of the most meaningful experiences of his life. A photographer captured a striking image of Rosh in a yarmulke, standing reverently at the Wailing Wall.

It was a tough race for Senator Rosh. The idea that he could just walk into the White House was a myth. Democratic candidate James Fisher represented Minnesota in the Senate from 1992 to 2000. He was also vice president and won the Democratic presidential nomination in 2000. Senator Rosh was running against an icon. It was like running against Mount Everest.

Mary Mackenzie knew that she would face a challenging job. She carefully selected her associates and adequately delegated them to perform certain important tasks.

Mary started her work by pushing this logo: "Rosh the unifier, Rosh the strongest; people in America can unite behind his strength." She then sent a letter signed by Senator Rosh to the Federal Election Committee, requesting funds for the presidential campaign. In that letter, Rosh agreed to abide by the overall spending limit and to other legal requirements, including a post-campaign audit.

To raise more funds, Mary advised Senator Rosh to announce himself as a born-again Christian, meaning even though the majority of his life was spent pleasuring himself, he has now found Christ and renounced all his past indulgences. He and his wife should be looked on as examples of the perfect Christian couple.

After the resignation of the president of the Christian Coalition weeks earlier, Mary diffused through TV and radio, and spread through the main newspapers, that Senator Rosh was the new leader of the religious right in America. The newspapers argued that Rosh was the movement's de facto leader, that his election to the White House was due to a divine plan. An evangelical magazine reported that Senator Rosh was God's man at this hour. Another magazine said that Rosh was able to go over the heads of the religious rights groups and reach individual activists.

During his campaign, Rosh impressed many religious rights activists when he named Jesus Christ as his political philosopher. He also spoke several times in his speeches about how his religious conversion helped him quit drinking and changed his life in other ways. Rosh assiduously courted religious rights and frequently spoke at movement conferences and meetings arranged by Mary.

Mary also arranged for Rosh to give political speeches before delegations from the Jewish lobby. In addition, she arranged visits to several political organizations such as the National Association for Uniformed Services, National PAC INC, Americans for Good Government, Women's Alliance for Israel, US Reform PAC, US Immigrating Reform PAC, Arab American Leadership, Citizens Organized, Young Jewish Leadership PAC, and several others.

Apart from the $67 million in federal funds received from the Department of the Treasury for Rosh's campaign, Mary was able to collect $1,250,524 million from political organizations.

After a strong and close fight between Senator Rosh and Democratic candidate James Fisher, John Rosh barely won the presidential election.

CHAPTER 7

Up in the New York sky, Elizabeth Rosh, the daughter of John W. Rosh, the president of the United States of America, was flying her single-engine airplane. The wind was light, and the clouds were high and scattered, almost a perfect day for flying.

Elizabeth climbed with little effort to 1400 feet and was soon on top of the world. It was beautiful to enjoy the solitude and the views, and it was quite pleasant to leave the world down there. Flying away from the turbulent earth and into a clear sky had always eased her soul. Here above the clouds, where the space was infinitely extended and stillness stretched along the space before her, she could find the peace that had escaped her since her husband died. She wanted to forget the tragedies of the past and get on with the remainder of her life. The small but powerful airplane was flying smoothly like a bird. Elizabeth was elated by enhancing speed and making sharp turns and steep diving.

In order to forget the bitterness of the past, Elizabeth was always running as if she were afraid of staying in one spot too long. There was nothing like work to take one's mind off things. That was why she kept herself constantly busy by joining several international humanitarian organizations and being an important working member of their boards. She was even frequently sent on missions abroad to evaluate aid programs directed to the developing world.

In two hours, she would be giving a lecture for the developing world about family planning in an international conference held at the Centre of the American Council for Voluntary International Action. And that very night, she would be heading to Kosovo to see for herself the proper delivery of humanitarian aid to refugees in a camp sponsored by the United Nations High Commissioner for Refugees.

After one hour of continuous flying, Elizabeth smoothly landed the airplane close to her fancy Cadillac. She slipped off her overalls and placed them on the rear seat. When she stepped out of the airplane, she pushed her hands in the pockets of her elegant jacket and swung her head so that her long golden hair swung out. It came to well below her shoulders. She looked outstandingly beautiful and chic. Her outfits were expensive, extremely cut, and feminine. Elizabeth strode swiftly to the Cadillac. She turned the ignition. The engine roared, and her foot pressed the accelerator against the floor; the car bolted forward.

In the main auditorium of the Centre of the American Council for Voluntary International Action, Elizabeth stood on the stage delivering her lecture. She addressed the issues of sexual promiscuity and sexual education, sexual freedom, making contraceptives widely available, reducing male fertility, legalizing abortion, and opening special clinics for such purposes. After finishing her lecture, she received enthusiastic applause from the one hundred female delegates from ninety nations.

Her Boeing to Kosovo was due in four hours, so she hurried back home, had a light lunch, took a brief nap, and then had her chauffeur drove her to New York International airport. Once the Boeing was airborne and she was settled in her seat, the floodgates of recall opened in ceaseless flow. Scenes of the past crashed back into focus.

Elizabeth Rosh was the only child of her parents and the apple of their eyes. Throughout her childhood and girlhood, her freethinking parents emphasized that her obligation was to exist in the way she felt right for her. Elizabeth was so certain of her decisions that no one ever questioned her entitlement. Her parents encouraged her inborn sense of selfhood. She therefore grew having a flawless confidence about the choices she made for herself.

At home with her parents, she was protected, cosseted, and fussed over. She was seen as the centre of their world, and they revolved around her like attendant planets.

In her final year at York College, where she studied political science and psychology, she was voted beauty queen. Due to her ravishing beauty and family wealth, she was an object of envy and a sense of inspiration to all who knew her. It was there in York College where she met her late husband, Roy Connery, and her dearest friend — or at least she had once thought she was — Mary Mackenzie.

Mary Mackenzie also had many attributes that attracted colleagues to her. She was beautiful with her creamy skin, brilliant brown eyes, and bright red hair. Her figure was rich and firm, and the sight of her always filled men with desire. Her father owned a series of grocery stores in Brooklyn and Manhattan. Mary was raised in a rich family, but of course not as rich and famous as Elizabeth's. If Elizabeth was as constant as sunrise, Mary was as changeable as the weather. Mary's life knew no boundaries. Although she never lacked for anything, she adored being the centre of attention. Mary had always played the role of the tough, arrogant little rich girl who did not give a damn what anyone thought, living for the mood of the moment. Life had always come on her terms. Mary was stubborn and sometimes impossible, and as she grew older, she became more sophisticated, more amusing, and more poisonous.

Mary Mackenzie had known Roy Connery since childhood. The two families knew each other well because they lived in the same neighbourhood. Roy's father owned a diamond and gold trading centre on Forty-Seventh Street in Manhattan. Mary's childhood relationship with Roy continued through primary and secondary education, until both started York College. Anyone who watched their relationship would have realized that Mary and Roy were deeply in love with each other. But the moment Roy laid eyes on Elizabeth and saw her beauty that caused heads to turn, let alone her immense wealth, he forgot all about Mary and became deeply enraptured with Elizabeth.

Roy was a slender man of twenty-two, with pale skin, an intelligent face, and thoughtful blue eyes. His voice inspired confidence. During their four years at York College, Roy and Elizabeth's love grew stronger, and Mary grew envious and vengeful. She wanted to slip them up so she could get her nails into Roy.

After graduation, Roy and Elizabeth got married. The wedding was the talk of New York City. It was a splendid event, held in the grand mansion of the Rosh family, and Senator Rosh invited all his distinguished acquaintances.

Mary attended the wedding with a bitter smile on her face and with a blind jealousy eating at her heart. With the passage of time, the love Mary carried for Roy didn't fade away but became more ardent and covered with black rage.

The wedded couple moved to the elegant mansion that Senator Rosh had gifted Elizabeth as a wedding present. The house was in Manhattan and set on a large estate of rolling green acres. The mansion was a charming two-story house with a master bedroom, two guest bedrooms, servants' quarters, a huge kitchen, a dining room, an elegant living room, and a library. The interior of the house was lovely, and the spacious rooms were filled with antiques and beautiful paintings.

After graduation, Mary joined *Time* magazine as a political reporter. Because she was ambitious and a hard worker, she became very efficient in writing about political events and influences affecting them. Due to her accumulated experience in political issues, she was frequently invited to attend TV sessions, thus debating with senators from both parties and abating their views. Her logical political analysis mingled with her amazing beauty, in addition to the latest fashion she wore, made her a popular TV figure in all of the American states. That is why Senator Rosh appointed her to run his election campaign. She ran the campaign with cleverness and firmness for nine consecutive months, and in the end, Senator Rosh won the elections and became president of the United States.

It seemed, however, that none of this success was enough for Mary. So with her own money, and some support from her rich father, she purchased a local TV station through which she was able to cover local news and particularly those congressional reports submitted to Congress by the senators of the different States.

Because she confined her heart to only Roy, Mary didn't get married. There was no other man worth sharing her heart but Roy. Roy, however, had betrayed her, and he was going to pay dearly for that.

Mary sought physical solace in the company of Abraham Ajami, a Jew working in the crime research division at *Time* magazine. Abraham was mild and decent. He was impressed by the way Mary successfully accomplished her diversified work. Mary tested him in bed, and he proved to be a skillful lover. He was always capable of bringing her to a climax, after which she would delightfully relax. She did not love him a bit, although he loved her immensely and thought that he was the only man in her life. She did not give a damn about his strong feelings towards her. To her, he was just a man satisfying her hot passion that sometimes exceeded the bounds of normal physical need, especially after the stress of a hard day work. Mary shared a luxurious apartment in Manhattan with Abraham and kept her friends at a careful distance. This distance, however, did not include Roy and Elizabeth. On the contrary, she became more attached to them by being a constant visitor. She was waiting for the opportunity to rob Elizabeth of her husband.

Roy was the vision of handsome young manhood. He was energetic and robust, easy to get on with. Elizabeth loved him dearly. Life went smoothly between them, and everyone knew that their love was exemplary. Occasionally, the Connery family invited their acquaintances to formidable parties. The elegant mansion with its twinkling lights frequently hosted the cream of New York society. All were wealthy people, including among them senior administration officials, successful lawyers and businesspeople, and diamond merchants. Mary attended all these parties as a distinguished guest. The Connery family spent weekends at the most exclusive clubs, or on the most expensive golf courses, or riding the best horses, or sailing in their private yacht.

After the retirement of Roy's father, Roy succeeded him in running the family business, the diamond and gold trading centre.

Seven years went by, and Mary's and Elizabeth's families became more attached. Mary had all the advantages to consolidate this relationship over the years. She was an old friend of the Connery family, a reputable TV political interviewer, and an eminent commentator on political issues in *Time* magazine. Not to mention her close relationship with President Rosh after she successfully ran his presidential election campaign.

Mary continued to climb the ladder of success without quarter. She kept looking for exciting political and criminal reports to be diffused through her TV station or published in the magazine. She was like a mad dog, searching for anything to bite. Her egotism was the only motive moving her to fame and success.

CHAPTER 8

One evening after a long day of work, Roy and Elizabeth were sitting in the living room watching television. Elizabeth was leaning her head on his chest, and he was surrounding her with his arm. Mary Mackenzie was on the screen, sharing important news in her one-hour weekly program called *Corruption in the Nation*. She looked beautiful, sharp, and elegantly dressed.

Mary started reading a report: "Money laundering is the process by which illegally obtained cash is made to appear as if it has been obtained by legal means. The funds are moved into valid accounts or businesses in order to hide or disguise the financial trail that leads back to the criminal activity. At present, the Colombian drug barons make twenty-five billion dollars each year in the United States alone. The drug barons are now seeking new ways to get the money out of the country. The money must somehow be shipped out of the States without arousing the attention of the American authorities. I am now addressing the people and Congress in order to establish a special American task force to combat the phenomenon."

A frown covered Roy's face after Mary had finished. He looked seriously concerned at what Mary was saying. Elizabeth commented," I have always admired Mary. She is a lady of accomplishments."

Roy kissed her hair and said, "Yes, my darling, you are quite right."

Abraham Ajami, Mary's lover, had an uncle called David Ajami. David Ajami was a devout Orthodox Jew and a member in the Addas community. The Addas congregation, of which David was a prominent member, was the strictest of the strict and as orthodox as they come. The men were dressed from head to foot in black, with just a white shirt to break the pattern. The boys wore their hair in curly side locks, while the men had beards and the women shaved their heads and covered them with wigs. All were forbidden to watch television, listen to the radio, or go to the cinema. Alcohol and tobacco were banned, as were most newspapers, and contact with the opposite sex outside of marriage was forbidden.

David Ajami was reluctant to see his nephew Abraham Ajami living in adultery with Mary. In the absence of Mary, David paid Abraham several visits trying to reform him. But Abraham rejected his uncle's attempts and insulted him rudely.

During one of those visits, Mary came home and saw David. She saw a man in his mid-fifties with a long black coat, long beard, big black hat, and wire-rimmed glasses. Mary did not like his appearance and the way he was dressed. She shot Abraham a look of extreme annoyance. Abraham told her that the man was his uncle and that he was just leaving. With a curt nod, Abraham left quickly, as if he were escaping from Satan. Astonishingly enough, Mary remembered that she had seen Abraham before, at one of Elizabeth and Roy's parties.

The match between the drug barons and Forty-Seventh Street was ideal. The diamond and gold industries circulated large amounts of cash. The diamond traders were accustomed to transporting large amounts of money in cash, from one state to another, efficiently and without leaving a trace. Large amounts of money passed from hand to hand on Forty-Seventh Street, without arousing suspicion. A diamond trader might launder five million dollars every day without arousing special attention. It was difficult to monitor the deals, to locate the sources of the money, and it was very difficult to infiltrate that closed field, which was based on personal acquaintance and trust.

The diamond and gold industries had recently become the core of the drug barons, due to the numerous possibilities for laundering. One of the popular methods was laundering by means of trading in gold. The drug money was converted into gold, which was smuggled to Colombia. From there, it was exported to Milano, where it was used to make jewelry. Then it legitimately returned to Forty-Seventh Street under import conditions because the gold seemingly originated from Colombia, and that country had trade conditions with the States.

There were also other methods. Drug money was deposited in the accounts of diamond merchants in the guise as profits and was later transferred to Colombia. Sums of less than ten thousand dollars were deposited in various bank accounts, converted into travelers' cheques, and then transported to their final destination.

But in spite of the ingenuity, undoubtedly one of the most popular and successful ways to launder money was through Jewish religious institutions, such as yeshivas and synagogues. Since the majority of the Forty-Seventh Street diamond and gold merchants were religious Jews, the process was easier. The Jewish religious institutions badly needed funds. The Colombian drug traders could be generous. They transferred their drug money as donations, which went to the Jewish religious institutions one way and came out the other, way back to the donors. On the way, the synagogue or yeshiva got a respectable per centage for its pious uses. Everyone was happy: the drug barons who laundered their money quickly and efficiently and the synagogue or yeshiva, which made easy money.

When Roy Connery succeeded his father in running the diamond and gold trading centre, he did very well during the first five years, but then the diamond and gold industries went into a deep slump, leading many traders into bankruptcy. In such a critical situation, traders might choose either bankruptcy or making easy, quick, and relatively safe money.

Roy Connery was not strong enough to withstand the temptation. Through a Jewish diamond trader on Forty-Seventh Street, Roy discovered the laundering business. Roy reached a laundering scope of two hundred thousand dollars per week. His laundering activities reached amazing heights. His trading centre on Forty-Seventh Street became one of the greatest laundering centres in the entire United States. Three times a week, Roy received the cash. It used to arrive in canvas sacks, in cardboard boxes, or in suitcases. Sometimes there would be a million dollars in one shipment.

Ricardo Lopez, representing the Colombian cartels, would arrive from Miami equipped with a document sent from Colombia that contained detailed coded instructions about where to send the money. Roy's role was to see that the money would be transported out of the United States and arrive in the bank accounts of the Colombian cartels in Panama and Colombia. For that purpose, Roy deposited money into his bank accounts in the form of profits from his diamond centre, purchased assets for the use of the drug cartels, bought and sold gold at inflated prices from merchants who were part of the conspiracy, and concealed money through various manipulations. Finally, all the money was turned into cheques drawn on the accounts of Jewish religious institutions. For his labours, Roy received from the Colombians 6 per cent of the turnover. Within a short period, he became a multimillionaire. Roy turned out to be one of the biggest sharks of laundering drug money in New York City. In just a few years, he was able to launder $500 million for the Colombian drug cartels.

And here came the role of the pious Orthodox Jew David Ajami. For fifteen years, David Ajami had been visiting his bank in New York twice a week. He would pull from his pockets or from plastic bags a mixture of $50 and $100 notes that would be sorted into bundles of ten thousand dollars. Ajami would deposit this money into a special account that the bank had provided for him in the name of United Charity. Providing Ajami with an account in the name of a charity would give the international transfers a gloss of authenticity and would minimize official scrutiny. Ajami would then go to the main banking hall and hand over instructions for the bank to telex the money to Israel. In an average week, he would send $150,000 offshore in this way. In an average year, he would export $7 million. The notes were often damp, soiled, and crumpled. Yet the bank never bothered to inquire where David Ajami had come by so much cash. Nor did its tellers object that rabbis they had never seen signed the telex instructions. They simply assumed that David Ajami was collecting all this money for charities in Israel and doing the Lord's work. The vast amounts of cash were made to look more genuine by a smattering of cheques made out to genuine charities.

United Charity did not exist. It was not a registered charity or a registered company, not even a business name. Nor were the huge wads of soiled notes, which David Ajami unloaded every week as charitable donations. David Ajami was a master money launderer who was helping some New York businesspeople evade taxes and exporting the money of Colombian barons to Israel. Once the money got to Israel, it could easily go to any other part of the world.

The many articles Mary Mackenzie wrote in *Time* magazine and the continuous news she broadcasted via her weekly TV program about laundering drug money led to the establishment of a special task force to combat drug money laundering. The task force was staffed with two hundred agents, officials of the US customs and internal revenue agencies. In the first two years of its operations, the task force captured $60 million and arrested 120 launderers; most of them were Jewish diamond traders from Forty-Seventh Street.

In cooperation with the head of the taskforce, Mary was constantly broadcasting his achievements in her weekly TV program *Corruption in the Nation*. In order to perfect its work, the task force found it important to use translators from Hebrew to English to work as undercover agents. When Mary learned that the task force was appointing Jewish Americans for that reason, she recommended Abraham Ajami as a suitable candidate. Abraham was pleased to do anything Mary wanted, and he gladly accepted the new assignment since it was also an extension to his original work in the crime research division at *Time* magazine. Abraham joined the agents of the task force and was given the mission of watching certain diamond shops on Forty-Seventh Street. Because Abraham spoke fluent Hebrew, he was able to make acquaintances with several Jewish diamond traders in a short time. However, he didn't get any clue that might help indicate involvement in illegal operations.

For a year or more, Mary had been writing and talking about the connection between drug money laundering and leading financial institutions in the United States. She commented on this subject in her TV program. Amazingly enough, while the United States spent billions of dollars trying to interdict illegal drugs from abroad, the country's banking system had been making it easy for drug barons to launder their profits. About half of the estimated trillion dollars in dirty money that came in large part from drug trafficking – and from criminal activities such as gambling, auto theft, and child prostitution – moved through the US financial systems, according to governmental estimates. This startling revelation became known when the US Permanent Subcommittee on Investigations released a report that identified four of the six largest US banks as having weak due diligence practices and inadequate money-laundering controls. The suspected banks had a don't ask, don't tell policy towards its wealthiest and sometimes dirtiest clients. In reality, the United States had two systems in place, one for ordinary customers and another for the rich, who were allowed to take advantage of a special unit within banks known as the private bank. Such banks worked hard as the bagmen for their wealthiest clients. The US State Department, in its annual International Narcotics Control Strategy Report, noted that private banking facilities continued to be vulnerable to money laundering. Under US laws, engaging in such activity was criminal, and the US government and Congress were now moving aggressively to punish the suspected banks. Accordingly, the banks involved in such criminal acts were forced to put adequate safeguards in place to screen and monitor their clients and be familiar with their customer's money.

While Abraham Ajami was on duty, he saw his uncle David emerging from the diamond and gold trading centre carrying plastic bags that he had not taken into the building. On the following day, he went to his bank to deposit the money. The trip from the diamond and gold trading centre to the bank was repeated twice a week. David, who hated his uncle for his constant interference in his private life, visited him at his house and told him about his suspicion that he worked in money laundering. A hot discussion took place between them. Abraham accused his uncle of masquerading as a pious and respectable citizen when he was in fact a thief. David, on the other hand, accused his nephew of adultery and said that he would burn in hell. Abraham left his uncle angrily, not knowing whether to report him or not.

After a hard day of work, Mary came home late. She took a shower and went to bed naked. She stretched her hands out to Abraham and roared like a lioness," Come and take me." Abraham plunged into the bed and worked Mary's body into violent shudders of ecstasy. After hours of hot passion, Mary relaxed in Abraham's arms; sleep began to banter her eyelids.

Only now did Abraham's mind begin to work as he tried to put things together. Was it not that the diamond and gold trading centre belonged to Roy Connery, the son-in-law of the president of the United States of America? Bearing in mind that Mary was Elizabeth's dearest friend, and that she was also highly appreciated by the president, what would the situation be if he passed that information to Mary or to the task force? It would be the scandal of the century!

Abraham glanced at Mary sleeping contentedly beside him and felt a tremendous love for her. He eased his body next to her and went into a deep sleep.

CHAPTER 9

Mary woke up in the morning in high spirits. After a hot shower, she put a robe on and strode to the kitchen for breakfast. Breakfast was already waiting for her on the table, thanks to Abraham, who was always trying to please her by making himself useful in many ways. At that moment, the sense of being serviceable and useful to Mary heightened in him immensely. His thoughts about the connection between Roy and his uncle jumped on the tip of his tongue.

After they finished breakfast and were sipping their coffee, the words flowed out of Abraham's tongue to surprise Mary tremendously. The surprise was agonizing yet thrilling — agonizing because she wouldn't have imagined in a thousand years that Roy could do such a thing and thrilling because now she could finally take Roy for herself and rob Elizabeth of him. Yes, now she could make Roy feel the agony she felt when he forgot all about her the moment he set eyes on Elizabeth.

Mary asked Abraham if he had released a word about this to anybody, and he answered that he wouldn't do that before consulting her. Mary wanted to be assured of Abraham's complete discretion and warned him seriously that if he released a word, she would consider their relationship over. Abraham swore to God that this secret would remain buried in his chest as long as he lived.

Later that day, Mary telephoned Roy from her office and asked him to meet her in an hour at her apartment. When he asked her about the reason for such a visit, she said that it was a very important matter. Through the glass barrier that separated her large office from the section of the Crime Research Division, Mary could see Abraham busy at his work. In an hour he would be going to Forty-Seventh Street to start his daily routine watch. Her apartment would then be a perfect place to meet Roy.

The moment Mary opened the door of her apartment and saw Roy standing there, her heart hammered in her chest. He looked strong and filled with the juices of life. She received him with a large smile on her face and greeted him with two light kisses on both cheeks. Mary took his hand and led him to the living room, where he eased his body onto a sofa. She then went to the bar and fetched him a scotch. She handed him the whiskey and then sat opposite him looking silently beautiful. Her fragrance, a special French perfume that she used, had delicately changed the quality of the air. Her scent came to him in small wafts; it tickled his nose, teased his senses.

Roy studied her with a smile, as if he were seeing her for the first time: vivid face, her bloom of mouth, the sumptuously full lower lip flirting with the delicate upper lip, her red hair, her beautiful eyes. Her skin was so white that it almost looked translucent.

Mary contemplated Roy. He was still very handsome. A man sure of himself, loaded with sex appeal. She had difficulty suppressing her smile of pleasure. Something burned along her spine, and her knees trembled. Oh God, why did he always have this effect on her?

After long moments of silence, Mary collected her thoughts with an effort and then said at last, "I am sure Elizabeth would be furious if she knew you were here."

His smile dissolved into a frown. "She fumes if I am not at home," he said.

Jealousy swept over Mary. She looked at him defiantly and said, "You are in considerable danger. Do you know that?"

"Danger of what kind?" His expression hardened.

"I've been watching you for a while. You are working in money laundering. What do you say to that?"

His stomach went cold at her words. Clouds of fear and confusion crossed his eyes. Beads of sweat broke out on his forehead; his hands trembled a little.

The urge to wound him swept over her. She said with a challenging voice, "I'm furious with you. You have acted selfishly and irresponsibly. You are interested only in collecting money. Haven't you considered Elizabeth and the president?"

There was a storm raging in his mind. He shot her a glance of annoyance and said, "You quite crushed me. You enjoy keeping me off balance."

She replied with artificial innocence, "Why on earth do you say such a thing? It's your doing, not mine."

Trying to understand her intentions, he asked, "Are you trying to say that you will give me away?"

She said, enjoying his distress, "Why should I do something like that? I love you Roy, and you know it."

Perplexed, he said, "Perhaps an accommodation can be reached between us."

She said with a laugh, "Really? And what would this accommodation entail?"

"Name anything you want." He felt his heart beating in his throat.

She looked him straight in the eyes and said plainly, "Now we come to the heart of the matter. Elizabeth lured you away from me, and I want you back. Either we become lovers again or you bear the consequences."

Aghast, Roy said, "Ah, now that's more like it. It's my life you are playing with. Because you think you love me, you assume you have a right to blunder into my life, causing hurt and harm you cannot even imagine. You'll expose me to shame and pain. If this is love, the hell with it."

He was gripped by combined feelings of grief and fear and anger. An odd mixture of vulnerability and strength overwhelmed him. He felt sorry for himself. The peaceful world he lived in with Elizabeth was about to collapse around him. Now he was entirely in Mary's hands, at her mercy.

Mary's voice came to awaken him from his thoughts. "I'm too open. That's my big problem. I wear my heart on my tongue. I want you back, and I want you now."

It pained him that she talked to him like that. Mary had left him no choice. He knew that he was sailing in a dangerous sea, but there was no holding him back now.

Roy raised the glass to his mouth and drank several long swallows of whiskey. The scotch did nothing to calm his rage down. He stood up and went to Mary. He took her by the shoulder and drew her to him.

She whispered in his ear, "Don't fear anything darling. It is only a storm in a teacup. I will not give you away. How could I do that when I love you so much?"

She kissed his lips hard and murmured huskily, "I love you. I have always loved you. You are fascinating when you are outrageous; make love to me now, please."

He was not proud of what he was about to do. But the fear and rage inside him had numbed any feelings of morality.

Mary needed the sex desperately; she could concentrate on nothing else. And Roy made love to her maniacally. His lovemaking was as if it were an act of vengeance. No amount of penetration could gratify him, until exhaustion had caught up with her. She fell into a deep sleep even before Roy got to the shower.

That is how the affair between Roy and Mary started.

CHAPTER 10

With the passage of time, the love affair between Mary and Roy was further strengthened. Mary's demanding body always needed Roy's love. The comparison between her two lovers was not in favour of Abraham. Roy was more skillful and more robust. He knew how to give her endless orgasms and then make her relax in his arms while showering her tenderly with his kisses. Along the way, she was able to convert his lovemaking into a sensual passion. The strong feeling that she had always carried for Roy further heightened this new exciting ecstasy. All these qualities were missing with Abraham. It was true that Abraham was young and robust too, but she only sought physical solace with him, nothing more. On some nights, however, she had to offer Abraham her exhausted body in order not to make him suspicious.

As for Roy's feelings towards Mary, he was reluctant at first, treating Mary's body ruthlessly as if he retaliating for her intrusion in his life and exposing his back to a situation in which it might harm him. But the more he made love to her, the more he became addicted to her special brand of taste. His reluctance had turned into an ardent longing. To him, she became like an exotic flower emanating a strong sensual odour from a distant tropical paradise. She gave him a feeling of pleasure and enthusiasm. She was a lovable woman with a zest for life.

Roy purchased a fancy private apartment in Brooklyn to nestle with Mary away from intruding eyes.

Although several months ago, Abraham had told Mary his speculations about the involvement of Roy and his Uncle David in drug money laundering, he was somewhat astonished to see that Mary didn't attempt to pass a word to the authorities. Abraham justified her silence as a kind of loyalty to the president and his daughter Elizabeth, Mary's best friend. A scandal like that would certainly ruin Elizabeth's marriage and shake up the president.

Elizabeth was so confident in Roy that it never occurred to her that he was betraying her with Mary. She would not have thought either, not even for a moment, that he was also involved in drug money laundering. Her day was divided between her duty as a wife and work in humanitarian institutes. No sign of distortion ever interfered in her daily routine life with Roy, except maybe those frequent night-time telephone calls from Roy: "I've got a business dinner tonight, and I can't make it home until late. Please, darling, do not wait up."

Roy was keen not to make Elizabeth suspicious of any kind of infidelity on his side, and whenever the opportunity was available, he made love to his wife compassionately, as if he were restoring his sanity.

On the other hand, the hot nights Mary spent with Roy were enough to make her reject Abraham. Her drained and exhausted body after the long nights with Roy could not stand Abraham's touches. The touches that were sensual and magical before became annoying and disgusting.

Abraham's pride was terribly hurt, and fear that he might be losing Mary's love overwhelmed him. He knew well the nature of her passionate, demanding body, but her attitude with him lately was amazing. She refrained from having sex with him as before, and he always had to beg for it. If she had to, she did it out of pure obligation. Had she found another man who satiated her body to the extent of not needing him? Abraham's mind began to whirl in his head. What happened to Mary, his big love? Something had surely gone wrong, and he must find out the reason behind Mary's strange behaviour.

The next day after work, Abraham followed Mary to Brooklyn. She disappeared in a building for hours. He stayed by the building's front door until she emerged with Roy at her side. Roy kissed her before they disappeared into their separate cars. Abraham's heart sank to his stomach. He felt severely humiliated. Was that it, a love affair between Mary and Roy! Mary had never loved him, although she made him think that he was the only man in her life. He was just a man to fill the void in her busy life.

For months, he endured her rejections with the hope that she might come back to her senses, but she insisted on rejecting him with disgust, as if he were some kind of dirt. She stepped on his heart and shattered his pride into pieces. And who was the new lover but the president's son-in-law! The husband of Elizabeth, her closest friend! Mary did not care about other people's feelings. She only cared about her own enjoyment. He would not reproach her or even open this despicable subject with her. But he would slaughter her heart bit by bit. He would report to the task force about what he saw on Forty-Seventh Street, and he would tell Elizabeth about what was going on between Roy and Mary.

Elizabeth Rosh received an unknown telephone call telling that Roy Connery was betraying her with Mary Mackenzie. Elizabeth did not believe it at first, but the private detective she hired confirmed that Roy was having an affair with Mary. When she faced Roy about his relation with Mary, he denied it, but guilt was clearly showing on his face.

Elizabeth shouted at him, "Did you ever lay her?" But she received no answer.

Roy couldn't tell her that he was a big drug money launderer and that if he didn't have an affair with Mary, she would have given him away.

Elizabeth couldn't believe that her exemplary happy life was falling apart around her. How could Mary do that to her? Oh, no. This nightmare could be just a rumour. She must face Mary in person to be sure.

The confrontation took place in Mary's office. Sitting at her desk, Mary was not quite surprised to see Elizabeth entering her office blazing like an erupted volcano.

"Is it true what I hear about your love affair with Roy?" Elizabeth demanded.

Mary answered coolly, "You know, dear, that Roy and I have loved each other since childhood. The matter is simple. I loved him first, you lured him away, and I got him back."

Elizabeth shot her a glance of disgust and snapped at her, "You are a woman without morals. You do not give a damn about other people's feelings. Nothing moves you in life except your own interests, your detestable egoism, and the contemptible needs of your body."

Mary said with an envious smile, "Don't lose your temper, dear. Nothing really happened. Roy is still your husband."

Elizabeth couldn't stand it anymore. After Mary had ruined her life, she was envying her for still having Roy as a husband.

Elizabeth stepped forward and slapped Mary's face severely before hurriedly leaving Mary's office to find the nearest lavatory. She felt the need to vomit, to expunge the disgust that had settled into her stomach.

Mary stood up and went to the glass wall of her office, which overlooked the compartments of the other employees. She put her hand on the slapped cheek rubbing it smoothly. There was a mean yet victorious smile on her face. She saw Abraham standing there, smiling at her victoriously. Her smile changed into a frown. Her mind worked fast. What was the name of the Jew who was captured today in accusation of money laundering? Mary hurried back to her desk and picked up that day's newspaper, where she read the following: "David Ajami was caught carrying bags full of cash. He refused to cooperate with the police in any way and did not identify his customers. David Ajami, who claimed not to have known the source of the money, will be convicted of forging bank documents and is likely to be sentenced to eight years in prison."

The name of the suspect was David Ajami, Abraham's uncle. Mary went back to the glass wall, searching for Abraham. He was still standing there smiling. He shook his hands and head as if he were saying, "Well, I couldn't help it. I just couldn't keep my promise."

Fear crept into Mary's heart. Roy was in considerable danger.

The real trouble began when American Customs and Internal Revenue agents raided the diamond and gold trading centre. Roy was arrested to stand trial, but his lawyer was able to release him on bail. It was clear that Roy would be sentenced to ten years of imprisonment and a fine of two hundred million dollars.

At home in his study, Roy was watching television. Mary was speaking on the screen: "Our sending five heavy volumes of corruption documents to the inspector general of the US Treasury, as well as broadcasting through our weekly program *Corruption in the Nation* several solid evidences about money laundering in America apparently led to the arrest of Roy Connery."

On that very afternoon, Roy was found shot dead in his study with a recently fired pistol in his hand. Mary listened to the news of Roy's death without much surprise. That was the kind of business Roy had run, and he had finally paid his dues.

The scandal spread all over the world. Elizabeth was terribly wounded, and President Rosh was terribly embarrassed. His credibility as the president of the United States of America descended to the lowest level. His son in law had committed suicide after being accused of defrauding America out of eight hundred million dollars.

For weeks, Elizabeth shut herself off from the world in every possible way. She had never felt so humiliated, so insulted, so cheated, and so angry in her entire life. Her wounded heart was still very tender, the scars not yet healed. Inside, she was aching with loneliness and pain.

Although she hated Roy for his infidelity, she had cried silently within herself, mourning his death, believing she would never get over the agony of her sorrows. The sadness she went through after Roy's death coloured her attitude to men from that point on, making her wary, cool and often unresponsive to any approaches that had been made to her. She had been once a warm and vibrant woman, a woman passionately in love with her husband. But Roy managed to kill that love by betraying her with another woman.

Now, after Roy, she was not interested in cultivating new relationships or dating. It would take a very special man to get her attention again. Even with Senator Robert Hudson, who proposed to her five months after Roy's death, she had managed to keep herself detached and private, and she politely rejected his proposal.

The death of Roy had left a void in her life, and she managed to fill it with continuous work. By keeping herself always busy, she didn't have time to think of her wretched past. That is why when the mission to Kosovo loomed in the horizon, she rose to it. Her father tried hard to dissuade her from going to that dangerous spot, but she stubbornly insisted. She wanted to be alone in a different world to lick her wounds, even if this world was dangerous. Her future belonged to only her now, and she would plan it one step at a time.

An ache began behind her eyes, and she blinked quickly in an effort to dispel the threat of tears as she gazed sightlessly out of the Boeing's window. Elizabeth sighed suddenly and came out of her reverie. "Things pass. Time heals," she murmured to herself.

There was a soft thud as the Boeing's wheels hit the ground of the Prestina airport in Kosovo, followed by a shrill scream of brakes. The engine wound down to a muted whine as the large jet wheeled off the runway and then cruised slowly towards its allotted bay.

CHAPTER 11

In the Pristina airport, General James Douglas, head of the United Nations forces in Kosovo, greeted Elizabeth. Two weeks before, General Douglas had received strict orders from the United Nations headquarters in New York and the American Embassy in Belgrade to ensure the safety of Elizabeth during her mission in Kosovo. Elizabeth introduced to General Douglas the two secret agents that were appointed by the American National Security Agency for her safety. General Douglas greeted them and then took Elizabeth in his Jeep to the United Nations headquarters in Prestina.

The headquarters was twenty feet below ground level. It was impregnable, even to the heaviest artillery barrage. The floor was of heavy timber boarding, and the walls were designed to keep out the damp and the cold.

General Douglas ushered Elizabeth to a small room with a lavatory to relax and freshen up. He said while leaving the room and before closing the door behind him, "We will be meeting in two hours. I am sorry to say that the situation in Kosovo is rather awkward. I hope you can adapt yourself to things."

After half an hour, a corporal came with a tray full of seasonal fruits, a variety of cheese, and a bottle of fresh water. The corporal placed the tray on a small table and said politely, "A meeting will be held at six in the general's office." The corporal raised his hand in a brief salute, turned on his heel, and strode out.

At the appointed time, the same corporal came to lead Elizabeth to the general's office. With a broad smile on his face, the general received Elizabeth and seated her in a chair facing his desk. The general then pressed a button and asked his secretary to call for Major Omar Abdel Aziz.

The general addressed Elizabeth, saying, "Although our forces have been here for some time now, Kosovo is still a dangerous area. I was surprised to learn that you were interested in coming here. The road is dangerous from Pristina to the refugee camp in Prekaz. We have maps, however, showing the approved routes and those hazardous due to the mine and cluster bomb threat. Under such critical circumstances, I have no choice but to assign Major Omar Abdel Aziz, my right-hand man in Kosovo, to accompany you to Prekaz. He is an Egyptian, a man of great strength and fighting spirit. Under my leadership, he accomplished several impossible missions. He knows the land here like the back of his hand."

Elizabeth commented, "I'm not afraid of the risks I might encounter on the road to Prekaz. Just get me there."

"It seems you don't appreciate the gravity of the situation," General Douglas said with a look of surprise.

A faint smile crossed Elizabeth's face. She said sadly, "I've been through a lot lately. I'm ready to adapt myself to any circumstances."

There was a knock on the door. General Douglas said, "Come in."

Major Omar entered the room and saluted the general. General Douglas saluted back.

The general looked at Elizabeth and said, "May I present Major Omar?" He then looked at Omar, saying, "This is Mrs Elizabeth Rosh, the daughter of the president of the United States of America. She is here on a mission you already know all about."

Omar glanced at Elizabeth, unable to overlook how beautiful she was, and how elegant, as she sat there with quiet dignity.

Elizabeth looked up to see a large man. She felt the glow of his personality the moment he stepped into the room. She stared at him in mute amazement. Omar walked to Elizabeth to shake hands with her. He moved with grace like an athlete – his long legs giving him an easy stride. Elizabeth stood lithely and gracefully before him. With a smile like sunshine on her face, she stretched her hand to him. He reached for her hand and pressed it lightly. He seemed to tower over her, handsome and rugged. His dark intensity burned brightly in contrast to her generous blondness.

Elizabeth sat in her chair, and Omar sat in a chair opposite her.

Elizabeth inspected the Egyptian with a curiosity she could not completely conceal.

The man was impressive, well over six feet tall. He was broad-shouldered, narrow-hipped, and heavily muscled. His curious wide black eyes gave his face an exotic cast. There was something so intense about his eyes. They were midnight black, fringed by impossibly thick and long dark lashes. They were glowing intently like burning embers. His wavy hair was jet black. She could see arrogance in the aquiline curve of his nose, while his mouth was firm, controlled, and sensual. He seemed so powerful and looked so handsome. He was attractive in a dangerous, exciting way. There was a feeling of violence about him, ready to explode. He was in his early thirties she surmised. She wondered what background had created this man. Elizabeth had difficulty suppressing her smile of pleasure.

Omar gave Elizabeth an assessing glance. She was in her mid-twenties and had a stunning figure. Her wheat-gold hair was straight, cut to shoulder length in an attractive style. Her skin was dazzlingly white, and her eyes were arrestingly green with a dark shade of grey. She had a small waist, generous hips, and beautiful long legs. Her legs were beautifully moulded, with slim ankles and gently swelling calves, knees marked only by symmetrical dimples.

The general glanced at Omar and said, "Don't let Ms Elizabeth out of your sight. She is entirely in your hands now. You have been given a big responsibility, and I'm sure you will carry it through to the best of your ability."

Omar said firmly, "Sir, I shall do as you command. I'd be glad to assist in any way."

General Douglas continued. "In Kosovo, there is little room for a man without aggression. The situation here is on fire, and desperate times call for desperate measures. I am aware of what Major Omar is capable of doing under such pressing circumstances. In our business, there is no room for error, and Omar is quick, bright, and trustworthy. He is known among his soldiers as a ruthless, tough-minded officer untouched by sentiment. He is a thoughtful tactician and a skilled warrior. That's why I selected him to secure your trip to Prekaz."

Elizabeth glanced at Omar. The Egyptian sat before her with the stormy dark looks of his ancestors. His look was as sharp as a skinning knife, and his face had a granite hardness that Elizabeth had never seen before. Elizabeth was annoyed with herself for being so aware of him.

General Douglas continued, saying, "Omar comes from a prominent and wealthy family. Besides being a military man, he also graduated from the Faculty of Economy and Political Science at Cairo University. He is very knowledgeable about political and economical matters. He is also a good Muslim and strictly abides by the rules of Islam. So as you see, Omar is not a man who would rely on brute strength alone to obtain his ends."

"I'm sure my life has been placed in good hands," Elizabeth said appreciatively.

"Be sure of that, Mrs Elizabeth. Major Omar has been provided with a small military convoy to secure your trip to Prekaz. All the necessary precautions for your safety have been carefully considered," the general said with a reassuring tone.

"Thank you, General," Elizabeth said thankfully.

Omar rose from his chair, nodded curtly to Elizabeth, and then addressed General Douglas, saying, "Will you excuse me, sir? I have things to do before leaving to Prekaz tomorrow."

"Of course, but don't forget dinner tonight at eight," the general said.

"Yes, sir." Omar raised his hand in brief salute and walked out of the room.

CHAPTER 12

At eight sharp, General Douglas, Elizabeth, and Omar were having dinner in the meeting room. A small table for three persons was set especially for the occasion. The food served included beef fillet with smashed potato, green salad, and ice cream for dessert.

Elizabeth commenced the conversation. She said, smiling at Omar, "So I received the impression of a brutal, clever, competent man who in war matters would be pitiless."

General Douglas said, laughing, "Being a warrior at heart is not his only quality. He is also a good conversationalist. Omar looks at the world from his own perspective. A perspective based on his religion and tradition."

"I haven't heard him say much since I arrived in Kosovo," Elizabeth said, trying to push Omar to talk.

She did not know that he restrained himself from talking because her exquisite beauty momentarily silenced him. Everything was soft about her. Her eyes had the softness of flowers, her voice was soft and mellow, and her manner was as soft as a summer rain. There was a feeling of uneasiness touching his heart. Crossing with her the dangerous territories to Prekaz was a heavy load on his shoulders. Besides being the daughter of the president of the United States, which was a huge responsibility in itself, Elizabeth was so fragile and so delicate, and he would hate to see her hurt. The task that General Douglas gave him this time was much harder than all others.

Omar said quietly, "Mrs. Elizabeth, we live in turbulent times. You don't know what you are in for. Are you sure you feel up to it?"

Annoyed, Elizabeth said, "I intend to continue my job here and see it through to the finish."

General Douglas quickly interjected in order to change the course of conversation.

"Allow me, Mrs. Elizabeth, to give you some background about Kosovo. Kosovo is the disputed region between the Albanian majority and Serbia. Once an autonomous federal unit of Yugoslavia, in 1989 it was stripped away of its autonomy by the government of Slobodan Milosevic. After the revocation of Kosovo's autonomy, the Serbia authorities closed schools in the Albanian language, massively dismissed Albanians from state-owned enterprises, and suspended Kosovo's legal parliament and government. Serbia instituted a regime of systematic oppression of the Albanian population in Kosovo, and flagrant violations of basic rights of Albanians occurred frequently. Initially, the Albanians responded to the repression with peaceful and massive resistance.

"In 1992, the people of Kosovo held free elections in which they chose their leadership, expressed their determination for the independence of Kosovo in the 1991 referendum, and in the same year, the Kosovar parliament declared the independence of Kosovo. They formed a parallel government, found means of continuing Albanian language education outside of occupied premises and providing health care.

"In early 1998, the Serbian government began to crack down against the Kosovo Liberation Army – the KLA. It became apparent then that the peaceful approach was ineffective in face of the brutal regime of Milosevic. After 1998, Serbian security forces conducted a scorched earth policy in Kosovo, razing villages to the ground, creating an exodus of over one million refugees and internally displaced persons, and committing horrific atrocities against unarmed civilians, including women and children. The NATO bombing campaign forced Milosevic to withdraw Serbian security forces from Kosovo. United Nations Security Council resolution 1244 established a United Nations Mission in Kosovo and allowed a NATO-led peacekeeping force to enter Kosovo to ensure security. In this respect, I would like to emphasize that the withdrawal of Milosevic security forces is not yet complete and violation of Albanians human rights continues."

Omar glanced at Elizabeth and said, "Mrs. Elizabeth, what exactly is your main interest in humanitarian work?"

Elizabeth replied, "I've a specialized team working with me for establishing programs that strengthen people's ability to help themselves in the developing world. Our programs promote economic development and self-reliance, improve health and education, and provide relief to victims of disasters and wars, assisting refugees and advancing human rights. When finished, these programs are submitted to the boards of humanitarian institutes for discussion, financing, and implementation."

Omar commented, "It is amazing that humanitarian aid usually comes after disasters have taken place and not before."

Elizabeth said sharply, "Are you implying that my trip is meaningless because I came here too late?"

"You came here to dress the wounds of the dead." His eyes had a hard look, and sadness was drawn on his face.

A deep silence engulfed the room, and then his words came to squeeze the hearts of his listeners. "It's an ethnic cleansing. They are killing men and women alike, boys and girls, even babies. The only guilt of the victims is that they are Albanian Muslims. The killers are the meanest cowards I have ever seen. They kill and burn because they know that their victims are armless and unable to defend themselves."

Elizabeth throat dried up. "Has it come to this?" she said, trying to pull herself together.

Omar saw the grief in her eyes. He said comfortingly, "The good times will come again. The war can't go on forever."

Elizabeth said, "You made it crystal clear that I am not welcomed here. I am not afraid of whatever might happen to me. I am looking for a world in which I can be of service. Could you help me do that?"

Omar looked intently in her eyes, trying to understand what was behind her firm insistence of going to the refugee camp. No sane woman would think of coming to this hazardous part of the world. He knew all about her husband's scandal. The news of the scandal had spread all over the world. The news had also said that Elizabeth had plunged herself in humanitarian work to forget her bitterness and hurt. *Is she here to forget the agony she experienced? And if so, the land she ran to was a blazing hell.*

"Of course I will, Mrs Elizabeth. I'm glad to see a lady who does not turn aside from a goal or a responsibility."

When Omar said that, he stopped eating and stared into space as though his thoughts were miles away. There was a thin edge of anger in his voice when he said, "God has created the world in order and justice, and it is for us to put ourselves in unison with this order and justice. But sometimes life can be unfair, and it's up to us to straighten things out. The war in Kosovo created over one million refugees and internally displaced persons, leaving over three hundred thousand people without shelter, an estimated ten thousand dead, and mass graves containing bodies of up to one hundred civilians, including women and children."

Elizabeth was astounded by what she heard.

Omar kept silent for long moments. When he spoke again, Elizabeth could feel echoing sadness in his voice. "The brutal terrorism witnessed in Kosovo is also taking place in the Arab world where I came from. Torture, illegal detention, assassination, assaults against civilians with missiles, helicopters and jet fighters, annexation of territory, transportation of civilians from one place to another for the purpose of imprisonment, mass killing – as in Qana, Jenin, Sabra, and Shatila, to mention only the most obvious. There's been denial of rights to free passage to schools, hospitals, and markets; use of civilians as human shields; humiliation of individuals; punishment of families; house demolitions on a mass scale; destruction of agricultural land; expropriation of water; illegal settlement; economic pauperization; attacks on hospitals, medical workers, and ambulances; killing of UN personnel … All of these policies have been carried out by Israel with the unconditional support of the Unites States."

Omar then looked intently in Elizabeth's eyes and said, "Not only has Washington supplied Israel with the weapons for such practices and every kind of military and intelligence aid, but it has also given the country upwards of one hundred and thirty-five billion dollars in economic aid."

"The State Department in Washington has issued a report charging Israel with serious human rights violations in the occupied territories,"

Elizabeth replied. "The United States keeps calling for a solution to the Palestinian problem."

Omar said, "In Palestine, the Palestinians are long-suffering at the hands of the Israelis. Entire Palestinian villages have been bulldozed and replaced with Jewish settlers. Barehanded and armed only with rocks, the Palestinians face automatic rifles, machine gun fires, tanks, and helicopters. It is a conflict of an unarmed people against a well-equipped modern military machine. It is men with guns against men with slingshots. If the things that are being done to the Palestinians were being done to Jews, Western outrage would have been overwhelming and the persecution of the Jews would dominate the news. The injustice exercised by the Israelis against the Palestinians in the occupied land is the result of the biased American foreign policy in the Middle East that is consistently pro-Israel and anti-Arab."

Omar's words were fanning Elizabeth's hot temper to the kindling point. It was on the tip of her mouth to tell him to go to hell, but she withheld. Instead, she shot him an indignant look and said, "America is always there when freedom is threatened. America has its own free will, which is not affected by any political lobbies. I work in the humanitarian field, and I know what America is doing to wipe out the tears of the oppressed and spread peace all over the world."

Omar said, "The truth is no insult, even if unpleasant."

Trying to lighten Elizabeth's mood, General Douglas said, "Because I know Omar well, I listen to his words with good-humoured tolerance. Wild though his views are, and no matter how provocatively expressed, there is a sort of nobility in them. His indignation was directed against oppression and cruelty. His deep sense of justice and rejection of oppression raised him to fury. This is perfectly understood among soldiers fighting for noble causes in battlefields. They become very close to death and witness all sorts of human sufferings."

Omar continued. "Being the strongest superpower on earth, being the defendant of democracy, America should stand strong and clean to lead the world to a bright and peaceful future. This would never happen unless America followed an unbiased international policy that was based on straightness, justice, and equity. America must help establish true peace to quench the anger of the oppressed and stop bloodshed of the innocents. Imposing biased and unjust policies on the weak is not workable with Allah, who is always there to descend his punishment on the oppressors."

Elizabeth said, "I understand exactly what Major Omar meant. As a woman working in a humanitarian field, I have a good idea about how the Palestinians are suffering. But I still insist that the United States is doing its best to spread democracy and freedom all over the world. The United States is doing a lot to the world in several domains, and that must be fairly recognized."

Silence beclouded the room for a while. Elizabeth realized that Omar had such a great gift of expressing himself clearly, straightforwardly, and effectively. She had to suppress the temptation to enter into another fully fledged argument with him.

The dinner ended, and Elizabeth rose and shook hands with General Douglas. When she shook hands with Omar and looked into his eyes, she felt that he had reached deep down to the depths of her soul. The tight grip of his hand and the warmth emanating from it made her body tremble a little.

She said with a beautiful smile covering her lovely face, "You are a remarkable conversationalist. I was deeply impressed by your views.

We come from different lives, and perhaps I'll never understand you and you'll never understand me, but we can be friends even so."

Because she had placed her life in his hands, she wanted him to feel at ease with her. She wanted to befriend him.

She added, nearly whispering, "Call me Liz. That's what my dad and mom call me."

Astonished by her simplicity, he said, "Liz? Yes, of course."

CHAPTER 13

The next morning, Elizabeth was waiting in her room, ready to leave for Prekaz. She heard a knock on the door and opened it to see Omar looking surprised at the way she was dressed. Her outfit, although simple, beautifully expressed her exquisite body. It consisted of a creamy transparent short-sleeved blouse over a beige skirt stretching down to her knees. On her feet were brown half boots of fine leather, matching the colour of the outfit.

"Haven't you got something else to put on? You can't go around like that," Omar exclaimed.

With an expression of anger on her face Elizabeth, snapped at him, "This is what I would like to wear on a trip like this."

"Wait a minute," Omar said, and then he disappeared. After a few moments, he returned with military overalls. "Put these on and twist your hair into a topknot," he ordered.

Elizabeth was going to protest, but there was firmness in his voice that impelled her to obey.

After thanking General Douglas for taking care of her, and the preparation he'd made for her trip to Prekaz, Elizabeth joined the convoy. The United Nations military convoy was comprised of four armoured vehicles with four soldiers each. Omar had his own Jeep, so he could easily inspect the road a few kilometres ahead or behind the convoy. Omar gave instructions that Elizabeth was to get into the second vehicle in the column. The first vehicle in the front was the leading vehicle that would change the direction of the convoy according to Omar's instructions if any danger arose.

The convoy set off from Prestina at 6.15, just as the sun appeared over the horizon. It had to cover forty kilometres to reach Prekaz. Omar was three kilometres in advance to inspect the road. The road was narrow, with little room to maneuver on either side due to the rocks and bushes.

The convoy continued over the rough, hilly country for fifteen kilometres. Suddenly, incendiary rockets hit the first and last vehicles of the column. The Serbs then started firing onto the road from an adjacent hill ahead and from the ridges on either side of the convoy. The Serbs were well hidden, and the two remaining vehicles shooting back did not seem to have much effect on their fire. The convoy had no choice but to stay in the narrow pass. Upon hearing the sound of gunfire, Omar hurried back to the convoy. To his big disappointment, two armoured vehicles were completely destroyed, with their men burned to death inside. Fearing that the remaining vehicles might be similarly hit, the soldiers jumped out and lay with faces to the ground. Elizabeth was lying on the ground beside them, hiding her face in her arms. Omar threw himself on Elizabeth to protect her from the stray bullets. The Serbs were able to fire on the two vehicles from the ridges and from the left rear. Serb shells supplemented the intensive rifle fire.

Omar grabbed Elizabeth by the arm and led her to a narrow channel cut into the ground at the side of the road, and from there, he battled with the remainder of his soldiers through the afternoon and evening against repeated assaults by waves of Serb troops. The battle seemed to last forever. All Elizabeth heard was the constant roar and echo of the ratatat chatter of machine guns and the whining of stray bullets.

Bullets from all directions were whizzing over her head. Another set of bullets landed close by, and the ground shook crazily around her. Her nose was filled with the stink of cordite and fire; the stifling air of hell surrounded her. She screamed internally, *Oh God, when will this nightmare end!*

As it grew dark, firing was sustained by rifle flashes on both sides and sniping continued for a further two hours. Another three incendiary rockets were fired almost simultaneously, hitting the two remaining vehicles and the Jeep. The crashing gave way to a deadly stillness.

Not willing to be identified, the Serbs took advantage of the darkness to withdraw. Omar and Elizabeth managed to survive because they were well protected in the channel at the side of the road.

Omar searched for his men. They were all dead, except for two who were severely wounded. They were lying in the middle of the road screaming. One had his left leg with a part of his lower abdomen blown off and he was staring at his wounds stupidly. The other was laughing hysterically as he crammed his entrails into the gaping hole.

Elizabeth watched the terrible seen in horror. Dead soldiers and human organs were scattered all over the place. The screams of the dying soldiers were unbearable. A feeling of panic washed over her. She had not been prepared for this terror and violence. Elizabeth shivered uncontrollably and began to weep brokenly.

"I have never witnessed anything as violent as this. You're putting me in jeopardy. You are putting my life at risk," she sobbed.

"It was an ambush, and we were outnumbered. Do not get all panicky. I hate it when women panic." Omar words were strong and hurtful, designed to wound.

He was mad because he did not have the chance to fight effectively against the Serbs. His convoy was besieged from all sides, outnumbered, and now all his men were killed.

Elizabeth wanted to run, but there was no place to run to. A big disappointment engulfed her, and her confidence in Omar began to erode. She knew, however, that under the present circumstances, she had no other alternative but to continue to cling to her faith in him.

From the wrecked vehicles, Omar was able to get some provisions, a bag of first-aid items, and a sleeping bag. As for weapons, he was heavily armed with a powerful handgun, a sharp knife, a machine gun, and a sporting rifle with a silencer. On his back was a leather bag full of explosive packages against tanks and armoured vehicles. He looked like a moving arsenal.

That night, Omar and Elizabeth camped on a grassy bluff above the unpleasant darkness of the thick bush. Elizabeth slid into the sleeping bag and fell asleep almost instantly. Omar kept awake to guard her. During the night, Omar called General Douglas with difficulty from his mobile phone, which was dying. Omar gave him a full report about the present situation and ensured the safety of Elizabeth. General Douglas said that he expected something wrong had happened when the convoy did not arrive at Prekaz at the appointed time. General Douglas tried to send troops for help, but they were stopped at the Serbs' strong checkpoints spread all over the borders of Kosovo villages. The international troops of General Douglas were not even allowed to check or investigate the sites where the Serbian troops killed innocent civilians. The troops were ordered to return to Prestina.

The Serbs were besieging all the villages and evacuating the ethnic Albanian inhabitants towards the borders of Albania. The villagers resenting evacuation were mercilessly killed on the spot. The S e r b s did not distinguish between men, women, and children. The Serbs were furious because of the severe NATO air raids over their military installations. Omar realized that since the mission of Elizabeth to Prekaz was no secret, the Serbs were either trying to kill her as a sort of retaliation against the United States, which was supporting the NATO air raids over Serbia, and then claim that her death was due to NATO's attacks, or they were trying to capture her in order to pressurize the United States to stop the NATO air raids.

The only available way to get Elizabeth safely to Prekaz was to rely on the total concealment of Omar and Elizabeth's whereabouts and on the warring skills of Omar. General Douglas asked Omar about the time needed to get Elizabeth safe to Prekaz. Omar answered quickly, "Seven days."

The conversation was cut off suddenly, and Omar's mobile phone was dead. Omar threw the useless instrument away.

Two hours after this conversation, a spokesman in the office of General Douglas said that the Serbs had ambushed a United Nations military convoy fifteen miles from Prestina. The convoy was heading to Prekaz for humanitarian purpose. The Serbs killed sixteen soldiers, and all the armoured vehicles were destroyed in the ambush.

A Serbs spokesperson disputed General Douglas account and held the Kosovo Liberation Army responsible for the ambush.

As a security precaution, no further news was released by General Douglas's office about Elizabeth and Omar. Their whereabouts must be concealed until they safely reached the refugee camp in Prekaz. Both were alive, and that was what counted. The camp in Prekaz was well protected by United Nations troops, and it was full of international groups and observers reporting to the world the brutal massacres the

Serbs were exercising against Muslim Albanians. The camp was also provided with Doctors Without Borders, working under the supervision of the International Relief Agency.

John Rosh, the president of the United States, was informed about the details of the ambush and that his daughter was safe and in good hands. General Douglas advised that no interference of any sort be undertaken by the United States before the end of the seven days appointed by Omar. President Rosh agreed hesitantly and promised to interfere vigorously against the Serbs if Elizabeth failed one way or another to arrive safely at Prekaz at the appointed date.

CHAPTER 14

When Elizabeth woke up in the morning and remembered what had happened last night, she felt a terrible sense of loss and desolation. She began to cry softly, nodding her head vehemently through the tears, unable to speak. The ambush was a nightmare that seemed to have no end.

Omar said soothingly, "I know that you are strong, Elizabeth, strong enough to do what has to be done. Please try to believe that."

She wished she could believe it. She did not feel strong. She felt weak and terrified.

"Now, let's have some breakfast," he said, trying to draw her attention to something else.

Omar offered her beef sandwiches, hard chocolate, and barley sugar. While having breakfast, Omar told Elizabeth about his conversation with General Douglas and said that her safety depended totally on obeying his orders. But how was she going to survive a week of this? She sobbed silently.

Omar could not stand seeing Elizabeth in pain. Since leaving Prestina, she had been facing dreadful terror. Guilt washed over him. He wanted to promise her that nothing would ever hurt her again.

Crushed by the pain in Elizabeth's eyes, he pleaded, "Please don't make this any difficult than it is. We are fighting a battle we could win. I will guard you with my life. Will you forgive me for what happened?"

She looked at him with tears shining brightly in her eyes. His black hair was blowing in the breeze, his beautifully boned face looking more arrogant and more handsome than she had ever seen it. The tenderness in his eyes was beautiful to see. Her heart was deeply touched.

She smiled at him through her tears and murmured, "You are forgiven."

"Now let's go to work." Omar said earnestly. "You and I together could form a team that would fight its way out to Prekaz."

"How?" she said, close to crying.

"We will move together as one body. We will mix with the refugee masses. We will live in the wilderness, in the forest, in the deserted houses of the Albanians. We might mix with the Serbs and use their weapons against them. I might shoot and fight and kill."

"You scared the shit out of me. I'm not prepared for these sorts of things, you know." She was terrified.

"What I want from you is to adapt yourself to whatever situation you might encounter and also to obey my orders without hesitation. It's not going to be a picnic but a dangerous adventure."

Although Omar's words had terrified her, she knew she could not succumb to weakness. Elizabeth nodded approvingly.

"I want you to trust me, to believe in me. Whatever I do, no matter how dreadful it is, it will be for establishing justice and for the sake of your safety. You understand?"

She nodded approvingly with a resigned look in her fine eyes.

The slight breeze wafted a limp strand of hair into her face, and she brushed it away. Her beautiful blonde hair cascaded around her shoulders like a fall, framing a face of perfect loveliness. She looked heartbreakingly beautiful. Omar looked at her, fascinated. To him, her beauty was almost unbearable. He felt vulnerable to her. It took all of his self-control not to reach for her and touch her face. He did not like the tender feeling her beauty caused in his chest.

Omar continued explaining his plan. "For our safety, we mustn't go along one road but zigzag our way across the villages until we reach Prekaz. If the Serbs were after you, they would come searching the areas adjacent to our wretched convoy. This means that we have to move out of here fast. The closest settlement we can get to in is the village of Polac. From Polac, we can cut off ten miles to reach Glogovac. Then we move to the nearby village of Prekaz, where the refugee camp is located."

Omar continued to instruct her. "Fasten your hair in a bun at the back of your head. Come on; let's get going while it's light."

Omar began to walk in long strides, and Elizabeth tried hard to keep pace with him.

They walked through the densely forested valleys and smooth grassy hills that stretched in miles ahead of them. After seven miles of continuous walk, they reached the bottom of an elevated hill. Elizabeth was fighting her way up the hill behind Omar. She was extremely exhausted, and only her dogged will kept her feet moving. Her face and her hands were scratched from the clawing weeds. But still she climbed.

On the top of the bushy hill, Elizabeth lay back against a rock and closed her eyes, her body crying out for rest. It was already after sunset, and Omar decided to spend the night on the hill. It was an ideal spot, for the hill was overlooking the valley where far below the village of Polac lay dark and silent under the full moon.

After having a dry meal, Elizabeth fell into a deep sleep in her sleeping bag, while Omar's sleep was interrupted by sudden waking during which he inspected the surroundings several times.

Early in the morning, Omar and Elizabeth walked down the valley to the village of Polac. An uneasy silence seemed to hang over the village. After three miles of walking, Omar suddenly stopped. A lethal stillness came over him. The stench of the village penetrated his nose. The musty smell of earth and mud was overlying with the odour of rotting flesh and sewage as well as the stale lingering whiff of burned cordite and high explosives.

Omar realized that the village had been under attack for days by the Serbs. The stillness of the village made him wonder about what had happened to its inhabitants and whether the Serbs were still around or had left to attack another village. Omar spoke his thoughts to Elizabeth and asked her to stay close to him. They moved together as one body, cautiously circling around the houses of the village. Most of the houses were totally or partially burnt, and some were still set on fire. Omar traced signs of tank chains on the ground. It was evident that joint police and military attack had hit the village. The army usually started its attack by bombing the houses and then left the villages to the Serb police and militia to do the theft, killing, burning, and expelling of the villagers to the Albanian borders. That was the common procedure undertaken by the central Serb authorities in all villages under attack.

The dead bodies of the villagers lay all around, in the gardens, in the yards, and in the fields. Seeing such a horrible scene, Elizabeth was filled with such a deep agony that she began to shiver violently and in sudden uncontrollable spasms from the lingering shock.

In her terror, she ran uncontrollably to the nearest deserted house to hide inside. She was not thinking sanely but was just trying to shut out the memory of the decaying corpses. Omar ran after her to prevent her from entering the house, but she was already inside. The decaying bodies inside the house further memorized her. She saw bloodstains, broken teeth, broken bones, brains, and bullets all over the place. Four bodies were lying dead in separate rooms. The Serbs had slaughtered them to death using shotguns and other hard and sharp objects, massacring innocent people. All the victims wanted was to be able to live freely on their own land and in their own houses.

Elizabeth raged around the rooms, screaming her anger, hate, and fear at the deaths of the innocents. She was trembling all over and began to cry helplessly.

"Oh God!" she shouted. Her legs collapsed, and she crumpled forward. She started to fall, but Omar caught her before she hit the ground and took her in his arms, holding her close. She sagged against him and felt secure in his arms, protected from the hazards of life and death.

"Pull yourself together. We must move. I sense danger in the air."

Elizabeth disengaged herself and looked at his eyes. There was no innocence in them; instead, there was a touch of cruelty.

They left the house and continued inspecting the village for inhabitants or Serb soldiers. After long minutes of cautious searching, they heard women screaming and men shouting. From behind a cottage overlooking a large field, Omar and Elizabeth lay belly down in the long thorny bushes growing behind the cottage. They could see ten Serb militia with semi-automatic weapons standing guard over a quivering line of displaced men, women, and children. The militia was wearing black uniforms with black camouflage make-up on their faces, and they had red bandanas around their heads. Their commander, however, had a black bandana covering his hair. He was tall, fat, and muscular. He had a white face painted with black and green camouflage paint. He was armed with a big knife and carried an axe in his right hand. The commander ordered his men to search the villagers for deutsche marks, gold, and watches. After they took all valuable possessions, they put them in a bed sheet stretched on the ground. The women and children were then separated from the men. The men were divided into two groups and were ordered to put their hands behind their heads. They were then kicked by boots and hit with weapons on their heads, legs, and backs.

They forced the first group of men to lie on their backs. The commander ordered his men to stand on some blocks about a metre and a half high and to jump off and land on their chests. They broke their chests and killed the men that way. That was the hardest for Elizabeth, seeing their ribs broken, sticking out through their skin. One man was still alive, breathing his last. The commander went to him and with his big knife castrated him. The commander cut his body, and then cut his scull open with his axe. Elizabeth saw his brain. When the commander moved, the brain moved. Elizabeth felt sick and vomited in her place.

The remaining men were made to kneel with their hands and faces touching the ground. Lying flat on their bellies, they were beaten with stones, weapons, and shovel handles. The women, seeing their husbands and sons beaten with such cruelty, were screaming all the time. One of the men could not stand the beating. He stood up and began to run. But one of the militia quickly caught him. The commander stepped forward and killed the man with a single blow from the axe. The axe cleaved the man's brain in half, and his blood splattered against the face of the militia. The commander handed his axe over to one of his soldiers and borrowed his handgun. He advanced to the villagers lying on the ground and executed them one by one. Each person was fired on twice with a burst from the gun aimed at his head. The commander then returned the gun to the soldier and took back his axe.

Watching the killing, Elizabeth was paralyzed. Chills swept through her, and she closed her eyes in pain. This torment must be stopped. Her face was white as chalk when she reached for Omar's arm and drew closer to him, seeking his direct protection.

"Contain your panic," Omar whispered firmly.

In all that happened, Omar's stillness was that of an animal sizing up its prey, waiting for the perfect moment to make its move. The militia was now relaxed, and that was the chance Omar needed.

"You stay put," Omar whispered to Elizabeth, and then he moved in for the kill.

Omar crawled on his belly for several yards and then rose to his feet and walked swiftly to his adversaries. The element of surprise was on his side. Omar fired his machine gun into the militia. He aimed high at the level of their heads and upper parts of their chests and backs. In just a few seconds, they were all dead except their commander, who was armed with the axe. Omar spared him for a while because he wanted to see the terror in his eyes when he did kill him. The commander threw his axe away and attempted to pick up a weapon from the ground, but Omar fired a burst of bullets between his legs, thus paralyzing him in his place. When Omar was within twenty paces of him, he put aside his machine gun and his sporting rifle. He said in the Serb language, "I'll smash your bones with my bare hands first and then blow your head off with a bullet."

The two men turned around each other, looking for an opportunity to attack. The commander dashed into Omar, and Omar's hard body crashed into the commander. In the first moment of direct encounter, the commander knew instantly that Omar's strength was far greater than his own. Omar's body seemed not to be made of flesh and blood but of brutal iron. Omar gave him steely punches on the nose, eyes, and jaw. The commander fell to the ground, groaning with pain. Omar pulled him from his hair with his left hand and punched his chest several times with his right fist. The severe punches broke his chest ribs and forced the air out of his body. The commander struggled to drag more air into his lungs. Omar then hit the commander's face with his forehead. He gave him several blows that crushed his facial bones. Omar's fists and forehead were lethal weapons. The commander fell nearly dead to the ground. Omar whipped his handgun from the holster around his hips and aimed at the commander's head and fired. The head was blown off, expelling a large part of the brain.

Omar ordered the women to restore their stolen valuable possessions and then asked them to dig two massive graves, one for the villagers and one for the Serb's militia. He could have left the dead Serbs to ravenous birds, but it was important to hide their killing for fear of the Serbs' retaliation that was only performed against Muslim Albanian villagers.

Omar walked back to Elizabeth. She was sitting on the ground surrounded by the long thorny bushes. He saw fear in her eyes. He realized with sorrow that after she watched the killing he'd done, she'd also become afraid of him.

She said, shaking with fear, "I've never approved of brute force. It never gets anyone anywhere."

Omar went down on one knee and said, "There is no ecstasy in killing. Such accidents frequently occur during war. No room for mercy under such circumstances. I want you to pull yourself together so you can face any critical situation that might arise in the coming days."

Elizabeth buried her head in her hands, trying to shut out the memory of the killing. She didn't want to go through the pain of it again.

"I have had enough of this. You must get me out of here, you hear me?" Tears sprang to her eyes.

"Now go to the women and share with them digging the graves." His low voice penetrated her ears like a lethal poison.

Elizabeth stood paralyzed in shock, her heart racing and her mouth dry.

"Are you crazy? I cannot do that. You are cruel and heartless!" She shouted at him.

"I have no time to pamper you. Go to the women now and do as you were told." Omar's voice held a tone of finality.

Omar caught Elizabeth by the arm and pushed her towards the women. His vice-like grip hurt.

Elizabeth walked with Omar to the women, and he handed her a shovel. With the women, Elizabeth shared digging the graves and carrying the corpses to their last abode. The women were crying all the time while burying their husbands and sons. An agonizing sorrow clutched Elizabeth's heart. What she saw was the horror of a lifetime. She wanted to burst into tears, but there were no tears to be shed.

In the meantime, Omar disappeared into the village to bring more corpses. Most of the corpses were so burned out that their relatives could not identify them.

After the bodies were covered with earth, Omar and the women performed Islamic funeral prayers, and he then advised the women to head to the Albanian borders.

Although she was terribly exhausted, Elizabeth looked more tenacious.

"I feel stronger now, ready to face whatever you have to throw at me," she told Omar more confidently.

Omar admired her courage. What else could harden one's heart but facing death?

The horrible massacres that Elizabeth had witnessed so far were also occurring in the other villages. And she and Omar had to pass through one more village before they reached the refugee camp in Prekaz. She must be strong enough to obey Omar's orders. This could save her life as well as his while crossing the dangerous spots to Prekaz.

CHAPTER 15

Omar started walking towards the next village, Glogovac, taking such big strides that Elizabeth had to run to keep up with him. They walked on for two hours while darkness fell. The time was near eight o'clock, and the moon had risen in the sky. The fatigue of the long, horrible day finally caught up with Elizabeth. She felt drained, swept by exhaustion. Each pace became an enormous effort for her.

Elizabeth stopped suddenly and refused to walk one inch farther. Omar stopped and looked back at her in surprise. Elizabeth's face was pale with fatigue, and her eyes were tight with unshed tears.

She shouted at him, "I'm tired of running! I have no energy left for it. All this running has to stop!"

"You know perfectly well that we must get to Glogovac on time," Omar said, annoyed.

"I'm not a wild creature waiting to be led around. I am not like you, a creature made of steel. I'm a woman made of flesh and blood."

"What is your problem now?" Omar said, astonished.

"You're ruthless and callous and completely lacking in any human feeling," she said hysterically.

"What's the matter with you?" Omar said.

"You're the most astonishing man I've ever come across. You know nothing about women's needs."

"And what are women's needs?" he asked impatiently.

Elizabeth put both her hands on her hip nervously and snapped at him defiantly, "Well, Mr. Know-It-All, I'm awfully tired. I am starving. I want to pee and to bathe. I want to get some rest."

Omar felt utterly embarrassed. No women had ever accompanied him on any of his missions before. He treated Elizabeth as one of his men soldiers. How inconsiderate of him. Yes, women were more fragile, especially this woman, whose immense delicacy showed in every word she uttered and in every move she made.

"All right, we're only six miles away from Glogovac village; we can camp here for the night," he said quickly, trying to hide his embarrassment. We have arrived at Bistrica River, and you can bathe in its fresh water. In the meantime, I'll prepare some food for you."

Elizabeth walked over to the river. The water glittered in the moonlight, inviting her to plunge into it. Elizabeth took off her clothes and waded through the water, allowing the light waves to soothe her tired body. As she bathed in the moonlit lake, she felt a little like a wild animal; it was a pleasant experience for one who often felt stifled in city environs and fettered by the codes and etiquette of civilization. Elizabeth stayed in the water for an hour, a matter that worried Omar and made him go in search of her.

In the moonlight, the river and its surroundings were all silvery gold. Suddenly, Omar saw Elizabeth coming out of the water. She was naked, and Omar gasped. He stood looking at her, astounded. He wanted to run back to the camp, but his feet were nailed to the ground. He was on the point of mistaking her for some river goddess.

With glistening water running off her firm contours, she was a stunning sight. Elizabeth came out of the water like Venus rising from the waves. Her waist was naturally small though so well developed. She was very slender; her breasts were firm and stood out from the chest as though carved in marble. There was a melting look in her fine eyes.

Omar felt as if his bones were melting inside him. Her beauty was almost unbearable. Omar stared at her with fascination, all his emotions in upheaval. He had never seen anything so beautiful or been so completely captivated in all his life. Elizabeth's skin was milky white, tipped with palest pink, and her wet hair was a light golden brown. Her body was soft, with the gentle yielding spring of woman's flesh. It had a plasticity that intrigued and excited him. He saw her as a silvery flower of the night that only gave its perfume to the moonbeams.

Omar's body trembled to feel her near him. He blushed to the very roots of his hair and turned around to give her his back. He closed his eyes. This might serve as a barrier against his passion.

Elizabeth smiled at his shyness and passed by him so closely that she noticed his confusion. There was no innocence in her eyes, and she wondered why, though naked, she was not embarrassed before him. On the contrary, she felt confident and sure of her outstanding beauty.

Somehow she felt victorious when she realized that Omar – this solid rock – was vulnerable to her exquisite charm.

The effect Elizabeth had on Omar was incredible. She had awakened his long-suppressed and tightly controlled sexuality.

Elizabeth bent over to pick up her clothes and disappeared in the wood.

Omar whispered after her, "What the devil is the matter with me? I can hardly breathe."

Omar was so shy and confused that he could not join Elizabeth at dinner. Watching her eating alone with a healthy appetite pleased him.

CHAPTER 16

Elizabeth slipped into her sleeping bag and tried to get some sleep, yet she could not sleep. She lay awake for hours, tossing in her sleeping bag. She turned over restlessly in the direction of Omar, but he was not there. Being alone in the wood at such an hour made her jump from the sleeping bag like a frightened bird. She ran to the river, hoping to find Omar there. She found him sitting by the river with knees drawn up, hands clasped loosely around them. She stood still, watching him from behind a nearby tree.

Omar sat for a while, contemplating the silvery river, and then rose and stripped out of his military clothes. His body was huge and lean, stretching gracefully from waist to shoulders. Elizabeth watched him, watched the massive muscles in his shoulders and back move subtly under his skin as his arms moved. His motion was smooth, fluid. He was beautiful, and the sight astounded her.

She whispered to herself, "Lord, he is so beautiful." She became sharply aware of something she had felt in the far reaches of her senses.

Omar soaked away his longing body in the cool water of the river, trying to put aside the waves of temptation that flowed up through his body.

Elizabeth kept watching him with a heart beating at an uncommonly rapid rate. She was aware that his maleness and closeness had a potent effect on her, and she knew that he could quite devastate her.

When Omar emerged from the water, Elizabeth was still watching him, fascinated by his beautiful body. He was definitely solid. His ribs were hard, his muscles firm. There did not seem to be an ounce of fat on him. There was no single turn of flesh, no line or muscle that did not blend in perfect symmetry.

She could look at him naked for hours. His perfection fascinated her. Before Omar could see her, Elizabeth retreated in haste to the camp, slipped into her sleeping bag, and pretended to be asleep.

Omar appeared after a short while and lay down on his prayer mat. A shocking awareness of Omar's closeness rippled along Elizabeth's nerves. She was suddenly much too warm. She pressed a hand to her racing heart, trying to catch her breath.

"Omar, are you awake?" Her voice was barely a whisper.

"Yes," he answered, surprised that she was still awake.

"You are ill mannered and unforgivably rude," she whispered softly. She didn't give him a chance to understand her reproach but crawled towards him while saying, "You shouldn't have left me by myself in the wilderness without warning."

Before he could explain, she was in his arms, covering his mouth with hot kisses. Omar jerked his mouth from hers, surprised by her daring. He struggled in her embrace, and in attempting to wrench himself free, he triggered a reflexive action that made her hold him tighter. With an effort, he sat stone still, but she was still holding him tight.

"Have you taken leave of your senses? Get hold of yourself," he pleaded.

"You are a beautiful man, Omar. I liked you from the first moment I saw you. I'm dying to make love to you."

Elizabeth was so beautiful and so full of fire that Omar found himself physically aroused by her. She noticed the beads of sweat forming along his forehead and the nervous quivering of his lower lip.

Elizabeth stared into Omar's face and refused to lower her gaze. The midnight darkness of his hair, the power and magnetism of character so evident in his face, and the enigma of his wide black eyes fascinated her. His beauty mesmerized her. She had never seen anything lovelier. Omar lowered his eyes against her piercing gaze.

"Look at me," she ordered softly.

He raised his eyes up to her. Lovely blonde hair hung in long curls along her petal-white cheeks, and her beautiful green-grey eyes were openly curious as she surveyed his face. Omar had no choice but to fight the hurricane of emotions swirling within him. With a great force of will, he attempted to pull himself together.

"I'm sorry. I can't be of help." A shy smile twisted his lips.

Elizabeth stiffened as if she had just been slapped. "And why not, may I ask? What are you so afraid of?"

"I can't. It would be death to me. It would be the betrayal of my soul."

"You are quite an enigma, Omar. I can read you. You cannot hide your emotions. It showed in your eyes. Is there another woman in your life?"

"No."

"Then what's holding you up from making love to me?"

Something fluttered inside him, and he damped it down hard, refusing to give it space to grow. He said with difficulty, "Adultery is forbidden in Islam. It's a sin, and I'm a good Muslim."

"How damnably pretentious you are," she shot at him. "I could feel the passion in you, could feel the heat rising in you." Elizabeth trembled with an overpowering desire to slap his face, but in his eyes she saw the isolation of him.

"Don't make it worse, please," he pleaded.

"Is that how you see me — a woman trying to seduce you! Aren't you a bit out of date? It's the end of the twentieth century, not the middle ages. Nowadays we live as we like. You are a virgin, I presume. You haven't had much experience with women, have you?" There was a hint of mockery in her voice.

She wanted to reproach him further, but her mouth had gone dry. She moved her tongue in an effort to moisten it.

Omar knew that his rejection was hard on a person of her sensitivity. Her hair was spilling over his arms, her skin was as luminous as the finest mother of pearl, and her beauty was a miracle that excited him beyond anything he had felt in his whole life. His resentment melted, and a great wave of tenderness washed over him.

Elizabeth eyes suddenly welled up with tears. "Please forgive me for causing this unpleasantness." She tried to pull herself away from his arms, but Omar captured her tenderly against him. She looked at him with surprise and saw a compassionate smile on his face. She would have had to be made of stone to resist the power of that smile, and she was not made of stone.

Omar brushed away her tears and raked his fingers through her hair. His hands, though thick and strong, were surprisingly gentle.

"Your hands are made for breaking bones and smashing heads. Those same hands tremble when they touch my face, shake when they stroke my hair." She was enjoying being in his arms.

He whispered tenderly, "You are such a beautiful woman, Liz. You are so rare. You look saintly."

His warm words penetrated the cold chambers of her heart. This encouraged her to say, "I came to you driven by a need that I couldn't control. Maybe I just wanted to lean my head against your chest and pour out all the fears that were churning inside me. Or maybe I had come hoping to establish a feeling of belonging, but you made me feel a deep loneliness."

Omar carried Elizabeth to the sleeping bag and sat with her, rocking her like a child. He stroked her hair as if she were a little girl, and patted her patiently and comfortingly. Elizabeth seemed to flourish with his affectionate interest and protection. The moonlight poured into their spot. She looked into Omar's eyes – serene, calm, and watchful, floating like shining stars in a black sky.

His voice came soothing into her ears. "You are the first woman in my life." Elizabeth melted in his arms with relief.

Omar was silent, enjoying having Elizabeth in his arms. As for Elizabeth, she was lost in her own thoughts. Fate had brought Omar into her life. She had kept saying to herself that types like him disagreed with her constitution. He was a conservative Muslim who had been brought up to believe in God, while she was unreligious and liberal. Although her parents were Catholic, she never went to church except for funerals and weddings.

Omar was too big, much too large, and too dangerous, definitely the wrong man. Everything about him frightened her — his great self-assurance, his striking good looks, and the physical power that radiated from him — but particularly her feeling that he could so easily look deeply into her soul. A man like that could never be tamed. Even the most casual of involvement with him would be like accompanying him barefoot on a walk across a mile of broken glass. But since she had laid eye on him, she had been exercising all the self-control she possessed to prevent herself from falling for him. Was her feeling true love or just a sort of attraction that would perish after the end of her mission in Kosovo? She knew deep inside her that with only a little relaxation of her self-control, she would love him madly. Her self-control was already so fragile that only a few moments ago, she'd thrown herself into his arms without any advances from him, seeking his love. She reproached herself several times for allowing him to cause such a violent reaction to rage within her, but she felt utterly helpless.

It was rare that she opened the door of the past to anyone, but this time she opened it to Omar. She told him about her husband trading in money laundering, how her dearest friend betrayed her with her husband, and how her husband disgraced her family and ruined her life.

"Every day seemed to narrow the boundaries around me, leaving me little room to find my own happiness. I have lived with that pain so long that it has become a part of me," Elizabeth said, ending her story.

Two tears escaped from the corners of her eyes and ran down her nose. "You must forgive my stupid tears. I don't know what came over me." She laughed apologetically.

"There's no point clinging to the painful past," Omar said soothingly. "The world goes on. Time and faith can heal the wounds. Remember that. Liz, I wish you everything wonderful," he whispered.

She felt a rush of deep affection for him that created an area of warmth around her heart. Between them, a warm friendship had ripened.

Elizabeth could feel Omar's warm breath in her hair as she leaned back against the solid wall of his chest. The aroma of him was strong and male. She wished he knew how much she needed him now.

This compelled her to ask him, "Does sex in your religion have to be allied to marriage? You know, a betrothal may be broken easily enough. The world is different now, and one must move with the times."

"Nonsense. A betrothal is a solemn and most binding commitment. Marriage is a serious matter on which rests the security of the family and the stability of the state. Yes, sex in our religion is allied to marriage. I was brought up to believe that a man should take care of a woman by loving her and making her the mother of his children."

"My marriage ended up a total failure. I do not think I will repeat this experience again. It's better to live free without commitments." Elizabeth sighed deeply.

"I don't understand. What exactly do you mean?" Omar inquired.

"Well, in America and in most Western countries, men and women can live together without marriage. It's easier. Men are afraid of marriage because if they get divorced, the women get custody of the children and take most of their husbands' salaries."

"Men and women living together without marriage are sinners. This has been mentioned in the great three religions: Judaism, Christianity, and Islam," Omar said firmly.

"Omar, be practical. The world is different now. Do I have to marry you in order to sleep with you? It is absurd. Women are free and educated now, and they can look after themselves. No woman wants to be treated as a second-class citizen by a man."

"In order for me to sleep with you, we have to tie the knot," Omar said seriously.

"Oh, shit." Elizabeth said. "You know well that you and I are totally different, and I doubt that our paths will cross again."

Omar said, "There are evil, terrible consequences coming from unlawful union with a woman. There is either disease without cure or a child without a father, a bastard to darken a man's honour. Men and women alike must revere Allah, their creator, who brought them into being from one single soul — Adam. And from Adam, he created his mate— Eve. And from joining both in matrimony did he propagate multitudes of men and women. Marriage is the sacred bond that ties the members of the family together. The family is the nucleus of society, and woman as a wife is the pillar on which the family is founded. Inside the family, woman is the uncrowned queen. She is stronger than man. She gets pregnant, she raises her children patiently, planting in them the principles of her religion, and she guards her husband in his honour and in his money. Her success in meeting her commitments as a wife is what makes her strong and dignified, respectable and worthy of appreciation.

"Women living with men without marriage, besides both being sinners, will suffer a painful chastisement on the Day of Judgement. They are like animals in the forest, living without laws, or like ancient primitive tribes in the wilderness, living without ethics. Women accepting this kind of living disgrace and humiliate themselves to the extent of being slaves to men. This manner of living makes men move to other women, and women move to other men, without any sort of commitment, thus spreading debauchery and laceration of family ties. New generations raised in societies admitting such corruption will think that this kind of lifestyle is normal and will follow suit. Societies raised in such a manner are subject to deterioration no matter how advanced their technology is. Is that what you call freedom? Sex outside marriage is backwardness and deliberate deviation from religion."

"I don't quite agree with you. Try to be realistic. Your explanation is based on religious aspects. Many people are not religious. They are living in a free world. Their relationships are based on mutual understanding, free love, and superiority of materialism."

Omar withdrew into himself for long moments. He knew that he and Elizabeth were utterly different. Both came from different worlds. She might never agree with his views. But there was something common between them. She liked him as a man, and he loved her loveliness and exquisite beauty. She was nestling in his chest, and he was holding the whole world in his arms. Was he falling for her? Maybe it was the thrill of the moment or the magic of moonlight penetrating the tops of the trees and illuminating the peaks of the mountains far ahead of them.

Elizabeth snapped at him while nestling in his arms.: "It's the age of equality. Many women don't appreciate men who take control. You think I am silly, don't you? You think I'm being trivial and horrid."

"No, I don't. You came from a different world, a world immersed in materialism. Money and power could ease many situations, but it counted for nothing against the blessing for happiness. Money is only a means, not an end. In the material world, people enjoy comforts that materialism has brought them. People in such systems attach a lot of importance to financial possessions and physical pleasure without restriction. Under the pretence of liberty and free love, people have committed all the sins God has forbidden. Surprisingly enough, the governments of the so-called industrialized capitalist countries encourage their people to do so as long as they pay taxes! Under materialism, people deviated from the path of God and thought that they would only live this life. They forgot that God only created them to worship Him by following the instructions of the divine books He sent to His messengers. They forgot that on the Day of Judgement, Allah would be there to judge their deeds. All the power and money they gained during their lives on earth would not protect them from a painful chastisement. So as you see, happiness is not only physical but also, more importantly, spiritual. To Muslims, seeking physical pleasures without clinging to Allah's instructions is a kind of barbarism, a kind of slavery to materialism. It's ugly." Omar said this with icy disapproval.

The warm of his body radiated through hers. She said while resting contentedly in his arms, "Happiness is unattainable without money, power, social distinction, and physical pleasure. In your opinion, what is happiness?"

Omar's voice was deep, penetrating her heart. "Unconditioned recognition of Allah and the sincere believe in Him, acknowledgement of the truth of Resurrection and Judgement, and deeds must be crowned with wisdom and piety, and that all must go together. If you do that, happiness will fill your heart. This is happiness. This is Islam."

Elizabeth began to feel a growing admiration for him. He really got to the heart of things, but in his own way. She knew where his power lay. He was a true believer. He believed that God existed and that the teachings of his religion were true. How easily and logically he was driving her into his world.

Omar said in a low, clear voice, "I wish I could make you see how much fuller the life of the spirit is than anything you have the conception of. It is illimitable. It is such a happy life. It is as if you were put on a plane by yourself, high, with only infinity surrounding you. You would be intoxicated by the boundless space. You would feel such a sense of exhilaration that you would not exchange it for all the power and glory in the world."

"I can understand that. I'm a pilot myself," Elizabeth said. She then surprised him, saying, "I long ago gave up the faith of my childhood. Now I believe in the power of modern science. Prayer seems an arbitrary frill."

"Do not make a mockery of this. Those who live lives apart from religion in this world will regret every moment of their lives. They were warned before and invited to the straight path. They had enough time to contemplate and embrace the right way. Yet they did not listen when they were warned, ignoring the hereafter as if they would never die. In the hereafter, they will have no chance to get back to this world and correct their errors. Islam warns people against a day when they will regret saying, 'Had we only not rejected the signs of our Lord.' Islam invites people to live for God while they still have the chance to correct their wrongs."

Elizabeth gazed up into the moon and wondered why Omar's words held the ring of truth.

"Omar, who is your God?" she inquired.

"Allah has indicated His nature in the Koran. I will recite to you a few verses showing some of his descriptions: 'He is Allah, there is no God but He. He is the knower of the unseen, and the seen, He is the Most Gracious, the Most Merciful. He is Allah, there is no God but He, He is the Sovereign, the Holy, the Peace, the Giver of Faith, the Overall Controller, the Almighty, the Compeller, the Majestic, Glory be to Allah above that they associate! He is Allah the Creator, the Maker, the Shaper; to Him belong the most Sublime Attributes. All that in the Heavens and the earth glorifies Him, and He is the Almighty, the All-Wise.'"

"I feel as if there is a light illuminating my heart," Elizabeth whispered, overwhelmed by the spirituality that suddenly invaded her soul.

Omar smiled and recited further: 'Allah is the Light of the heavens and the earth. The similitude of His Light is as if there were a niche wherein is a luminary, the luminary is in a glass, the glass is as if it were a planet glittering like a pearl, lit from a blessed olive tree, neither of the east nor of the west, whose oil is almost luminous, although no fire touched it, Light upon Light, Allah guides to His Light when He pleases, and Allah sets similitudes for people, and Allah is All-Knowing of all things.'"

To Elizabeth, Omar's submissive voice was like the ripple of a piano when the violins with great sweep sing the several themes of a concerto.

Omar whispered as if dreaming, "The purpose of creation is to worship God and serve Him as He wills. God is not in need of human worship. He did not create human beings out of a need on His part. If not a single human worshipped God, it would not diminish His glory in any way, and if all humankind worshipped Him, it would not increase His glory in any way. God is perfect. He alone exists without any needs. All created beings have needs. Consequently, humankind needs to worship Allah. Sincere worship necessitates living righteous lives through obedience to God's commandments."

The moon paled away in the coming of the dawn. Elizabeth said with a yawn, "How wise you are. It seems that the East has more to teach the West than the West conceives."

After a few minutes, Elizabeth went into a deep sleep in Omar's arms. Omar eased her body back into the sleeping bag. He kept looking at her. She looked like an innocent baby while sleeping. She was so beautiful that it tore at his heart. A strong feeling washed over him. He wanted to care for her, to protect her from unhappiness and wanton damage.

Elizabeth slept for hours and awoke in the forenoon. She yawned and stretched luxuriously like a cat. Her eyes roamed the place, searching for Omar. She found him prostrating on his prayer mat, praying in gratitude to God.

"What were you saying to your God?" she asked him after he finished his prayers.

He said with a smile, "I said, 'My Lord, if you do not turn away her guile from me, I may be caught in her snare and become one of the ignorant.'"

She laughed heartily and realized that no matter how deep the differences between her and Omar might be, he would always remain close to her heart.

CHAPTER 17

The Yugoslav Army and Serbian police began a major offensive against the Kosovo Liberation Army. The offensive, which involved heavy artillery, tanks, and occasionally air power, was highly effective in driving the Kosovo Liberation Army from most of its established positions into pockets in the mountains and woods. In the end, however, very few of the Kosovo Liberation Army's fighters were killed or captured.

More than two hundred villages were destroyed, and at least three hundred thousand people were internally displaced. The brunt of the suffering was borne by Muslim Albanian civilians who lived in the areas of conflict. In Kosovo, Muslims had become the main victims — if not the actual targets — of the fighting.

President Milosovic and his military planners knew that they had little time left to complete their objectives in Kosovo and then avert a Western military response by ordering a rapid and dramatic pullback of forces.

Through the woods, Omar and Elizabeth marched towards Glogovac, the largest village in the Drenica region. They emerged from the woods to reach a hill overlooking the village of Glogovac. They could hear the roar of continuous shelling and women's screams in the distance. Omar reached for his binoculars and lay belly down on the edge of the hill to examine the village in the valley below. Elizabeth lay beside him with a terrified look on her face.

While looking through his binoculars, Omar said, "The whole village is burning. It would be impossible to set an entire village on fire without the use of an accelerant. Someone clearly moved through the houses and set them on fire, as it would be impossible due to the distances between the houses for the fire, however fierce, to jump from one house to the next. As I see from here, the Yugoslav Army is shelling the village with various types of artillery and mortars. It seems that the village is deserted, with most of its inhabitants having fled to the adjacent forest. The forest could be a good hiding place for them. The militia avoids going into the forests for fear of the Kosovo Liberation Army, which is usually hiding there. I can see forty tanks and armoured vehicles moving towards the village. The tanks are firing at the houses. There are three types of forces moving behind the tanks and armoured vehicles: the special police, distinguished by their blue camouflage uniforms; the special antiterrorist force, distinguished by their darker brown camouflage uniforms; and contingents of the Yugoslav Army, recognizable from their green uniforms. There is no question that all these forces work in concert with each other to execute the ethnic cleansing plan put forward by the Yugoslav authorities."

"What are we going to do now?" Elizabeth asked, trembling all over.

"We will stay here until sunset. By that time, the Yugoslav forces might leave for another village. However, they always leave behind some forces to continue the cleansing process. There is no other way but to cross Glogovac to the nearby forest, and from there we move to Prekaz. We must also get some provisions from the deserted houses because right now we are living on the bare minimum."

Omar ceased looking through his binoculars. Elizabeth could see a dangerous look on his face.

"I would prefer to change our overalls for the blue uniforms of the Serbia special police," he said. "It would be good camouflage, don't you think?" Omar's eyes were as cold as hell boring down into the valley.

"The logical, sensible thing to do now is to retreat and find a safer road to Prekaz," Elizabeth said, trying to dissuade Omar from exposing himself to danger. "You can't mess with them. There are too many, and they are well armed. They will blow you away like smoke." Elizabeth had concern clouding her expression.

"We must be ready to confront them," Omar said decisively.

"Omar, please don't make a martyr of yourself." Elizabeth squeezed her eyes tightly, refusing to think about Omar being killed.

Omar stared at the valley before him for a long time. He seemed locked in his mind, forecasting the probable moves of the Yugoslav forces below.

Elizabeth reached for Omar's arm and pressed it gently. She pleaded, "Omar, talk to me, please. I'm scared."

Omar said, while engaged wholly in observing the movements of the forces below, "The injustice of the Serb's government and the oppression they impose on the poor Muslim villagers makes me apply an Islamic rule called 'jihad'. The Muslims of Glugovac need someone to help them by alleviating injustice. Under the present circumstances, I use my own laws and I stand by them. You know what the meaning of jihad is in Islam? It means fighting in the cause of Allah. Jihad is common in Islam because Allah ordered Muslims to perform jihad when they sought to drive out their oppressors. Because God's reward for those who fight for His cause is great in the hereafter, Muslims race to die in order to please God and do not even think to return to their families after the fight is over. That is why their fight in the cause of Allah is severe. Muslims think that at the moment of death, a martyr will feel no more pain than if he were being pinched. God Almighty said about Jihad, 'Let those who sell this worldly life for the hereafter, fight in the cause of Allah, and whoever fights in the cause of Allah then is killed or conquers, we shall reward him with a great reward.'"

Elizabeth listened to the Koranic verses and realized that no power on earth could now dissuade Omar from starting his own jihad in the cause of Allah.

One hour after sunset, Omar and Elizabeth galloped down the hill, heading towards the silent village of Glogovac. Omar was fully armed, and Elizabeth carried on her back a leather bag with a tin of first-aid supplies. They ran close to each other and in concert as if one body. A strange feeling washed over Elizabeth. She felt that she was an integral part of Omar's being. Yes, with Omar even danger could be faced with elation. Confidence in God and submission to whatever fate might bring them radiated from Omar to her. Although she was terrified of the danger she and Omar might encounter soon with the Serbs, she felt that God was on their side. Their fate was now is in the hands of God. Weren't they fighting now in the cause of God? Weren't they fighting for a noble cause? Alleviating Albanian misery was certainly a noble cause. A mixture of fright and submission to God were pushing her to run side by side with Omar in long strides. They were heading towards their enemy. Just two persons against a whole army! In that particular moment, she didn't think about the consequences of such an unequal encounter. She just ran and ran with her man. Her man – a man with whom she felt protected and secure.

What an exciting and beautiful feeling. A man who moved and acted with the words of God was surely supported by divine care.

Omar and Elizabeth moved silently in the darkness to one of the many deserted cottages of the village. The cottage was elevated from the ground by short wooden stanchions. Omar and Elizabeth hid under the cottage for half an hour, during which Omar thoroughly inspected the place. Through his infrared binoculars, he was able to locate thirty armoured personnel carriers and twenty tanks. Each armoured vehicle had a three-man crew: the commander, the driver, and the gunner. Each tank also had a three-man crew. That equaled 150 armed persons. Adding the number of the infantry that was moving behind the tanks and the vehicles, the total number of the Serbs would amount to approximately 250. The tanks and the armed vehicles seemed deserted. The officers and the soldiers were totally relaxed, sitting in one large circle and eating, laughing, and smoking.

Omar examined the deserted armoured vehicles. To enter the vehicles, the crew must climb through the roof hatches in front of the turret. The vehicles also had two hatches behind the turret for mounting and dismounting the passengers. The gasoline engines were mounted at the rear of the hull.

Omar focused on the command vehicle that served as the fire direction centre for wheeled artillery. Mounted externally on top of the turret was a 30 mm cannon. A 14.5 mm heavy machine gun was mounted to the right of the cannon. Mounted on either side of the cannon were electrically operated heavy machine-guns. The vehicle had full side doors, each consisting of an upper half that opened forward and a lower half that opened downward and formed a stepladder for troops entering and exiting.

Quite close to this vehicle, Omar spotted a vehicle with a turret boasting a rotating rocket launcher. The Egyptian Army had similar Russian armoured vehicles, and Omar was well trained on them.

Omar's eyes roamed around the place. He sighted eleven villagers herded like cattle by two soldiers from the special police. The villagers were blindfolded, and their hands were handcuffed behind their backs. They were stumbling on weary feet, their faces grey with fatigue. The two policemen interrogated them for a while, possibly about the hiding places of the Kosovo Liberation Army, and then made them lie on the ground. The two soldiers kicked their heads and backs. Blood was dripping from their heads and mouths. The soldiers removed the blindfolds from their eyes and cut off the plastic handcuffs. Some of the villagers tried to stand up but were shoved to the ground by the machine guns. The soldiers then put pieces of cloth into their mouths and started to burn their backs with a torch. The villagers were screaming for mercy. After half an hour of such torture, the villagers were led into a house. Close to the house was a deep trench, possibly dug by the Kosovo Liberation Army. Omar realized what was going to happen to the villagers inside the house. The two soldiers would execute them and then the house would be set on fire. It was a common procedure exercised by the Serbs against Muslim Albanians.

Omar knew that he was outnumbered, but he would try, by God. Omar groped for the bag containing the explosive packages. Everything was ready. He could move now.

Omar motioned Elizabeth to stay put until he got back, and then he slid through the shadows. Fat black clouds billowed over the moon, yet Omar had no trouble moving through the area. Instinctively, he knew where to place his feet so as not to make the slightest betraying noise. By the time he reached the trench, he heard the sound of machine guns spraying the innocents inside the house. He stopped and leaned against the wall of the trench, waiting with a gun fitted with a silencer in his hand for the two soldiers to emerge from the house. After a few minutes, the entire house was ablaze. One soldier in blue uniform came hurriedly out of the burning house, and Omar aimed at his head and pulled the trigger. The man spun around and smashed to the ground. After a few moments, the second soldier appeared at the door, finishing off the fallen men with his pistol. Before he realized what had happened to his colleague, Omar turned his gun on him and cut him down with a bullet between his eyes. Omar jumped out from the trench, stripped the two men, and then threw their bodies into the burning house. Dancing flames, billowing smoke, and burned corpses all blended into an inferno.

Omar took off his overalls and put on the blue uniform of one of the men he killed, keeping the other for Elizabeth. Omar looked in the direction of the troops. They didn't even bother to look at the burning house, as if killing and burning was a common practice to them. Omar paused to listen. Now he had to keep his guard and move cautiously. Omar silently rushed to the tanks and armoured vehicles. He moved lightly, hiding in the shadows of the night. Swiftly and efficiently, he taped the explosive packages to the bottom of fuel tanks, close to the gasoline engines, and inside the hatches of the gunners. He set the timer on the clock to go off after half an hour. Omar didn't have enough explosive packages to cover all the tanks or vehicles, so he chose some of them randomly in a manner that would cause the highest explosion density and the utmost confusion to the troops. The command vehicle was left intact, as was the vehicle with a rotating rocket launcher.

Omar did not forget to pick up some canned food and hard bread from the vehicles.

"Where have you been? I was sick with worry," Elizabeth whispered, heaving a sigh of relief at the sight of Omar.

"Put this on," Omar said, giving her a blue uniform.

Elizabeth felt a little embarrassed taking off her overalls before Omar. But it seemed just a trifle silly to be worried about her privacy. He had seen every inch of her.

"Let's move now," Omar ordered.

Omar crawled silently from under the cottage and ran with the shadows, Elizabeth following close behind. They headed across the dense bushes to the command vehicle. They got in through the stepladder of the side door that opened downward. Omar checked the 30 mm cannon and the 14.5 mm heavy machine gun. They were loaded and ready for use. Through the infrared searchlight, he was clearly able to locate the troops gathered in a large circle.

"We have to fight our way out of here by dispersing the troops relaxing over there. They're blocking our path to the forest through which we should cross to Prekaz. The element of surprise is a crucial factor in winning battles. The Serbs don't have the slightest idea that we are here. They will drink from the same cup of agony they forced the innocents to swallow. After just a few minutes, all hell will break loose." Omar said this in a low, lethal voice.

Omar waited for the remaining minutes to pass. He waited with the patience of a hunter, the quiet stillness of a man in control of his body and emotions. Elizabeth was closely watching him. She knew that under this stillness, Omar was filled with a rage pushing him to kill.

Suddenly, the entire place blew up. The tanks and the vehicles began to explode at short intervals. Before the troops dispersed and discerned what exactly was happening, Omar shot at them from a near distance with the 30 mm cannon. The soldiers lay with faces to the ground, trying to avoid the shooting. They became thus immobile, giving Omar the chance to shoot at them right and left with ease. The turret system, which could turn 360 degrees, allowed Omar to swiftly direct the shooting in every direction he chose. Those who tried to escape were confronted with the blazing splinters coming out from the exploded vehicles. Omar then shifted to the 14.5 mm heavy machine gun and sprayed both alive and dead bodies scattered on the ground. Figures that rose from the ground while trying desperately to escape were easy targets. Omar kept firing in all directions for fifteen minutes and then set the electrically operated heavy machine guns into motion.

Omar caught Elizabeth by the arm, and both hurried out to the vehicle with the rotating rocket launcher. Omar quickly reloaded the launcher through a small hatch located behind it. Through a sight mounted on the front right of the vehicle, he controlled the direction of the rockets to successively hit the centre of the circle and its peripheral boundaries. The whole place turned into a blazing hell.

Amid the inferno, Omar and Elizabeth jumped out of the vehicle and vanished like smoke into the forest.

CHAPTER 18

They ran non-stop for a mile. Elizabeth unable to catch her breath came to a halt. There was no doubt that she was delaying him. They still had ten miles to go in order to reach Prekaz. They had to cross the forest as quickly as possible because one or more of the Serbs might have observed them disappearing in the forest. He was certain that the Serbs usually avoid going into the woods for fear of the ambushes set up by the Liberation Army, but the dense casualties they'd suffered a few minutes ago would surely make them search for Omar to the very gates of hell if necessary. He must stay alert and constantly on guard.

"Omar, I want to pee. I'll go behind that tree and—"

"All right, all right. But hurry up," he interrupted nervously.

After a few minutes, he shouted at her, "This delay could jeopardize everything! I haven't got all day so hurry up, please."

"Who the hell do you think you are?" she shot at him, emerging from behind the tree. "I'm tired. I don't know whether I'm standing on my head or my heels." Elizabeth felt a sudden urge to burst into tears.

"This is a dangerous spot, and we must move fast," Omar said.

"I'll spend the night here, you understand? That's final." She spoke with cheeks burning with fury.

"Now you listen to me and listen well. You aren't the boss up here. I am. And what I say goes." Omar called forth every shred of self-mastery that he could claim.

"Go to hell." She turned away from him to hide the sudden glitter of tears burning her throat and swimming in her eyes. "I've been through a lot with you, and I passed bravely through all this terror without complaint. It's my right to get some rest."

"What did you expect me to do – pat you on the back and give you a medal?"

"You are a cold-blooded killer. It goes against everything you are standing for," she said furiously.

Omar was hurt. He did not utter a word. Elizabeth instantly felt his hurt. The look of pain in his eyes was so overwhelming that Elizabeth thought she might faint just looking at him. Her soul twisted.

"I'm sorry. I didn't mean to hurt you. It's just a slip of tongue." Her eyes were still misty.

Omar looked into Elizabeth eyes. He saw fear, pain, and exhaustion. He was too hard on her. She had still not recovered from the shock of the day's events, yet he was pushing her too hard. How insensitive he was. He would not stand seeing her in pain. His heart went out to her.

"Liz, I'm sorry. I was too hard on you. You're the only thing that made this nightmare endurable." Omar smiled at her. It was a painful smile, expressing all his regrets and sadness, a smile that was also so incredibly warm.

"Do you mean that or you are trying to calm me out of my fears?"

"I mean every word of it." He was still smiling.

"I was beginning to wonder if you knew how to smile," she said sadly.

"God, do you have any idea how beautiful you look when you are angry like that – with your cheeks red and your eyes glittering in the moonlight like jewels?"

"Don't be nice to me or I'll cry." She began sobbing.

"I wouldn't dare hurt you; I'm here to protect you with my blood and soul. You must be sure of that."

She saw his pain and sorrow. She saw the crashing torture of the continuous fighting pressing him too hard. And he was taking all this patiently and bravely – and only because of her. She wanted him to relax and lose himself completely in her arms. She wanted to hold his head against her bosom.

"Omar, I want to cry in your arms. I want to hold you and wipe away your pain. Would you allow me?" She was wavering like a young tree in a storm.

A steady stream of crystal tears slipped down her cheeks. Omar stretched his arms to her, and she ran to embrace him. He wrapped his arms around her, holding her tightly, unable to bear being on the side-lines of her sadness a second longer. Elizabeth exploded in his arms. She cried and cried and cried.

She said through her tears, "The waiting for you under the cottage was unbearable, the fight was unbearable, the endless running was unbearable."

Omar pressed her face into his shoulder and laid his cheek on top of her hair. A mixture of comfort and bewilderment had befallen her. She feared him yet ran to him at the breath of danger. He was dangerous, but she knew that he would never hurt her, not one hair of her head. Yes, he was ready to slay dragons for her. In his arms, she felt loved, cherished, and protected. Somewhere deep inside her, a gentle warmth blossomed in her heart, a heart that had known only resentment and sadness lately. Why hadn't they met before? He was a real man, a man she would like to have for herself. In his arms, the world ceased to exist.

Feeling Elizabeth in his arms was amazing to Omar. He felt that her heart beat in his chest.

"I'll sleep in your arms tonight; it's safer, you know. Don't say no, please." She was enjoying the warmth emanating from his body.

"Liz, you are a very beautiful woman. Being so close to you is very tempting. Our religion, as you know, forbids ..."

She laughed and interrupted him, saying," All right, man of virtue. I can see that you are strong enough to control your feelings. I'll sleep innocently in your arms like a babe."

Omar held her tighter to his chest and said mockingly, "You know what I'll do with you? I'll turn you over my knee and hit your backside so hard that you won't sit down for a week."

She laughed merrily and kissed his shoulder.

Omar carried Elizabeth and sat with her under a tree. She buried her face in his chest, relaxing in his arms. She felt the same solace and relief as when she had so frequently run into her mother's arms as a little girl.

Before Elizabeth went into a deep sleep in Omar's arms, the events of the day whirled in her head. The manner in which Omar had outwitted the Serbs at the village, and the way he alone effectively and courageously fought a whole army, was the most ingenious bravery she had ever witnessed. He had killed dozens of them in just few minutes. He had been certainly trained to deal and cope with the unexpected. She discovered that the advantage of highly trained soldiers and weapons technology was nullified when put against a courageous fighter in a restricted environment. She did not know how he had managed it, but she just guessed God was on his side.

She said in a low voice, "You are a brave man, Omar; I haven't seen such rare courage before."

He said modestly, "Belief in the one true God inspires bravery in man. There are two things, which make a man cowardly: fear of death and the idea that there is someone else besides God who can take away life. The believer in the one true God knows that his life, his property, and everything else really belongs to God, and he becomes ready to sacrifice his all for God's pleasure. He knows that no weapon, no man, and no power can take away his life; God alone has the power to do so. A time has been ordained for him, and not all the forces of the world combined can take away anyone's life a moment before the appointed time, nor can they delay his death in an instant. It is because of his firm belief in one God and dependence upon Him only that is no one braver than a believer."

His words penetrated her soul. The man in whose arms she lay confidently did not know disappointment under any circumstances. He understood that power was in God's hands and that God bestowed it as He wished. He knew that success and failure depended on God's grace; if He willed to give, no power in the world could prevent Him from doing so; and if He did not will it, no power could force Him. Omar considered his struggle for helping the oppressed ordained by God. Omar, by helping the oppressed, was doing his hardest to deserve God's grace.

from doing so; and if He did not will it, no power could force Him. Omar considered his struggle for helping the oppressed ordained by God. Omar, by helping the oppressed, was doing his hardest to deserve God's grace.

CHAPTER 19

Just before dawn, Omar awoke sensing danger. Sounds of bullets mingled with men's and women's screams were heard in the far distance. Omar's prediction proved correct. The Serbs were already in the forest. They were either after him or after the villagers who fled seeking shelter in the forest. Omar awoke Elizabeth gently and instructed her to stay put until he got back, for God knew what was behind those trees.

Omar walked cautiously for half an hour. He breathed the smell of fired bullets in the air. About sixty feet down the forest path was the temporary shelter the villagers had constructed, a wooden frame with a great tarp covering three foam mattresses. Omar could see from his hiding place civilian bodies scattered around the place. Gunshot wounds, knife cuts, and mutilations found on the bodies were disturbing. It was clear that this was not an accidental killing during combat but rather a direct attack on a group of civilians. All bodies were dressed in civilian clothes, and there was no evidence of any resistance to the attack. Bullets of different sizes were scattered at the scene of the crime. He would not get himself involved in a fight right now. It was wiser to go back to Elizabeth and move swiftly ahead to Prekaz. Prekaz was the only safe village in Kosovo. It had UN forces guarding the refugee camp and was immune to any sort of inspection from the Serbs. Omar ran back to Elizabeth like the wind.

Under the tree, Elizabeth sat frightened while waiting for Omar to return. She had absolutely no way to tell the time. She could not even be sure how long Omar had been gone. It could not have been a few minutes. It could not have been an hour. It felt like an eternity. She got angry with the passage of each minute. What was Omar doing? He was playing with her life!

A boot in the ribs brought Elizabeth to the ground. She rolled over and sat up, gasping with the pain of it. There were four men wearing red scarves on their heads, carrying axes and long knives on their belts. They also had semi-automatic weapons. One of the men was short and had a round head like a cannonball. His body was stocky and solid, with broad, thick shoulders. He had the look of a killer. The other three were tall and had the heavy shoulders of a wrestler.

The men noticed her blue uniform and began to interrogate her about its source. But Elizabeth didn't answer them because she didn't understand their language. The stocky man hit her face hard, and blood oozed from her wounded lips. She squeezed her eyes tightly in pain as the stocky man lifted her off her feet. The men talked among themselves and decided to take Elizabeth back to Glogovac for interrogation by the special police.

While the men were talking to each other, Elizabeth ran aimlessly in panic. Horror squeezed her lungs and made her heart pound severely in her chest. Her legs felt weak and rubbery under her. Racing footsteps were close behind her, steady, gaining on her. She could run no faster. Her legs aching, Elizabeth hammered her feet on the ground in a final burst of speed, but her legs gave out. The stocky man was suddenly over her, crushing her body. His forearm, like a heavy iron bar, was across her throat. He angrily scooped her up as though she were a sack of flour and slapped her face several times. Blood was dripping from her nose and mouth, and she felt she was going to die. The assailants marched towards Glogovac with Elizabeth walking before them.

When Omar returned to Elizabeth and did not find her, he searched the whole area, but there was no sign of her. Omar felt his heart sink. Omar climbed up a nearby grassy bluff and surveyed the forest below. Through his binoculars, he was able to spot the assailants moving fast. The stocky man was pushing Elizabeth ahead with his weapon. The assailants were about five hundred metres away from him. With the determination of a shark that had tasted blood, Omar raced after them with swift ground-eating strides.

Suddenly, Elizabeth heard a single shot. The head of one of the assailants snapped backwards as though he had taken a heavy punch. He tumbled backwards, falling heavily to the ground. The other three assailants turned back, and another bullet split open the skull of one of them. His head wrenched backwards, and his body turned heavy in mid-air.

The stocky man and his companion, seeing the two men dead, started to shoot blindly in all directions. When no shots were returned, they ran forward, pushing Elizabeth before them. After ten minutes of running, they suddenly stopped, for they saw far in front of them a figure watching them from the shadows. Here the assailants realized with alarm that their attacker had moved more swiftly than they had anticipated and become in a position of command. The assailants wondered how their attacker could vanish into thin air or be in two places at the same time!

The two assailants opened fire in the direction of their attacker, but the attacker was not there. He was swiftly turning around them and crawling amidst the clusters of trees. Now he was right behind them, lying on the ground, hiding in the long thorny bushes. He had trapped them.

Omar raised his right arm, steadying his sporting rifle with the left as he took aim. A neat hole appeared in the centre of one of the assailant's back. Omar's second shot spun the man around; a jet of blood spurted from his mouth as he fell to the ground.

What remained now was the stocky man. He felt panic spur him and started to run, pushing Elizabeth ahead of him. Omar hunted him through the wood like a persistent wolf.

Omar's main concern now was that the stocky man was pushing Elizabeth ahead towards the place of the carnage. Omar did not want Elizabeth to see the mutilated corpses, but it seemed that in order to cross the forest to Glogova, one must go along the path in which the carnage took place.

When Elizabeth and the stocky man got there, Elizabeth turned in shock at the sight of the corpses and ran away, stumbling and falling against the dead bodies in her haste to escape the site of the carnage. Elizabeth gasped when the strong arms of the stocky man came from behind. She was hauled back against a body that was as hard as a block of granite. She struggled even though she knew that her pitiful attempts to break free were no match for the man's strength.

Suddenly, the stocky man felt an iron hand on his shoulder digging into his flesh and heard someone commanding him to let her go. It came as a worse shock to find himself staring into Omar's cold black eyes. With his forefingers and middle fingers, Omar pierced him in the eyes. The man felt a terrible pain and dropped his machine gun while trying to rub the pain out of his eyes. Omar took advantage and kicked the man hard in the stomach. The man bent downwards but quickly straightened up. He then drew his long knife and charged forward. Omar clamped his right hand above the man's wrist and with his left hand gripped the fingers wrapped around the knife. He snapped the wrist downward, facing the blade inward, and then plunged it into the stomach, up to the hilt. The man's face contorted and began a terrible scream, which was cut off by death.

Elizabeth was trembling all over, and in her terror, she threw herself against Omar, who put both his arms round her.

"Don't be frightened, Liz. It's all right now," Omar said, heaving a sigh of relief.

"I was eaten alive with worry. Where the hell have you been? They have frightened the life out of me." Elizabeth began sobbing into his chest.

"Sorry I gave you such a fright. The men I killed were the assassins. They deserved to die," Omar said with relief.

Elizabeth clung to him. She held him closely, as though she might drown if she left him for an instant.

"You have saved my life, and for that I will be eternally grateful." She was still crying. "I've missed you," she added gently.

Omar held her close and spoke in a soothing tone. "Liz, all your troubles are over; it will all turn to the best."

Eventually, her tempest of misery began to die down to individual sobs and sniffs. She slowly pulled away from his arms and began to look around her, frightened. With Elizabeth close beside him, Omar walked around the place examining the corpses.

In the temporary shelter the villagers had constructed in the forest, they found the bodies of an old man and an old woman. The woman had a gunshot wound to the head and her throat was cut. Her right foot was almost severed from the body, apparently in an attempt to remove the foot with a knife. Only a small piece of skin waskeeping the leg together. The woman was lying on her back, and her legs were spread. There was a lot of blood around her. The man was lying on his stomach and part of his head had been blown off. The left side of his head was missing, and his brain had slipped between the mattresses. The mattress was filled with blood.

Down the forest path, a small gully veered off to the right. Omar found bodies of eleven persons, mostly women and children, along the narrow gully, which measured only a few hundred feet in length. Most were shot in the head. It seemed that they were executed at close range, possibly as they attempted to flee from their pursuers.

Just a few feet up the narrow gully, Omar found the youngest victim of the attack, a two-year-old boy with a blood-splattered face. A nine-year-old boy was found close by, his throat cut from the jugular to the lower lip by a knife or a bullet.

Nearby was the body of a pregnant woman, about to give birth any day. The woman was cut all over, starting from the shoulder and going down to her stomach, and her internal organs were spilling out through a big hole in her back. It looked like an explosion not from a gun but from a grenade.

Up the narrow gully, Omar and Elizabeth found a body of a woman lying on her right side, and next to her lay her six-week-old daughter. The woman's face was cut all over, and her left arm above the baby was cut with a knife. The baby's mouth was full of blood from her mother's left arm.

Omar knelt down on one knee to examine the baby. At that moment, the baby opened her eyes, not totally but halfway. The baby was alive! Omar tried to clean the blood out of her mouth, and the baby stuck her tongue out a little. Omar took her clothes off. The baby was not wounded, so he dressed her again.

"She's a baby girl. She is alive," Omar said, giving the baby to Elizabeth.

Every nerve in Elizabeth's body throbbed to a savage beat as she stood carrying the baby.

"I've never carried a baby before." She was frightened.

"Let's get out of here." Omar took Elizabeth by the arm and walked away in long strides.

The baby was weak and silent during the long walk. Omar suddenly came to a halt. "Elizabeth, the baby must be hungry by now. Feed her, please." He sounded concerned.

"And how do I do that?" Elizabeth asked with surprise.

"Give her your breast or something." He said this seriously, as if he had resolved the problem.

"In order to do that, I have to be pregnant and give birth — then milk will come." His ignorance of women astonished her. "You certainly know nothing about women, do you?" She loved his virginity. She looked in his eyes and saw embarrassment and confusion. She said, trying to sound casual and normal, "We have been walking for an hour now, and the baby hasn't moved."

Omar turned ashen. He examined the baby. "She's dead. I'll bury her under that tree. Stay here till I get back." He took the baby from Elizabeth and walked to the tree.

Elizabeth's heart sank to the pit of her stomach. She had looked at Omar's eyes while giving him the baby and felt his agony in her soul.

Omar was kneeling on the ground, busy burying the baby. After he finished the difficult task, he sat for long moments looking sadly at the grave before him. His sadness was so agonizing that he felt weakness and emptiness. He felt conquered and defeated. He wished to be left alone. He did not want Elizabeth to see him in such a state of weakness. It went totally against his pride. Yes, he had a heart of a lion and could fight a whole army by himself when necessary, but he just couldn't stand watching the assassination of the innocents: old men and women, mothers and children, and even babies!

His whole body trembled. He wanted to weep, but he fought back the tears. If he had any soft places, they were well hidden. He prayed in silence. *Oh, God, you are the one who knows my deepest thoughts and understands my hurts. Give me strength, for I'm falling apart.*

A soft hand came from behind and rested on his shoulder. "Do you mind if I join you?"

Her compassionate hand touched his soul deeply, and he found himself shaking terribly inside. Waves of tears raced to his eyes.

"Omar, are you okay?" Elizabeth asked while kneeling down beside him.

"The hurt I have, the pain I feel, I can't explain." He turned his face to her.

Elizabeth felt tightness in her throat. Omar's face was stiff, but his eyes were watering. He tried to maintain his cool, but he could not prevent a torrent of tears from rolling down his face. Elizabeth's face turned deadly pale and looked with disbelieving eyes at his tearful pain-filled eyes. Her heart went out to him.

He said through his tears, "The cruel twists and turns of fate are just unfair. This misery slices through me like a knife. Please forgive my stupid tears. I do not know what came over me."

She couldn't help but take him in her arms and rock him gently, as though he were an injured child. He exploded into her arms, clinging to her as if she were the only shelter left in the world. She was astonished to see tears still streaming down his face. It was the only time she'd seen him cry. It must take an enormous pain to make a rocky mountain cry.

Holding him tightly in her arms, she said, "Just open up your heart and let your feelings show."

He said with a sob, "Sorry. I just couldn't ..." The words caught in his throat.

Consoling him, she said, "Omar, don't cry, please. The clouds of sorrow will depart." She was sobbing with him.

"Do you still think I'm a cold-blooded killer? Injustice goes against everything I stand for. It's oppression that I fight against."

Loving his momentary weakness, she said, "No, my love, you are just full of righteous indignation. In your heart, you yearn for love, not death."

"I've put you through misery and fear which will haunt you for the rest of your life." He felt sorry for her.

He looked tired and so handsome that her breath caught. She found herself kissing his wide black eyes.

Omar looked at her lovely face. The sunlight caught the thick waves of her hair, setting them on fire. He loved the way the sun turned her hair to dark gold. Waves of golden hair fell loosely around her shoulders, and he lost himself in eyes so green. He saw in her eyes a spring of light. He saw her like a radiant rose with lovely petals falling free. His heart melted. She had stolen his heart from deep within.

Omar's heart began to beat quickly. In that moment, he felt that he loved her to the depth and breadth and height his soul could reach. In that moment, he knew that she was the only woman in the world for him.

"I've wasted my life fighting. It was all darkness before I met you. I saw light when I realized that I care for you."

She held him closely and wept in his arms when he uttered the tender words. Her face bloomed like a sweet flower, and she melted in his chest like a candle burning in the dark. She buried her face in his neck and whispered, "Keep me safe and warm all through my life. Make my life worth living."

He held her tightly and felt her slim body like the fair light of dawn, like the earth giving birth to a field of beautiful flowers. He loved her as freely as men strive for right. He loved her with the breath, smiles, and tears of all his life.

Suddenly, his sad voice came to awaken her from her sweet dreams. "My heart aches at the thought of you leaving me. I'll miss being by your side."

She had forgotten that she was here on a mission that was supposed to last for only few days. Her face contorted with pain, and clinging strongly to him, she said, "I know that nothing is forever or always, but for now I don't ever want to lose you."

"After you depart, it will all fade away and I will go about my lonely way."

"I just don't ever want you to leave my life," she said, feeling his pain.

"We are different, and I'm only a soldier."

She looked at his eyes and saw the hurt. "I know that we will never truly part. Together we will find a clearer path to follow through the twists and turns of life."

"I'll miss your special light, although it will always shine on in me. One day you'll be mine and only mine." He held her as tightly as if he were holding his own heart.

CHAPTER 20

Omar and Elizabeth continued their trip to Prekaz. They walked cautiously, scarcely moving by day, covering a long distance by night. In two days, they covered a distance of eight miles without interruption from the Serbs. Four miles were still ahead of them to reach Prekaz. Along their way, they passed through scattered smaller deserted villages. Most of the houses had been torched and were completely destroyed. The food units had also been burned, and valuable possessions such as appliances, satellite dishes, vehicles, and televisions had been stolen, destroyed, or were severely vandalized.

Shot cattle lay strewn around the villages, and many haystacks and other food supplies had been torched. The pattern of destruction clearly showed the systematic and premeditated nature of the actions of the Serbian police and the Yugoslav army, without any form of resistance by local Muslim Albanians.

After a long walk, Omar and Elizabeth reached a small hedge surrounded by dense bushes. It was overlooking a small village in the near distance. The hedge was a perfect place to spend the night, as it was unexposed to the Serbs.

In the morning, Omar spotted a small convoy of armed vehicles leaving the area and heading back to Glogovac. The convoy, however, had left behind six police officers torching the deserted houses and setting them on fire.

The hedge in which Omar and Elizabeth were hiding was only fifty metres away from the police officers. Their shouting was clearly heard, and the smoke arising from the burning houses was thick and suffocating. Omar ushered Elizabeth to stay motionless until he returned. Omar intended to explore the area in order to find a safer path to their final destination. He also needed to find a strategic location to dominate the situation when necessary. Omar crawled lightly and vanished in the adjacent bushes. After waiting half an hour for Omar to return, Elizabeth got tired from lying with her face to the ground. She tried to move, but the police heard the crack of the dry leaves and fired at her location. Elizabeth lay on the ground, hiding from the bullets. She could feel the dirt flying against her legs as the bullets hit the ground. The police no doubt thought she was one of the Kosovo Liberation Army.

From his comparatively advantageous location, Omar was clearly able to spot the attackers. He quickly put the silencer in place, and with his sporting rifle, shot down three of them.

The shooting stopped for a while, for the attackers didn't know from where the silent bullets had come. The attackers hid behind the trees and decided to circle around the hedge. They retreated calmly, crawled amid the heavy bushes, and disappeared in the forest.

Omar did not like their sudden disappearance, and he realized with a pang of alarm that Elizabeth was in extreme danger. Omar hurried back to Elizabeth, trying to figure out the direction from which the assailants might start their attack.

Figures swarmed from the forest and raged to the hedge. Bullets blazed from their machine guns, targeting the hedge. Omar cut one down and then another.

Elizabeth was lying on the ground, hiding her face with both hands, when Omar arrived. Omar knelt down on one knee beside her, examining her. She was panicky and shaking terribly, but she was safe and alive.

"Let's get out of here." Omar urged Elizabeth to stand up. Instead of responding to him, she looked at him with terrified eyes, unable to move. At that instant, they heard the chatter of a nearby machine gun. Omar threw himself over Elizabeth, protecting her with his body. The assailant fired again, rapid lethal bursts, at the two unclear figures covered by the bushes. One bullet slammed into Omar's side. A fiery pain spread all over his body.

Omar whispered through his unbearable pain, "Don't move, Liz. Stay still. Don't even breathe if you can."

The eyes of the assailant were filled with loathing and hatred as he approached the two figures lying on the ground, covered by the thorny bushes. He moved slowly forward, the machine gun ready in his hand.

Omar could hear the sound of his footsteps by the sound of the cracking leaves. In order not to be tricked, the assailant paused for long moments to be certain that the bodies before him were dead. He then stepped forward and continued marching towards Omar and Elizabeth. With the speed of lightning, Omar turned around, drew his handgun, and squeezed the trigger. Four bullets tore into the assailant and slammed his head and chest. The man fell dead to the ground. Omar fired again, and the man's body jumped with the impact of the bullets.

Omar's body was on fire, every fibre of his being screaming with pain. Slowly, every move in agony, he managed to draw himself up on his knees, holding his right side. Blood was oozing from under his hand. The bullet had scored the intestine deeply and then had entered the right thigh. Blood seeped heavily, but it was not spurting.

Elizabeth stared at Omar and turned ashen. Omar's wound filled her with horror. She stared at him helplessly, watching his blood ooze across the ground. Elizabeth began to cry hysterically, not knowing what to do.

"Such accidents occur during war. Don't worry; I'll be whole again," Omar said, trying to reassure her.

Omar opened the small tin box of first-aid supplies and took out a bottle of alcohol and sulpha powder. He was trying desperately not to think of anything but becoming mobile and rejecting the pain as an unwanted state of mind. Omar took off his shirt. Gritting his teeth, he doused the wound heavily with the alcohol. Omar lit a small fire and heated his knife in it. He then put the red-hot knife into the wound and the alcohol caught. The pain was enormous. He felt near death, and he fought for strength. Omar cauterized the wound and probed deeply and quickly. He knew that if he did not do the burning carefully, the wound would rot and he would certainly die. Omar sweated profusely while extracting the bullet with the hot knife from his thigh and then repeated the same treatment he'd made to the side wound. Omar sprinkled sulpha powder over the two wounds and then neatly bandaged them.

Slowly, torturously, Omar began to stand up. Each moment was agonizing. The pain in his belly was knife-like; the sounds in his head were cracks of thunder. Elizabeth tried to assist him.

"Let go of me. I can make it on my own."

Elizabeth looked at him with a face white as chalk. "Omar, you almost died. Don't walk; you'll tire yourself."

"We must get out of here as quickly as we can. We will walk as my wounds permit."

Elizabeth stared at Omar disbelievingly. There was no fear in him, only a resigned acceptance of fate. She could see in his suffering a strong will to keep moving for their lives. They walked until darkness came on.

"Omar, you are too hard on yourself. I am tired myself. Let's get some rest, please," Elizabeth pleaded.

"We will spend the night here," he said at last. "Oh God, I feel like death." He felt the roots of exhaustion curbing into the deepest tissues of his body.

"You have to eat something; you have lost a lot a blood. I'll prepare some food for you." She opened the handbag and searched for food with a shaky hand.

Ice spread through his belly and into his legs. A tingling weakness went down his spine, and the ground rushed up at him as he fell down, tumbling in an echoing chaos of blackness. Black fear wrapped its cold arms around Elizabeth, gripping her tight.

Crouched to the ground, Elizabeth searched desperately for Omar's pulse and began to count his heartbeats. Omar's pulse was so slow that she had great difficulty feeling it. Tears were streaming down her face, blinding her. She cradled Omar's head in her lap, wiping the sweat from his face with her sleeve, stroking his hair. Elizabeth was worried sick about Omar, and that night she lay awake holding his fevered body in her arms.

When Omar opened his eyes in the morning, he did not know how long he had been unconscious. He'd lost all awareness of time. Omar felt helpless, his face grey and his body hot with fever.

"Omar, where does it hurt? Omar, talk to me," Elizabeth said, trying to get him back to full consciousness.

Omar's eyes gradually began to focus. Even talking was a great strain for him. "My throat is dry as hell. Please give me some water."

Elizabeth supported him with her arms and brought some water near his lips. He swallowed hard but drank plenty of water. He then slid back into semi-unconsciousness.

Elizabeth realized that she must keep talking to Omar. He must not slip into deep oblivion. She kept talking to him while wetting his forehead with water to reduce his high temperature.

"You have been unconscious all night. Lying helplessly like this will make things even worse. You must rise above your pain and get up. You will be all right in a bit, I assure you. You are only lying here waiting for the waves of pain to recede, and then you will be whole again. You have lost a lot of blood, but no vital organ was hit. You'll live to a ripe old age, you hear me?" Elizabeth was speaking through her tears.

Although Omar's body was on fire and he had difficulty breathing, he clearly heard Elizabeth's sad words, word by word. He felt her agony and fear. He was here for her, and now he'd become a load over her shoulder.

Omar prayed in silence. *I feel her hot tears falling on my flesh, urging me to rise, yet I cannot move. My knees are weak, and my body is burning up. I cannot stand seeing her in pain. Lord Almighty, give me strength.*

Omar lay cradled in Elizabeth's arms, gathering strength. After an hour of stillness, he opened his eyes and emerged into consciousness. There was dizziness, his vision was blurred, and everything was moving in and out of focus. Omar tried hard to concentrate. Now he could see clearly above him Elizabeth's face, framed by the cascading hair that touched his face. There were tears in her eyes and running down her cheeks. He tried to wipe away the tears, but he could not reach the lovely yet tired face above him. Omar smiled through his pain and managed to utter some words.

"I went where others feared to go and did what others failed to do. I have cried and hoped for a better world. But the thunder roared and the earth became a shattered night. With peace alone can this earth mend. Someday there will be colours and rainbows – and peace will live for real."

Elizabeth smiled down at him through her tears. She knew that he would live.

Weeping with joy, she said, "I've seen the face of terror, felt the stinging cold of fear, and enjoyed the sweet taste of your caring. The power of love made you sacrifice yourself for me."

"Liz, I was traveling in darkness, far away from you. I missed you so much." He was shaking in her lap.

"I missed you too." She was sobbing, her face mirroring her emotions, her eyes revealing her heart.

Her abundant tears were warm on his face. To him, her encouraging words were like the thread of life that holds a human soul.

"Help me to my feet," he said, trying to rise.

"Yes, my love. Let's move together along the road of life." She was watching the enormous effort he was having trying to rise to his feet.

Omar stood with difficulty, leaning heavily on Elizabeth. She held him whilst they walked, cutting the two miles left to Prekaz. The two miles seemed like eternity, with Omar walking on weary legs, stumbling, falling to his knees, walking again, and then staggering, until they reached the refugee camp in Prekaz.

As soon as they reached their destination, images went out of focus and the buildings spun; darkness descended. Omar fell into a void. The doctors in the camp carried him to the clinic. Elizabeth did not leave him for one second. She told the doctors about his wounds and the way he treated them. The doctors were astonished to see how brilliantly Omar was trained to face the unexpected. He had mended his fatal wounds wonderfully. The doctors told her that Omar would have died if he were not trained to mend his wounds. The wounds needed nothing from them but injection with strong antibiotics and to change the bandages for clean ones.

Omar also needed blood. It was a coincidence that Elizabeth's blood group was similar to his. She gave him one litre of her blood. Now her blood was running in his veins. Now a part of her was living inside him. The doctors reassured Elizabeth that Omar would recover fast. Omar was discharged from the clinic after three days. The doctors needed every available bed for the wounded refuges.

During Omar's stay in the clinic, Elizabeth crawled in the night into his arms, where it felt safe and warm. He wrapped her in his arms, enjoying her tenderness, her charms. She was his sanctuary. She'd brought the gift of life to him.

In the camp, Elizabeth roamed around the place. Thousands of refugees were living under severe conditions. Elizabeth met a sixty-five-year-old man squatting beside his wife's unconscious body. His twelve children and grandchildren huddled around him in a tiny open tent. The man brushed away tears as he described his prospects in the coming Kosovo winter. Freezing rain and snow would cover the camp, which contained twenty thousand refugees. Temperature would drop to minus ten centigrade, and the filthy roadside ditch from which the refugees fetched their grey fetid water would freeze. Already the ground was too hard to dig graves. Instead, the bodies of those killed by starvation, dehydration, disease, or exposure were covered with earth and weighed down with stones against storms.

Elizabeth also met a seventy-five-year-old man. He had already watched a thirty-year-old son and a ten-year-old grandson starve to death. The refugees had exhausted their savings, and after a while, they ate leaves, and even those were gone now. War and hunger had taken everything from them — their families, their neighbours, their lives, and their hope.

Many refugees were going to die, the children and the elderly first, then the others. In bitter irony, thousands of tons of food, clothes, and medicine were stockpiled about two hundred miles away, across the border in Serbia, which had managed to send only a few tons to the refugee camp.

With the help of a number of humanitarian organizations currently operating in the refugee camp and in Kosovo in general, Elizabeth prepared a report to be submitted to the United Nations. The report described the damage caused during the fighting in Kosovo.

The war in Kosovo had created over one million refugees and internally displaced persons, left over three hundred thousand people without shelter, an estimated ten thousand dead, and mass graves containing bodies of up to one hundred civilians, including men, women, and children.

General Douglas's deputy in Prekaz informed him about the safe arrival of Elizabeth and Omar to the refugee camp. President Rosh was reassured that his daughter was safe and was to leave Kosovo to return to the United States within the next few hours. General Douglas sent a helicopter to Prekaz to take Omar and Elizabeth back to Prestina.

CHAPTER 21

Omar and Elizabeth spent a whole day in Prestina with General Douglas. Omar briefed General Douglas about all that had happened during their trip to Prekaz. Omar did not mention his entanglements with the Serbs, although Elizabeth did. She narrated in detail the battles Omar rushed into and ended up confirming General Douglas's previous opinion about Omar, that he was one of his cleverest and courageous men in Kosovo.

General Douglas frowned and said seriously that what Elizabeth saw during her trip to Prekaz was not entanglements between Omar and the Serbs, for the role of the United Nations in Kosovo was only to preserve peace and see that the refugees were getting humanitarian supplies. Therefore, the Kosovo Liberation Army could be the one responsible for such entanglements and not at all one of his men. However, the courage of Omar in penetrating the lines of the Serbs, and the sacrifices he made to save the life of Elizabeth Rosh – the daughter of the American president – deserved to be celebrated in the Prestina airport.

On the day of Elizabeth's departure to her homeland, soldiers lined up at the airport in orderly rows to fly the United Nations flag. General Douglas, Major Omar, and the soldiers saluted the flag. General Douglas then gave a small speech: "As commander of the United Nations troops in Kosovo, I was most impressed with Major Omar's military record. In direct support of the many manoeuvre battalions throughout Kosovo, Major Omar provided important assistance towards the accomplishment of the overall mission. Major Omar has every reason to be proud of those contributions and sacrifices he made on behalf of the United Nations."

The soldiers were then dismissed. General Douglas realized that Omar and Elizabeth needed to be left alone. He shook hands with Elizabeth, said that he hoped to meet in better circumstances, said his farewell, and left.

The airport seemed deserted except for Omar and Elizabeth, in addition to a private jet waiting nearby to take off.

In a few minutes, Elizabeth would be away from Omar and she would go through forcing herself to forget him. They walked up and down the airport, trying as people do in such occasions to think of something to say.

Omar wondered if it passed through her mind that in all probability, they would never see one another again. It was odd to think that for eight days, they had been almost inseparable and in an hour it would be as though they had never met.

Saying goodbye to her was going to be the hardest thing he ever had to do.

Elizabeth reached for Omar's hand and held it, smiling faintly. "What would have I done without you? I can never thank you enough. In truth, I owe you far more."

"It wasn't anything." Omar said sadly, hating her near departure.

The thought of never seeing Omar again was too much to bear.

The slight breeze wafted a limp strand of hair into Elizabeth's face, and Omar brushed it away. He saw her eyes swimming with bright tears and her lips quivering. It took all his self-control not to hold her and kiss her.

"It's frightening to think of you out in the world unprotected." He was dying inside from the hurt.

"I'm a very self-sufficient woman, you know." She wiped away her tears with delicate fingers. "I know it's hard to say goodbye. Goodbyes wound the soul." She said this with a broken voice. "Come close and hold me while we walk." She clutched his arm and drew him near her.

Omar wrapped his right arm around her, and they walked slowly together along the airport path.

"No matter where you are, you will always remain my eternal rose," he said, feeling a hand clutching his heart at the thought of separation.

"I feel your pain. I wish that I could heal your heart." She stopped walking and buried her face against his chest.

Omar held her close for long moments. She felt his agony. A glitter of tears burned through her throat and swam in her eyes.

"If you come with me, a new life awaits you," she said, knowing that she was just throwing some words into the air. "I can take you with me along the paths of wealth and power."

"I have visited your country before, and I already know a lot about it. I am well off. I came from a rich, dignified family. There's only one thing I like better than getting out of Egypt, and that's getting back to it." He kissed the top of her hair.

Agonizing minutes passed. They pulled away from each other's arms and started walking again hand in hand. Elizabeth suddenly stopped.

"Omar, I'm heading for home. Am I ever going to see you again?" Hot tears brushed her cheeks.

He said with a trembling voice, "I wonder if I will be just a memory to you. I just want you to be happy. Leave if you must but remember me."

"I cannot count the ways you have cared for me. You sacrificed your life for me. The love you brought into my life makes me believe that we will meet again, for in spirit we are whole." Sadness showed in the depths of her eyes. "Say a wish and whatever you wish, imagine it's true." She hid her face against his neck so as not to see bitterness in his eyes.

"I hope that one day you will be mine," he said, holding her tightly and rejecting her disappearance from his life.

She lifted her face up to his. A smile lit up her beautiful face.

"That's exactly the wish I would like to make for myself. Even your scars will remind you of me, am I right?" she said, touching his right side tenderly.

Omar tried to maintain his cool, but he couldn't prevent a tear from rolling down each of his cheeks as he looked down at her.

"I love your tears; they are expressing the tenderness of your daring heart." She said this with a pang, realizing how sorely she would miss him.

"You are mine and only mine," his broken voice whispered in her ear.

But the parting had to come. Elizabeth's legs refused to walk away. She felt as though she were leaving some of herself behind.

Elizabeth released herself slowly from Omar's arms. She looked in his eyes and saw tears and sadness. She leaned forward and kissed him on the edge of his hard jaw. It was a gentle kiss filled with kindness and gratitude. It was a kiss goodbye. Elizabeth then withdrew her lips and hurried to the airplane. She resisted the urge to turn around for one last look.

Omar stood watching her, afraid to blink for fear she would disappear.

The airplane moved on the runway and then flew to the sky. Omar kept watching it until it disappeared in the air.

No more Elizabeth in his life now. She was like a beautiful dream that gave meaning and beauty to his dry life. He would miss her tender touches and encouraging words. The moments she took him in her arms, smoothing away his pain, were the moments that made him realize the importance of a woman in a man's life. This beautiful tender creature had a hold over him, so strong and powerful. Her strength lay in her compassion and caring. She comforted him, consoled him, and solaced his heart.

In her arms, she was an understanding shelter for his tormented soul. In her embrace, he felt newly born, serene, and happy.

Omar walked back to his Jeep with an afflicted heart. His life without Elizabeth would be meaningless and empty.

Elizabeth sat in the airplane listening to the screaming of her heart, the whisper of her soul. She was in a place where time had stopped. What she saw in Kosovo was the horror of a lifetime. She had to get away; she had to force the images out of her mind. They were too clear, too real, and too horrible. She should have been filled with relief because she was going back home, but the only thing she felt was a crushing depression. Elizabeth closed her eyes in pain.

Funny how one trip to a different world could change a person! For only eight days, she had known a remarkable man who'd slipped out of her life as quickly as he had smashed into it.

How had it all begun? Thoughts whirled in her mind. Roy Connery — the man she had married — was rich and smart, but he was also weak and betraying. Roy was weak to the point of committing suicide. She got nothing from him in the end but a broken heart and family disgrace. Did she really love him? Or was her love for him just a teenage crush? She had promised herself that she would never fall in love again, but destiny had brought Omar into her life.

What did she see in Omar that made her care for him so much? Was it because he was different from Roy? No doubt that he was a man different from all those she knew before. He was a very special breed of person, with special qualities and skills. Was it because he came from the land of the prophets? People strived to seize the chance to reach power and influence, yet his unworldliness and spirituality took him high above all those who attached importance to the material world. Pure materialism was not on his horizon but rather spirituality and ethics of Islamic culture. Now she knew where the power lay. He moved by the words of God. He moved by God's light, hoping to live in a world of virtue and not of depravity or vanquish. In all his movements, he was applying Allah's message of righteousness. His belief was so strong that he offered his brave heart to those beset with suffering and misery. He fought alone a whole army, without a moment of hesitation or fear. He had the heart of a lion. He had battled long and hard, and she wondered how far he could go. How far could he fly? He flew to the peaks of the lofty mountains. He flew where eagles proudly fly. He was a rare specimen of human being. He was a winner.

She thought that a man like him could never be tamed. Yet the killing of a baby made him weep in her arms. How lucky she was to take all these qualities in her arms — qualities that harmoniously united to give a delightful perfume reflecting his thoughts in life. A perfume that strongly attracted her to him as moths were attracted to light. His hot tears on her lips were like a delicious drink to her soul.

The love of his heart was so precious and rare. He'd sacrificed himself to save her life. Was that love in his opinion. He had been a shoulder to lean on, a chest to contain her pain, a heart to assuage her fears. In eight days with him, she matured, she grew wiser, she understood better. Her darkness grew light when he taught her that together they rise or fall; together they stand as equals. He was her grounding rock. He was the world to her in fullest measure. She would be forever in his debt.

Now she realized the exact meaning of manhood; now she realized what love was meant to be.

No matter how the hands of fate separated them, but he would always be remembered.

Omar's mission in Kosovo ended six months after Elizabeth's departure. Elizabeth was not to be forgotten, for she was embedded in his soul, dominating his thoughts. She was the legend of his life, the first and only love his heart ever knew.

CHAPTER 22

In the White House, Elizabeth sat with her parents, telling them about all that had happened to her in Kosovo. She counted the heroic actions of Omar, the Egyptian major who sacrificed his life to save her – how he protected her with his body to receive the bullets that were originally aimed at her; how he rescued her from the brutal militia; and how, on their way to Prekaz, he fought alone a whole army, leaving behind dozens of dead corpses. He was like a voice coming from the wilderness, roaring angrily to alleviate injustice. He was like a whale rising from deep down in the ocean to inhale the breeze of freedom. With him, she felt utterly safe and protected. Yet a man with such tremendous fighting spirit had tears to shed over a baby girl who died from hunger and neglect because her mother was slaughtered among others in an unsightly massacre. A man with such unselfish dedication and breath-taking military talent was also remarkably knowledgeable in political matters and in the doctrines of his own religion. Islamic laws bound his attitude to the world, and Koranic verses flew from his tongue when trying to ascertain his ideas and thoughts. Although she had been in real hell, she enjoyed his company and felt the agony in his heart – the agony of injustice and the toil of defending the oppressed in a ruthless environment.

With the heart of a mother, Amanda Rosh asked her daughter, "What does he look like?"

"Without exaggeration, he is the most beautiful and powerful man I have ever seen." Elizabeth said with admiration.

Smiling, Amanda Rosh asked, "You're not falling for him, are you?"

The question surprised Elizabeth for a second, but she replied quickly. "I fell in love before, and I got nothing but heartbreak, but as it seems, we cannot choose who we fall for. I have found myself caring for him much sooner than I ever imagined. Was it because of his unworldliness and strong belief in God or was it because he was a lifesaver and an angel of mercy within a sea of pain? I never thought it was possible to care so deeply for someone after such a brief time."

A frown covered president Rosh's face. He said, not wanting to hurt his daughter's feelings, "I know, dear, what you've been through. It was hell out there. It is normal to be impressed by the heroic actions of your lifesaver. But he was only doing his job. Your safety was his responsibility, and it seems he has done a good job, a matter deserving a thank-you letter to the UN forces in Kosovo and another to the Egyptian authorities. I must warn you dear, however, that Muslims are different from us. Their strict fundamentalism threatens our civilization. Their extremists fight our interests in the Third World. Under the pretension of contradiction with Islamic rules, Muslim fundamentalists oppose globalization as the New World Order. Believe me if I say a man like Major Omar could make your life a living hell."

Elizabeth noticed her father's worry, so she tried to reassure him. "Perhaps the events I came across in Kosovo are still fresh in my memory. Yes, Major Omar is so different from any man I ever knew. Beautifully different, I must say. Together we were unbeatable. He almost died trying to save me. I owe my life to him. As I slowly came to know Omar, I discovered him to be gentle and a lovable man with a never-satisfied passion for his duty. He listened to my fears and banished my agony.

Perhaps I wished so much to fall in love again, but I am still afraid to get hurt like I got hurt before. Don't worry, Dad. I don't think our paths will cross. And maybe my admiration for him will perish with time."

The United Nations High Commissioner for Refugees was waiting impatiently to hear Elizabeth's report about her mission to Kosovo. A conference attended by the press was held in the main auditorium for this purpose. Elizabeth read the report she had formerly prepared in Prekaz refugee camp. She terminated her report by thanking the Egyptian major who'd saved her life by exposing his body to the militia bullets. She even mentioned in some detail the frequent Serb's assaults on them and the major's impressive courage in fighting back until they safely reached Prekaz.

Omar's heroic achievements in the report were so interesting that it became the round of the press. Omar's remarkable courage passed from mouth to mouth, and the press and TV reporters hurried to Egypt to interview Omar. According to Egyptian military rules, reporters were not allowed to interview officers. But the reporters from several parts of the world were pressing the Egyptian authorities to grant them permission to interview the man who'd saved the daughter of the President of the United States. Their insistence was so pressing that the Egyptian Ministry of Defense had to contact the president of Egypt, asking his view about the matter. The president, who was also the chief of the army, gave his orders that the army would celebrate the bravery of Omar by inviting only the army's high officers and the reporters. The celebration would start with a short speech from the Ministry of Defense, after which Omar would be awarded the Medal of Honour. The reporters could take all the pictures they wanted, but they would not be allowed to interview Omar.

The picture of Omar in his military suit receiving the Medal of Honour from the Ministry of Defense hit the front pages of newspapers and television screens all over the world.

In the White House, while president Rosh was having breakfast with his wife, Amanda, the picture of Omar receiving the Medal of Honour in the morning paper stared him in the face. He passed the paper to his wife, who examined Omar's photo carefully and said, "He looks young and robust. I must say he is a very good-looking man. Don't you think?"

"I hope her relation with him was infatuation and not love. Thank God that he lives on another continent," president Rosh said, feeling a great sense of relief.

Omar derived from a wealthy Egyptian family owning vast agricultural land in the Nile Delta. The family was also famous for breeding Arabian horses. Because Omar's erupting soul always sought solace in seclusion, he sold his land in the Delta and bought five hundred hectares in a remote desert area in the northern part of Egypt. The Mediterranean Sea was in sight.

Omar subdivided the land into sectors and planted each with a certain kind of high-quality fruit tree. The edges and borders separating the orchards were planted with indigenous palm trees of good quality. Some other high varieties of palm trees were imported from Saudi Arabia and Gulf Estates. A drip irrigation system bringing fresh water from a nearby canal was used to water the farm. A small dairy factory was established for the harvesting of animal milk and processing it into milk products such as butter and cheese.

The Arabian horse held a unique place in Omar's heart. The beauty, grace, and grandeur of the Arabian horse had always inspired Omar. Developing Arabian horses with unique characteristics was Omar's passion. Right in the middle of the farm, a wide horse arena was established, surrounded by a beautiful white fence.

Up on a hill overlooking the farm, Omar built a grand villa offering beauty, comfort, and privacy.

Omar loved the land and the horses. It was the delight of his soul to sit for hours under an acacia tree watching the horses coming in with their attendants. Hours would go by with Omar sitting quietly, selecting the most outstanding traits for horse breeding. Their variable colours would glitter in the fading sunlight.

He remembered his days of struggle and love in Kosovo. In Kosovo, he'd met Elizabeth. She'd blazed into his life like a ray of pure sunlight, thawing him with her warmth. She marched through his dreams. He could not get through a day without her hounding his thoughts. He remembered her proud bone structure, the beautiful eyes, and the stubborn chin. Her hair was a luxuriant blonde cascade. Her smile was like the rippling of moonlight on water. She had the serenity of a summer evening when the light fades slowly from the unclouded sky.

Her tender voice was ringing in his ear. Her tears were swimming in his eyes. Her embrace was holding his soul. Her remembrance was his motive to live and work in this unpredictable world. He wondered whether she still remembered him or if to her he was nothing but a shadow from the past. Would fate re-join them again or was that wishing just a dream?

Elizabeth was not just an ordinary woman but also the daughter of the president of the United States. It was hard to contact her. She was certainly strongly guarded, her moves under strict surveillance. Elizabeth always kept herself busy, submerged in humanitarian works and surrounded by elite acquaintances, and he was here, quite distant from her eyes and heart.

Elizabeth belonged in a far more elite world. Most certainly, she was surrounded now with fans and admirers. She was beautiful, famous, and rich, and it was her right to get herself a husband of her status who could make her happy.

Omar was different. He was a strict Muslim. His strictness might annoy Elizabeth if she could not understand his religion. People in America lived freely, without limits. But Muslims lived within certain divine laws that might be an obstacle to those living open lives without boundaries.

Did she still love him or had her love for him faded away? He must wake up now, before this hopeless love destroyed his peace of mind. He would try to bury his feelings so deeply that they would never resurface to torment and haunt him.

Omar looked at the far horizon before him and whispered, "Elizabeth, you are a fragrant rose I breathe every moment of the day. You are a gentle ray of light brightening my soul. If only you could see how my soul flees from emptiness to emptiness while seeking your nearness. You may only be a person in this world, but to me you are the world. You are always in my thoughts, and how I wish you were here with me. May God bless your soul and shine his light upon you."

CHAPTER 23

In a cloudy sky, Elizabeth flew her small but powerful aircraft. Masses of clouds were floating in the air. Rays of sunlight penetrated the clouds and revealed colours of white and gold. Up in the sky, she could feel pure and serene. She looked at the golden rays mingling with the clouds as if searching for a ray of hope. Thoughts whirled in her head.

One year had flown by since she had last seen Omar. During that entire year, she had not been able to get him out of her thoughts. The more she tried to put him out of her mind, the more she thought about him. Her days with him had blossomed in her memory. Every word and every action had been relived a thousand times, until her mind had memorized the smallest detail, right down to the male scent of him. There was an overpowering quality about him. His brave heart was a special corner of peace in the troubled and turbulent world. She needed him as she had never needed anyone in her life. She had a great yearning to feel his arms around her.

Ever since she came back, she worked herself to death, but nothing really helped. She knew that she was escaping from something missing that made her empty inside. Omar was missing. Being away from him was a killing loneliness. She wondered why of all the men in the world, it had to be Omar. Maybe because he was the type of man she would trust with her life. She felt safe with him. He gave her a sense of being cared for, of being completely protected.

Elizabeth wanted to know for sure if the future would hold anything at all for them. Was their love worth fighting for? "You are crazy," she told herself. "Omar is nothing but a man you met in Kosovo. Just forget him and move on." She was angry with herself for not being able to forget him.

After the return of Elizabeth from Kosovo, and noticing this strong infatuation with the Egyptian, the first lady and the president decided to fill their daughter's life with work. Since Amanda owned half of Rosh's wealth, she and the president agreed to assign Elizabeth as deputy chairperson of Rosh Enterprises. Now Elizabeth could run the huge family business while her father was busy running the country. Elizabeth delightfully accepted the new position, but this was not at the expense of the humanitarian work she loved.

Humanitarian work became an integral part of her being, especially after her experience in Kosovo. She had suffered in her marriage and had seen injustice in Kosovo, so giving became an agreeable duty to her. She would give anything to wipe out the tears of the oppressed and launch war without quarter against those suppressing human rights. This is why she established an office in Rosh Enterprises for human rights. The words of Omar about the injustice the Palestinians were suffering at the hands of the Israelis still lingered in her mind. So the first assignment the office had been given was to investigate the true causes of the Palestinian-Israeli conflict and the reasons behind the Palestinian uprising against the Israelis. Elizabeth gave instructions that a report about this vital matter should be ready for her in ten days. She also instructed that the sources of information should be realistic, accurate, and unbiased.

As an active member in the Human Rights Commission of the United Nations, Elizabeth flew to Durban in South Africa to attend the

United Nations Conference on Racism. The American and the Israeli delegations also attended the conference.

The conference witnessed a mass demonstration in which tens of thousands of people took to the streets of Durban. The demonstration was not only joined by the conference delegates but also by thousands of South African activists, trade unionists, and students who arrived by bus and train from all over the country.

Those who came from far away provinces were mostly landless people who, in striking resemblance with the Palestinian situation, were forcibly removed from their lands and were subjugated to abject poverty. The people of the landless movement came to demand their right to land and to protest globalization and privatization, the main causes of a new economic apartheid in post-1994 South Africa. Upon their arrival, the International Landless Assembly was held. Their struggle was supported by solidarity messages from people in similar situations.

In the two days leading to the demonstration, supporters of Palestinian causes and Zionist groups had daily verbal confrontations at the conference site. A small group of Zionists set up a table and distributed flyers: "Arabs are hijacking the conference — the conference is not a conference about racism; it is a racist conference." A spontaneous demonstration by Palestinian supporters broke out in front of the table, led by South Africans and joined by hundreds of Arabs, Burmese, Japanese, Indians, Americans, Europeans, and many others holding up signs, posters, and Palestinian flags. The police formed a line to separate the groups. The Zionists, mainly several white males dressed in dark suits, kept singing the same verse — "All we are saying is give peace a chance" — from a John Lennon song. They also tried to hand flowers to Palestinian supporters, who rejected by chanting "No justice, no peace."

To the South Africans, the resemblance between theirs and Palestinian situations required no explanation. Thousands of Palestinians and South Africans raised signs in the air that read, "Israel is an apartheid state"; "Zionism is racism"; "Land for the landless"; "Sharon is a war criminal" …

Having defeated their own apartheid with the help of the international community, it was now the duty of the South Africans to lend hands to the Palestinians to fight against the Israeli apartheid. A number of speeches were made in solidarity with the Palestinians; after several moving and powerful speeches, the demonstrators declared the official kick off of a new movement. The birth of the movement was presented by a declaration read by a South African activist. The declaration challenged many of Israel's conceptions about the noble ideas of a "Jewish" state. The declaration made people consider how it can be acceptable for Israel to enshrine principles of racial superiority and segregation into its legal system and structure in the twenty-first century when people fought so vigorously against these same principles in the United States and South Africa in the twentieth century.

The declaration stated that Israel was simply an Apartheid state and that the State of Israel rested on overt repression, a system of structural violence and institutionalized discrimination that dehumanized one group to the advantage of another. Apartheid Israel had developed an elaborate system of racial discrimination that was embedded in its legal system – even surpassing apartheid South Africa's laws. These laws included the law of entry, the law of return, citizenship law, legally sanctioned discriminatory rabbinical rulings, and the military service law. Palestinians were denied various welfare benefits, access to many jobs, and the leasing of homes and land controlled by government bodies. Electricity, sewerage, roads, and water supplies were provided free to Israeli households, whereas many Palestinian communities in Israel, let alone the occupied territories, had existed for decades without adequate services. The Israeli education system was racist in practice and in content. Almost no Arab history was covered, and there were no Arab textbooks in the Israeli curricula. Palestinians also faced significant barriers in gaining access to universities. In South Africa, similar factors contributed to the uprisings in 1976 and the 1980s.

The declaration also stated that the suffering in the West Bank and Gaza was the continuation of the colonization of all of Palestine. Zionist militias seized 75 per cent of the land and drove out eight hundred thousand Palestinians through a series of massacres between the partition of Palestine in 1947 and the formation of Israel. With the declaration of the State of Israel in 1948, 385 out of 475 Palestinian cities, towns, and villages were razed to the ground, disappearing from the map. The 90 remaining were denuded of land and confiscated without compensation. Israel was an apartheid state, founded on pillage and predicated on exclusivity. Rights flowed from ethnic and religious identity.

The declaration emphasized that South Africans who had lived through apartheid could not be silent as another entire people were treated as non-humans, people without rights or human dignity and facing daily humiliation. They could not permit a ruthless state to use military jets, helicopter, gunships, and tanks on civilians. They could not accept state assassination of activists, the torture of political prisoners, the murder of children, and collective punishment ...

As the declaration ended, Elizabeth felt a knife of guilt pierce her heart. America was supporting Israel without limits. Why did Israel have to occupy the West Bank? This was not part of Israel at its creation and was not now. America and the NATO response to the Iraqi invasion of Kuwait in 1991 was swift and unequivocal. Why was there no such response when there was a continuous occupation of a foreign nation state by another? American double standards condemned one action yet supported another, thus harming her credibility before the world.

The secretary general of the United Nations hijacked the conference for turning into a world court on Israel when dozens of countries spent up to two years of their time preparing for the conference to present their own country's important issues as well.

The American delegation, headed by the US Secretary of State as well as the delegation of Israel, had chosen to boycott the deliberations. They insisted that the future of humanity was hijacked for political causes of the worst possible kind.

While Elizabeth was watching the hot events of the conference, Omar's face drifted into her consciousness. "Omar," she murmured to herself, thinking about him intently.

She heard his voice ringing in her ears: "It is for a lasting peace that man has to strive."

"Yes, my love. It's something worth fighting for," she'd replied, feeling sad for him. He was so idealistic, so innocent, so brave, and so very much alone.

Her tears fell on the papers before her. At that moment, she felt so deeply in love with him that it was painful.

She whispered to her secret soul, "If only you knew how much I love you. Fate has brought you into my life. Will I see you again? Who knows what lies in store?"

When Elizabeth returned from Durban, the declaration of South Africa that Israel was racist and apartheid was still fresh in her mind.

With a great pain piercing her heart, Elizabeth realized that the media's treatment of Israel's brutal and inhumane actions against the Palestinians was totally biased. The American media adopted the US political agenda, which blindly supported Israel. The truth about Israel's aggression against the Palestinians was hidden from the American people. She had always wished to see an effective US policy pressing for a just Middle East peace. There had to be a US constituency that demanded such a policy.

The policy of demolition of Palestinian homes was horrendously inhumane, and with its racist concentration on Palestinian homes, it was reminiscent of Nazi practice. She had read several stories on the web issued by several committees and groups, describing army demolitions that pushed out Palestinians virtually without notice. The stories were dramatic and heart-breaking. The stories stressed the racist essence, the widespread Palestinian fear of being demolished, and the murderous character of the policy.

The US mainstream media closely followed their government's agenda of giving Israel carte blanche in dealing with their Palestinian subjects, both within Israel and in the occupied territories. The American media did not give substantial detail on the brutality of the Israeli violations and suffering of the Palestinian victims. It even gave the Israelis rationale that the demolished Palestinian homes were illegally built or that it was a response to Palestinian violence. The media never, or only rarely, suggested that the demolitions and settlements in the occupied land violated the Oslo accords as well as the Fourth Geneva Convention.

In media reporting on Intifada II, "violence" means stone throwing and shooting; it never refers to the structural violence of expropriating land; evicting people from their houses and demolishing them; seizing and diverting their water resources for the use of the chosen people;

building roads that destroyed communities and access to former neighbours and jobs; and tolerating and protecting settlers' attacks, destruction, and seizure of gentile property. This massive violence had been entirely acceptable to Rosh and preceding administrations, so for the mainstream media, it was not classified as violence or given serious attention.

But even within their limited conception of violence, the media's bias displayed during Intifada II had been spectacular in giving far greater attention and exclusive indignation to stone-throwing and suicide bombings by Palestinians than to the more cruel and deadly violence of the Israeli army.

The US mainstream media used words like terrorism and violence to describe the retail acts of the Palestinians, not the wholesale killings and coerced structural changes imposed by the Israelis. They also refused to use the words "ethnic cleansing" to describe Israeli policy, despite the excellence of the fit.

Elizabeth had been to Kosovo before and seen the atrocities committed by the Yugoslav army against Muslim civilians. She might as well go to Palestine to see the violations committed against the Palestinians by the Israeli forces.

CHAPTER 24

Elizabeth's first working day after returning from Durban was rather busy. She found on her desk a compilation of reports, among which was a report about the Palestinian-Israeli conflict. She read the report and realized that it was matching some of the accusations launched against Israel in the Durban conference.

The report mentioned that the Israeli atrocities in the Palestinian land relied on decisive US support and European acquiescence. The Palestinians saw no difference between Israel and America since the United States has always been and continues to be Israel's gigantic backer.

The report also highlighted the arrogant words of prime minister Ariel Sharon to Shimon Peres as reported on Kol Yesrael radio: "Every time we do something, you tell me America will do this and will do that ... I want to tell you something very clear: don't worry about American pressure on Israel. We, the Jewish people, control America, and the Americans know it."

After what Elizabeth witnessed in Durban's conference and what she read in the report, she decided to visit Palestine and see facts on the ground. She remembered Omar's words to her in Kosovo: "The Palestinians are long-suffering at the hands of the Israelis. They are disarmed and conquered. Their homes and lands are being confiscated so that the Jews can tear down the Palestinian homes and put up homes for themselves."

When President Rosh learned about Elizabeth's intention to visit Gaza, he warned her that the Israeli army had launched its attack against the city of Gaza a week earlier. Tanks and armed vehicles, backed by helicopter gunships, rumbled into the city centre and entered into full-scale battle with Palestinian militants. The Israeli army left behind ugly ruin and destruction, scenes she must not see. The president's warning, however, made Elizabeth more determined to visit the ruined city and see for herself.

Elizabeth decided to join the International Solidarity Movement and risk a trip to Gaza. The International Solidarity Movement was a non-violent direct action group that supported an end to the occupation. But how to travel to Palestine without being noticed by the Israeli authorities?

The government of Israel controlled access to Jerusalem and the West Bank. As the daughter of the president of the United States, the Israeli authorities would celebrate her coming and make a big deal out of it. Since she intended to work hard to keep Palestine issues in the Western consciousness, she feared that the Israelis might hide facts from her and make things look rosy. She must find another root that was not under Israeli control. Access to Gaza, however, was controlled by the Palestinian Authority. She would enter Palestine via the Gaza Strip.

The Egyptian authorities facilitated Elizabeth's entrance to Gaza by allowing Elizabeth to cross the Rafah crossing point. The Israeli authorities, however, knew about Elizabeth's trip to Gaza and declared that they were not responsible for her safety. At noon, Elizabeth entered Gaza and spent the night at the Al Deira Hotel.

In the morning, Elizabeth looked at the city from her room's window and went deathly pale. The city was in ruins, the walls in the buildings were crumbled, and the city looked like a ghost town.

The Centre of International Solidarity Movement in Gaza sent Elizabeth a station wagon. As the wagon moved on, she was horrified to see a Palestinian youth holding a Palestinian flag seized by six Israeli police officers. The boy was brutally beaten, punched in the face, and kicked in the groin.

Elizabeth turned her face in pain and looked through the other window, only to see Palestinian boys collecting their belongings from the rubble of their homes, which were destroyed by Israeli army tanks and bulldozers. Women were sitting in front of their houses weeping after the Israeli army tanks and bulldozers took their houses to the ground.

Elizabeth muttered, "Enough to turn a Palestinian into a suicide bomber."

Elizabeth arrived at the centre with a broken heart. The head of the centre introduced her to the other members, who were mostly Palestinian activists and a few others coming from different parts of the world.

The members of the centre convened to organize their work. They decided that each activist should visit one or more families in the ruined houses to provide them with UN provisions. Elizabeth was given the task of visiting and helping a Palestinian widow called Khadija.

Khadija's husband was shot on his way to buy school supplies and books for his children. He left behind his wife, Khadija, and three boys, who were fourteen to eighteen years old. The elder boys were arrested after throwing stones at the Israeli soldiers. The boys in prison were tortured and beaten to death. The younger boy, Mahmoud, was not arrested, and he stayed with his mother to look after her. He told his mother that he would retaliate for the killing of his father and brothers. Khadija had nothing to do but weep and pray.

Khadija set the table and loaded it with the food Elizabeth brought. The three of them sat eating in silence. Khadija began to talk with bitterness: "They have dissected the leftovers of my country into bits and pieces of ghettoes and concentration camps. They have cut off our water supply and left us thirsty while they bathe in cooled pools not far from where we live. They have uprooted our trees and desecrated our fields. They have cut off medical supplies and detained at their checkpoints wounded Palestinians who were in dire need of medical assistance."

Elizabeth said, "I am really sorry to hear that."

Khadija said, "They shoot to kill little children who in defiance and courage wield small stones in the name of liberty against the fiercely armed enemy."

"There must be something to be done against the Israeli injustice."

"Allah has created all men equal, yet the Jews have made it their protocol that they are better than all others and that they have the right to come to my land committing killing and plundering."

"Take it easy, Khadija," said Elizabeth. "Things could get better in the future."

Khadija said, "How come they slay Palestinian children while going to school? They kill Palestinian children when they fight them with their bare hands."

"I must admit that it's a barbaric cruelty."

"They shell the homes of Palestinian families, instantly killing the occupants, and then pretend shock when finally, a Palestinian human bomb blows himself up."

Mahmoud burst in: "I will not rest without revenge. I will avenge my father and my brothers."

Khadija looked directly into Elizabeth's eyes and said, "Do you know that this house is slated for demolition? They considered my boys, whom they tortured and killed, enemies of the Israeli army. Imagine grieving the loss of my husband and sons – and now my house is slated for demolition!"

Elizabeth replied, "My heart goes out to you, and I pray you find peace. No one would dare hurting you. I will stand by you until the end."

"The Israelis are murdering innocent people whose only crime is being born in their own homeland." Khadija then raised her hands to the Lord, saying, "Lord, take care of us. Let us see another day."

Elizabeth whispered as if talking to herself, "We send men to the moon, but we cannot stop ethnic cleansing."

Elizabeth toured the house. She realized that the Israelis were here before. Their bullets and splinters penetrated through the walls, breaking the windows, the sink, and the toilet.

When night fell, Elizabeth slept beside Khadija in one bed and Mahmoud slept on the floor. But the night was not peaceful. Israeli tanks and troops surrounded the whole area. They fired everywhere a barrage of bullets, and there was tank fire. Khadija and Elizabeth had to lie on the floor and keep silent for long hours in the darkness. They heard the troops shooting people in the streets and could hear them screaming. No ambulances were allowed through. The screams then stopped, and there was just silence.

In the morning, the situation became clearer. The Israelis had imposed a curfew on the area. The Israeli soldiers were arresting medics and ambulance drivers, including foreign volunteer medical workers. Large groups of people had been found shot dead in rooms, and there were blood marks where they had lined people up on their knees and shot them, with their ID cards lying on top of them. People were taken from their homes, blindfolded and clothes removed. They were taken away or lined up against a wall and shot. The hospitals had also been surrounded and invaded, and Israeli troops were taking the injured people and interrogating them.

After day five, the Israelis lifted the curfew, suddenly announcing that everyone had two hours to go out to get food. People ran around trying to make it to the stores, but the Israelis looted the stores and there was no bread or anything.

Protected by her ID, as being American and the daughter of the American president, Elizabeth went out to see what exactly happened during the night.

It was a massacre. Not since Kosovo had she seen the innocent slaughtered like this. The Palestinian men, women, and children lay murdered in heaps, their hands or arms or legs missing. There were well over a hundred of them. A baby lay without a head. The Israeli shells had scythed through them as they lay in their homes believing that they were safe.

In front of a burning building, a girl held a corpse in her arms, the body of a grey-haired man whose eyes were staring at her, and she rocked the corpse back and forth in her arms, kneeling and weeping and crying the same words repeatedly: "My father, my father."

A Palestinian stood amid a sea of bodies and, without saying a word, held the body of a headless child. Elizabeth walked unconsciously towards the man, but she slipped on a human hand. It was the hand of a baby.

With abundant tears in her eyes, Elizabeth walked and walked, not knowing where to go. She saw a Palestinian guard muttering oaths to himself as he opened a bag in which he was drooping feet, fingers, and pieces of people's arms. "I would like to be made into a bomb and blow myself up amid the Israelis," he said.

Elizabeth suddenly felt that she had become not a part of the International Solidarity Movement but Israel's ally, an object of hatred and venom. A Palestinian stared at her with fierce eyes, his face dark with fury. "You are American?" he screamed at her. "Americans are dogs! You did this. Americans are dogs!"

Elizabeth's tormented conscious screamed at her, *And who cares if the whole world knew?* The Israelis knew the whole world was powerless to stop them as long as the United States backed them up. The Israelis were assured that thanks to the Zionist-controlled media, millions of Americans were as politically ignorant and brainwashed as it was possible to be, and they would do absolutely nothing to stop the US government from fully supporting Israel's endless war crimes.

She has seen with her own eyes a one-sided slaughter. Using American tax dollars, the Israelis had purchased all the latest weapons of mass murder. Israel Defense Forces were murdering children, using state-of-the-art Merkava 3 tanks, which fired 120 mm shells and high-calibre bullets into crowded villages and refugee camps. Israelis had assault rifles, Uzi machine guns, depleted uranium shells, CS gas, tear gas, gigantic armoured D9 bulldozers, gunboats, high-tech satellite communications equipment, reconnaissance planes, snipers, grenades, and missiles fired from American-made F-16 jets. And as if

all that were not enough, the Israelis also had nuclear bombs, including three submarines with nuclear missiles – all paid for by American taxpayers.

The Palestinian Authority police forces had small-calibre arms, but 99 per cent of the Palestinian people had nothing unless they wanted to hurl rocks. The Palestinians, however, had something more powerful than all the tanks and helicopter gunships in the world – a righteous and incredibly heroic determination to be free, not to mention the sympathy of all decent people in the world, and the Americans who were decent but brainwashed.

Mahmoud – Khadija's son – was now at the front of a group of young Palestinians, throwing rocks at an Israeli tank. As Mahmoud crouched to pick up a stone, he was hit in the neck. Several other boys were shot dead too. Because they were so close to the Israeli tank, their friends had to wait an hour before they felt it was safe to remove their bodies and load them into an ambulance. Mahmoud and his friends were pronounced dead upon arrival at the hospital.

Elizabeth returned to Khadija's house to find her weeping quietly, her shoulders shaking, her body trembling. Elizabeth put a compassionate hand on her shoulder, consoling her. Khadija raised her tearful eyes and said while sobbing, "Some birds are not meant to be caged so you let them go. They killed Mahmoud; they shot him dead." Khadija continued through her tears, "I do not know whether to grieve for him or rejoice. We belong to Allah, and to Him we shall return. My son has sacrificed his soul for the love of his Lord and Palestine."

Tears silently flew down Elizabeth's face. She was stunned and shocked by the death of Mahmoud. He was just a boy. It would take the rest of her life to come to terms with her grief.

Khadija pointed at a small paper in her hand. She said through her tears, "He left me just few words: 'Mother, I regret that I have but one life to give for my country.'"

Amid protests, tears, sobs and some enraged protesters, the coffins of Mahmoud and his friends arrived at the grand mosque wrapped in the national flag. It was noon prayer, after which the funeral prayer would be given. Elizabeth was hit by the most beautiful voice of mankind: the adhaan, the call to prayer. Her hair stood on end, and an unknown powerful force led her to the mosque with the other women. She wanted to share sorrow with Khadija by bowing and prostrating herself before her Creator.

Men lined up for prayer. Elizabeth watched them standing shoulder to shoulder in straight rows praying to Allah, all banded together in the equality of Islam. All men and women were participating in the same ritual, displaying a spirit of unity and brotherhood. Elizabeth had been at churches where the front pews were reserved for the people who gave the most money!

Elizabeth stood with Khadija and the other women in the back rows. She imitated the women in bowing and prostrating to Allah the Creator.

She was taken aback. The Muslims' prayers started making sense in her bones, in her heart, and in her soul.

The coffins were then placed in front of the imam, one in front of the other. After performing the funeral prayer, coffin after coffin seemed to float from the door of the grand mosque like blossoms on slow water. The crowd followed the coffins to their final resting place at the cemetery of martyrs, and there they buried them in the silent heart of the earth.

Khadija murmured, "O Allah, forgive them and have mercy on them, and join them with the righteous. O Lord of the worlds, make their graves spacious enough for them and make them sleep in peace until the Day of Judgment. Allah, there is no god but You; to You we belong, and to You shall we return."

Agony squeezed her heart, and she threw herself in Elizabeth's arms, sobbing. Elizabeth held her gently, her own tears overflowing.

As if she were singing a sad song, Khadija said in Elizabeth's arms, "Seekers of justice, enforcers of rights, sleep peacefully in your humble graves."

At that moment, Elizabeth wanted to open the coffins and set the boys free.

House demolition was a common practice justified by the Israeli Defense Forces in order to harm the parents and relatives of those who carried out attacks against Israeli forces. Mahmoud and his brothers were considered violent insurgents because they threw rocks at the Israeli army. When Khadija and Elizabeth returned from the funeral, they found the house already bulldozed and flat on the ground.

Elizabeth decided to host Khadija in her room in the Al Deira hotel. When Khadija stepped into the spacious room, she said bitterly, "My city has two million souls. Some are living in modest houses; some are living in holes."

Khadija turned to Elizabeth and said, "You have no mercy for yourself; your duty is to others. You have compassion for those in need."

Elizabeth tapped her back and said soothingly, "Things will get better. You will get over it and get on with your life."

"The light of my life has been extinguished. I don't know if comfort exists when they are all gone."

"Mourning over your sons won't change things," said Elizabeth.

"Taking action does."

Elizabeth did not understand what Khadija really meant.

Khadija stayed with Elizabeth for several days, during which Elizabeth watched her performing her five daily prayers. She saw her bowing and prostrating in humility to Allah, the Lord of creation.

Elizabeth asked her, "Khadija, why pray five times a day?"

"Praying five times a day is considered the second most important of Islam's five pillars, after professing that there is no god worthy of worship but Allah and that the Prophet Mohammed is Allah's Messenger. Muslims consider prayer to be a spiritual and physical act, with various standing, bending, and prostrating postures symbolizing devotion to Allah. The prayers symbolize what Islam considers the purpose of creation: to worship Allah. These prayers are considered an obligation for every Muslim by the time he or she reaches puberty.

Prayer protects against great sins of every kind and washes out sins; is a light for the believers in this life and the hereafter; raises in rank; and is one of the greatest causes to enter paradise with the Prophets and the righteous.

Elizabeth asked, "While prostrating, what were you saying to your Lord?"

"Merciful God, forgive me my sins and answer my prayers."

Since January 2002, Palestinian women had heightened their involvement in the Israeli conflict by joining the ranks of men who used themselves as human bombs and committed acts of suicide bombings.

Four Palestinian women shocked the world by strapping bombs to their bodies and detonating them in crowded places where Jewish people gathered. These women had responded to the call of war against Israel as a way of protecting their families and homes and as a way of retaliation for the injustice they had been made to endure.

Days had passed, and Khadija was completely absorbed in prayers. She spent many days and nights praying.

Elizabeth watched her pray. She liked her prayer, as it brought her a sense of ease she had never experienced. Between prayers, Khadija addressed Elizabeth with few words: "We are travelers, and our homecoming is with Allah alone. What an honour, then, to reach Him. I am cured forever of the fear of death. Death is not total annihilation but a shifting from the dungeons of worldly life to the gardens of paradise. I have found Allah in my soul. I long to be raised again in Him. I see the splendour of His beauty like a bright light shining over the meadows of paradise. It is but a loss to stay here."

Elizabeth did not understand the meaning behind Khadija's words, but she was touched by their sincerity.

Elizabeth started a conversation with Khadija: "In our schools, the teachers deliberately keep the students in the dark about Islam. They describe Islam briefly as a religion of destruction. They regard Islam as a serious threat to Western civilization."

Khadija replied, "The enemies of Islam spare no efforts to hide the true nature of our religion. They are aware that if they mention the virtues and good manners Islam calls for, Islam will take full control of people's hearts because it is the religion of truth."

"The American schools pay little attention to religion, whereas children learn about sex and moving out of their families' houses by the time they become teenagers." Elizabeth added.

Khadija said, "You live in an era of heightened materialism. People are obsessed with making money and accumulating material possessions. The entire culture is geared towards the marketplace. No time is left for God. God is the only One that can provide us with real, lasting contentment in our lives. Allah says in the Koran, 'O you who believe! Let not your wealth, or your children, divert you from the remembrance of Allah; and whoever does that, these are the losers.'"

Elizabeth said, "I came from a Catholic background. I was not a regular churchgoer. It was boring to stand up, sit down, kneel, sit again, stand up, and recite things after the priest. Each service had a booklet – a kind of direction book – and I had to follow along in order to know what to do next. I am in search of my Creator and the purpose of my creation. Why are we born? What is the object of existence?"

"One day we will leave this world and be accountable to God. Our purpose in life is to recognize our Creator, to be grateful to Him, to worship Him, to surrender ourselves to Him, and to obey the laws that He mentioned in His divine books."

"Can you explain Islam to me in just a few words?"

"The word 'Islam' is an Arabic word that means submitting and surrendering your will to God," explained Khadija. "Islam teaches that all religions originally had the same essential message, which was to submit wholeheartedly to the will of God and to worship Him alone, without associating with Him any partners. For this reason, Islam is not a new religion but is the same divinely revealed truth that God revealed to all prophets, including Noah, Abraham, Moses, and Jesus. Only by submitting one's will to God can one obtain true peace both in this life and in the life hereafter. Islam is both a religion and a complete way of life. Muslims follow a religion of peace, mercy, and forgiveness."

Elizabeth paused the question, "Who is Allah?"

Khadija said, "For various reasons, many people have come to believe that Muslims worship a different God than Christians and Jews. Judaism, Christianity, and Islam are one religion. They are all Abrahamic faiths, and all of them are classified as monotheistic. However, Islam teaches that other religions have, in one way or another, distorted and nullified a pure and proper belief in God by neglecting His true teachings and mixing them with fabricated ideas. In Arabic, the word 'Allah' means 'the One who deserves all worship'. This in fact is the pure monotheistic message of Islam.

"There are some people out there who are obviously not on the side of truth, who want to get people to believe that Allah is just some Arabian god and that Islam has no common roots with Christianity and Judaism. To say that Muslims worship a different God because they say Allah is just as illogical as saying that French people worship another God because they use the word Dieu, that Spanish-speaking people worship a different God because they say Dios, or that the Hebrews worship a different God because they sometimes call Him Yahweh. If Islam were presented in the proper way to the world, it is quite likely that when people find out that there is a universal religion in the world that teaches to worship and love God, while also practicing pure monotheism, they would at least feel that they should re-examine the basis of their own beliefs and doctrines."

"How is Islam a purely monotheistic religion?"

"The Oneness of Allah, known as Tawheed, is the first and paramount constituent of the Islamic concept, as it is the fundamental truth of the Islamic faith. Among all the belief systems and philosophies currently prevailing among human beings, only the Islamic faith can be characterized as having a pure form of monotheism. Allah says in the Koran, 'And We sent never a Messenger before thee except that We revealed to him, saying, "There is no god but I; so serve Me.'

"The Oneness of Allah has been the chief constituent and characteristic of all religions brought by the messengers of Allah. Unfortunately, after these messengers passed away, interpolations and deviations were introduced into Islam, the only religion of Allah.

"Allah teaches humankind in the Koran that associating partners with Him in worship is an unforgivable sin. Now we see the Jews confining God to their own race. The Christians consider Jesus as God or the son of God. They consider that God has a mother, a son, and a holy spirit connected with Him, which share in His lordship. Allah says in the Koran, 'Verily, Allah forgives not (the sin of) setting up partners with Him, but He forgives whom He wills sins other than that, and whoever sets up partners in worship with Allah has indeed strayed far away.

"It is also an unforgivable sin to direct any type of worship that belongs to Allah alone through idols such as statues of pious people or Jesus, Mary, saints, popes, angels, crosses, and so forth. The Islamic concept rests on the principle that Allah is distinct from His creation. Divinity belongs exclusively to Allah Most High, while creatureliness is common to everyone and everything else."

The moment came when Khadija received the order from the Palestinian resistance – an order to prepare for an outstanding journey.

One morning after the morning prayer, Khadija sat on her prayer mat to read the Koran. After she finished reading, she went to the bathroom. She washed her body to purify herself and dressed in her best clothes because in a few hours she was to stand before Allah, the King of Kings.

At the door, she held Elizabeth tightly and kissed her. She said while holding her, "I am not afraid to die for a good reason. I will sacrifice myself for Allah. I am going to blow myself up."

Terrified, Elizabeth said, "Have you gone out of your mind? Do be sensible, I beg you. Suicide attacks only defeat the cause; they provide the appropriate justification for Israelis to kill your people."

"Suicide bombings are the only means available to the Palestinians to defend themselves. I shall be like a star, like the sun."

"Please reconsider. I can't afford losing you," Elizabeth said through abundant tears.

"Do not cry for me, for I am now free. Allah has perfected his blessing on me by choosing me as a martyr. I can see my place in heaven – so peaceful up there."

"Your name will be engraved in my heart and in my memory," Elizabeth said, still weeping.

"I see you as clearly as a diamond reflecting the light of truth. You gave your soul and knew not pain in giving. May thousands of rays of Allah's light flow into your heart every day and illuminate your way. Do not grieve for me. Remember me. God be with you always."

Elizabeth held Khadija tighter while weeping incessantly. Khadija said, while disengaging herself tenderly from Elizabeth's arms, "Now you fly back to your country and we poor people turn back to our dying."

Khadija left the hotel quietly and marched forward to the target. She put on the explosive belt and held in her hand the wire that connected all the pins of all the grenades beneath her gown. She cried, "Allah is the greatest." She pulled the wire, and the place was filled with blood. She'd fulfilled her vow to her country.

After one hour, the national police spokesman announced, "A suicide attack on a busy Israeli restaurant killed at least seventeen people as well as the female bomber."

For eight days, Elizabeth did not leave her room. She was ill, dreadfully ill, morally more than physically. During those eight days, she lived through the horror of hell. She trembled at the pictures that passed before her.

During those long days in her room, Elizabeth thought about all that had led her to this hell. What in the hell had happened? Why did the Israelis have to bomb the people she was trying to help?

She was exhausted and wanted to relax. She wanted peace, and she would go home, where sorrow could not follow.

CHAPTER 25

Elizabeth returned from Palestine a mental wreck. In Palestine, she had shed tears that could saturate the earth from its crust to its centre. She had seen the anguish of the human soul; the corporal punishment of the innocents; the violation and humiliation of woman's dignity; the killing and maltreatment of little children.

She felt as if she were walking asleep in the darkness, searching for her own awakening. She felt a void within her that needed to be filled. She desperately wanted some kind of medicine to take her worries away.

President Rosh was at the oval office, awaiting the arrival of his daughter. He'd received a call from her a while ago, saying that she was in desperate need to see him. When Elizabeth entered the room, the president rose from his chair with his arms wide open. Elizabeth rushed forward to her father and hugged him. The president kissed her tenderly and then ushered her to sit in a leather chair facing his desk. A broad smile was drawn on the president's face when he saw Elizabeth's exquisite beauty radiating to fill the whole place.

"Tell me about your visit to Gaza Strip," he told her. "What conclusion did you come to from your experience there?"

Elizabeth said, "Life is not fair. In Palestine, I learned the truth that the media has been hiding."

"Truth has nothing to do with reality. You have to deal with reality."

"I am a woman plagued by her conscious. I pledge myself to the principles of humanity and justice, of freedom and equality. No might can give manpower to destroy ideas that are eternal and indestructible. If you are talking about reality, I can tell you in confidence that the Palestinian people are long-suffering at the hands of the Israelis. They are disarmed and conquered. Their homes and lands are confiscated. Entire Palestinian villages have been bulldozed and replaced with Jewish settlers. The Palestinians face automatic rifle fire, tanks, and American helicopter gunships with only bare hands and rocks."

"Wait a minute," he responded. "There are restrictions on using American aid to build settlements on Palestinian land."

"Despite these restrictions, Israel spent hundreds of millions of American dollars for importing Jews from across the world, confiscating Palestinian land, and demolishing their homes to make way for brand-new settlements for the new arrivals."

"It saddens me greatly when I am told that American aid is being used to commit atrocities against the Palestinian people. I feel their pain, and I am so sorry that they were suffering."

"Then do something to alleviate the oppression subjugating the Palestinians," she said.

"I tried, and I tried hard. I called on Israel to end occupation of Palestinian land. I called for an independent Palestinian state living side by side with Israel in peace. I proposed a road map to resolve the Israeli-Palestinian conflict."

"But the road map failed due to Israeli opposition. Ariel Sharon requested more than one hundred changes to the road map. He stated that a settlement freeze would be impossible due to the need of settlers to build new houses and start families. This is why talks between the two sides remained blocked."

The president laughed. "You know what Sharon said to our secretary of state? 'What do you want, for a pregnant woman to have an abortion just because she is a settler?'"

"Please, Father, take it more seriously. For fifty-three years, the Palestinians were forced to live in concentration camps, drink polluted water, have their loved ones killed, their homes razed, their futures shattered, deprived of all God-given rights. They were forced to flee for their lives from one place to another; they were imprisoned, tortured, and assassinated."

"The two sides should sit and talk. The Israelis are willing to talk, but the Palestinians answer with suicide bombers. The personalities of suicide bombers and their religion are the principal causes for such violence."

"It's politics, not religion, which has led the Palestinians to blow themselves up," she stressed. "The driving force is not religion but a cocktail of provocations, including politics, humiliation, revenge, and retaliation. The main motive for many suicide bombings in Israel is revenge for acts committed by Israelis."

"Both sides should conduct negotiations with regard to issues of peace-making. Violence will only lead to more hatred and dissension."

"When it comes to sitting down to the table, the Israelis seem to always find a reason for the deal not being good enough. Israel knows that the longer they delay a solution to the Palestinian problem, the more they gain. Each day that goes by, more settlements are built and more

Palestinians are displaced. The Israelis love the peace process, but achieving peace is not their goal."

The president said, "I have sent my envoys to Israel several times to stop violence and build peace, but the result was always unpleasant."

"As it seems, your envoys had an inherent tendency to see the Palestinian-Israeli conflict first from Israel's vantage point rather than from that of the Palestinians. In truth, not a single senior-level official involved with the negotiations was willing or able to present, let alone fight for, the Arab or Palestinian perspective."

"In order to understand the nature of the Israeli-Palestinian conflict, you must look at it from a wider perspective. You must understand that support for Israel is particularly deep in the American Jewish community and among a significant majority of Evangelical Christians. Evangelicals who support Israel do so from deeply held religious convictions. First, they believe God gave the Holy Land to the Jews forever; and second, they believe God has promised to bless those who bless the Jews and curse those who curse the Jews. In other words, if they want God to bless America they believe America must bless Israel. You can find Evangelicals everywhere: in Jewish- Christian coalition, Christian Right, neoconservatives, the Tea Party, and Congress, including Republicans and Democrats. Yes, most Americans will side with Israel in its right to exist. That does not mean blind support for everything Israel does or wants to do. Also, America gives a great deal of aid to the Palestinians as well as other Arab states, not just the Israelis."

"This shows that America can exert significant influence by being an honest broker with sufficient trust from both sides," she said.

"Do not forget that I am the first American president to officially call for a two-state solution to the Arab-Israeli conflict."

Silence reigned in the room for long moments. Suddenly, Khadija's torture and self-sacrifice emerged into consciousness. Elizabeth broke the silence with words that sounded blameworthy.

"You gave Israel a blank cheque in assault on the Palestinians. The Israeli invasion to the Palestinian territories could only have taken place with the green light from Washington. Palestinians are human beings and not faceless enemy terrorists. America has long ago proved unworthy of the title honest broker. Today America is totally siding with Israel, a matter that became almost a patriotic duty for anyone in public office. Only those who ignore reality can deny that such bias has tarnished America's reputation and undermined its interests abroad. Is it not enough that you support the plan of Kadima's party about outlining the borders of Israel without consulting the Palestinians! Is it not enough that you gave Israel clear permission to reoccupy the West Bank! You approved that the Israelis destroy the private and public properties of the Palestinians without restrictions during the annihilation of the West Bank. Was it not enough that you supported Israel by ignoring the resolution of the International Court of Justice, which compels Israel to pull down the separating wall! You have established the ugly fact that in your time, America stands against the international law and that she imposes by force her biased views about the Arab-Israeli conflict. Your administration has swallowed its declaration about the date for establishing the Palestinian nation, saying that there are no sacred dates! You sided with Israel when it refused the return of the refugees to their homeland. The Israeli-Palestinian conflict is damaging the image of Washington in the eyes of the Arabs."

"The United States is working toward a Middle East where Israel can be a key component in projecting American military and economic interests. The US project requires suppressing challenges to its local hegemony. Consequently, it has long been in the interest of the United States to maintain a militarily powerful, belligerent Israel. Real regional peace could undermine this crucial relationship. The United States therefore has pursued a policy that could bring stability in the region while falling carefully short of real peace."

Elizabeth was amazed. "The so-called peace process, then, is not about peace but about imposing a Pax Americana!"

"I told you that the Palestine-Israeli issue is complicated. In a region where radical nationalism could threaten US control of oil and other strategic interests, Israel has successfully prevented victories by such movements, not just in Palestine, but in Lebanon and Jordan as well. It has kept Syria, with a radical nationalist regime once allied with the Soviet Union, in check. Israel has missiles capable of reaching the former Soviet Union and has cooperated with the US military-industrial complex with research and development for new jet fighters and anti-missile defense systems, a relationship that is growing every year. Another function Israel performs is that its frequent wars have allowed for battlefield testing of American arms. Israel's own arms industry has provided weapons and munitions for governments and opposition movements supported by the United States."

The president ceased talking for a moment, during which he cut the tip of a cigar with a cutter and then lit it with butane lighter. He held the cigar in his mouth enjoying the tobacco fragrance.

The president continued. "The United States has been involved in and assisted in the overthrow of foreign governments without the overt use of US military force. Often such operations are tasked to the CIA. Israel assisted the States in such operations."

"It's like Israel has become just another federal agency, one that is convenient to use when you want something done quietly."

"The stronger, more aggressive, and more willing to cooperate with US interests that Israel has become, the higher the level of aid and strategic cooperation. In other words, a militant Israel, in a constant state of war — technologically sophisticated and militarily advanced yet lacking an independent economy and being dependent on the United States — is far willing to perform tasks that might not be acceptable to other allies that would an Israel at peace with its neighbours. So as you see, Israel's obstinacy serves the purposes of both our countries best."

"You've turned the Jews in Israel into mercenaries fighting wars of what the ruling elite in America consider to be American interests," she said. "We give them food to eat, and they bite those whom we tell them to bite. Is this what you call strategic cooperation?"

"American interests are what matter in the end."

"For decades, Israel has violated well established precepts of international law and defied numerous United Nations resolutions in its occupation of conquered lands, in extrajudicial killings, and in its repeated acts of military aggression. Most of the world regards Israel's policies, and especially its oppression of Palestinians, as outrageous and criminal. Only in the United States do politicians and the media still fervently support Israel and its policies. For decades, the US has provided Israel with crucial military, diplomatic, and financial backing, including more than three billion each year in aid. Why is the United States the only remaining bastion of support for Israel?"

"Today, though barely two per cent of the nation's population is Jewish, close to half its billionaires are Jews. The chief executive officers of the three major television networks and the four largest film studios are Jews, as are the owners of the nation's largest newspaper chain and the most influential single newspaper, the *New York Times*. The role and influence of Jews in American politics is equally marked."

"But Jews are only two per cent of the nation's population."

"Yet they comprise eleven per cent of the nation's elite. Jews constitute more than 25 per cent of the elite journalists and publishers, more than 17 per cent of the leaders of important voluntary and public interest organizations, and more than 15 per cent of the top ranking civil servants. Jewish economic influence and power are disproportionately concentrated in Hollywood, television, and in the news industry."

The president blew the smoke of his cigar and then continued. "Let alone the amount of money they contribute to election campaigns. Jews alone contributed 50 per cent of the funds for President Bill Clinton's 1996 re-election campaign. They are a major source of money for Democratic candidates."

"Jews may have great power in the States, but they should have a greater sensitivity about the issue of people who are suffering."

"I'm afraid it is a fact that the Jews wield immense power and influence in the United States. The Jewish lobby is a decisive factor in US support for Israel."

"As long as the powerful Jewish lobby remains entrenched, there will be no end to the Jewish-Zionist domination of the US political system," she said.

"I told you, honey, that the matter is not simple. Under these circumstances, my role as a president is to make decisions taking into account the weight of the several powers, influencing the political texture of our country."

Elizabeth said, "As the president of the United States, you represent what America always stands for: fairness, openness, and justice. In all your analysis, you did not touch any of these principles. You just talked about America's interests. The Palestinian people are slaughtered every day, and you talk only about the American interests. The Zionist extremists and their Christian supporters in your administration are working together to create chaos and bloodshed and may thus be engaging in a self-fulfilling prophesy of a great Armageddon. They clearly appear to place their loyalty to Israel above the true interests of the United States."

The president said angrily, "The members of my administration, whether Jews or Christians, are loyal to the United States and are efficient in their work."

"It's no secret that the Zionist lobby in America is dramatically influencing the American administrations, and in the end, the Palestinians pay the price."

"The Israeli lobby has many think tanks that provide advice to the various administrations, both Republican and Democrat. During my predecessor's administration, the Israeli lobby provided officials from the Washington Institute for Near East Policy. During my administration, many of the officials that the Israeli lobby provided are from their Republican think tanks, like the American Enterprise Institute (AEI) and the Jewish Institute for National Security Affairs – JINSA."

"Do they take into consideration the interests of the Palestinian people as well or do they only serve Israel and its unlawful gains in the area?"

Elizabeth ceased talking for a while and then said sarcastically, "Jews call the tune; the world dances. Palestinians won't get their independence until Americans get theirs."

Elizabeth rose from her chair and looked straight into her father's eyes. "Palestine has the right to exist under international law, and granting Palestinians statehood should not be looked upon as a favour by the US, EU, or Israel. You make deceiving announcements favouring Israel by giving it the green light to attack and assassinate, at the same time numbing the Arabs by promising them a Palestinian state when you know that it will never be established. Your cunning promises will come back to you. Being a president is more than talk; there is responsibility here."

"Israel is the only democratic nation in the Middle East. The Palestinians are the aggressors. They started the suicide bombings and all acts of terrorism. Such indiscriminate murders of Israeli civilians are immoral, non-defensive acts of vengeance. Israel will continue to defend herself, and the situation of the Palestinian people will grow more and more miserable."

Elizabeth headed for the door. She opened it and then turned to her father and said sadly, "Dad, please save me the embarrassment. Israel defends itself against disarmed people fighting back with slings and stones! The Palestinians have the right to live freely on their land, yet we slaughter them like cattle. America is responsible for all this bloodshed. Our hands are stained with the Palestinian blood. I fear God might send down upon us a painful chastisement of wrath for our evildoing."

CHAPTER 26

At the White House, Amanda Rosh was having breakfast in bed. Thoughts about Elizabeth's future rushed around in her head. Elizabeth, her only child, the apple of her eye was living alone in her mansion in Manhattan. After the tragic death of her husband, Roy, Elizabeth passed through a trauma that was about to cause her psychological damage. Despite the fact that Elizabeth kept herself busy all the time with humanitarian works, she looked like a piece of pain moving aimlessly without a goal. Her soul was sorely shaken, and her belief in marriage was broken.

Elizabeth's sadness pierced through Amanda's heart. She could not leave her only daughter like that, troubled and forlorn. It was horrid for a woman of such beauty and wealth to be left alone without love and marriage. Elizabeth had more than enough to keep going, but money counted for nothing compared to the blessing of happiness.

Lately it was plain to see upon Elizabeth's face a tint of grief, and sometimes her eyes were shadowed with unshed tears. What could the cause of her grief be? Was it because of that Egyptian who stole her heart? That man must have cheered her heart, yet if hope had flown away, Elizabeth had to go out and find life.

She thought that Elizabeth must marry someone of her status, someone who could protect her, cherish her heart, and be the father of her children. There was no one better than Senator Robert Hudson.

Senator Hudson was a promising Republican senator. The president appreciated his past political achievements and sought his consultation in several political issues.

Senator Hudson was the keynote speaker at the state conventions of the California, Michigan, and Texas reform parties. The *Washington Post*, Fox Network Television, and CNN had profiled Congressman Hudson. Hudson also appeared on a number of national talk and news shows, including *The Phil Donahue Show*; NBC's *Meet the Press*, CNN's *Crossfire*, and *Good Morning America*.

Senator Hudson was also a noticeable businessperson. He was a stock owner and shareholder in several global American corporations. He owned a farm run by a Mexican named Carlos. He also owned an old boat that needed to be repaired.

Senator Robert Hudson was the majority leader of the Republican Party. He presided over the Senate in the president's absence; exercised the powers and duties of the president in his absence; and assumed other duties as assigned by the president.

Senator Hudson was a close friend of the Rosh family, and on several occasions, he was invited to private dinners in the White House to discuss with the president certain political matters. Elizabeth joined few of these dinners. Amanda had noticed that Senator Hudson was infatuated with Elizabeth. Amanda also knew from her daughter that Hudson had once proposed to her five months after her husband's death, but at that time, Elizabeth was not in a position to accept the idea of another marriage.

It was true that Senator Hudson was in his early forties and Elizabeth was in her late twenties, but Amanda thought that he was still the most suitable for her. The difference in age between them would create the environment of understanding and patience required for Elizabeth to accept a new life with another man. Now was the time to avow her thoughts to her daughter.

Amanda Rosh thought highly of Ohio Representative Robert Hudson, but Hudson had a secret life that Amanda didn't know about. Hudson was a man who would use any method to win. Hudson liked to play on the winning side, and long ago, he had decided there was only one side to consider in his fight — the side of the president — the side of the neoconservatives and their allegiance with the Christian Right and the Jewish lobby.

Amanda paid Elizabeth a visit in Manhattan. She wanted to know Elizabeth's plans for the future. "It's about time, Liz, that you start thinking seriously of getting married. I can see that Senator Robert Hudson is willing to propose to you if you give him a chance. I find him the most suitable for you."

Elizabeth trembled a little. There was a mass of many images crowding like waves upon her. Raising the subject of marriage was a sudden shock to her. She needed time to sort out her feelings and prepare an answer that would express exactly what she felt about this delicate matter.

Elizabeth delayed her answer by shaking a small bell placed on the table before her. The butler wheeled a tea table into the room. Amanda realized that Elizabeth had a lot to say, so she respected her silence and occupied herself by sipping tea and tasting the delicious cake.

After long minutes of silence, Elizabeth began to talk.

"I knew the wisdom of life with the man I met in Kosovo. I learned that man is not just a person with male characters but also the spirit of God moving to establish the divine justice on earth. My heart bled within me when I saw him standing alone confronting the unjust world. Together we passed the forests of hell. With him, I shed tears and saw torture in the silence of the terrible nights. But he was like a tempest shaking the earth beneath the enemy. He stood tall and proud to defend me. I have seen him in the middle of utmost danger bowing and prostrating in worship to God. I saw that through his hands, God speaks, and from his eyes, God smiles upon the earth. He looked as if he owned the world and everything in it. His love was pure and incorruptible. I am the only woman he ever loved, and he is the only man I have ever trusted with my life. Swept by the tempest of his love, my heart enjoyed a touch of thrill. What could be more purely bright than the love I felt for him? The days I spent with him will never become a memory, for profound bonds tie me to him. Since I returned from Kosovo, I have lived with no other thought than to love him."

With eyes wetted with tears Amanda took her daughter in her arms and said in a shaky voice, "Oh, my dear child, you have suffered a lot. Do you love him that much?"

"He made me feel safe when everything else was frightening. I owe my life to him. He almost died trying to save me." Elizabeth's whole body quivered with sadness.

Amanda released her daughter from her arms, looked intently in her eyes, and said, "Be realistic, my child. Don't cling on to memories; those days are over."

"I grew stronger in his hand. He is everything I could want in a man."

"You are praising him to the skies. He couldn't possibly be a match for you. Forget your foolish heart. Show some sense. Listen to your head."

"No matter how hard I tried, I was unable to get him out of my mind."

"So where did that leave you? No good would come of knowing him. Get your head together, Liz, and start thinking straight. In all of life's lessons, you have yet to learn the simplest of words: letting go. Life goes on. It's time you start living again, my child."

"But how does one live without a heart?" Elizabeth said with a tormented soul.

"My philosophy has always been to look forward, not backward, to consider the future rather than the past."

"You don't know the ways of fate, mother. Everything that happens has a reason behind it. I met him when I needed a man to listen to my pain and banish my agony. It's hard to shut him out of my life. What he did for me goes beyond friendship."

"Liz, my love, you are the blessing of my life. I just do not want you to be hurt unnecessarily. Show some sense, dear. The man you love belongs to a different world. Being a Muslim would always prevent you from forming any permanent tie with him. Now he is but a shadow from the past. He couldn't possibly be a match for you. You simply have to adjust to that fact."

"My love for him was overwhelming. It enveloped my whole being. But do not fear anything, mother. I know what pain and misery can do to me. I got hurt before, and I don't want to fall again. It's true that my heart has become troubled, but I am aware that feeling sorry for myself will not get me anywhere. But in all circumstances, I shall be forever in his debt. To me, he will never be a shadow from the past but a living reality embedded in my soul."

"You will get over him, I'm sure."

"I'll live with it, but I will never get over him."

"That's my girl. Do not trouble your life away. Love causes havoc and creates chaos. Time is a good healer. Time is what you need." Amanda patted Elizabeth's shoulder.

"I must be going now, dear," Amanda said, rising from her seat. She said while walking with Elizabeth to her car, "I was wondering lately if your life wouldn't have fallen into a more perfect pattern if you'd married again and had children like everybody else. By the way, your birthday party is two weeks from now. I promise you that it will be the talk of the city. I have already made arrangements. Your mansion will be like a star twinkling in the sky."

Elizabeth Rosh's birthday party was indeed the talk of the city. The mansion sparkled in the night like a shining star. The joy in attending was not only because of Elizabeth's birthday but also because the Republican Party seized control of the Senate midterm elections. With such a result, Republicans would control all three branches of government, allowing them to shape the political battles to come, including how to stimulate the economy and manage free world trade. The guests were Republicans, a few Democrats, and a group of tycoons.

With a broad smile on his face, the president stood in the lobby and congratulated dozens of Republican winners. Amanda Rosh stood beside her husband, chatting with one of her acquaintances, her eyes fixed on her daughter's room on the first floor. She was waiting impatiently for her daughter to descend. The whole gathering was waiting for Elizabeth to appear in order for the party to begin. The whiskey kept coming on the silver trays, and now it was champagne cascading into crystal glasses in showers of golden bubbles.

Elizabeth appeared from her room and started to descend the staircase. She was wearing a long white chiffon dress with delicate silver slippers and a diamond necklace. She looked exquisitely beautiful. Amanda glanced at Senator Robert Hudson. He looked stunned. Elizabeth's beauty clearly fascinated him as well as all the others. Amanda smiled and hoped that Hudson would be the right man for her daughter.

Elizabeth walked among the guests and greeted everyone. When she reached her father, she kissed him lovingly. She also embraced her mother appreciatively for the effort she'd devoted to the success of her birthday party. Elizabeth then headed to the spacious dining room, pushed the door open, and walked in. The elegant dining room was bathed in flickering candlelight, and the tables glittered with silver and crystal. Every table was set for four persons, but there was only one table set for only two: Elizabeth Rosh and Robert Hudson. This, of course, was arranged by Amanda Rosh. Within a few minutes, the dining room was a sea of elegantly dressed men and exquisitely dressed women.

The dinner was rich and delicious. Appetizers included grilled marinated gulf shrimp; the main dish was seared sea scallops; and there was maple ginger crème brûlée for dessert.

Elizabeth and Hudson ate in silence at first, and then Hudson surprised her by saying, "This is my birthday gift for you; I hope you like it."

It was a large piece of emerald cut into a dome shape and placed in a small box of navy blue velvet.

"Oh! How nice of you to bring me the queen of gems. I just adore emeralds." She appreciated his valuable gift.

"I brought it for you because emerald is the birthstone for the month of May. Emerald is also the gem of queens, and you are a queen." He gave her a charming smile.

His tender words were touching. Elizabeth kept contemplating the gem with interest.

"The most prized is pure green or slightly bluish green," Elizabeth said, admiring the precious stone. "The stone is pure green. I can see all sorts of lovely patterns resembling foliage in a garden."

"The ancients held the emerald in great esteem, believing it sharpened the wearer's eyesight and mind. Travelers relied on emeralds as protection against the hazards and perils of long journeys," Hudson said, watching Elizabeth examine the stone.

Elizabeth was about to tell him that the green gem was also said to give its owner the power to predict the future, but she didn't.

The green gem would be her magic ball. She would ask the emerald about her dreams, her future. Her mind drifted to Omar, and her heart raced in uneven beats. She whispered in her soul, *I can see you in the emerald, wandering about the crystals trapped within. Every moment with you is as fresh as a teardrop. I still carry your tears in my eyes and your words in my heart. Is your fighting soul still seeking justice in a restless world or are those days over? You filled my heart with pride, and you have put meaning into my life. We walked arm in arm, soul in soul, heart in heart, and together we were unbeatable. can I just forget you and move on? Can I find someone else to love? Has destiny sentenced me to a bitter end with another man? But my heart is beating for you, and your love in me never dies. Oh, what a heaven love is. O, what a hell!* Elizabeth wanted to cry. Tears streamed down her face.

Hudson thought that her tears were those of gratefulness because of the precious stone he'd just presented her.

Elizabeth glanced at Hudson unreservedly, as if trying to study him. He was handsome, attentive, and smooth talking. But that was all. Omar struck a cord deep within her that no other man had ever managed to do. Hudson was all surface polish, shallow. Omar was a cold block of steel, but he had depth and heart when he cared to reveal them.

"I wonder if you would care to have dinner with me one evening," Hudson said hopefully. "I hate eating alone."

"Maybe," she said with difficulty, trying to rise from her shattered dreams.

CHAPTER 27

Senator Robert Hudson insisted that Elizabeth had to go out and enjoy life. She must find time for herself. The touch of sadness that was always showing on her beautiful face must disappear.

Hudson bombarded Elizabeth with calls. He called her each day a number of times to tell her about the good feelings of comfort and love that come from a meal prepared with care and eaten in the company of a good friend in a well-selected restaurant. In order to stop his persistent telephone calls, Elizabeth had to accept his dinner invitations at the city's fanciest restaurants.

Elizabeth was spotted having dinner with Hudson at Aquavit and Daniel restaurants. The *Rendezvous* magazine claimed, "Hudson was watching the door like a hawk until Elizabeth got there. The two had a very intense conversation and gazed into each other's eyes throughout the dinner."

During the frequent dinners, Hudson insisted that visiting exotic places where nature takes precedence over civilization could make life more inspiring. In such exotic remote places, Elizabeth could use her mind only in peaceful thought and find a spiritual solution to every problem.

Hudson's sweet talks appealed to Elizabeth. She liked his pragmatic sense of humour and decided to go along with his plans designed to make her days more palatable.

While having dinner at L'Impero restaurant, Hudson seriously suggested a seven-day Costa Rica cruise aboard the ship *Royal Caribbean*. When Elizabeth asked him why Costa Rica in particular, he said that Costa Rica was a unique place with exceptionally diverse scenery, including tropical rain forests, nine active volcanoes, hot spring spas, unspoiled white sand beaches, rivers and waterfalls, and many national parks. Hudson noticed that Elizabeth was considering the matter and seemed interested.

"Elizabeth, please give it a try. You have nothing to lose. Well, do I make reservations?" he said, pressing her to accept his offer.

"Okay," she said after a moment's hesitation.

Hudson's face radiated with happiness. He would be alone with Elizabeth at last. She would be totally his, and he would be able to impress her with his charm and cleverness.

Elizabeth and Hudson started their sea trip to Costa Rica. The ship was beautiful, the food was excellent, and the service was outstanding.

In Costa Rica, they lodged in Sol Playa Hermosa Beach Resort, overlooking one of the most beautiful beaches there. Hudson cleverly planned the trip. On horseback, they passed through the jungle with a guide. The jungle hosted a huge diversity of birds in a lush, peaceful environment. The next day, they watched the hourly eruptions of Arenal volcano. At the Playa del Coco, a small village located fifteen minutes from Playa Hermosa, they went fishing and tanned on the excellent beach.

The well-equipped boat took them to dive in the Gulf of Papagayo. A professional guide took them sixty feet underwater to watch yellowtails, turtles, stingrays, angelfish, and many species of eels.

The seven days went too quickly. The trip was a wonderful experience for Elizabeth. It was relaxing and memorable.

As the days passed, a good relationship was established between Hudson and Elizabeth. They were frequently seen skiing in the mountains of the Midwest or camping and fishing at Lincoln Rock State Park in Washington.

One month later, the *Washington Post* wrote, "It sure looks like Elizabeth Rosh and Robert Hudson are becoming an item. While the two continued to deny any serious involvement, Hudson recently unloaded a pair of diamond-studded dog tags to Elizabeth. Her pair, featuring the initial *E*, is a match to his, featuring the letter *R*, and they have been wearing them everywhere lately. Arriving together at the Iridium Jazz Club earlier this month, Elizabeth still insisted that they are just good friends and that the dog tags were actually a token of their close friendship."

Robert Hudson was right, Elizabeth thought. She must live her life beautifully and far from anxiety and fear. She was young, beautiful, and rich; and a bright future awaited her. It was true that her marriage to Roy had been a complete fiasco, but this was not the end of the world. Although she carried no feelings for Hudson, the man was enthralled with her and was doing his best to make her happy. She must also admit that Hudson, besides being a reputable Republican senator with a bright political career, was also sensible, considerate, and understanding.

But could a relationship work out if she were not in love with Hudson? A start of fear went through her. She was scared and not sure she wanted to marry Hudson. It was like being stuck in a river and getting whisked over a waterfall. Was marrying Hudson what she wanted from life? The answer stared back at her. She wanted Omar. Her life without him would always remain boring and incomplete.

At first, the mere thought of marrying Hudson had frightened her. She felt a tightening in her chest, feeling that she had been trapped into marrying him. But she wanted to live a normal life with a husband and kids. She wanted a family of her own. She wanted a husband who would love and cherish her.

Although she didn't love Hudson, it was her duty as a wife to make him happy — then Omar would go away and leave her thoughts. She must show Hudson that her relationship with Omar was platonic and just a shadow from the past.

Hudson had been thoughtful and considerate. He had been attentive and affectionate. He was a man of intelligence, and he was handsome. She could be proud of him.

Robert Hudson was waiting for the suitable moment to propose to Elizabeth. The proposal must be incredible and unique. Hudson took Elizabeth in a rented four-seated plane and flew over a vast area of green fields. The pilot suddenly yelled joyously, "What the hell is that?" Startled, Elizabeth looked to where the pilot was pointing to see a two-acre field with the words "Elizabeth, will you marry me?" The words were written in fluorescent orange paint. When Elizabeth turned back to look at Hudson, he was down on one knee holding a ring for her. The ring was an oval Ceylon sapphire, set in platinum and surrounded by ten diamonds. It was the most incredible proposal Elizabeth could have ever imagined.

Elizabeth said yes.

As he placed the ring on her finger, Hudson said, "I promise to honour and cherish you forever."

The *New York Times* reported the following: "Republican Senator Robert Hudson and Elizabeth Rosh, deputy chairperson of Rosh Enterprises and the sole inheritor of Rosh's wealth, began appearing in public together more than one year ago. The Senator has popped the question, asking Elizabeth to marry him, and Elizabeth accepted his proposal. Elizabeth was just beaming when she arrived with Senator Hudson at the Iridium Jazz Club showing off a diamond ring on her engagement finger. Both looked ecstatic. It looks as if they are knee-deep in wedding plans."

The news of their future marriage began to appear on TV stations and newspapers: "Republican Senator Robert Hudson and the president's daughter, Elizabeth Rosh, are to marry in the autumn. Their wedding ceremony will take place in the Hamptons, the exclusive beachside resort near New York, at a property owned by the Rosh family. The bride and the groom will live in Elizabeth's mansion in Manhattan."

Five months after the proposal, Elizabeth and Hudson got married. The news of their marriage flew all over the world: "Elizabeth Rosh, the president's daughter, married in a lavish wedding in the Hamptons. Some two hundred people attended the ceremony, which included four bands, a gospel choir, fireworks, and tens of thousands of flowers.

CHAPTER 28

In Egypt, while Omar was in his office at the headquarters of the Egyptian Special Forces, his secretary informed him that he received a call requesting that he meets with the minister of foreign affairs. Astonished about such an unusual call, Omar went to the ministry at the appointed time.

In his elegant spacious office, the minister of foreign affairs welcomed Omar cheerfully and ushered him to sit in on one of the two seats opposing his desk. The minister sat at his desk and looked plainly at Omar.

"I am glad to see you, Major Omar, especially after the heroic deeds you did in Kosovo and Bright Star 1996. You know, of course, that sometimes, due to political reasons, we appoint ambassadors from the army. Our former ambassador in the United States has terminated his period, and you will replace him. Yes, we have appointed you the ambassador of Egypt to the United States of America for many reasons.

"Your records as an aid to General James Douglas in Kosovo and your heroic actions to save the life of President Rosh's daughter, as well as Commander Kenny Walker in Bright Star 1996, have been very much appreciated by the United Nations and the American administration. The vast knowledge you have reported to your superiors about your visit to America and the brilliant analysis you made regarding the internal and external factors moving the American foreign policy worldwide is the real reason behind your appointment as Egypt's ambassador in America. Your work as ambassador comes during a crucial time for Egyptian-US relations, which have increasingly fallen under the shadow of intensified conflict in the Middle East region.

"I must remind you of some facts that you should keep in mind while representing Egypt in America. Do not ever forget that America is a superpower and her trade connections are worldwide. Do not ever forget that we live in hazardous times and America and Egypt are ancient allies.

"Israeli-Palestinian violence is reaching new levels of intensity now, but the optimist in me still thinks that if both sides showed more trust in the other's intentions, gradual progress could be made. The United States will have to act like the 'honest broker' it once called itself; otherwise, we can only look forward to more disappointments and ever-deepening distrust. Currently, however, violence and instability in the occupied Palestinian territories are affecting US interests in the region. It is your duty to urge the US government to take a more direct and consistent role in the Middle East affairs in order to curb the violence in the occupied territories and revive the peace process.

"Peace is essential for regional prosperity, and a just brokerage of peace in the Middle East would help reverse the widespread loss of prestige and trust in American foreign policy.

"You must call attention to Egypt's commitment to regional peace and the eradication of terrorism, along with the need to address religious and socio-economic factors.

"The American administration must understand the danger that might result from the interference in the affairs of a country like Egypt, which is highly sensitive to anything that may touch its sovereignty, culture or religion.

"For the continuation of a good relationship between America and Egypt, the American administration should understand that Egypt must be allowed to develop its regional role the way it finds most suitable for her interest.

"Our responsibility with regard to Egypt's relationship with America in the future is virtually connected to your ability to make your voice heard."

The minister finished his talk, then stood up and shook hands with Omar. He said while accompanying Omar to the door, "You are a great warrior, Omar, but this time you will negotiate with words and not with weapons, right, Major?"

"I appreciate the confidence you put in me, sir. I will do my best to serve my country," Omar said respectfully.

"Now you have to prepare yourself for the heavy task awaiting you. You must fly to New York in two weeks or so," the minister added.

Omar sat in his study with a sad heart. He opened the drawer of his desk with a shaking hand and took out an old issue of the *New York Times*. The newspaper was opened to a certain page – Elizabeth and Hudson marriage. The news of Elizabeth's marriage had splintered Omar's heart into a thousand shards. He felt as though he had been hit with a log. He was terribly hurt. Without Elizabeth, life had no meaning.

The image of Elizabeth and Hudson kissing sent a wave of familiar pain through him. It wrenched his heart in two to see her kissing the senator.

Omar stared at the void before him. The past was not yet over, and the memories of how they met were still vivid in his mind. He whispered with a tortured heart, "While I'm sitting here alone drowning in tears of pain, you are enjoying the company of another man. You are the one who brought happiness into my life, and now you are the one who gave me pain. Do you know how it feels to be dead while alive? I knew the moment I looked into your eyes that I was born to love you. You are the love of my life, the sunshine of my days. My heart fights to keep my dream alive. Is love lost somewhere in your heart? Maybe I cannot fit in your world and you cannot fit in mine, but still I love you with every atom in me. Until the day I die, no other woman will touch me. I would instead prefer to wait and wither. I will endure the pain and bear the agonizing hurt because I knew in my heart that you are the only one for me."

Elizabeth became fond of long vacations with Hudson in far exotic places. They travelled to Malaysia to spend a week at the Sheraton Langkawi Beach Resort.

Hudson knew in his heart that Elizabeth was not in love with him, so he tried hard to impress her with his honeyed words and his experience about exotic places. Elizabeth was, to him, the love of his heart. He loved her with a passion that seemed to get deeper and more intense with each passing day. In addition, she was also a golden chance for further brightening his political career.

The resort was located within a natural unspoiled rainforest that fringed the sandy white shores of the Andaman Sea. The mystical island of Langkawi offered the married couple a myriad of sights like jungle-clad mountains, hills enveloped in mist, rice paddies, and lush tropical rainforests. The combination of bright sun-filled skies and natural beauty made the resort a perfect summer place for Elizabeth and Hudson.

Elizabeth was impressed by the beautiful exotic places that she saw. However, she longed for a normal life with Hudson. She didn't love Hudson. He was not her true lover; he was not her soul mate. Her heart was deeply enthralled with another man, a man she met in Kosovo, and since then, their souls had been entwined together.

First comes love, then comes marriage, but love never happened between Elizabeth and Hudson before marriage.

Elizabeth had always expected to have children with Hudson, but she was so amazed by the chilliness she felt towards him. The more Hudson tried to entice her to be better in bed, the colder she got. Even his words in bed — "my little bird, my special darling, my sacred angel" — seemed artificial and annoying to her. She tried her best to fulfil his sexual desires, but she couldn't. She never had fulfilling sex with him. Their lovemaking was only partial and incomplete. Hudson never satisfied her sexually in bed, and she doubted he ever would. She knew that their relationship had been all wrong from the start, but she didn't care anymore. She would try hard to keep up appearances for the sake of her image before the people. She didn't want to succumb to disappointment because of an unhappy marriage, which, if made public, would again embarrass her and her father. She would maintain a good front; make things look good even if they were not.

Omar arrived in the United States one year after Elizabeth's marriage to Hudson. In the White House, he presented his credentials to President John Rosh. The president realized from the first glance why his daughter fell in love with the tall and strong man standing before him. Even though Omar was elegantly dressed, the president could sense the sheer power of his physique, the wide, strong shoulders of the athlete tapering down to a small waist and narrow hips. Omar looked proud, calm, and totally in control of himself.

Thoughts whirled in the president's mind. When Elizabeth had returned from Kosovo, he'd asked the CIA to provide him with a full report about Omar. This beautiful devil that saved his daughter's life by sacrificing his own, also saving the life of an American military officer in Bright Star 1996, had killed more than one hundred Serbian militants in a one-week period. And now he was standing before the president of the United States as a diplomat! *Those Muslims are strange,* he thought. *When they raise the flag of jihad, nothing can stop them.* In jihad wars, fighting in the cause of Allah, the purpose is not only to fight and win but also to die as a martyr because this kind of death is highly rewarded by God. The martyr would join the prophets and messengers in the highest ranks of heaven. How could these people be stopped in a fight when their ultimate goal was to die? That's why they were strong warriors.

A man of such heroic deeds must be received kindly in a ceremony at the White House. Omar would be the guest of honour in a well-prepared ceremony. This was the least he could do to honour the saviour of Elizabeth's life. This tactful ceremony would also improve relations between Egypt and the United States, which had been deteriorating lately due to the blindsiding of America with Israel against the Palestinians. The Arab ambassadors to the United States would be invited, as would the senators from both parties.

After examining Omar, President Rosh was sure that Elizabeth, if left alone with him, would find the old romance flourishing again. Thank God Elizabeth was already married to Hudson. A sort of uneasiness befell the president. He wondered what Elizabeth would say if she knew that Omar became the ambassador of Egypt to America. Women were likely to do the unpredictable. Would Elizabeth be rational enough to keep a distance between her and Omar or would she give the reins to her feelings and fly with him to dangerous skies?

President Rosh told his wife about the ceremony that he intended to have at the White House. The purpose was to celebrate the heroic action of Omar, the new ambassador of Egypt to the United States, for saving Elizabeth's life. President Rosh asked Amanda to tell Elizabeth that Omar would be the guest of honour. Elizabeth – the rescued – must of course attend the ceremony with her husband, Senator Robert Hudson.

CHAPTER 29

Amanda Rosh visited her daughter in her mansion in Manhattan. Elizabeth looked relaxed after a long vacation in Malaysia.

"How are things between you and Hudson?" Amanda started.

"Things are okay, I suppose," Elizabeth said, not willing to open the subject further.

"Do you love him?"

"You know perfectly well that our marriage is not based on love," Elizabeth said quickly, trying to hold her mother back from probing further.

"You and Hudson are invited to a ceremony at the White House next week."

"What for?" Elizabeth asked carelessly.

"Ambassadors of the Arab countries and senators from both parties will attend the ceremony. It will be an opportunity for your father to make amends with the Arab world."

"Count me out, mother; I'm not interested."

"The ceremony is principally arranged to celebrate a particular event. The ambassador of Egypt will be the guest of honour." Amanda looked intently into her daughter's eyes.

"Why the ambassador of Egypt in particular?" Elizabeth wondered aloud.

"Egypt has appointed a new ambassador. It happens that you knew the man. He is the man you met in Kosovo — the man who saved your life."

Elizabeth was totally caught off guard. Her heart stopped for what felt like many seconds. She looked at her mother open-mouthed. Stunned into speechlessness, Elizabeth struggled to maintain her composure. Her whole body trembled, and she took a deep breath to calm her frantic heartbeat.

"You still love him, dear, don't you?"

Elizabeth murmured, "Did he ever think of me at all or was I shoved into the past?"

"How vulnerable to him you still are, Elizabeth. Stand up and walk away from the past — best to maintain a certain distance and best to hold yourself apart," Amanda pleaded.

"No one can ever take his place. He has haunted me in my days, in my nights, in my dreams. I haven't been able to get him out of my mind after all these years."

"The press has frequently published your story with him, but the news faded away with the passage of time. Now he is here. Gas is put beside fire. If you don't get hold of yourself, an explosion is about to happen. The media will be at the ceremony."

Amanda saw that her daughter's eyes were filled with tears. "My baby, I love you so much. I just don't want to see you hurt." Amanda said this with a tremulous voice.

"I can't help it, mother. He is not a man to be easily forgotten. He carved his own niche in my heart. I just couldn't contain the love I felt for him because it was so great. He is docile like cascading water and daring like a lion. He is pliable like green nature and wise like a prophet. He memorizes the words of God and applies them in his daily life. His heart contains the whole universe, and in a second, he sacrifices his life for others. Have you seen him in person, mother? Have you talked to him? Have you listened to his words? In Kosovo, alone in a forest, I wanted him so much for myself. I tried to seduce him, but he treated me piously, without hurting my feelings. I spent the whole night resting in his arms and listening to the words of God, words that calmed my fear and rested my soul. I still feel the warmth of his protecting arms holding me. I still hear the echo of his deep voice in my ears. I shall never lose the marks he made on my soul."

"But, dear, you are married to another man now."

"I feel sorry for myself and for Hudson too. I can't really love him. We are far apart. I can't even stand his touch."

"What's going wrong, Liz?"

"I'm not happy, mother. My first marriage was a scandal, and father was extremely embarrassed. I don't want the second marriage to become another fiasco. Hudson and I are just keeping up appearances."

"But Omar belongs to another culture, dear. He cannot fit in your world."

"Do not fear Omar. He must have learned about my marriage and drawn a line he would never cross. But fear me, Mother, for Omar has the power to melt my reason and ignite feelings that are most unwise."

In a spacious dining room at the White House, tables were arranged in circles to seat the Arab ambassadors and the senators and their wives. At the head of the room, a round table was ready for President Rosh, the First Lady, Elizabeth, Hudson, and Omar. The guests came in succession to be greeted at the doorway by the president and the First Lady. The president shook hands with Hudson and kissed his daughter. Amanda saluted Hudson and hugged her daughter for long seconds. The guests were led to their tables, and Elizabeth and Hudson were seated at the president's table. Elizabeth's eyes were anxiously staring at the doorway, expecting the arrival of Omar.

Omar was the last to arrive. He was neatly dressed and tall enough to fill the doorway. While he was shaking hands with the president and exchanging brief words, a broad smile covered Amanda's face. Omar was the best-looking man she ever laid eyes on. She could not help thinking how wonderful he looked. Amanda saw the strength in his stance, his frame, his face, and the steady black of his eyes. She felt as though his presence alone righted the world, making it a safe and sane place to be. It was a shame that he came alone without a wife – what a waste of a beautiful and strong man. Amanda could not help but sympathize with Elizabeth. Now she realized why Elizabeth had fallen in love with Omar. The man definitely had a charm that women would find irresistibly attractive.

Omar's deep black eyes that looked so dark lit up as he shook hands with Amanda. His face beamed with a pleasant smile.

Since Omar was the last to arrive, Amanda kindly held his hand and walked him to the table where Elizabeth and Hudson sat. The president followed at their heels. Omar stood tall and handsome, smiling at Elizabeth. It was then that Elizabeth met Omar's eyes. When her eyes rose to his, her pulse started to race. Their gaze held, and for an instant, the world became still.

Omar looked down at the green-grey eyes that had stolen his heart from the first moment he laid eyes on Elizabeth. He was thrilled to see her. Elizabeth looked more beautiful and had blossomed in the years since he had last seen her. He was certain she was the most beautiful woman on earth, and his love for her spread out to fill his soul.

There was joy in his eyes, and it touched Elizabeth to see that. His eyes were gazing at her with an expression that squeezed her heart.

Elizabeth was filled with mixed emotions. She did not know whether to laugh or cry. All the emotions and memories she had worked so hard to bury over the years came rushing to the surface at the sight of him. It was as if they had never been apart. Her pulse quickened, her heart melted, and the old romance flourished in spite of her – God, how she wanted to run into his arms and show him how much she missed him.

"I am Omar. Do you remember?" he announced, extending his hand.

She gave him a trembling hand and said in a shaky voice, "This is an unexpected pleasure."

Omar's smile grew until it filled his eyes. Elizabeth introduced Omar to her husband, Robert Hudson. Omar saluted him politely.

Hudson had been watching Elizabeth's quivering and trembling since Omar first stepped in the dining room. Hudson felt a pang of jealousy and hated Omar on sight.

Elizabeth smiled and said, "A great warrior and now a diplomat. You don't cease to surprise me!"

Omar smiled in return. "Sometimes, due to political reasons, Egypt appoints ambassadors from the army."

Elizabeth laughed lightly, saying, "What's a great warrior like you doing here? Are you going to start a war on our land?"

"My battles in Kosovo were to protect you. Am I going to protect you here also?" He laughed.

She glanced at him and whispered within her soul, *I want to sleep in your arms as a child sleeps, knowing that you are protecting me from all evil and danger.*

The president, Amanda, and Omar all sat at the table to have dinner. The dinner was superb: jumbo shrimp cocktails, a salad with smoked salmon and avocado, whole lobsters, and sautéed spinach.

During dinner, Elizabeth was at a loss of more words. The feel of Omar's nearness burned intently in her soul. Her breath quickened and followed in waves, and her heart hammered in her chest. She had to initiate a conversation with him but she was afraid to look into his eyes. Those black eyes had always been trouble for her. They could melt her bones and turn her life upside down in a second. She tried hard to keep her emotions safely locked inside but she was still trembling all over.

With a big effort, Elizabeth raised her eyes from her plate and looked at Omar. Their eyes met. His smile bloomed. God, she loved his smile. He was gorgeous to watch. His dark gaze jolted her heartbeat. Her whole body warmed at the look in his eyes. Yearning pierced her heart. He was beautiful, in a wholly masculine way, with his dark wide eyes, a perfect nose, and luxurious jet-black hair and close. Temptingly close. She fought the temptation to reach out to touch his luxurious black hair with her fingers.

With pretty eyes mirroring the love reflected in his, she managed to say something at last. "Do you still remember our days in Kosovo?"

"I'll never forget," he murmured in a husky voice that sounded very much like a vow.

She found the courage to say, "Where do you live in America?"

"In Washington, DC."

"I have an apartment in Washington, but most of the time I live in Manhattan. I'll see you soon, I trust," she said shyly.

"Of course," he said, feeling the quickening of his heartbeat, although his face was as calm as a resting sea.

After dinner, the president rose to his feet and gave a small speech, thanking Omar for his heroic action in saving his daughter in Kosovo and Kenny Walker in Bright Star 1996. The president then introduced Omar to the attendants and pointed to a microphone located in a corner of the room. Omar went to the microphone and began his speech.

"Mr. President, First Lady, senators, ambassadors, ladies and gentlemen, it is a great honour to be here tonight with this distinguished gathering. I thank President Rosh for making this opportunity available. Maybe this is not the time and place to mention political issues, but I find myself pushed to touch on some points I find relevant to my presence here tonight.

"We Arabs live in a hazardous time in our part of the world. The Palestinian uprising against Israeli oppression has been going on for years now. The uprising is not an act of terrorism but a just fight against Israeli persecution. Under the guise of the Palestinian uprising, Israel launched a ruthless war against innocent Palestinians. Israeli tanks blast away Palestinian buildings while helicopters hover ahead, firing down civilians. Surely a Palestinian child wielding a stone in the name of freedom is no match for an Israeli tank, or helicopter, or gunship. The Israelis are waging genocide against the indigenous inhabitants, making them an endangered species. The Palestinians are living a holocaust.

"The Arab world is hoping that America will be more just in solving the Palestinian-Israeli conflict. Mr. President, you have been born Christian again. We Arabs expect that such a rebirth in faith will make you more committed to the justice and liberty of all, regardless of religion or ethnic background. Israel should not be America's only ally in the Middle East. America should be concerned about the friendship of all.

"Mr. President, distinguished guests. As I understand, this gathering is meant to celebrate my attempt to rescue Mrs Elizabeth Rosh in Kosovo. If I were to be known for anything, I would like it to be for admiring Elizabeth's extraordinary courage and for desiring this courage to be recognized.

"Elizabeth is an American lady living a comfortable life, yet she rushed into danger and watched all the calamities of a ruthless war. She broke into hell to be certain that the persecuted had their needs met. In such a dangerous spot in the Balkan, we shared hopes and disappointments. I was hit with a bullet during our struggle to safety. Her encouraging words, her support and help, healed my wounds and helped me to stand firm on the path to freedom. She leaned on me, and I leaned on her. We were a team digging its way out to freedom. I will always keep memories of her close to me, supporting me.

"Elizabeth lives a conscious life. She has made an outstanding effort to establish human rights in a struggling world. Her continuous endeavours to apply human rights on vanquished dispersed people in several parts of the world had left a lasting impression on me. I am proud to have known her. I will always cherish the time I knew her. Elizabeth, to me, is the conscious mind of America when America is concerned about bringing a legitimate, equitable, and comprehensive peace in the world, where the rights and dignity of everyone, without exception, will be protected and respected. This is why I am here. This is why I have been appointed the ambassador of Egypt to the United States — to urge the United States to build peace where there is war and bring about justice where there is none.

"I pray for the awakening of the human conscience. I yearn for a world of justice and peace. To all the heroes who care for truth and a world without tyranny, I remain eternally grateful.

"Mr. President, we all wish for world peace, but world peace will never be achieved unless we first establish peace within our minds. We must recognize that the suffering of one person or one nation is the suffering of humanity, that the happiness of one person or one nation is the happiness of humanity. Now more than ever, we need to come together as a planet and show compassion for each other and end the unnecessary battles over land, resources, and greed. Mr. President, spreading peace prevents humanity from its own destruction. Thank you."

Omar's brief speech touched Elizabeth deeply. His words were evidently reflecting his love for her. He did not mention the sacrifices he made to save her life. He gave her all credit instead. He became the rescued, not the rescuer.

His speech about injustice and his being proud of her touched her to the core. He'd mentioned the Israeli-Palestinian conflict and emphasized their agony and despair. She perfectly understood that. She shared their pain, and she had wept at the coffins of their dead. Abundant tears dropped silently on Elizabeth's cheeks. Amanda had to lend her a handkerchief to wipe the falling tears.

The attendance applauded Omar, who smiled in return. On his way back to his seat, a man and a woman obstructed him. Omar shouted with joy, "Jennifer and Walker, what a pleasant surprise!"

Jennifer held him dearly and kissed his cheek. Kenny Walker hugged him and shook hands with him heartily.

"I don't want to interrupt anything. Jennifer and I will see you later," Walker said, pointing at the president's table.

"Okay," Omar said, laughing. He started to head back to his seat, but some Arab ambassadors obstructed him to discuss some political issues he'd touched on in his speech.

Elizabeth was watching Omar across the tables as he talked to the ambassadors. Familiar warmth enveloped her at the sight of him standing there tall and straight, with his broad shoulders and pleasant smile. The urge to reach out and touch him was overwhelming. She found herself rising involuntarily to her feet and walking over to him. His face broke into a broad smile as he saw her.

She stood looking at his face with misty eyes. He saw perplexed tears about to drop on her cheeks. He excused himself and took her aside.

"Are you happy Liz?" he asked in a caressing tone that made her love for him flows like a river. The way he said Liz broke her and released her tears like broken diamonds. He saw her tears as the brightness of a night star.

"I am happy only because you are here. Thanks for the kind words you said about me in your speech." Elizabeth saw tears swimming in his eyes. She knew that she was the only woman in the world who could bring forth his tears.

Omar stared at her, enthralled. She was soft, beautiful, and filled with love for him.

He stood saying nothing, a huge smile spreading across his face, his love spilling from his dark eyes.

Elizabeth wanted to hear his caressing voice once more. She whispered, "I was lost before you came along." Her voice broke.

"Omar, say something, please."

Omar tried to maintain his cool, but he could not prevent a tear from rolling down each of his cheeks as he looked at her.

Lost in the wondrous glory and magic of her love, he softly whispered, "Thank you for colouring my world. I have come for you. I care."

Her green eyes lit up. His love for her was like a balm to her troubled soul.

They stood looking at one another for one eternal moment, ignoring the crowd around them. Women gazed at Omar longingly and eyed Elizabeth enviously.

It was unwise to see Elizabeth so attracted to Omar. The president tactfully ended the ceremony by leaving his table with Amanda and heading to where Elizabeth and Omar stood. The president and Amanda kissed their daughter and shook hands with Omar. They then raised their hands, greeting their guests and smiling while heading to the doorway. The attendants applauded them respectfully.

Hudson came to take Elizabeth home. He saluted Omar with a brief nod and then took Elizabeth gently by the arm and headed to the door.

Omar stood alone with a broken heart, watching Elizabeth leave. His soul whispered after her, "Don't leave me behind. I have just found you. Why do you have to leave? I love you."

During the drive back to Elizabeth's apartment in Washington, Hudson grew irritable. He wanted to reproach Elizabeth for being so influenced by Omar, but he withheld.

Elizabeth was silent all the way back home. She was reliving her rare moments with Omar at the ceremony. It was fascinating to see him again – so attractive, so proud of himself, and so in love with her. His kind words in his speech about her captured her soul and lifted her to a better place.

"I wonder what it was you saw in him," Hudson said sharply. "Sorry, but that wasn't a tactful speech. Instead of giving a thankful speech, he included sensitive political issues, accusing America of siding with Israel. This accusation was, of course, primarily directed to the president. That's enough vulgarity. I must say I did not like him. Don't put so much trust in him."

"Omar is all human and more conscientious than you'll ever know, Hudson. He is as easy to read as an open book. We have run through fire together. We have opinions in common. And above all, he saved my life."

Hudson's stomach went cold at her words.

Elizabeth could not sleep well that night. She went on an hour's ramble through Omar's words: "She leaned on me, and I leaned on her. I will always keep memories of her close to me, supporting me. I will always cherish the time I knew her ..."

She was happy because she had seen Omar after such a long time, but she was also sad because now she belonged to another man. She wanted to cry and be comforted in strong, warm arms. She wanted Omar.

In the morning, Amanda phoned her daughter and said, "Omar summarized you in words that made me very proud of you. He understood your giving heart to the extent of calling you the conscious mind of America. I was eager to see the man who had stolen my baby's heart. Yesterday I saw him in person. It was as if the sun shines and sets on him. I did not know that your taste in men was so charming and exotic."

Amanda stopped talking for a while, then said hesitatingly, "Don't fear anything, darling. The future will bring you the best of what you hope for."

In his fancy apartment, Omar lay flat on the bed with his hands behind his head and stared up at the ceiling. He had never been so happy. Elizabeth was the best thing that ever happened to him. She was so fascinating the previous night that he was captivated by the grandeur of her beauty. He was absorbed in the beauty of her eyes that had stolen his heart from the first moment he saw her. Without Elizabeth, life would be unbearable. He needed her. His life revolved around her. She was the other half of him, the solid centre of his world. But Elizabeth was not just an ordinary woman. She was the daughter of the president of the United States. She was also married to a man of distinction, a Republican senator. It was not his right to have intimate relations with a married woman, for this was prohibited in Islam. And even if Elizabeth were not married to another man, was she ready to commit herself to a totally different life with him? His image as the ambassador of Egypt to the United States must always remain respectable and intact. He was no fool, so why think of dipping his feet into water that he knew would be boiling hot? This love was dangerous. He really would have to get a grip on himself.

Elizabeth's private life was none of his business. It was her life, and he was not getting involved. From now on, he would take a step away from Elizabeth. He would put some distance between them so he could start to control his rebellious thoughts and dreams. He would draw a line between him and her, and he was never going to cross it, no matter what.

CHAPTER 30

After the ceremony, Hudson had been looking forward to enjoying a pleasant night with Elizabeth. Now they were finally alone in their bedroom. No phone calls, no distractions, no interruptions. He wrapped his arms around her and felt her stiffen. Elizabeth couldn't seem to respond. The more he tried, the more anxious she became.

She struggled out of his arms. Her stomach lurched. She was about to throw up, but she pressed her lips together so she wouldn't.

The more Hudson tried to entice Elizabeth to be better in bed, the colder she became. She was cold in bed, and Hudson was never able to bring her to orgasm. For several nights, she lay in bed unfulfilled.

Hudson's failed attempts to have complete sex with Elizabeth irritated him to the core. When the following weeks produced more of the same, he couldn't take it anymore.

When Elizabeth appeared for breakfast, she looked pale and drawn. Hudson confronted her over their morning breakfast.

"Elizabeth, we need to talk," he said irritably.

"What about?"

"You know what about." He got up from his chair and began pacing the room. Now the moment had arrived. She'd known it was going to come to this sooner or later.

"I'm not sure what you mean."

Hudson stopped his pacing and ran a hand through his short hair. "Love should have more flow and ease than this. I am very stressed due to lack of sex. You still love him, don't you?"

"Love who, exactly?"

"The Egyptian, the one the press talked about."

"Please don't bring that up. It hurts."

"How does it hurt?"

"I'd rather not get into it. You are making me nervous."

"I love you so much, and I don't want to lose you. I am not pressuring you, honey, to do anything you don't want to. We are already a couple, and making love is not so bad. But the more I try to entice you in bed, the colder you get." He was feeling sorry for himself.

"Let's learn to be friends with one another," she said, annoyed.

"You should at least give it a try. Don't knock it until you try it."

Elizabeth slowly stood. Hudson reached out, taking her shoulders in his hands. She looked down, not meeting his gaze.

"I know I am not perfect, but you have to put up with me the best you can."

"I tried hard, and I failed."

"Why are you so repulsed?" he asked tenderly.

"I need space. I need time."

"Time waits for nobody. Time is running out for us all. I won't wait forever."

"No, Robert, you will give me all the time I need."

"We'll start over and ..."

"I'm sorry, Robert," Elizabeth interrupted. "I am so sorry, but I'm afraid we lack sexual intimacy."

"Oh, please, Elizabeth. Our failed attempts have ruined our sex life. We could try again and again." Hudson suddenly grabbed her shoulders, pulling her roughly against him, and kissed her lips in a demanding way that roused more anger than anything else. She pulled away, her anger flaring.

"You don't help much, Hudson. You turn my stomach," she said, terribly annoyed and frustrated.

Her words were tearing him apart. "It's OK, honey. It doesn't matter; being together is enough." But it wasn't. They both knew it.

Over the coming months, Elizabeth and Hudson felt more like roommates. They were only keeping up an appearance of a happy marriage. Since she had met Omar at the White House, their already poor sexual relationship has further dwindled.

The news spread with incredible speed that Omar, the Egyptian officer who saved the life of the president's daughter in Kosovo, was now the ambassador of Egypt to the United States. The newspapers published excerpts from Omar's brief speech, emphasizing his words of praise for Elizabeth's bravery in Kosovo. The excerpts surrounded their photo, both standing in the middle of the dining room and looking deeply into each other's eye. Other newspapers even reported that the good-looking ambassador had fascinated Elizabeth with his heroic actions in Kosovo. This news terribly annoyed Senator Hudson and certainly was not to the president's liking.

CHAPTER 31

In his office at the embassy, Omar received a telephone call from Walker and Jennifer, offering to show him Washington, DC, attractions. Omar considered their offer a rare opportunity to reunite with his two dear American friends.

The next morning, Walker and Jennifer picked up Omar and toured the city, seeing the Lincoln, Jefferson, and Washington memorials; the Smithsonian museums and the national gallery; and the Capitol and the Library of Congress, where they had lunch in the cafeteria. That night, they cruised for an hour on the Potomac River, going past all the monuments. The scenery was exceptionally beautiful.

At nine that evening, the three of them dined in a Middle Eastern restaurant. They ate in the courtyard-like dining room, where oriental music played and the walls were hung with prayer rugs. They enjoyed a variety of oriental food: demi mezze with pita for dipping, hummus, tabouleh, baba ghanoush, pastry-wrapped spinach pies, and chargrilled kebabs of chicken and shrimp. The diners chatted about old times and their latest news.

"You still work for the Department of Defense, Walker?" Omar asked.

"I work for the CIA now. I am the director of the Office of Military Affairs of the United States Central Intelligence Agency," Walker said, proud of his important new job.

"Congratulations. This is surely a sensitive post. So you are the man who calls the shots regarding support of American plans and operations."

"Precisely. We also conduct functions related to national security as directed by the president, as well as face the issues of the post–Cold War world, such as terrorism and international organized crime."

"And you, Jennifer – what happened to you with this guy since I last saw you?" Omar asked, laughing while pointing at Walker.

Jennifer sighed deeply. "We have two children, two-year-old twins, a boy and a girl. I am trying hard to raise them decently. But how can I do that in a society opened to deviation and abuse? The prohibited is allowed, and the unlawful is permitted. I still remember your preaching about moral beliefs, about right and wrong. Your utopian ideas are hard to adapt to our present society." Signs of concern were drawn on Jennifer's face.

"Just do your best, Jennifer, and leave the rest to God. He will invest your efforts for the well-being of the kids," Omar said comfortingly.

"People are becoming more and more materialistic. I want to stick to the remaining traces of my humanity by abiding God's law. I want to raise my children in chastity, in a pure environment," Jennifer said hopefully.

"You see what you have done to her, Omar?" Walker said in an annoyed tone. "You corrupted her mind. Your words were of great influence on her. She became captivated by your conservative ideas. She became meticulously concerned about the most ideal way to raise the children and to guarantee a healthy, moral life for them. Could you ever believe that she is trying to protect the kids from our society, the most progressed in the world? I just can't understand why she is doing this."

Jennifer explained further: "Walker is a wonderful husband. He has been patient with me so far. But after I had my babies, I became obsessed with the idea of protecting them from the infatuations of life. I don't want them to live as I lived.

"As the years passed, I became increasingly concerned about the loss of religiousness in American society at large. American culture has increasingly appeared to have lost its moral and religious compass.

"Yes, corruption has appeared in the land for what the hands of the people have earned," Omar confirmed.

Jennifer continued. "Anywhere you look in American society, there is a reminder that the female body should be flattered, displayed, and used to attract men. Mode of dress and sexuality are inextricably linked, and this link is recognized universally, especially by the fashion industry, which strives to bring us more attractive clothing designs, manipulating American vanity and egoism. Unfortunately, in the midst of all this babble about fashion, modesty has fallen by the wayside, with a steady and intentional push towards immodesty over time. Our society makes up the rules as it goes along, so the norms on modesty, like those on sexuality, charity, prayer, and marriage, are continually evolving and subject to change."

"Jennifer dear, who cares about modesty in a world where the human body has become a piece of meat consumed in every imaginable form?" Walker said, challenging Jennifer's views.

"Muslim women wear decent, respectable clothes," Jennifer commented.

"Muslim women are exhausted mothers chained to the stove, victims suppressed in a life of indoctrination," argued Walker. "They are covered from head to toe and are not allowed any freedoms or rights.

The veil is an obstacle clouding their minds. Female converts are either brainwashed, stupid, or traitors to their sex."

Jennifer said, "In my youth, when I started to meet people in bars and nightclubs in order to socialize in the so-called 'society of equal rights', I realized that this equality was not so true in practice as it was in theory. When I went out with my friends to those places of entertainment, I found everybody interested in talking to me, and I thought that was normal. But it was only later that I realized how naive I was, and I recognized what these people were really looking for. I soon began to feel uncomfortable, as if I were not myself. I had to dress a certain way so that people would like me, and I had to talk a certain way to please them. Everybody was saying that they were enjoying themselves, but I don't call this enjoying.

"In our society, all people have beliefs that they live according to. If having sex is some people's belief, they do everything to achieve this. If they believe drinking is one way to enjoy life, then they do it. If making money is their belief, they do this. But this leads nowhere; no one is truly satisfied. In the society of equal rights, you are expected to have a boyfriend and to not be a virgin or you are weird. This is a form of oppression, even though women do not realize it. The respect women are looking for is diminishing this way.

"Our society defined such terms as liberty and freedom, and then these definitions were accepted by women without even attempting to question or challenge them. Everything seems to be degenerating backwards. I don't want my girl to go through all this.

"I reject the freedom that American women claim to have. Women in our society are often portrayed as sexy, ladylike, and independent enough so that men have no real responsibilities toward us or the children they help create, but we're dependent enough that we are continually in search of a new man. The average woman on the street is honked at, whistled at, has had her butt or breasts fondled. I never agreed with any of that and never found a come-on flattering."

"In Islam, marriage is an important part of life, the making of society," Omar said, supporting Jennifer's point of view. "Therefore, a woman should not go around showing herself to everybody, only her husband. Even the man is not allowed to show certain parts of his body to anyone but his wife. Allah has commanded Muslim women to cover themselves to ensure their modesty. If we look around at any other society, we find that in some cases, women are attacked and molested because of how they are dressed."

"The appeal of Islam to liberated Western women is difficult for many to understand, largely because of the widespread perception in the West that Muslims treat women badly," Walker added.

"What you have picked up on about Islam, Walker, came from media representations of a stern and unforgiving God, fanatical followers, terrorists, subjugated women, and all the usual negative and untrue images," Omar commented.

Jennifer cut in: "Just because a Muslim wife must obey her husband and cooperate with him, it does not mean she is oppressed."

Walker said with annoyance, "Jennifer, why don't you go with the flow? You are trapped in a prison of morals."

Walker looked at Omar and begged, "Omar, put some sense in her head, please."

"Jennifer knows what she is doing. Let her raise her children the way she likes." Omar smiled broadly at Jennifer in approval of what she had said.

Walker changed the subject. "Let's move to a more important subject. The media has brought attention to the intimate relationship between you and the president's daughter. This is rather unwelcome to the president's family and the American people. Elizabeth Rosh is jealously guarded by my administration. Don't forget that she is already married to Senator Hudson. Keep away from her or you'll get yourself into trouble." Walker rose from his seat and went to the cashier to pay the bill.

As if something important was troubling her, Jennifer asked suddenly, "Omar, do you really love Elizabeth Rosh? I always admired her humanitarian work. She is kind and very beautiful. I loved the way you described her as the 'conscious mind of America'."

Jennifer's sudden words touched Omar's heart like a beautiful dream. Instead of answering her, he prayed for her in an audible voice:

"I pray to Allah the exalted to keep you on the right path and help you raise your children in the righteousness you desire for them. May Allah bestow on you a blessing from Him; He is indeed the Most Merciful, the Most Compassionate. Ameen."

CHAPTER 32

The Egyptian embassy was located in Washington, DC. In addition, Egypt had consulates in New York, Chicago, and San Francisco. Omar had to travel for short periods to these consulates to check their work. The ambassador had an office in each consulate and a fancy apartment in the states in which the consulates were located.

While in his office in the New York consulate, Omar received a phone call. A feminine voice said that this was Elizabeth Rosh's office and asked Omar to hold on for a second. Omar's heart throbbed strongly in his chest. His whole body shivered when he heard Elizabeth's melodious voice.

"Omar, is that you?"

Omar tried to sound normal. "Liz! How nice to hear your voice again."

"It's ridiculous that you are here in New York and I don't see you. I called you at the embassy in Washington, but they said you are in New York's consulate.

"Yes, I am here for a few days."

"Splendid. I want to take you out. How about having lunch with me at Daniel today? It's one of the best restaurants in New York."

He wanted to gently refuse her invitation so as not to get deeply involved with her, but he said hesitantly, "All right. As you wish."

"Okay. Do you know the place or should I send you my driver?"

"My driver knows New York like the palm of his hand. At what time do you want me there?"

"How about twelve?"

"Okay."

"Just ask the waiter about my table and he will take you directly to me."

"What should I wear?"

"I want to see you refreshingly informal," she said, laughing. "See you there. Please don't be late. Bye for now," she added, ending the conversation.

Omar put down the receiver. Several months had passed since he'd met Elizabeth at the White House, but he'd done nothing to contact her. During these months, she must have felt the red line he had drawn between them, the line he would not cross, not even if he wanted to. He must not subject his relationship with Elizabeth to outside influences. Elizabeth was now married to another man, and it was improper to meet her in public or in private places.

He had been dreading this moment. Elizabeth could simply make him forget his conservative manners. She could so easily blow his mind and wreck his control. He'd never forgive himself if he put Elizabeth at risk, but what choice did he have?

Common sense screamed at him to be careful, to get back to his conservative world where he belonged, but when Elizabeth came into his world, he felt reborn. Allah had made her for him.

Elizabeth forgot all about her marriage to Senator Hudson. And as she hurried to the restaurant, she wondered if she had committed the ultimate foolishness in succumbing to her feelings for Omar. The last thing she needed was to form a lasting relationship with a man who was completely different from her. To love a man like Omar would be as foolish as depending on the seas to be forever calm, and she was too sensible to try to calm stormy water. Could she just forget him and move on with her life with Hudson? But she loved Omar more than she ever thought she could. He had touched her life in so many ways. He made her feel again. Her mind screamed, *Turn back now!* But she could hardly wait to see him.

The waiter recognized Elizabeth immediately, smiled broadly, and showed her to her preferred table. Atop the table sat a white rose sustained by fresh water in a slender fluted glass.

Only a few minutes had passed before Elizabeth spotted Omar coming towards her. He looked like a man sure of himself, a man in full command of his own life.

Dressed in white trousers and a light blue short-sleeved shirt, which showed off his dark colouring and muscular build, he looked very sexy, and he held every female's eyes as he made his way towards Elizabeth. A tiny stab of unexpected jealousy caused Elizabeth a moment's pain.

"Hello, Liz. It's great to see you." He stretched his hand out to her. She took his hand in hers and smiled at him. To Omar, her smile was like the sun on a dark, rainy day. The gleam in her eyes brightened the room. Omar sat down in the seat across from her.

"I am very glad that you came." Her natural skin glowed. Her eyes sparkled with happiness and enjoyment, reflecting the satisfaction of a woman in love.

"For months and months, I was sitting by the phone waiting for a call. I wanted to hear your voice; it gives me hope for tomorrow. I can't believe my eyes that you are here with me now. Omar, I want to cry." Her eyes blurred with tears.

"Always glad to see you, Liz," he said, regarding her from under dark thick lashes. She was soft, sweet, and happy with her love for him.

The waiter came with the menu. They chose scallop with porcini, lobster with fennel and caviar, and veal shank with Swiss chard and cranberry beans. They were soon chatting while eating.

"I loved the way you spoke my name – Liz." Love glimmered in her eyes.

He said, smiling, "This is how you wanted me to call you when we first met, remember?"

"You didn't forget our moments together. How cruel it is when memories are lost without any recollection. You fought with honour and pride, trying to make the world brighter. You risked your life for me. You live a hero within my heart."

"You see me through rose-coloured glasses. I am nothing special, just an ordinary man," he said modestly. Memories stirred in his mind. He added, "Kosovo was our own playground: struggle, adventure, caring. Then the time came for us to live our lives, to dream and to recall.

We cannot repeat the past. To you, I am just a memory." His sadness was building.

Feeling his sadness, she quickly changed the subject, "If you could relive one wonderful moment of your life, what would you choose?"

Omar could not resist the love pouring from her eyes. He said without reserve, "I would choose the moment we first met. What could be treasured more than every precious moment I spent with you? That moment I'll remember forever."

She leaned over the table towards him and said, "I could go on for days, telling of what I feel. You're the one I've waited for all these years. You brought happiness into my lonely heart. No one is as special as you are to me. Now tell me that we belong together. Tell me that you love me."

Omar leaned back and closed his eyes for a few seconds. He must take a firm hold of himself. Omar opened his eyes and said politely, "I have to realize that you have gone your separate way. Now you are married to another man. It would be better if I make myself scarce. But I will always love you, even from a distance. I just want to see you happy." His smile at her hid beneath it a whole world of pain.

Elizabeth felt a lump rise in her throat. There was a moment of frozen silence, followed by another moment of awkward silence.

"I married Hudson because you were far away and I thought I would never see you again. I thought Hudson was someone I could live with." Omar could hear the regret in her voice.

"You don't marry someone you can live with. You marry the person you cannot live without. Maybe I am not cut out for your kind of living; maybe you and I would never mix. Now you have found someone of your status. I do not want you to get hurt because of me. For your own sake, I prefer it this way – shut off from you."

Omar's eyes were flat with hurt. His sadness was such that she could touch it. Elizabeth's heart was bleeding for him and for herself.

"What's a relationship without a little risk and faith? Tell me you love me, please," she demanded insistently.

"I have no choice but to accept my fate. It is too late now to tell what has been in my heart for you. Things have changed. I cannot let you enter my life and live with the fear of losing you. I must step back from your way."

"Omar, who am I to you, exactly?" She sounded on the brink of tears.

"You are my inspiration; you are a wish, a dream, and so dear."

"Omar, it was my fate to know you. Don't sentence me to a fate worse than death – life without you." Tears trembled in her eyes.

"Love without hope is an agonizing death. I haven't lived my life to the fullest yet. Your love holds me here in this brutal loneliness. Let destiny manifest itself. If it is fate, then it will be. We have no say in it."

Elizabeth was pouring herself out to him, yet Omar seemed distant.

"Why must you feel this way? You are the only man that I can see. I never found true love until I found you." She touched the petals of the white rose with her delicate fingers. "The white rose stands for pure love. My heart is an open door waiting for you to enter."

He stared at the vibrant young rose and said with regret, "It stands for friendship. Friendship is a golden thing. I'll always be there for you when you need a friend."

"I thought I could live again. Did you ever think how often you made me weep?" She was now crying silently.

"Liz, please have mercy on me." Her tears were like a knife piercing his heart.

She said through her tears, "I just wanted you to know that after all these years, I still can't forget you. You are the one I want for life until the day I die."

Sadness devoured him. Her true love and agonizing sadness broke him. He felt tears burning the back of his throat.

"Hey! Loosen up. Your pain is my thorn. You mean so very much to me. I am here for you. It makes me happy just being by your side."

She said with saddened eyes blurred with tears, "Then talk to me. Don't shut me out. Tell me what you feel inside."

"I have poured my entire soul into you right from the very start. There is one thing that will never change between you and me. I will always keep falling in love with you."

She smiled through her tears. Those were the words she had been praying for.

"Do you love me that much?" Happiness radiated from tearful eyes.

"Only Allah reigning in heaven knows."

"Love is beautiful and life-giving. There is no remedy for love but to love more. I want to love you and be loved in return. Let a fresh start be at hand. We will begin anew."

"And how can this be? Love means marriage in Islam." Clouds of confusion crossed his eyes.

"I know your religion, and I respect it. I wouldn't do anything that might hurt you. But for now, hold my hand. I'll hold you for a lifetime if you just hold my hand."

He held her hand in silence. He closed his eyes for a moment. It was as if he were holding the whole world in his arms. Warmth radiated out of him, and his love shined brightly.

"How life seems worth living when you are holding my hand. I feel the warmth of your hand as it covers mine. Touch my heart and ease my pain," she whispered.

"Your eyes draw me to a place of peace. I am home," he murmured absorbed in her lovely green eyes.

"Love forgives, and love is kind. I have never been in love like this before. Come into my world. Colour my world with your love." She held on to him with her eyes.

Omar drowned in her shining eyes and saw her as a gentle ray of light.

"From your soul spills the sweetest scented perfume," he said. "Let me breathe you; you are a fragrant rose. You are my pride and joy. How lonely these last years have been without you."

His words touched her to the core. Her heart skipped a beat at the tenderness of his words. A smile played upon her lips.

With love pouring from her eyes, she said, "We are two parts of a whole. Nothing could have kept us apart. We are like an angel with only one wing, and we only fly embracing each other. Loving you gives me hope to free this misery. Now that I have found you, there's nothing I wouldn't do."

"You are the daughter of the president and the wife of a senator," he said suddenly, as if awaking from a beautiful dream.

"It's my private life; I am free to live it as I please." She spoke quickly, as if escaping from a fact staring her in the face.

"You know that I love you for what you are, not who you are. But listen carefully, Liz. No matter what we do, we are watched and monitored. We are in a relationship that is public, and we are under a microscope. Our freedom is but an illusion."

"Don't worry about my being watched. The job of my guards is to protect me, not to interfere in my private life."

Elizabeth was so filled and overflowing with happiness that she wanted everyone to experience the joy that such a love could bring.

Time flew by, and the romantic lunch ended. They stood in the restaurant's doorway, waiting for their cars.

As if she had forgotten something important, Elizabeth glanced at Omar and said, "I want you to know one thing, Omar. If you stop loving me, I will stop loving you. My love feeds on your love."

Before she disappeared in her car, Elizabeth surprised Omar by leaning over and kissing him lightly on the cheek.

When Omar got into his car, he could still smell the spice of her perfume and the touch of her hair that had brushed his face with her kiss. He closed his eyes, basking in the warmth of her love and reliving every precious moment he'd spent with her at Daniel. He did not know where love would take him. When he'd first met Elizabeth, it was not by chance or luck. His true life began when he fell in love with her.

A flash of guilt crossed his eyes. Elizabeth was now married to another man, and the realization that the kiss was unlawful sunk in his stomach like a stone. But one does not know the ways of fate.

CHAPTER 33

The two lovers hadn't noticed that Mary Mackenzie was also having lunch at Daniel. Mary's table was not that far from Elizabeth's. From her seat, Mary easily spotted the waiter leading Elizabeth to her table. When Omar entered the restaurant, Mary couldn't drag her eyes from him as he passed her table. She stared at him in disbelief, devouring him with her eyes. Her eyes drank him in. He had the sort of charm that drew women to him like moths to a flame. As a woman, she saw him as the handsomest man in the world. He was simply irresistible. He was the kind of man any woman would want to find on her pillow. She was so aware of his vitality and his virility that her heart began to slam inside her chest.

The media talked a lot about him. Three years earlier, the media had portrayed him as a magnificent beast that fearlessly killed nearly one hundred soldiers in Kosovo and saved Elizabeth's life. Now he was the ambassador of Egypt to the United States — how brilliant. Diplomacy and military did not coincide well. A man doing both was surely fascinating. The media also waded through gossip about a strong love affair between Elizabeth and the Egyptian.

Mary's gaze rested on Elizabeth sitting with Omar. Elizabeth was so in love with Omar that she could hardly bear to let go his hand. To Mary, Omar was an enigma. Who knew what lay beneath that calm, assured face? There was vulnerability about him when he talked to

Elizabeth. It was only then that his face softened. Mary wondered how long this had been going on.

So this was Elizabeth's suitor, Elizabeth's lover! Didn't he know that Elizabeth was married to Senator Hudson? She knew Senator Hudson well because she'd hosted him several times on her famous TV program, *Corruption in the Nation*. What would happen if she passed a word to Senator Hudson about this jubilant launch? Mary kept glancing at Omar and Elizabeth with a jealous grin on her face.

When Omar rose from his chair, she realized how tall and huge he was. Mary wasn't used to a man she had to look up to. She glanced at him, trying to read him. He looked dangerous and very attractive. Her heart almost leaped into her throat at his beauty.

Heavens! Her face, her whole body, flushed and throbbed. She felt the heat rising in her face. Desire dried her mouth. She started to shake. Mary tried hard to control herself to look composed and casual, but her heart flopped about in her chest like a fish on dry land.

It was almost midnight before Mary finally lay down to sleep. She tossed and turned in bed, thinking about her lonely life. She sighed as she sat up and ran her nails through her fiery red hair. Since her quarrel with Elizabeth and the death of Roy, she nearly lived alone, without a man. She was like an isolated island. The loneliness tore open a deep rift in her heart. Time could not take the pain of loneliness away; it just buried it deeper in her soul. Fear of isolation and more hurt led her to a gloomy feeling of alienation. Except for her work, she had convinced herself that there was nothing worthy about herself to love. These thoughts kept endlessly spinning in her head. She was afraid to spend time with acquaintances because she knew that her hands only brought pain and death. She never wanted to hurt anyone, but she did hurt her dearest and closest friends. Had not she pushed

Roy to death? Hadn't she embarrassed the president and caused Elizabeth shame? The media severely attacked her and talked a lot about her relationship with Roy and how she sacrificed him for the sake of her ego and more fame. How she sacrificed her dearest and closest friend, Elizabeth, for her burning passion and fiery lust. She lured Roy and tricked him into adultery although she was already living with another man. She did not care about morals or friendship but only lust and greed. The severe media attack on her had left deep scars in her soul that would never heal. She discovered the nature of her soul. She was treacherous and betraying like a snake. This was the reason that although she was terribly lonely, she preferred to live isolated.

But her loneliness was also special and unique. No one else had her inherited genes and distinguished characters. She was an independent, aggressive, bold, and brilliant woman, not just a shadow drowning in her miserable loneliness. Her talents, her self-determination, and her brilliance were things she developed alone. She had too high a forehead for a woman, and she was not going to cover it up. The media world was tough and she had to fight every day for her existence. She always fought like a tigress to achieve her goals, and she wondrously won. Struggling to survive in a man's world was nothing new for her.

Her individuality and uniqueness reflected in her work. She was still the most eminent TV commentator in her field. She did not work for others anymore; now she owned her own TV station. She started her own cable TV network by launching four hours per week and then expanded further by leasing her own satellite time. In this manner, she managed to have instant access to five million Dish owners. Since its launch two years ago, her company's reach had extended to two cable and satellite television networks and three websites. Her program, *Corruption in the Nation*, the most famous compared to all other similar programs, was now eagerly watched by most Americans nationwide.

What else might she desire that would take her out of the emptiness surrounding her? She could find more meaning in life through love. Love could fill the void in her heart, but in the world of men, she was always in control of her feelings. She broke up with Abraham Ajamy after he called her a scandalous whore. She overcame her loneliness by choosing the men she wanted only for a short time and then dropped them when she grew tired. Now she found herself aching to live again. Now she wanted to be loved by a man in control, a man who could carve his presence into her heart to the point where it ached as badly as it did now, a man who could ease her pains and take her out of this terrible loneliness. In life, she was rich and powerful. At work, she was tough and strong. But in bed, she didn't want the power. She wanted to be conquered. She liked being told what to do. Omar looked strong and seemed to be in control. He could give her that sense of satisfaction in the loss of control.

Mary lay on her back again, her long red hair fanned against the pillow. She pictured Omar in her mind; he was fine specimen of the human animal. Her eyes shined with her lust. She held her pillow and wrapped herself around it, wishing she could feel the strength of his arms squeezing her lustful body.

"Oh God, what kinds of feelings I have for this stranger. It cannot be love. I simply do not know the man at all. It has to be lust. I want that man." She coiled in bed like a viper.

CHAPTER 34

On September 11, 2001, four hijacked airlines ploughed into the World Trade Centre, the Pentagon, and a field in Pennsylvania. The attacks killed more than five thousand people and destroyed the World Trade Centre. The Americans lost their sense of security and for the first time experienced feelings of fear and vulnerability, long known to many in Africa, Asia, and the Middle East.

Within hours of the attacks, the FBI released the names and in many cases the personal details of the suspected pilots and hijackers. By midday, the US National Security Agency and German intelligence agencies had intercepted communications pointing to Osama bin Laden. On September 27, 2001, the FBI released photos of the nineteen hijackers, along with information about possible nationalities and aliases. Fifteen of the men were from Saudi Arabia, two from the United Arab Emirates, one from Egypt, and one from Lebanon. But were these the real perpetrators of 9/11 attacks?

After September 11, the Americans were ready to believe that all Arabs and all Muslims hated them and were plotting to ruin their country and all that it stood for.

Omar analysed the consequences of the attacks. It was strange to see that no one exactly knew the perpetrators behind such ruthless attacks!

Could Osama bin Laden and his followers that were living in caves be capable of committing such sophisticated attacks? If not, then who was? Who had the capacity and opportunity to carry out the crime? Who benefited from the crime? What did the mode of the crime indicate about the perpetrators?

The 9/11 events raised unanswered questions about the unprecedented failure of the US air defense system on the morning of the attacks and the contradictions and dubious evidence the American administration presented to the people about the alleged hijackers.

Substantial evidence was presented by many investigators to show that elements within the US government must have been involved in facilitating or orchestrating the attacks. In other words, 9/11 was possibly a classic case of false flag or synthetic terrorism such as corrupt states have often perpetrated on their own citizens.

What motive would people in the US government have to commit crimes of this magnitude? The outrage caused by September 11 allowed the Rosh administration to launch instantly the War on Terror, actually a war against all enemies the US government might designate.

FBI agents started sweeping through mosques, arresting Saudis, Pakistanis, Palestinians, and Yemenis. The American administration forgot that the FBI even arrested five Israelis on a rooftop near the twin towers, videotaping and cheering the entire event. When the *New York Times* asked Benjamin Netanyahu about his view regarding September 11, he replied, "It's very good." Then he edited himself: "Well, not very good, but it will generate immediate sympathy."

The attack on the World Trade Centre was obviously good for Israel. Israel was the only nation who benefited from it. Israel's fifty years of unrelenting terrorism became completely overshadowed by the horror of this one spectacular terrorist attack. When the Jewish-dominated American media repeatedly showed a few long-suffering Palestinians celebrating the attacks, Palestinians became unfairly painted as being behind the trade Centre terror, even though every Palestinian organization condemned it and not a single Palestinian was proven to be involved.

Immediately after the September 11 attacks, the political playground was prepared to tarnish the religion of Islam with dirt and consider Muslims terrorists!

Some of the negative perceptions highlighted through the biased Western media campaign included the following: Islam was projected as a monolithic bloc, static and unresponsive to change; it did not have values in common with other cultures and was seen as inferior to the West; it was seen as barbaric, irrational, primitive, and sexist; it was seen as violent, aggressive, threatening, supportive of terrorism, and engaged in a clash of civilizations; it was seen as a political ideology, used for political or military advantage.

Hostility towards Islam was used to justify discriminatory practices towards Muslims and exclusion of Muslims from mainstream society; anti-Muslim hostility was seen as natural and normal.

Severe attacks by the Christian leaders and televangelists on Muslims and Islam as a religion were also launched by Franklin Graham, Benny Hinn, Pat Robertson, Jerry Falwell, Jimmy Swaggart, Chuck Baldwin, and many others.

Arab and Muslim Americans had been compelled repeatedly to apologize for acts they did not commit, to condemn acts they never condoned, and to profess openly loyalties that for most US citizens were merely assumed.

After the events of September 11, Omar saw how Muslims were badly treated in America. The aggression played out so soon after the attacks; every other day there was a report on the news about a hate crime against Muslims. Muslim businesses were empty, and people refused to buy from them. A firebomb damaged the Islamic Society of Denton Mosque in North Texas. Over one hundred demonstrators chanted "USA" outside the Chicago mosque to protest foreign nationals.

Arab Americans were already experiencing the double burden that accompanied being an ethnic "other" in the United States. People would yell out terrible things to them in the street, such as "Go to your country, terrorist Taliban!"

The FBI rounded up hundreds of Muslims in the United States and kept them in jails without charging them or allowing them to communicate with family or lawyers. Of the eighty-two thousand Muslims who voluntarily registered at the request of the Justice Department, thirteen thousand faced deportations.

Omar wondered, *Why are people saying these things to innocent people? People who attacked the World Trade Center were certainly horrible people, but why blame people who did not have anything to do with the attacks!*

Such acts and threats were unwarranted because whoever executed the attacks, whether from the Middle East or not, they definitely were not Muslims.

The divine religion of Islam is a religion of peace, mercy, tolerance, kindness, and benevolence. It stands upright against all brutality, wanton violence, and viciousness in order to promote and protect justice and peace.

Allah the Wise and Sublime characterized the mission of Muhammad as a mercy to all when He said, "We have not sent you but as a Mercy for all creation."

Allah urged Muslims to live in peace and harmony: 'O believers, enter the peace, all of you, and follow not the steps of Satan; he is a manifest foe to you.'

Allah also said, "Whereby Allah guides whosoever follows His good pleasure in the ways of peace, and brings them forth from the shadows into the light by His leave; and He guides them to a straight path."

As Omar expected, right after the attack of September 11, hundreds of articles, tens of books, and dozens of websites attacked Islam and distorted the image of Arabs and Muslims in the West. Hardly a month passed without Islam being directly attacked and Islamic values being ridiculed. Hardly a week passed without Arabs born Muslims or individuals who reverted to Islam being portrayed as threats to Western civilization.

The prejudiced journalists and biased authors also reinforced wrong ideas, namely that Arabs and Muslims were enemies of democracy; that the majority of Arabs and Muslims were ill-educated; that oil-rich countries were gradually moving towards poverty; that many young Muslims were oppressed, frustrated, and turning into professional terrorists; that most reverts to Islam were former criminals who had discovered their new religion in prison cells; and that Arabs and Muslims hated America. They even ignored the fact that Muslims and Jews were Semitic cousins and accused Muslims of anti-Semitism.

Rosh's administration provided the Americans with simple answers to their pressing questions: Arabs and Muslims hated Americans because America was the only superpower in the world. Arabs and Muslims hated Americans because they envied them their prosperity, cultural superiority, and the quality of life and freedom they enjoyed.

President Rosh further elaborated: "They hate us because we are the beacon light of freedom. They hate us because we are good. They hate us because we are the land of opportunity."

Omar listened in amazement to the words of President Rosh. Did he mean what he said or was he just camouflaging his people? With all due respect to the president, his justifications for his people were not correct.

Omar analysed the facts on the ground and understood the motive behind the September 11 attacks. The attack on the World Trade Centre would be an excuse to launch wars against Islam and Muslims. The Israeli-American agenda against Islam and countries of the Middle East was well known to the Egyptian military intelligence and the ministry of foreign affairs. Egypt was fully aware of the negative Western theories and plots that went against Islam.

Egypt knew that war had begun against the religion of Islam as well as Muslims. The war would first be launched against Afghanistan, then Iraq, Syria, Yemen, Egypt, Lybia, and Saudi Arabia. The purpose was to divide the Arab countries into small sectors based on ethnicity and racism. By dividing the Arab countries into sects, factions, and small dominions without borders, Islam would be defeated and Israel would best serve the American interests in the region. Israel must be the sole power in the Middle East.

The damage inflicted by Israel on Lebanon during the 2006 Israeli-Lebanon war was so damaging and devastating that Lebanon was torn apart. Houses were demolished, families were dispersed and displaced, and Lebanon slipped into a terrible chaos.

In June 2006, Under Secretary Condoleezza Rice welcomed the chaos in Lebanon and stated that a project for a New Middle East was being launched from Lebanon. She meant that the chaos tearing Lebanon apart would be the beginning of other chaos devastating the countries of the Middle East.

Secretary Condoleezza Rice stated during a press conference, "What we're seeing here [in regards to the destruction of Lebanon and the Israeli attacks on Lebanon], in a sense, is the growing — the 'birth pangs' — of a 'New Middle East', and whatever we do we [meaning the United States], have to be certain that we're pushing forward to the New Middle East and not going back to the old one." Secretary Rice was immediately criticized for her statements both within Lebanon and internationally for expressing indifference to the suffering of an entire nation, which was being bombed indiscriminately by the Israeli Air Force.

In Tel Aviv with Prime Minister Olmert, Condoleezza Rice introduced the term "New Middle East" to the world in June 2006. The announcement was a confirmation of an Anglo-American-Israeli "military road map" in the Middle East. This project, which had been in the planning stages for several years, consisted of creating an arc of instability, chaos, and violence extending from Lebanon, Palestine, Egypt, and Syria to Iraq, the Persian Gulf, Iran, and the borders of NATO-garrisoned Afghanistan.

The New Middle East project was introduced publicly by Washington and Tel Aviv with the expectation that Lebanon would be the pressure point for realigning the whole Middle East, thereby unleashing the forces of "constructive chaos". This constructive chaos, which generates conditions of violence and warfare throughout the region, would in turn be used so that the United States, Britain, and Israel could redraw the map of the Middle East in accordance with their geostrategic needs and objectives.

As for Egypt, the largest country in North Africa and the Arab World, the third largest in Africa, and the fifteenth most populous in the world, the plot was to bring it to its knees by dividing it into a Bedouin Sinai, Muslim Lower Egypt, Coptic Upper Egypt, and a new Nubia farther south. The intention was to separate Sinai from Egypt and give it to hired Islamic militia that would destroy Egypt from within by spreading dissensions among the people prior to dividing the nation into insignificant territories without borders. Muslim brotherhood and Islamic militants were the sects chosen to divide the country into sectors and parts.

The plot against the Middle East known as the Arab Spring was entirely designed by the United States. Islamic militants and the Muslim brotherhood were trained, funded, and equipped by the United States. In particular, a coalition between the US State Department, NGOs, corporations, and organizations entirely contrived for the sole purpose of fomenting unrest in foreign nations began as early as 2008, preparing for what was now unfolding in the Middle East and North Africa.

The *New York Times* itself conceded in an article titled "US Groups Helped Nurture Arab Uprisings" that it was beyond a mere conspiracy theory. A number of the groups and individuals directly involved in the revolts and reforms sweeping the region were the April 6 Youth Movement in Egypt, the Bahrain Center for Human Rights and grassroots activists like Entsar Qadhi, a youth leader in Yemen, received training and financing from groups like the International Republican Institute, the National Democratic Institute and Freedom House, a non-profit human rights organization based in Washington. Also implicated in the *New York Times* report was the National Endowment for Democracy, which provided these organizations the bulk of their funding.

The Egyptian April 6 Movement was in New York City as early as 2008, receiving training and an opportunity to "network" at the US State Department–sponsored Alliance for Youth Movement's summit. In 2009, the April 6 Movement then attended training at the US-created CANVAS organization in Serbia before returning to Egypt to partake in out setting President Mubarak.

In an April 2011 AFP report, Michael Posner, the assistant US Secretary of State for Human Rights and Labour, stated, "The US government has budgeted fifty million dollars in the last two years to develop new technologies to help activists protect themselves from arrest and prosecution by authoritarian governments." The report went on to explain that the US "organized training sessions for five thousand activists in different parts of the world. A session held in the Middle East gathered activists from Tunisia, Egypt, Syria, and Lebanon, who returned to their countries with the aim of training their colleagues there." Posner would add, "They went back, and there's a ripple effect."

Omar's political analysis was also based on an article published by the Hebrew language magazine *Kivunim* (*Directions*), the official organ of the World Zionist Organization. The article was published in 1982 and was entitled "A Strategy for Israel in the 1980s. The editor of Kivunim was Yoram Beck, Head of Publications, Department of Information, of the World Zionist Organization.

The article explained the detailed plan of the present American Zionist regime for the Middle East, which was based on the division of the whole area into small states and the dissolution of all the existing Arab states. The real aim of Israel was clear: to make an imperial Israel into a world power.

The plan was based on the fact that the Arab states were

fragmented into ethnic minorities, factions, and internal crises, which are astonishingly self-destructive.

In the end, this Arab world would be unable to exist within its present framework in the areas around Israel without having to go through genuine revolutionary changes. The Muslim Arab World was arbitrarily divided into nineteen states, all made up of combinations of minorities and ethnic groups that were hostile to one another so that every Arab Muslim state nowadays faced ethnic social destruction from within, and a civil war was already raging in some.

What remained, then, was to invent false excuses in order to launch wars against the Middle East. The war would start with Iraq because it was a major threat to Israel from the Israeli point of view, and most of all, it contained huge oil reserves that America was after.

After destroying Iraq into small ethnic groups, war would extend in the region to divide Syria, Libya, Yemen, the Gulf Estates, Saudi Arabia, and Egypt into small ethnic and racist areas devoid of power or authority.

But who was going to do that? America, of course, the country blindly siding with Israel all the way.

The political fabric of the United States helped prepare the ground for executing such a treacherous plot. The plan was designed by the Israelis and the prominent Zionist Americans in the White House. President Rosh stuffed his administration with Jews who, with the Israeli officials, designed the plot for dividing the Middle East into small pieces. To mention just a few: Richard Perle, Paul Wolfowetz, Douglas Feith, Edward Luttwak, Henry Kissinger, Dov Zalkheim, Kenneth Adelman, and nearly forty others.

Moreover, the Zionists had many lobby groups. The Israeli lobby had many think tanks that provided future advisors to the various administrations, both Republicans and Democrats. During the Clinton administration, the Israeli lobby provided officials like Martin Indyk from the Washington Institute for Near East Policy. During the Rosh administration, many of the officials that the Israeli lobby provided were from their Republican think tanks, like the American Enterprise Institute (AEI) and the Jewish Institute for National Security Affairs (JINSA).

In order to achieve their goal, the warmongers in the Rosh administration propagated false excuses for launching wars against Muslim countries. They frightened the American people to death when claiming that the Arabs and Muslims were terrorists; the Muslims adopted a violent religion that oppressed women and urged Muslims to kill Americans if they did not embrace Islam. The biased media would promulgate such lies perfectly well.

Pursuing the Republican attitude of bigotry, Senator Robert Hudson championed a hearing about what he described as "radicalization" of American Muslims. Hudson claimed that US Muslims were being radicalized by al-Qaeda operatives, accusing Muslim leaders of not cooperating with law enforcement authorities in fighting terrorism. He also called for the banning of practicing Shariah in several US states. Hudson charged that preaching in some US mosques was leading to radicalization.

Republicans and the Tea Party movement had made the political calculation that bashing Islam and Muslims was a winning issue for them.

Hudson had been at the centre of a political maelstrom that gained national attention since he published comments on social media warning people to be wary of Muslim Americans and then refused to apologize in the face of mounting criticism.

In a lengthy presentation, Hudson outlined a history of the Islamic faith and his views that Islam is a socio-political movement intent upon destruction of Western civilization and world domination. Hudson launched several announcements against Islam in several meetings: "Their goal is the destruction of Western civilization from within; Islam is a cancer in our nation that needs to be cut out. I'm not going to stand back and let them push Islam into our nation. Islam has no place in these United States."

Older Americans, Republicans, conservatives, and evangelical Christians were much more likely to link Islam to violence.

Omar quickly analysed the situation. The Rosh administration hawks were taking American foreign policy to dangerous levels. Chaos in the Middle East was their plan. They thought that the invasion of countries in the Middle East one after another was only the first move in a wider effort to reorder the power structure of the entire Middle East. They would begin with Iraq, followed by other countries. The undersecretary of state had already told Israeli officials that after defeating Iraq, the United States would deal with Iran, Syria, and North Korea. A war of such reach and magnitude should be seen as tactical events in a series of moves and countermoves stretching well into the future.

The thinking was that America must first bring down the terror regimes beginning with the big three: Iran, Iraq, and Syria. And then America had to deal with Saudi Arabia. Once the tyrants in Iran, Iraq and Syria, and Saudi Arabia had been brought down, America would remain engaged. Stability was an unworthy American mission. America did not want stability in the Muslim countries. America wanted to destabilize.

From a leaked report talking about "Grand Strategy for the Middle East", Omar read, "Iraq is the tactical pivot, Saudi Arabia the strategic pivot, Egypt the prize."

What these neoconservatives and Christian Right sought was to conscript American blood to make the world safe for Israel. They wanted the piece of the sword imposed on Islam and American soldiers to die if necessary to impose it!

The plan of the Christian Right and the American Zionists was to destroy Islam and cleanse the earth of this great religion, and President Rosh was their tool for achieving their goal. It began with Afghanistan and was now in Iraq. The plan was to change school curricula by removing the message of the Koran from the education process and brainwash young Muslims to think and behave anti-Islam. Would they succeed? Of course not. One thousand years of European history of hate and opposing Islam and three hundred years of direct rule and tyranny had failed. Sometimes Muslims suffered temporary setbacks, but they rebounded even stronger. Islam was like the phoenix, re-emerging from its own ashes.

The Rosh administration was trying to roll the table to use US military force, or the threat of it, to reform or topple virtually every regime in the region, from foes like Syria to friends like Egypt, on the theory that the undemocratic nature of these regimes was what ultimately bred terrorism. Actually, there were plenty of good reasons not to purposely provoke a series of crises in the Middle East. But that's what the hawks were setting in motion, partly on the theory that the worse things got, the more their approach became the only plausible solution.

These negative scenarios had not been shared with the American people. President Rosh had not even told the public that such a clean-sweep approach to the Middle East was in fact his plan. This broke new ground in the history of pre-war presidential deception.

The plan was to use deceit to create facts on the grounds that then made the administration's broader agenda almost impossible not to pursue. Once America began the process of remaking the Middle East, it would be extremely difficult for America to pull back.

CHAPTER 35

The Zionist plan for Iraq was planned before Rosh entered the White House and years before the September attacks. A group of Zionists and neoconservatives hatched a plan to get Saddam out of power.

The Project for the New American Century, or PNAC, was founded in 1997. Among its supporters were Donald Rumsfeld; Dick Cheney, and Paul Wolfowitz.

In open letters to Clinton and GOP congressional leaders the next year, the group called for "the removal of Saddam Hussein's regime from power" and shifted towards a more assertive US policy in the Middle East, including the use of force if necessary to unseat Saddam.

And in a report just before the 2000 election that would bring Rosh to power, the group predicted that the shift would come about slowly, unless there were "some catastrophic and assassin event, like a new Pearl Harbor".

That event came on September 11, 2001. By that time, Cheney was vice president, Rumsfeld was secretary of defense, and Wolfowitz was his deputy at the Pentagon.

The next morning, before it was even clear who was behind the attacks, Rumsfeld insisted at a cabinet meeting that Saddam should be "a principal target of the first round of terrorism".

President Rosh was influenced by the Zionist neocon agenda after 9/11. What started as a theory in 1997 was now on its way to becoming official US foreign policy.

President Rosh sensed that he was guided by a divine purpose and that the Americans had now become the chosen people, with a divine duty to deliver the world to God's dominion. He said, "I see myself as a priest of a divine mission to rid the world of its demons."

President Rosh told two high-ranking Palestinian officials, "I was told by God to invade Afghanistan and Iraq and then create a Palestinian state to bring peace to the Middle East." He further added, "I'm driven with a mission from God."

The mantra was revealing. Quite simply, this was the president's case for military action against Iraq.

But the president had to create a diversion in order to hide the true purpose of his mission, which was remoulding the Middle East. He deceived his people by claiming that Saddam Hussein had weapons of mass destruction; he was about to unleash those weapons of mass destruction on the United States; he tried to buy uranium yellowcake from Niger; he was in bed with al-Qaeda – a creation of the CIA – and was therefore responsible for 9/11; he was a brutal dictator that had his own people tortured and killed; therefore, America had to liberate the Iraqi people and help them set up a democracy.

On the other side of the Atlantic, American ally Tony Blair was lying to the House of Commons about Iraq, Saddam Hussein, and weapons of mass destruction. He knowingly, deliberately, and consciously misled parliament, the public, and the press. In the under-reported words of Lord Butler, speaking in the House of Lords in February 2007, Blair was, at the very minimum, "disingenuous".

The scare about the danger of Iraq on world peace was just a public relations scam to obscure the obvious: The United States, not Iraq, was the rogue country that the world feared.

The secretary of state briefed the United Nations Security council in an effort to convince the international community that Iraq was hiding weapons of mass destruction. He provided the UN Security Council with charts, diagrams, and photographs to prove that Saddam had weapons of mass destruction. He showed very specific spots where such weapons were being developed and stored.

The UN secretary general announced, "Iraqi war is illegal because it is not in conformity with the UN Charter."

But America didn't care a bit about the resolutions of the UN or the announcements of its secretary general. In 1994, an American official who in 2005 became the ambassador of the United States to the United Nations said, "There is no United Nations ... There is an international community that occasionally can be led by the only real power left in the world, and that's the United States, when it suits our interests and when we can get others to go along."

He also said, "The secretariat of the United Nations in New York has thirty-eight stories. If you lost ten stories today, it wouldn't make a bit of difference."

No wonder that the Rosh government did not want the UN to get involved in the political process in Iraq, but the UN job would be to clean up the mess of death and destruction created by the American troops. The UN job was to bring money and labour for cleaning up the country and install a puppet dictatorship, supervise it, and pump oil to make money for the American oil companies.

For decades, the US policy towards Iraq had been nothing but a heinous exercise of gangsters against a small country that was virtually defenseless in comparison to the massive high-tech firepower of the Pentagon.

On 6 August 1990, the United Nations Security Council imposed economic sanctions on Iraq in response to its invasion of Kuwait. Under these sanctions, all imports into Iraq and all exports from Iraq were prohibited. These sanctions were the toughest and most comprehensive sanctions in history. The sanctions were unprecedented in terms of longevity and their comprehensive nature.

The sanctions imposed on Iraq have led to great human catastrophe of unpredictable destructive impact in the short and long terms. Low birthweight babies — less than 2.5 kilograms — rose from 4 per cent in 1990 to around a quarter of registered births in 1997 due to maternal malnutrition. As many as 70 per cent of Iraqi women suffered from anaemia. Almost the entire young child population was affected by a shift in their malnutrition status towards malnutrition. Malnutrition stemmed from the massive deterioration in infrastructure in the water supply and waste disposal system. Hospital and health centres had degraded further from shortages of water and power supply, lack of transportation, and the collapse of the telecommunications system. Communicable diseases, such as waterborne diseases and malaria, which had been under control, came back as an epidemic in 1993.

As for the cumulative effects of sustained deprivation on the psychosocial cohesion of the Iraqi population, the following aspects were frequently observed: increase in juvenile delinquency, begging and prostitution, anxiety about the future and lack of motivation, a sense of isolation bred by absence of contact with the outside world, and the development of a parallel economy replete with profiteering and criminality.

The Iraqi victims were innocent civilians who had no part whatsoever in the decisions which led to the events that brought on United Nations sanctions in the first place.

During the ten years of sanctions, Iraq was bombed with weapons built with uranium components. When the uranium bullets, missiles, or bombs hit something or exploded, most of the radioactive uranium instantly turned to tiny dust particles, too fine even to see. When Iraqis breathe even a tiny amount into their lungs, as little as one gram, it is the same as getting an X-ray every hour for the rest of their shortened lives. There is no treatment or cure, and the uranium will last in the affected bodies virtually forever.

Prolonged sanctions in addition to bombing with radioactive weapons led to the deaths of more than half a million children, not to mention more than a million Iraqis.

When US Secretary of State Madeline Albright was asked if the death of half a million Iraqi children was a price worth paying, she replied, "This is a very hard choice, but we think the price is worth it."

Yes, the time was ripe now to invade Iraq. Iraq was now easy meat. Although President Rosh would lead the invasion, the former president, Bill Clinton, had laid the groundwork with the sanctions and with the previous bombing of Iraq.

The invasion of Iraq began on March 20, 2003, without UN approval. Forces belonging to the United States, the United Kingdom, Australia, and Poland, as well as naval forces from Denmark and Spain, also took part. All these nations invaded an already defeated country unable to defend itself.

The Iraq war was an armed conflict that consisted of two phases. The first was an invasion of Iraq. The second was a longer phase of fighting, in which an insurgency emerged to oppose the occupying forces and the newly formed Iraqi government.

Yet for all the blood spilled, there's no good reason why. Almost 4,500 US troops were killed and more than 32,000 wounded, including thousands with critical brain and spinal injuries. Estimates of the number of Iraqi civilian fatalities were staggering, ranging from 100,000 to 600,000.

The Iraq war had nothing to do with weapons of mass destruction, zero to do with al-Qaeda, and zilch to do with implanting democracy in Iraq. The strategic doctrine at the heart of the US Middle Eastern policy was the installation of Israel as the regional hegemon.

The United States attached high moralistic rhetoric to its invasion of Iraq. At first, it was supposedly to save the world from the threats of Saddam Hussein's weapons of mass destruction. When those weapons were not found, the US rhetoric immediately found another anchor. We were told that the object of liberating Iraq from the brutal rule of Saddam was noble enough of a goal to go to war. The United States did everything since then to underscore how much better off the Iraqis were going to be under the American version of secular democracy. But one of the major problems related to the global war on terrorism was that it was also based on good and evil and on black and white. The perpetrators of violence were depicted as "evildoers". Thus American forces emerged as "forces of virtue" which could do no wrong.

The Iraqis defending their country against the American invasion were described as "dead enders", "terrorists", and a "mixture of outsiders" who were there to cause trouble. In other words, anyone who opposed American forces – the forces of virtue – was nothing but a representative of the forces of evil.

The war contributed to a destabilization of the Middle East and a move away from democracy in the region. President Rosh declared war as part of the US War on Terror, but the war had laid the foundation for even more terror.

The Iraqi war was a massive crime – a criminal and immoral war of aggression. Those who executed the war must be prosecuted for their crimes.

From late 2003 to early 2004, during the Iraq War, military police personnel of the United States Army and the Central Intelligence Agency committed human rights violations against prisoners held in the Abu Ghraib prison. They physically and sexually abused, tortured, raped, sodomized, and killed prisoners.

Under the American concept that her troops are the "forces of virtue", it is hard to believe that the American perpetrators of abuse of Iraqi prisoners did not regard themselves as doing something evil while abusing those prisoners, humiliating them, and having fun at their suffering and misery. After all, how could forces of virtue do anything wrong?

In November 2003, President Rosh flew to Iraq under extraordinary secrecy and security to spend Thanksgiving with US troops and thank them for defending the American people from danger.

In December 14, 2008, President Rosh made a surprise appearance in Iraq, but he was not welcomed with open arms. During a news conference with the prime minister of Iraq, Iraqi journalist Muntazer al-Zaidi from Al-Baghdadia television network threw both his shoes at President Rosh. Rosh dodged both shoes, and neither of them hit him.

Throwing a shoe in the Arab culture is the most disrespectful act ever. Muntazer threw his shoes at Rosh when he heard him saying, "The war is not over; there is a lot of work to do". While throwing his shoes, Muntazer was yelling, "This is from the widows, the orphans, and those who were killed in Iraq. I hate Rosh. He deserved it."

After Rosh was attacked by the flying shoes, he joked, "I'm okay. All I can report is that it was a size ten!"

CHAPTER 36

It was a remarkable day when Elizabeth Rosh asked Hudson, "You don't mind, of course, if I invite Omar to dinner?"

Hudson became highly irritated, but he said coolly, "On the contrary. It will be an opportunity to challenge him in a series of debates."

Omar received a handwritten invitation to dinner:

> *Elizabeth Rosh and Robert Hudson invite you to dinner and conversation at the home of Elizabeth Rosh.*
> *Date: May 26*
> *Time: 7 p.m.*

Omar felt a sense of uneasiness when he read the invitation. For him, Hudson represented everything he hated in the political life of the United States. But he didn't want to offend Elizabeth by refusing her invitation. He was anxious to see her any way, at any time, in any place.

Elizabeth was happy to see him. She met him at the door. His glorious appearance and their memories together cheered her beyond limits. He whispered, smiling, "How charming you are in such wonderful dress. It is a joy to look at you. Seeing you brightens up the days of a lonely man." She laughed aloud, took his hand in hers, and led him to the dinner table.

Hudson met Omar with an artificial smile, and they both shook hands coldly.

Hudson said, "I'm certainly pleased to meet you. Elizabeth has spoken about you often. She's very proud of you."

"I am very proud of her too," replied Omar.

The dinner started with lobster medallions and Belgian endive and was accompanied by some glamorized olives and nuts. Then the main course — beef filet — was served.

During dinner, Elizabeth looked at Omar's face. She detected a glint of sadness in his eyes.

"I'm happy to have you here tonight. How have you been?" She said this with inquisitive eyes.

"My life has been going the same as usual. Busy at work in the mornings, and in the evenings, I spend my spare time in the gymnasium or running long distances. I am well, praise to Lord."

After dinner, they settled in the library. Elizabeth pressed a buzzer, and a servant entered with a tray of coffee and Danish pastries. The coffee was poured. It smelled wonderful, and the Danish pastry tasted great.

It had been a tense and awkward dinner, however. The animosity between the two men was still quite obvious. Hudson did nothing to ease the oppressive atmosphere. He was rather deliberately allowing it to deepen.

Hudson threw one leg over the other and lit a cigar. He took a long drag on it.

Omar said, "I watched your hearing about radicalization of American Muslims. You accused Muslim leaders of not cooperating with law enforcement authorities in fighting terrorism."

Hudson replied, "We are in the middle of a religious war with Islam. I urged lawmakers to seek a ban on the practice of Shariah in the US states."

"Your continuous attacks against Islam speak volumes about how many of your politicians are more interested in distracting the public's attention away from more important issues, such as improving your economy and ending racial profiling," said Omar.

"The Republicans always look after the interests of their voters. I accused the Muslim community of refusing to cooperate with law enforcement and charged that preaching in some US mosques was leading to radicalization. Islam is the babble that will destroy the Western world."

"Am I wrong if I say that the new perception is that the United States has entered a war with Islam itself?"

"Well, more or less."

"Muslims are part of the American fabric," Omar said. "Muslim Americans love this nation and work with the government to protect it against danger. However, many law-abiding Muslim Americans face discrimination and charges that they're not real Americans, simply because of their religion."

"I have warned people on social media to be wary of Muslim Americans, and I refused to apologize in the face of mounting criticism. I outlined a history of the Islamic faith and my views that Islam is a socio-political movement aiming at destroying Western civilization and world domination. Its goal is the destruction of Western civilization from within. Islam is a cancer in our nation that needs to be cut out."

"You've put all Muslims in America in one group, associating them with terrorists and encouraging fear and wariness to spread among Muslim and non-Muslim Americans!" Omar retorted.

"Half of Americans now believe that Islam is more likely to encourage violence than other religions."

"What would you say if I told you that the American Christian fabric and its association with other political entities are behind the tribulations the Muslim world is suffering from?"

"What do you mean by other political entities?"

"The Christian Right, Judeo-Christian coalition, Christian Right Republicans, Tea Party Republicans, neoconservatives, and the AIPAC."

Hudson said, "Sorry, but you are terribly mistaken. I am myself a Christian Right Republican with strong bonds with the Judeo-Christian coalition. Our goal is to see the world at peace."

"The Christian Right Republicans and their strong bond with the American Zionists are behind the chaos the Muslim world is suffering from. The Christian Right Republicans strongly favour US military interventions in the Middle East. The Tea Party–affiliated Republicans are spreading hatred against Islam without any reason. Joe Walsh warned that Muslims were trying to kill Americans every week, and were lurking in the Chicago suburbs, and Allen West linked the entire religion of Islam to terrorism. The House Republican caucus is the place where the ugly head of Islamophobia rests comfortably. Many members of the Republican Party remain wedded to that hateful ideology. But sometimes the truth will appear to overshadow the falsehood they promulgate."

"I am afraid you can't do anything about it," said Hudson. The Christian Right is a strong power now and has successfully infiltrated the Republican Party, and its supporters took over numerous state parties. The Christian Right is highly resilient and continues to influence US foreign policy. Our purpose is to see that democracy and freedom cover the Muslim nations. We are trying to reform the world by taking it back to the teachings of Jesus."

"Who gave you the right to reform the world? The American political groups and Christian cults and factions must not exert their religious and political power over Muslim countries. Their influence must be restricted only to their own people. Congress must not legislate for other countries, only for its own people."

"I wonder when all this chaos in the Middle East is going to end," Hudson said, changing the subject.

"You brought your tyranny to our door. You fix it."

"Why are you so upset? We have done a lot for you. The president proposed a road map towards a Palestinian state. It is a proposal that would establish peace between the Palestinians and the Israelis."

Omar said, "Israel has demanded one hundred revisions in the road map, effectively rejecting it without total renovation in accordance with its specifications. The main demand is for the removal of all mention of an 'independent' Palestinian state. There will be no 'further withdrawals' from territory meant for the Palestinians under the Oslo accords. This would leave the Palestinians in control of just about nineteen per cent of the West Bank and only fifty-five to sixty per cent of the Gaza Strip. America has not lifted a finger to protest. Support for Israel is so entrenched in American politics that the United States has lost credibility and influence in the Middle East."

Elizabeth joined the discussion: "How does Muslims fit into all this?"

"I'll tell you how," said Omar bitterly. "The war against Muslims expanded to fight the religion of Islam itself. Islam must be defeated! Army Lieutenant Colonel Matthew A. Dooley taught young American officers that America's real terrorist enemy wasn't al-Qaida but the Islamic faith itself. He taught them that there was no such thing as moderate Islam and that it was time for the United States to make its true intentions clear. Islam as a barbaric ideology would no longer be tolerated. Islam must change or America must facilitate its self-destruction. Matthew's plan was to reduce Islam to a cult status and threaten Saudi Arabia with starvation. He thinks that the protection of civilians in wartime is no longer relevant, and he opens the possibility of applying the historical precedents of Hiroshima and Nagasaki to Islam's holiest cities, bringing about Makka's and Medina's destruction. He further suggests annihilating the one point five billion Muslims inhabiting the four corners of the world! This was the military strategy of Dooley, to wipe out Muslims from the surface of the earth! We've had enough of your tyranny. You break the world. We help repair it. For you, the Middle East is some other place; for us, it is our home."

Hudson said, "To make a long story short, we are the only superpower on the planet, we own the world, and we are the mightiest ones yet."

Omar couldn't stand Hudson's arrogance. He shot at him, "First, you are not the only superpower on earth. The Russians can destroy the whole world in minutes as well. Russia has more nuclear warheads than you have. Second, do you not see that Allah, who created the heavens and earth, is infinitely greater in power and far mightier than you are! He destroyed nations before because they spread corruption in the land. Whosoever desires glory, the glory altogether belongs to Allah. Allah destroyed the generations before us when they disobeyed him and spread mischief in the land. The annihilation of evil nations is thus a reality. But man is arrogant and quickly forgets the lessons of history. Allah says in the Koran, 'How many a city We have destroyed! Our might came upon it at night, or while they took their ease in the noontide."

"We are developed people who rely on facts. We do not rely on the tales of people of old."

"The words you just heard are derived from the Koran. They are the words of your Lord, Hudson. What do you think of me, Hudson? A male Muslim who beats his wife, kills babies, and is a terrorist in his spare time!"

"Don't start that, Omar. Back off, please." Elizabeth pleaded.

Omar continued angrily, "Why do you people think you are superior over others? Is it because of the technological advancements you enjoy? This could be destroyed in a minute if Allah's wrath touches a rebellious country committing sins every day or a rogue country oppressing others under the pretext of protecting the American interests. Is it because our women are decently veiled and yours are walking naked without decency or maybe because we hold fast to our religion while your churches are empty and are now characterized by jazz bands, dancing, and yelling! Is it because you have a good movie industry spreading debauchery everywhere? Is it because you are living a modern lifestyle characterized by sex outside marriage, gambling, and drinking, or is it because your women are free to terminate their pregnancies through abortion? Or perhaps because you are living in a free society stained by narcotic and wine addiction, adultery, murder, shooting in schools, sex abuse, homosexuality, and lesbianism?"

"Omar, please calm down," said Elizabeth.

"Civilization is not advancements in technology or market surplus. True civilization is the civilization of ethics. If ethics and good manners prevail, the world lives in love and peace. This is what the Koran offers. Allah says to Muslims in the Koran, 'You are the best nation ever brought forth to men, bidding to honour, and forbidding dishonour, and believing in Allah.'"

"Oh, don't give me that shit, please," said Hudson

Omar couldn't contain his anger. He let it flow. "The words of Allah are not shit. Islam is the frame in which we live. We Muslims live by Allah and die for Him. Beware the fury of a patient man, Hudson."

"Hudson," Elizabeth shouted, "you're getting off the track here! A little respect, please. Both of you are out of line."

Omar said, "If you are looking for trouble, Hudson, I reckon you have found it. I am the last person you want to piss off."

"Watch your tongue; we have rules here in the United States."

"I live by my own rules. Take heed, for you might get hurt."

"We live in a free country, and our constitution allows us to express anything we wish to disclose!"

"You think you have complete freedom to reject and humiliate the truth?" asked Omar.

"Robert, you know, you are being irrational. You got so far of track," Elizabeth said to Hudson furiously.

"Your friend is becoming a pain in the ass, darling," Hudson said sarcastically.

"There is a lady present. Watch your language." Omar's nerves were beyond tense.

Hudson forced a smile. "Why are you so unfriendly? You are very entertaining to watch."

Omar glanced at Elizabeth and pointed at Hudson. "This arrogant Republican senator and his colleagues take politics as strictly business. To them, Islam phobia is a profitable propaganda for their electoral campaigns. Islam phobia is their main concern because their minds are empty of any meaningful issues that might benefit their voters. They demean the Muslim faith. They use deception, lies, and falsehood in their attacks."

"Sorry, Omar, but—"

Omar interrupted Elizabeth's attempt at an apology. "They burned the Koran, defiled it and the rulers of this country, haven't raised a finger to stop this despicable comedy."

Hudson said coolly, "America is a free country, and we enjoy freedom of speech."

"Freedom of speech has limits, Mr. Know-It-All. Freedom of speech is about taking responsibility for your words. Your senators have made a career out of opposition to Islam. Absolute freedom of speech is a myth."

"America is a capitalist country. Freedom of individual, ownership, religion, and speech are essential cornerstones of capitalism," said Hudson.

"In Islam, it is Allah who gave the right of speech to people and defined the limits on what is acceptable and what is unacceptable. The prophet of Islam said, 'Whosoever believes in Allah and the Last Day, then let him speak good or remain silent.' He also said, 'Every word a human being speaks is recorded by the two angels. Even the speaking of one bad word may lead someone to the hellfire.'"

"The United States is the land of freedom, the land of the brave. The president repeatedly argued that he would wage war to defend democracy, liberty, and all that is good and just in our world. The president depicted our soldiers as the world's greatest and most honourable fighting force, our willing servants in the cause of freedom."

"It would thus come as a tremendous shock when photographs of American soldiers inflicting torture on Iraqi detainees surfaced. Additional photos across the internet provided graphic evidence of the full extent of sadistic and degrading treatment to which the prisoners had been subjected." Omar added.

"You think America is brave?" Omar said. "Yet she turned a blind eye to the Palestinian cause and helped Israel demolish Palestinian houses, stealing the land and killing men, women, and children. Your brave men destroyed Iraq under the false allegation of weapons of mass destruction. Every American who voted Republican shares responsibility for the great evil America has brought to the Middle East. The evil that America brought to Iraq transcends the tens or hundreds of thousands of Iraqi civilians who have been killed. The violence and killing that you brought to Iraq has created more terrorism than the world has ever seen.

"The reasons given for the American invasion of Iraq have been exposed as lies, revealing America as either a country of fools and idiots or of war criminals. Worldwide polls show that America is no longer regarded as a guiding light but is tied with Israel as the second greatest threat to world stability. The two thousand three American invasion of Iraq is a war crime under international law. The invasion caused sectarian violence far beyond anything Iraq ever experienced under Saddam Hussein. The American people have never been told the real reasons that Rosh and the Republican Party rushed America to war in Iraq. Americans have only been fed a pack of transparent lies."

"The war has brought honour, glory, and tangible benefit," Hudson responded.

"The war has brought shame upon America for routine torture of Iraqi detainees and for the routine slaughter of unarmed Iraqi civilians — mothers, fathers, children, and grandparents."

"What I saw in Palestine was so awful that the mere thought of it breaks my heart." Said Elizabeth.

Hudson challenged Omar, "Bottom line: America is free to look after her own interests the way she sees fit. No one can stop us. All you have said is meaningless and nothing but shit. I don't value your opinions."

The hurt look on Omar's face was more than Elizabeth could stand. She shouted at Hudson, "Omar is my guest so behave!"

Hudson said ironically, "Sorry, I take that back. Omar, are you mad at me? Let's shake hands."

"You cannot shake hands with a clenched fist," Omar said angrily. "I don't have to listen to this. I'd better get going." Omar rose from his chair.

"I'll see you to the door," Elizabeth said, rising too.

At the door, they stood talking for a few minutes.

"Sorry, Elizabeth, but he drove me mad," Omar said sorrowfully.

"I understand. Omar, I'm scared."

"With a man like him, you ought to be. But remember, I'll always be next to you."

"My marriage doesn't seem to be working. You were away and I had to have a life of my own. There is a void in my life that I can't seem to fill."

"It was nothing unexpected. You chose Hudson out of emptiness and boredom. Well, see you later." Omar was fighting an urgent need to hold her and kiss her at the door.

Elizabeth returned to Hudson. She looked at him out of furious eyes. "Why did you have to be so rude to Omar?"

Hudson said, "He deserves every word I said. I don't happen to like the man, that's all.

"He could tear you apart with his bare hands, you know."

"You still have feelings for him. I wondered what it was you saw in him!" Hudson said, laughing harshly.

"Look at yourself, how you become distorted. You know what I like about him? I can see through him how the world with morons like you has become twisted."

Hudson snapped at her, "I'm not blind, Liz. You think I didn't see how you stared at him? That I didn't see the look that comes into your eyes when he talks or moves? Don't pretend this isn't about him. You both stayed at the door for long moments whispering. What were you saying to him? Words of love, of course. Don't forget that you are a married woman."

"You are such a big mouth, Hudson. You did not fight like Omar on the battlefield, but you sit here yelling like a woman. I will make you pay for that."

Elizabeth went to her bedroom and slammed the door.

CHAPTER 37

Omar had to raise his voice and tell the truth to the American people. This administration was taking the American people to a big loss. But how could he explain the truth? Most of the TV stations were owned by American Zionists or by televangelists spewing falsehood and outright hatred of all things Muslim. They judged the veracity of the Koranic teachings according to their negative observations of some Muslims who were merely Muslims by name, Muslims only by birth, and Muslims weak in faith and ignorant of the teachings of the prophet. They indulged in immoral practices and destroyed their lives.

Omar and the Arab ambassadors to the United States visited the undersecretary of state in his office and submitted to him two official memos, the first opposing the American war in Iraq and the second condemning the arrest of the American Muslims on flimsy conspiracy charges.

A correspondent from *The Nation* magazine managed to get to Omar before he entered his car and asked him to say a few words about the reason behind such a visit. Omar replied, "The Muslim world rejects the American invasion of Iraq. The war is an act of aggression. America violated the international law when she attacked innocent civilians in Iraq. We denounce the inhumane and degrading treatment of American Muslims under the Rosh administration. We strongly oppose attacking Islam as a religion. An anti-Islamic hate campaign launched to incite enmity against Muslims has been underway for quite some time. Fabricating the Islamic demon has not been difficult for the insider-controlled press. I wish I could have the opportunity to expose the plot against Islam and to explain to the American people the real reasons behind the Iraqi war."

The reporter asked, "What's keeping you from addressing the American people?"

"I contacted ABC, CBS, and NBC television and radio networks to allow me a little space in their programs, but they refused. I want to explain the truth to the American people, the truth they must hear before it's too late."

Mary Mackenzie was watching the TV in her office and heard every word Omar said. She decided she had to have him. She would go to any length to have him. She would lure him into her trap. As the ambassador of Egypt, the outstanding fighter in Kosovo, and the lover of Elizabeth Rosh, the daughter of the president of the United States, there was no doubt that his appearance on her show would give it an amount of class.

In his office at the embassy, Omar received a phone call.

"Hello. Is this the ambassador of Egypt?"

"This is he."

"This is Mary Mackenzie. I am a media proprietor and talk show host. My talk show, *Corruption in the Nation*, is a highly rated program in the United States and the world.

After a moment of silence, Omar said, "I heard about you."

"What did Elizabeth tell you about me?"

"She said that you are a very dangerous woman."

Mary lauded aloud. "Does that mean you don't want to see me?"

Again there was silence. Then Omar asked, "What do you have in mind?"

"Providing you an opportunity that will give you a thrill."

"What opportunity?"

"Three long interviews on my show. One about the Iraqi invasion, the second about the religion of Islam, and the subject of the third will be of your choice."

"Why would you do that?"

"I watched you on TV yesterday asking for space on TV shows."

"I certainly need your services," said Omar.

"Would you care come to my office? We must make plans in advance for such special interviews."

"I will meet with you in an hour; just give me your address."

Mary's secretary opened the door for Omar. He entered the room slowly to see a beautiful young woman with wavy red hair, beautiful brown eyes, and snow-white skin.

Mary was sitting at her desk. When she saw Omar, she contemplated him for a few seconds. She saw him as very handsome and robust. His sight made her heart melt. He mustn't know that a volcano was rumbling in her heart. She felt herself drawn to him, yearning him with everything feminine that was within her. She had never experienced such a strong feeling before.

She shook hand with him and led him to a table in the centre of the spacious room: "Very gracious of you to come."

"We have work to do, remember."

"Media is very important because it help shape the perception of the public." She sat in a chair facing him.

"But what food does the press dish out to the people? Is it not the worst poison? Their opinions consist only of lies and falsehoods."

"Tell me what made you so reckless as to put yourself in the den of lions," said Mary.

"There are times when a person has to stand and speak. I felt that I was screwed out of my right to talk. What kind of person would I have been if I didn't defend my religion? They are seeking to silence the Muslim and Arab voice, but I can tell you that I will keep on fighting until the American people hear my voice."

Omar was talking with a kind of eagerness, like a child bubbling over with the zest of life, and his eyes were lit all the time by his engaging smile, a smile that made Mary feel at home.

"Your federal government is trying to silence anyone who dares tell the truth."

"It's a terrible chance you take."

"Their impudent attack on Islam pushed me to the open field. How incorrect and biased have the Christian Right and their coalitions spoken and written of Muhammad and Islam! If we put their false accusations down to the true cause, it will be nothing but ignorance and plain hatred."

"You can get yourself killed with this kind of talk," Mary said.

"What do you mean?"

"You wouldn't find that easy. You will be burned by the press. You will be crucified."

"That's a risk I am willing to take," Omar said.

"I am afraid you don't quite understand the situation. The media has become the greatest power within the Western world, more powerful than the legislature, the executive and judiciary. TV is an irresistible power that reaches into every American home – the primary source by which most Americans learn about the world. This enormous power, however, is dominated by the Jews that fight the Arabs and support only Israel."

"Such control threatens American freedom. If Americans are not free to obtain unbiased news, democracy cannot work."

Mary said, "Please listen carefully. Jews dominate TV and radio networks. They also control the three most influential American newspapers – the *New York Times*, the *Wall Street Journal*, and the *Washington Post* – in addition to the majority of the remaining major magazines and newspapers. The Jews dominate the Hollywood movie industry as well as book publishing and even book distribution. They also hold immense wealth in business and banking and are thoroughly entrenched in entertainment and Hollywood, academia and judiciary, and the government. On top of this, they have the most powerful lobby in Washington and are responsible for the bulk of fundraising for both the Democratic and Republican parties."

"Are you asking me to back off? You are not afraid, are you?"

"Me, afraid? Not in the least. I've made my share of stupid mistakes, but this one tops them all." She laughed.

"Then why you are helping me? I don't want to put you to any trouble."

"The name of my program is *Corruption in the Nation*, and your words to the nation about the issues you choose would demonstrate such corruption."

"I promise that all my thoughts will be open to you."

Mary replied, "I couldn't have asked for more." She rose from her seat and ushered Omar to a comfortable big sofa. They sat on the sofa facing each other.

"So Elizabeth told you that I am a dangerous woman."

"More or less. You were supposed to be close friends, yet you had an affair with her husband and destroyed him. You simply ruined her life."

"Her husband was guilty, and it is my duty to expose any corruption in the nation. Besides, he was my lover before she even knew him."

"But still, you shouldn't have made love with a married man, your best friend's husband!"

Mary looked before her as if trying to unfold the mystery of her rebellious soul. So many thoughts seemed to be travelling in her mind. Long minutes passed before she started talking in a low voice.

"I am different. I know I'm different. All my life, I lived one dream. My dream was to be a success, to surpass everyone and bring others who stood in my way to their knees, make a name for myself, and live my life of success with someone, find someone to be mine. I had no competition because my competitors knew not to stand in my way because I would outdo them at any cost. I was the best, I got the job done, and I got it done right, with more than complete satisfaction. I was living my dream as I wished it to be, but I forgot all about love. After a while, my dream turned into a vicious cycle of eat, sleep, work. No love life, no true love, no intense pleasure, no passion."

"You will change your mind when you meet the right guy," said Omar.

"I am so sick of hearing that. I do not fit. I never have. I never will. I don't see the world as most people see it. My perception is that the world is wide open and available to me for the taking."

"You live a big lie, Mary! You are treading the wrong road. Only one road will turn your gloom into a holy glow: the road of God. Here you will find love that merits living."

"I rid myself of the toxic waste they are calling religion today. Enough with the fables. I don't follow a certain path, one chosen by a religion or God. I am different and make non-traditional choices. I am a free and independent woman."

Getting off the sofa, Omar said, "I'm late. I'm afraid I have to go."

Mary rose from the sofa and stretched her hand out to Omar, saying with a laugh, "Let's knock 'em dead."

CHAPTER 38

As previously planned, Omar appeared on Mary's famous program, *Corruption in the Nation.*

Mary started the conversation. "Ladies and gentlemen, good morning. Our program *Corruption in the Nation* welcomes Mr. Omar Abdel Aziz, Egyptian ambassador to the United States. We have many questions to ask the ambassador. This session is about the American invasion of Iraq. Mr. Ambassador, welcome to *Corruption in the Nation.*"

Omar said, "Thank you for having me."

"To begin with, I want to know the exact reasons behind the war in Iraq. The American administration has bombarded us with several reasons behind such war. Are these reasons true or false?"

"The Rosh administration strategy appears to be based on the proposition that if you repeat lies enough times, people will accept them as facts."

Mary said, "You mean the administration twisted the truth to drive the country to war?"

"Exactly. President Rosh justified the war with lies. This is an impeachable offense. This pattern of deception and deceit rivals the Nixon administration. Launching a country into war based on fabrications would make Watergate pale by comparison.

"Before the war, Rosh claimed that Saddam Hussein was dealing with al-Qaeda and that it was this connection which made Hussein a threat to America. US intelligence supposedly had evidence that Iraq was involved in the September eleventh attacks or that it supported the al-Qaeda terrorist network that planned and carried them out.

There was no credible evidence that Saddam Hussein helped al-Qaida target the United States. Nearly a year after US and British troops invaded Iraq, no evidence has turned up to verify allegations of Hussein's links with al-Qaeda."

"And how about the Niger documents that supposedly proved Iraq was developing a nuclear program?"

Omar replied, "This was a forgery to deceive your congressmen and senators into voting for promoting war in Iraq."

"You mean that Rosh and his aides made false statements about Iraq's weapons of mass destruction?"

"The facts revealed that no chemical, biological, or nuclear weapons have been found in Iraq."

"The American president convinced the nation to go to war by guaranteeing the people that he would free Iraq from Saddam's tyranny and save the Iraqi people," said Mary.

"Instead of freeing Iraq from Saddam's tyranny, he wrecked Iraq. You don't save by destroying Iraqi homes and hospitals and throwing their country into chaos. The invasion of Iraq caused the deaths of as many as a million people and displaced, internally and externally, another four point seven million. Today there are still more than a million Iraqis lost in their own country, internally displaced. They're living in horrible situations without government help, without hope for the future, surrounded by garbage, anticipating only more sectarian violence. Your invasion caused havoc on the physical and social infrastructure of the country. And the weapons you used, including depleted uranium munitions and white phosphorous, shattered its health. The city of Fallujah is experiencing higher rates of cancer, leukemia, and infant mortality than Hiroshima and Nagasaki did in 1945. The country as a whole has seen an enormous jump in cancer rates. Before the first Gulf War, there were forty registered cases of cancer per one hundred thousand Iraqis. Now sixteen hundred out of one hundred thousand Iraqis are registered with cancer. The city of Fallujah, in particular, has been devastated by an increase in birth defects, a two hundred fourteen times higher than the rate measured in Hiroshima and Nagasaki after they were bombed."

Mary said, "So you think America has lost the War on Terror. The invasion of Iraq has not secured America …"

"By any standard, this Iraq war is of no benefit to America. It only increased Islamic radicalism and worsened the terror threat. In fact, the war has increased more hatred and terrorism. For every one terrorist killed in Iraq, America is creating thousands more who hate and want to hurt America and Americans. This is the surest way to lose the War on Terror, not win it."

"America is liberating oppressed people, eliminating weapons of mass destruction, maintaining law and order around the world, and improving the lives of the less unfortunate in the developing countries. So why do you Muslims have such a negative opinion about us?"

"The United States has become the greatest obstacle to establishing the rule of law in international affairs. America has not lived up to her obligations under the International Covenant on economic, social, and cultural rights. America has violated all treaties of the international community."

"What treaties you are talking about?"

Omar read from a paper before him: "Anti-Ballistic Missile Treaty, nineteen seventy-two; Convention on the Elimination of Discrimination Against Women, nineteen seventy-nine; UN Convention on the Law of the Sea, nineteen eighty-two; Convention on the Rights of the Child, nineteen eighty-nine; Comprehensive Test Ban Treaty,nineteen ninety-six; Kyoto Protocol, nineteen ninety-seven; Chemical Weapons Convention, nineteen ninety-eight; Biological Weapons Convention two thousand one; Non-proliferation and Test Ban treaties, two thousand two; International Criminal Court, two thousand one. You have signaled to the world that the Vienna convention on the Law of Treaties no longer binds you! Instead you have been bullying and bribing other states to sign bilateral agreements to circumvent the jurisdiction of the International Criminal Court."

"Mr. Ambassador, America is the land of democracy and human rights."

"America has shown an utter disregard for international conventions on human rights by holding Arabs at Guantanamo. These prisoners have been tortured and denied rights under both American law and international law."

"You must realize that America is now under critical conditions," said Mary. "America is now suffering from international terrorism."

"You rounded up hundreds of Muslims in the United States, keeping them in jails without being charged or allowed to communicate with family or lawyers. Of the eighty-two thousand Muslims who voluntarily registered at the request of the Justice Department, thirteen thousand face deportation."

"Do you Arabs hate us because we are supportive to Israel?"

"America is too supportive of Israel. America's double standard is obvious. The largest stockpile of weapons of mass destruction in the Middle East is in Israel. The recipient of the biggest portion of your foreign aid is Israel. Israel has cost the United States more than one point six trillion dollars."

"President Rosh proposed a road map for peace in the Middle East. His vision is two states living side by side in peace and security."

Omar said, "Israel began building the separation barrier with the West Bank the very month Rosh proposed his road map for peace. If the road to peace would be realized, it would have to find a way through that barrier, but it hasn't. Further, Israel continued to build settlements in the West Bank. And the Rosh administration's diplomatic push was never sustained. Now Gaza and the West Bank are entirely walled off economically from Israel, and they will soon be physically walled off as well. The Palestinians must be content with unemployment and severe restrictions on movement. Palestinians traveling within the West Bank now face five hundred and forty-two obstacles, eighty-three of which are guarded by soldiers."

"Israel is the only democracy in the Middle East," Mary said. "It is a symbol of freedom, both collective freedom for the Jewish people and individual freedoms for all its citizens, with Jews, Muslims, Christians, and Druze having full equal rights in Israel. Israel has yearned for peace for a long while but has met with constant Arab and Palestinian refusal."

"Is that what you think – Israel has yearned for peace and we Arabs refuse such peace! Israel has all weapons of mass destruction, including at least two hundred nuclear warheads and delivery missiles, yet no one in the West raises a voice against it. Israel invaded Lebanon and Syria, murdered Arabs by the thousands, and demolished many towns and villages, but no one in the United States raised a voice against it. Israel is still occupying strips of Lebanon and Golan Heights, but the United States is doing nothing to remove Israeli illegal occupation. Israel occupied the West Bank illegally, but there is no action from the United States. We Muslims hate this double standard. Israeli government is destroying Palestinians, their homes, their businesses, and their economy. Attacks on civilian homes, arrests, jailing, and torture are routine; shutting down roads is routine; and the build-up of Jewish settlements on Palestinian lands never stops. The United States supports Israel with money and war equipment. It is American weapons killing Palestinians. Why should Muslims not hate America?"

"In the Middle East, Islamic imams openly preach jihad against the United States. America Is under attack from Muslim jihadists."

Omar replied, "Islam is the one that is under attack from America. A course for US military officers has been teaching that America's enemy is Islam in general, not just terrorists, and suggesting that the country might ultimately have to obliterate the Islamic holy cities of Mecca and Medina, without regard for civilian deaths."

Mary said, "Yes, but the Pentagon suspended the course. The FBI also changed some agent training after discovering that it too was critical of Islam."

"Yes, but it was too late. The course was offered five times a year, with about twenty students each time, meaning roughly eight hundred students have taken the course. Army Lieutenant Colonel Matthew

Dooley, the instructor, said in his course given to young officers that his war plan suggested possible outcomes such as Saudi Arabia threatened with starvation, Islam reduced to cult status, and the Muslim holy cities of Mecca and Medina in Saudi Arabia destroyed. In what he termed a model for a campaign to force a transformation of Islam, Dooley called for a direct ideological and philosophical confrontation with Islam, with the presumption that Islam is an ideology rather than just a religion.

"The problem with negative portrayals of Islam in federal government is not new. A six-month review the FBI launched into agent training material uncovered eight hundred and seventy-six offensive or inaccurate pages that had been used in three hundred and ninety-two presentations."

"I'm sorry to hear that. This is totally objectionable, against our values, and it isn't academically sound."

"War on Iraq is the second link in the chain of wars on Islam. The first link of the war on Islam was Afghanistan; Iraq is the second link; and Iran, Pakistan, Yemen, and Saudi Arabia are other subsequent links to be attacked to enslave the entire Muslim population of the world. The war on Islam is an ideological war because Islam is the only theoretically competing political-economic-social system with the capitalist-secular system."

"Will the West succeed in his war against Islam?" asked Mary.

"The answer is a big no. We read in the Koran: 'They desire to extinguish with their mouths, the light of God; but God will perfect His light, though the unbelievers be averse.' And again Allah emphasizes in the Koran: 'It is He who has sent His Messenger with the guidance and the religion of truth, that He may uplift it above every religion, though the unbelievers be averse.' Muslims who abide by Allah's commandments may go through many trials and tribulations in this life but will surely prosper in the life hereafter. Those who oppose Allah's plan may enjoy material prosperity in this life for a short period, but they will end up in hell for eternity."

"So you think America will never win a war against Islam under the label 'war on terrorism'?"

"The American government can fool its own people, but it cannot fool the Muslim world. America's best option is to return home and let the Muslims mind their own business. Muslims will let the American puppets fall, and they will bring true democracy in their own countries. Democracy is built into Islam, and Muslims will establish democracy their own way, not through the deceitful American way — war on terrorism."

"America's wars are for a just cause: to establish freedom and democracy and to protect her interests," Mary stated.

"Oppression is clearly obvious in the wars of America against the downtrodden people, as is happening in Iraq, Afghanistan, and Palestine. Under the banner of war on terrorism, America subjugate developing people to the interest of her own people, by placing her hand on their oil and natural resources and controlling the people's policies and security and even their cultures and religions."

"You think that oppression is America's policy in the Muslim world?"

"Yes, and it has severe consequences not only on the world order but also on America itself."

"How is that?"

"Oppression is the reason behind all the ordeals that inflict humanity. God has deemed oppression the reason behind the collapse of civilizations. God hates the oppressors. Nothing more than oppression hastens God's wrath, for Allah hears the call of the oppressed and answers all those who ask for their rights."

"Does that mean that America will be encompassed by God's wrath because of her oppression?"

"God says in the Koran, 'Have they not travelled in the earth and seen how was the end of those who were before them? Mightier than these were they in strength and in fortifications in the land, but Allah destroyed them for their sins; and there was not for them any defender against Allah.'"

Mary said, "Don't forget that as far as the third interview, the subject will be up to you. What do you want to talk about?"

"America's financial crisis and the impact of America's wars on Iraq and on the already sick economy."

After the interview with Mary, Omar found himself in the middle of a media firestorm following his attack on the American administration and Rosh's policy in the Middle East.

The Jewish organizations took out ads in the *Washington Post*, denouncing Omar and accusing him of resurrecting the dangerous anti-Semitic canard about Jewish influence and control of US foreign policy. Democratic leaders vied with Republicans in censuring Omar and claimed that he has neglected his diplomatic duties as an ambassador and adopted a hostile attitude against the American people. Six Jewish congress-men issued a statement demanding that Omar quit his job because he was unfit to serve as an ambassador to the United States.

Senator Robert Hudson called for President Rosh to suspend five hundred million dollars in aid for Egypt. He also called for Omar's expulsion from the United States.

A small crowd of Christian Right activists surrounded the Egyptian embassy, protesting against Omar's involvement in Washington's foreign policy in the Middle East.

Omar sensed danger surrounding him. He gave specific orders to his intelligence men and bodyguards at the embassy to open their eyes and watch any stranger roaming around his apartments or watching his movements and hereabouts.

CHAPTER 39

One month after Omar's TV interview with Mary, she phoned him to discuss the impact of their interview on the American people. Omar invited her to lunch, but she declined and invited him instead to dinner at her apartment. She wanted to impress him. She wanted him to walk through her fancy apartment and admire the decorating style.

Omar arrived at the appointed time, and she opened the door for him. A wide smile was drawn on her face. She was so aware of his vitality and his virility. The moment he entered her apartment, he sensed the profound silence and the empty echo of loneliness.

Mary had lit candles, and the food was served on white china plates. There were white linen napkins, silver that was polished to a shine, and china cups for coffee. The flowers were placed off centre so they could talk with the candles in between them. The dinner included Japanese appetizers, Italian entrées, and French desserts.

After dinner, Mary served tea. They sat on the couch talking while sipping tea. Mary's warmth and perfume surrounded Omar.

Mary started the conversation. "After our session on Iraq, the National Council of Churches officially took a stand against the Iraq War, calling it dishonourable and urging a change in US policy. The latest Gallup polls revealed that opponents of the war have tended to outnumber supporters. A majority of Americans believe the war was a mistake."

"Splendid. You are a brave woman. Having me in an interview is a big risk, especially in the wake of September eleventh and the hostility shown against Muslims and the Arabs. I am so thankful for your support that I cannot express my gratitude. We became good friends in such a short period."

"I am not exactly known for taking risks, you know."

"Great opportunities often come from risk taking."

"I don't need great opportunities. I'm already famous."

"I need to know something, Mary, and please be honest."

"I'm always honest. It's one of my faults."

"I know that you are not quite sympathetic with our cause, so why are you doing this?"

"Everything has a price." Without warning, Mary's eyes were flashing like a flood.

She fixed her eyes on him, contemplating him. He was like a huge untamed animal she had hunted on a savage shore and brought to ground. Now she all but owned him. What she wanted, she would have.

"What price you want from me, Mary?" he asked.

"I want a man who can say that I am more than a friend. I want mutual pleasure. I want cuddling, kissing, touching, and good sex." She muttered the last with a throaty, sexy moan.

Omar felt troubled. "Please, Mary, don't destroy our friendship and what we have accomplished together. Stay strong with me and keep exposing the corrupt and revealing the truth to the people."

"My heart longs for someone who will soothe it with care and concern. Your love can ease the difficulties of my hard life."

"Is that what this is all about? You want sex with me?" He looked at her with a puzzled expression.

"We can start an affair if you want us to. Are you up for it?"

"Let's be frank with one another. There's no place for me in your life."

"I thought that I meant more than that to you." She forced a smile to her trembling lips to hide her deep distress.

"I fear I'm the wrong person Mary. Is this all there is to life? Don't you have room for anything else?"

"Go ahead and make fun of me. You are a cruel man, blind to a loving glance, deaf to a passionate plea. You've discarded my heart. You are an enigma, a loner; you don't allow anyone to get through to the real you."

"No need to delve any deeper than that."

She glared at him, her eyes half filled with tears. He made her feel that she was ruined, tossed away, deemed insignificant, ignored.

"I am afraid I must be going," he said, rising from the couch and heading to the door.

She escorted him, feeling defeated. She opened the door for him. He shook hands with her in gratitude and said soothingly, "I hope you have a lovely life and hope all your days are special and memorable."

"We need to reconnect," she said with a broken heart.

"Of course we will. We still have two interviews to go," he said as he stepped out of her apartment.

A private detective hiding down the corridor was taking photos of Mary and Omar while standing in the doorway talking.

It was time for the second interview about the Islamic religion. Mary sat elegantly dressed. Her fiery hair was neatly combed in a fashionable style, and Omar sat before her, wearing a beautiful tailored blazer.

"As we see nowadays, Islam is under attack," Mary began. "Islam is under pressure from radio, television, print media, journalists, publishers, and politicians. They do not miss an opportunity to belittle and insult Muslims. Muslims are portrayed as fanatics, fundamentalists, and terrorists. They are called foreign infiltrators in the Western world. The result of this propaganda is that anti-Islam feelings and activities are on the rise. All this portrays that Muslims are a threat to Western way of life. Can you elaborate on that?"

"President Rosh has used the word 'crusades' against the Muslim world, while others have cried 'war of civilizations'. Franklin Graham has called Islam a 'very wicked and evil religion'. General William Boykin, US deputy undersecretary of defense, said that America is waging a holy war against the 'idol of Islam's false god and a guy called Satan, who wants to destroy us'. Evangelist Pat Robertson claimed that Prophet Muhammad was an 'absolute wild-eyed fanatic — a robber and a brigand'. He also claimed that Islam, at its core, teaches violence and that Muslims are crazed fanatics and want global domination. In his view, Islam is satanic and is not a religion of peace. He even went to the extent of saying to an American Christian who was generous enough to host a Muslim boy in her house for weeks after his father kicked him out of the house, 'Don't let Muslim demons inside your home. You don't have to bring an unclean soul inside your home.' Jerry Falwell claimed that Muslims are a threat to America.

"Those whom you call Christian leaders, and some of your people call them 'false prophets', forget that they have committed all the sins God has forbidden. Allah has forbidden indecency, sin, and unjust insolence, but look at what is happening in the churches: rock music, dancing, and sexual abuse. Some of these false prophets were caught with indecent women in private apartments, and others were put in jail for stealing church's money. Allah has forbidden associating partners with Him in worship, yet along with him, they worship Jesus, the son of Mary, whom he never authorized. Allah has forbidden that they say things about Him without knowledge; but see how they launch falsehoods about Him, saying that He is a moon god, a monkey god, a demon god!

"I am sad! I have lived long enough to see Allah – the Lord of creation – humiliated, the seal of the prophets slandered, and the Koran, the last divine revelation to mankind, burned.

"Do they feel secure against Allah's wrath? No one feels secure against Allah's wrath except for those doomed to ruin. Allah shall gradually seize them with punishment in ways they perceive not.

"The Koran says, 'And those that cry lies to Our signs, and wax proud against them – those shall be the inhabitants of the Fire, therein dwelling forever.

"These false prophets think they are rightly guided, but the truth is that they are far astray. By attacking Islam, they bar from Allah's way, desiring to make it crooked, and by doing so, they compile sins over sins upon their heads.

"Apart from these verbal attacks, the Christian missionaries are also working in almost all Muslim countries as humanitarian and aid workers, delivering food, medicines, blankets, and improving the water systems and so forth. Their hidden goal is to finally undercut Islam and spread Christianity rather clandestinely. They come to Muslim countries camouflaged as teachers, professors, consultants, and language students. Christianity is being promoted through children's toys and nursery level storybooks in schools. Multicultural students in secondary schools are being encouraged to participate in activities, schemes, and outings which are deeply offensive to Muslims. They say that Muslims must be reached by whatever means possible. They regard the Islamic world as a hinterland that must be penetrated before the Messiah can return. They say that Islam is the final frontier to conquer. They are at every UN food distribution and AID Supply Distribution Centre with food basket in one hand and the Bible in the other. They do all this because when a person is in a desperate situation and in despair, he is most vulnerable. Then he is told that it is Jesus who is doing all this for you. When persuaded further, the recipient is likely to even change his faith, belief, and religion."

Mary said, "America has think tanks and experts knowledgeable of the Middle East affairs and the religion of Islam. Based on their opinions, the American foreign policy in the Middle East is shaped and designed."

"These people you call 'experts,' because of their deceit and lying, I call them 'the gang'. The members of the gang are heavily sponsored by the Religious Right and Zionist organizations. Their aim is to implement an evil and imperialistic agenda against the Muslim world by tarnishing the religion of Islam and convincing people that Islam is a wicked religion and Muslims are terrorists and heretics. They took the religion for a laughing stock. Deep root prejudices overcome their senses, and ignorance and despicable bias stain their discourse and publications. In order to deceive the people and convince them with their lies, they published heaps of silly books and articles against Islam and Muslims, books characterized by erroneous information and false conclusions and assumptions. Their websites spit out their venom against everything Islamic. They try to seek everywhere vain proofs and groundless causes to refute the truth. They disdain indignantly to acknowledge Allah's signs and warnings and laugh them to scorn! They do not know that the minute they attacked Islam as a religion, the minute they uttered the word of disbelief.

"They have such a smug sense of self-righteousness that while they go on doing wrong, they think they are acquiring merit. Consequently, their works shall be doomed to worthlessness and Allah shall give them no weight on the Day of Judgement. Hell will be their reward because they denied the truth, made a jest of Allah's signs, and ridiculed His Messenger.

"As we read in the Koran: 'Shall We tell you who will be the greatest losers in their works? Those whose striving goes astray in the present life, while they think that they are working good deeds. Those are they that disbelieve in the signs of their Lord and the encounter with Him; their works have failed, and on the Day of Resurrection We shall not assign to them any weight. That is their recompense — Hell - for that they were unbelievers and took my signs and My Messengers in mockery.'"

"The West thinks that Islam, as a faith and as a way of life, encourages violence as a means of achieving political, spiritual, or other objectives," said Mary.

"This is in stark contrast to the prevailing view shared by one billion and five hundred million followers of Islam who see themselves as peaceful adherents of a great faith, those who have been the victims of Western exploitation and domination over the years. Addressing this schism necessitates dispelling the myth that an entire faith can be so simplistically held responsible for the evils of terrorism and violence. Propagating such a fallacy serves no one. The crimes of crusaders should not be attributed to the core philosophy of Christianity, just as the violence of modern-day Muslim radicals should not be the term of reference for judging the Islamic faith. The Koran, the sayings of the prophet, and the legal construction developed by Muslim scholars over the years collectively shape the framework of Islamic thought and practice and spell out in unambiguous terms the peaceful, compassionate nature of Islam. This is what Muslims believe in. A few radical Muslims along with many In the West seem to share a common tactic. They intentionally interpret texts out of context and claim that it is what Islam represents. They should not be allowed to impose their distorted reading or to define this great faith. A sober scientific discussion encompassing, inter alia, the three Abrahamic faiths, may lead to a better understanding of the realities and the nuances surrounding this vital issue.

"Any honest man, whether a believer or an unbeliever, is capable of reading the Koran without prejudice. He has only to approach it freely, to be concerned with it alone and not with the consequences which he may foresee resulting."

"The hostile statements of the Christian leaders against Islam have a tremendous impact upon their followers," Mary said. "Their followers trust them and believe in them. Their followers are in the millions."

"Those whom you call Christian leaders do not realize that in fact they are attacking their Lord, His seal of the prophets, and His last divine book to mankind, the Koran. They do not realize what is in store for them. The day will come when each soul will come pleading for itself. Every soul will be repaid for whatever it has done. On the day of Resurrection, they will bear the full weight of their own burden and some of the loads of those that they led astray without knowledge. How terrible their burden will be."

"The Christian leaders attack the religion of Islam because they do not believe in the Koran, in Allah, and in Muhammad," Mary said.

"Your Christian leaders belie the Koran, slander the prophet of Islam, and mock Allah the Creator by calling him moon god, monkey god, or demon god. Other messengers had been mocked before our prophet, but those who mocked them were overwhelmed in the end by the very thing they had mocked."

"You mean that the Christian leaders will be inflicted with divine wrath because of their attack against Islam?" asked Mary.

"The Koran is a decisive word; it is no merriment. It is the word that separates the truth from falsehood and commands strict laws for mankind to cut the roots of evil. None deny the Koran but every guilty aggressor. The deniers of the Koran will be held accountable for their words. They have taken Allah their Lord as a rival. Do they think they will be left alone without reckoning? How ill they judge. The Koran says about them, 'And who does greater evil than he who forges against Allah a lie? Those shall be presented before their Lord, and the witnesses {the angels, the apostles, and men of piety} will say, "Those are they who lied against their Lord." Surely the curse of Allah shall rest upon the evildoers.

"If only they knew that the time will arrive when they will not be able to ward off the fire from their faces and their backs. On the day of Resurrection, the fire will come upon them suddenly and confound them; they will be powerless to push it away; they will not be reprieved. Hell will be a fitting punishment for them. The Koran says, 'Surely those who oppose God and His Messenger, those are among the most abject.' The Koran also says, 'Do they not know that whosoever opposes God and His Messenger — for him awaits the fire of Gehenna [Hell], therein to dwell forever? That is the mighty degradation.'

"Allah has sent His Messenger with guidance and the religion of truth to make it victorious over all other religions, even though His enemies hate it. They wish to put out the light of Allah with the falsehood they utter from their mouths, but Allah will bring His light to perfection."

"What do you mean by saying that Allah will cause Islam to be victorious over all religions?"

"In terms of intellectual supremacy, all non-monotheistic beliefs about God were to be demolished and monotheistic belief was to be promoted as the predominant belief. All other beliefs were to be intellectually overcome."

Mary said, "Our God is different from yours. Most main-line churches believe in the Trinity — that is, the concept that the Father is God, the Son is God, and the Holy Spirit is God — and that these three persons are not three gods but one god: Jesus Christ. We believe that Jesus is God and he died on the cross to save us from all our sins. Whoever believes in Him will receive eternal life in heaven."

"Claiming that Allah has a son depicts Allah as deficient and unable to run his kingdom alone; therefore, He needs a son or sons to help Him manage His kingdom's affairs. Allah having a son also reduces Him to ordinary people of His creation. Both of these propositions are baseless. If this false accusation is combined with the doctrine of vicarious atonement, it amounts to a negation of Allah's justice and man's personal responsibility. These false doctrines are destructive of all moral and spiritual order and are condemned in the Koran in the strongest possible terms. Allah's power is beyond limits or imagination. The moment He wills a thing, it becomes His word or command and the thing forthwith comes into existence. Allah's word is in itself the deed. Allah's promise is in itself the truth. There is no interposition of time or condition between His will and its consequence, for he is the ultimate reality. He is independent of the proximate or material causes, for He Himself creates them and establishes their laws as He pleases. The Koran says, 'His command, when He desires a thing, is to say to it "Be", and it is.'"

"So the Koran condemns that God has a son?"

"Yes," replied Omar. "The Koran says, 'And they say, the All-Merciful has taken unto Himself a son. You have indeed advanced something hideous! The heavens are well-nigh rent of it and the earth split asunder, and the mountains well-nigh fall down crashing for that they have attributed to the All-Merciful a son; and it behoves not the All-Merciful to take a son. None is there in the heavens and earth but he comes to the All-merciful as a servant; he has indeed counted them, and He has numbered them exactly. Every one of them shall come to Him upon the Day of Resurrection, all alone.'"

"Has the Koran rejected the doctrine of the Trinity as well?"

"Christians believe that God is a Trinity of three persons – the Father, the Son, and the Holy Spirit – and these three are one God, the same in substance, equal in power and glory. Within Islam, however, such a concept of plurality is a denial of monotheism and foreign to the revelation found in Muslim scripture. The act of ascribing partners to God, whether they be sons, daughters, or other partners, is considered to be blasphemous in Islam. The Koran repeatedly and firmly asserts God's absolute oneness, thus ruling out the possibility of another being sharing His sovereignty or nature. The Koran says, 'They are unbelievers who say, "God is the Third of Three. No god is there but One God. If they refrain not from what they say, there shall afflict those of them that disbelieve a painful chastisement.'

"Muslims are now the only true believers on earth. They believe in Allah, the One and only God. They follow the teachings of the Koran and the Sunna of the prophet."

"And what about those who rise defiant against Allah?"

"They were born to be losers. For them, chastisement in the present life and the chastisement of the world to come is yet more grievous; they have none to defend from God. Their requital is the fire."

Mary said, "Muslims claim that Islam is a universal religion. Is that true?"

"It is our duty as Muslims to communicate the message of Islam because it is the road map to paradise. Islam is based on the concept of Tawheed, or unity of God. Muslims are strictly monotheistic and fiercely reject any attempt to make God visible or human. Islam rejects any form of idol worship, even if its intention is to get closer to God. Islam rejects the Trinity or any attempt to make God human.

"In Muslim understanding, God is beyond our sight and understanding yet at the same time nearer to us than our jugular vein. Muslims pray directly to God, with no intermediary, and seek guidance from Him alone because Allah knows well the secrets of the hearts.

"The religion of Islam is not named after a person, as in the case of Christianity, which was named after Jesus Christ; Buddhism after Gotama Buddha; Confucianism after Confucius; and Marxism after Karl Marx. Nor was it named after a tribe like Judaism after the tribe of Judah and Hinduism after the Hindus. Islam is the only true religion of God, and as such, its name represents the central principle of God's religion, total submission to the will of Allah. The Arabic word Islam means the submission or surrender of one's will to the only true god worthy of worship, Allah, and anyone who does so is termed a Muslim. The word also implies peace, which is the natural consequence of total submission to the will of Allah. Hence, it was not a new religion brought by Prophet Muhammad in Arabia in the seventh century but only the true religion of Allah re-expressed in its final form.

"Islam is the religion which was given to Adam, the first man and the first prophet of Allah, and it was the religion of all the prophets sent by Allah to mankind. The name of God's religion, Islam, was not decided upon by later generations of man. It was chosen by Allah Himself and clearly mentioned in His final revelation to man. In the final book of divine revelation, Allah states in the Koran, 'This day have I perfected your religion for you, completed My favor upon you, and have chosen for you Islam as your religion.' In another verse, we read, 'If anyone desires a religion other than Islam [submission to Allah — God] never will It be accepted of Him.' We also read, 'Abraham was not a Jew nor Christian; but an upright Muslim.'

"And here the question arises: did God gave Adam, Noah, Abraham, Moses, and Jesus a different religion than Islam? Of course not. Allah does not accept one religion one day and then change His mind the next day and send another religion with another prophet.

"The enemies of Islam capitalize on their foolishness and wickedness to destroy Islam. But they will never succeed in their evil plan, for Islam, as the religion of truth, will continue to prevail over all religions. Allah promised in the Koran to protect His book from any sort of corruption. The unbelievers plot and plan, and Allah too plans; He is the best of planners. The more that someone tries to suppress Islam, the more Allah will make it flourish."

Mary said, "The West claims that the Koran is outdated, a theft from the Bible, and a hate speech against Christianity. There are numerous articles saying that the Koran attacks the major doctrines of Christianity."

Omar said, "God has ordained for us the same religion which he enjoined on Noah, Abraham, Moses, and Jesus so that we should remain steadfast in religion and not become diverted in it. What God desires for His subjects is that they should be firm in the belief in the oneness of God. Any shift in this centre of attention amounts to polytheism. When the call of Islam is given, the Islamophobe hate mongers, the disbelievers, and the polytheists reject it out of jealousy, doubt, or a false sense of pride. This is the case with people who have attained an elevated status in society. Acceptance of truth by them would involve stepping down from their high positions. As they are not prepared to lower themselves, they set about belittling the call for truth in order to justify their stands. To them, God gives enjoyment a little and then He compels them to a harsh chastisement."

"So you think those who oppose Islam are great losers?"

"The greatest losers in their works are those whose striving goes astray in the present life, while they think that they are working good deeds. Those are they that disbelieve in the signs of Allah – the Creator – and the encounter with Him; their works have failed, and on the day of Resurrection, Allah shall not assign to them any weight. Hell will be their reward, for that they were polytheists and unbelievers and took Allah's signs and his messenger in mockery."

Mary said, "Judaism and Christianity are also divine religions. Do Muslims believe in them?"

Omar replied, "Of course. Muslims believe that God did indeed reveal His message of Islam to previous generations through many prophets. Each of these messages was for a particular people at a particular time in history. The message given to Moses was for the Jews of his time. The message given to Jesus was for the Jews of his time. The Koran, however, was for all people and for all time."

"But Muslims believe that the Torah and the Gospel no longer exist in their original forms."

"There are indeed copies in existence of the books which Christians and Jews believe were the revelation of Allah. Muslims, however, do not believe that these books are a true record of what was originally revealed. Either they were written down incorrectly in the first place or were corrupted by translation or by the deliberate actions of men. We read in the Koran, 'Some of the Jews pervert words from their meanings.' In addition, 'So woe to those who wrote the Book with their hands, and then say: "This is from Allah," that they may sell it for a little price. So woe to them for what their hands have written, and woe to them for their earnings.'

"The early Christian Church eventually chose four Gospels from among many, which roughly corresponded to what Christians already believed. Muslims, however, do not believe that these scriptures are indeed the Torah and the Injeel [Gospel] originally revealed to men by God. They believe this because the Koran tells them that they are not. The originals no longer exist.

"While science, no matter how much it progresses, can answer a lot of questions, two questions it will never be able to answer: one, what is the purpose of our existence; and two, what happens to us when we die?"

"If the Koran is the word of God and Islam means peace, why is the Islamic religion rejected by the West?"

"The West wants to live freely, without accountability. One of the major issues affecting Western societies is its lack of ethics and standards. In today's Western society, religious, moral, and ethical values have been declining. Families are falling apart, the divorce rate is increasing sharply, and excessive sexual indulgence is common in adolescents and young adults. These factors lead to conflicts, resentment, loss, of self-respect, loneliness, depression, anxiety, and a host of psychological symptoms.

"Because of the power of the Western media, your heroes are movie stars or pop stars. Science has replaced religion, and if something can't be logically proved, it doesn't exist. Such a culture is bound to cause psychological problems in a human being, as there is going to be an imbalance between the body and the soul.

"In the United States, which has shown the greatest materialistic progress while giving its citizens numerous rights, almost 60 per cent of the population consults psychiatrists.

"Religion plays a significant role in satisfying our physical as well as spiritual needs. Islam teaches us a code of behaviour and gives us a meaning for our existence. It helps in developing adaptive capacities for stressful events in life. It gives us a sense of self-respect and teaches us about the virtues of family life and a cohesive society with a sense of brotherhood.

"Muslims fear only their Creator and no one else. Islam is the balance between fearing the wrath of Allah and hoping for His mercy. This fear is healthy; it keeps you aware of your actions.

"We Muslims do not live the American dream. Our purpose in life is totally different. We offer our whole selves and our possessions to Allah, and Allah gives us salvation. This is the true doctrine of redemption. This doctrine is not only of the Koran but of all earlier revelations – the original Law of Moses and the original Gospel of Jesus. Any other view of redemption is rejected by Islam, especially that of corrupted Christianity, which thinks that some other person suffered for our sins and we are redeemed by his blood.

"The Koran says, 'O you who believe! Shall I guide you to a trade that will save you from a painful torment? That you believe in Allah and His Messenger, and that you strive hard and fight in the cause of Allah with your wealth and your lives – that will be better for you, if you but know. If you do so, He will forgive you your sins, and admit you into Gardens under which rivers flow, and pleasant dwellings in Eden Paradise; that is indeed the great success.' Islam is not something enforced on anyone. It tells you what to be mindful of in order to be successful in this life and the next."

"But Muslims always impose their religion on others by force."

"Wrong. In Islam, there is no compulsion in religion. It is our task to deliver the message of Islam to all because it is a message of mercy and a road map to paradise. People are free to believe or not to believe. Muslims are not their guardians. But those who deny Allah's oneness and associate a partner or partners with Him in worship shall come to know the fatal consequence of their denial of Allah's authority when the fetters and chains are on their necks and they are dragged in boiling water and then into the fire they are poured."

Mary said, "Can you summarize Islam in just a few words?

"Islam is the worship of Allah alone and the avoidance of worship directed to any person, place, or thing other than Allah. This should be crowned with good deeds based on the commandments of the Koran and the Sunna of the prophet.

The Koran states, 'I am only a mortal like you; it is revealed to me that your God is one God. So let him, who hopes for the encounter with his Lord, work righteousness, and not associate with his Lord's service anyone."

"Thank you, Mr. Ambassador, for being with us tonight," said Mary.

"You're most welcome."

CHAPTER 40

Mary's passion for Omar grew each day. She felt as if her heart were being burned. Her desire for him cut through her like a knife.

It was almost midnight before Mary finally settled down to get some sleep. But she was about to burst into flames imagining Omar with her in bed.

With a sigh, she got up slowly and walked up to the bathroom. She was leaning up against the sink studying herself in the mirror when a thought suddenly crept up on her.

She put on a short-sleeved sexy satin dress and covered it with a midi coat. She descended the stairs to the garage. She got into her car, thrust the key into the ignition, and gunned the engine with smooth expertise.

Omar was just dosing off when he heard a light knock at his door. He walked to the door and opened it to see Mary standing in the doorway. "Mary! What are you doing here?" he asked, astonished.

"I just thought I'd drop in for a bit and keep you company. You are surely lonely being here all by yourself."

Omar stood silently, bewildered as to what he might say in this awkward situation. Mary was like a wild animal, both beautiful and deadly.

"Don't you think it's too late to pay me a visit?" he said, not moving from the doorway.

"Aren't you going to let me in?"

"Come in," he said, embarrassed.

She followed his broad back and long legs to the living room. She sat on an elegant couch with a table before it. She took off her coat and placed it on the table. Omar had to make sure his eyes weren't playing tricks; Mary was almost naked under her coat.

Omar stood staring at Mary sitting on the couch. None of this made sense. Omar took a seat on a fauteuil.

"Why are you sitting there? Come here," she said, tapping the side of the couch.

"No, Mary. I am good."

"I'm not. Come here."

Omar rolled his eyes at her and finally sat beside her.

"I already sensed a bond growing between us, and I wonder if you do too. I keep hoping that one day you will see the love I have for you."

"Love takes a long time to happen. You loved me so fast?"

"Omar, you are absolutely wonderful, and I haven't been able to stop thinking about you," she cooed, tracing her claws gently over his face and smiling. She whispered in his ear, "My whole body tingles with a passionate heat that needs to be cooled. I'm longing, yearning, but you are nowhere near. I'm scared of being lonesome and empty. Hold me and caress me." She placed a hand gently on his chest and leaned over him. "I love you, Omar."

"It's an awkward thing to play with souls, Mary. I don't want to hurt your feelings, but sexual intercourse without marriage is a grave sin. I fear the torment of my Lord."

Omar's refusal only heightened her passion. "Loving you is like ripping out my heart. All I want to be is to be your woman," she pleaded. She ran a hand through her red hair before tossing it over her shoulder, then she leaned over Omar and wrapped her arms around his neck. Her arm encircled his neck tightly, and she pushed herself against him with a sort of detached hunger. Her breasts pushed against his breast, and he could feel the pressure of her thigh against his leg. Her heavy breathing was tickling his ears.

While disengaging himself gently from her arms, Omar said, "Mary, please stop that nonsense."

"Omar, I can't bear the hurt of being apart from you. With you, my life is whole."

"I shall not succumb to your evil ways," Omar said, getting off the couch.

"Why can't you realize the way I feel?" she asked, feeling a sharp pang of sadness.

"Mary, please try to understand. In our religion, there is no sex outside marriage. Fornication is a major sin."

"Oh, Omar, listen to me. I will enrich your heart with my love. I want to belong to you."

"You played me, Mary. You helped me in order to fulfil your bestial desire."

His rejection made her feel like a small crushed animal who'd been run over and thrown to the side of the road to bleed to death all night long. With her hands to her face, she burst into tears.

"Don't cry, Mary. I don't want to make you miserable."

"It's all very fine to say you don't want to make me miserable. You see, I love you. Demon. I'll break your pride!" she shouted, turning into a fierce crouching tigress. She leapt off the couch like a leopard, trying to hit Omar.

"You get mad at me when I don't do what you expect of me," Omar said, easily slipping to the side.

She looked more like a wild cat than a woman. Her eyes burned darkly, and a sly grin turned the corners of her lips. She sprung again, but Omar's arms grabbed her and heaved her back to the couch.

"Don't hurt me. I can hurt you worse if I wished to," she said, crying.

Sorrow, not wrath, had brooded in Omar, and he tried to calm her. "I am not the bad guy here, okay? Don't get so down on yourself."

Mary drew a shaking breath. Sad silence fell upon her.

"It's time to go home, Mary," Omar said, covering her body with her coat and escorting her to the door.

She obeyed him, realizing that there was no way to reason with him now.

In a nearby building, a private detective had set up a remote camera directed to Omar's rooms.

CHAPTER 41

Omar still had a last interview with Mary, and that was about the American economy.

The interview started with Mary asking this question: "In our previous interview, you said that war in Iraq would cost America billions of dollars, which would severely affect the already sick economy."

"America became embroiled in wars in Afghanistan and Iraq. These wars cost America billions of dollars. In addition to high defense and military expenditures in recent years, America has endured a collapse in the housing and stock markets. Many cities are experiencing decaying infrastructures. The US government does not have the resources to help build the infrastructures of these American cities. The government is spending more than it takes in and has obligated itself for future expenditures with money it does not have. Many Americans are struggling to feed themselves and their families and to take care of their daily needs. Approximately fifty million people in America are on food stamps. President Rosh has emptied the treasury on wars instead of helping his people."

"But our government is telling us that stocks have recovered all their losses. Real estate has rebounded, and unemployment and bankruptcies have dropped."

"Your government is not telling the truth. I expect there will be a near complete shutdown of the American economy. Your governments on both the federal and state level will shut down. Banks will not open. Businesses will at least temporarily shut their doors. I expect you will see martial law enforced by the US military."

"You are giving us a grave picture of our economy," responded Mary. "Of course, your allegations can be challenged by other economists."

"The economists would never deny the fact that every single hour of every single day, the US government spends about two hundred million dollars that it doesn't have. The public debt has more than doubled; it amounts to more than twenty trillion dollars. With each traditional commitment, you sink further and further into debt, closing in upon the moment that you can simply no longer afford even the interest payments on your obligations. That's exactly where you are today. You are trapped. There is no way out."

"But don't forget that we are the only country in the world who can legally print US dollars because the US dollar is the world's reserve currency. In other words, the dollar forms the basis of the world's financial system. It's what banks around the world hold in reserve against their loans."

"Your biggest advantage is about to disappear," stated Omar.

"How is that?"

"You have been able to consume as much as you want without worrying about acquiring money to pay for it because your dollars are accepted everywhere around the world. All you had to do was borrow and print more money. As late as the nineteen seventies, America was the world's largest creditor. But by the mid-eighties, you had become a debtor to the world. And since the late nineties, you've been the world's largest debtor. With all these bad debts piling up, you've had to begin repaying your debts by printing trillions of new dollars. The Fed is printing sixty-five billion dollars a month. That's nearly a trillion dollars a year."

"With America going through this financial crisis, what do you think the response of our creditors will be?"

"I believe your creditors will either completely stop accepting dollars in payment or greatly discount the value of these new dollars."

Mary said, "No, that sounds crazy."

"That's why China is now actively taking steps to phase out the US dollar because of its frustration with the US government's mismanagement of your currency. And how does your government respond? You have the audacity to label China a "currency manipulator"!

"People are getting truly desperate to protect their savings!"

"The result of this currency crisis, and the end of the US dollar as the world's reserve currency, is massive inflation in America, the likes of which you have never seen before."

"But our political leaders have come to believe that narrowing the tax base and printing billions of dollars is the formula for prosperity," she said.

"Many countries around the world want to diversify out of the US dollar as quickly as possible. In fact, in the past couple of years, China has signed international currency agreements with Germany, Brazil, Russia, Australia, Japan, Chile, the Unites Arab Emirates, India, and South Africa.

"Along with China, Russia, Japan, and France, Gulf Arabs are planning to end dollar dealing for oil, moving instead to a basket of currencies including the Japanese yen, Chinese yuan, the euro, gold, and a new, unified currency planned for nations in the Gulf cooperation council, including Saudi Arabia, Abu Dhabi, Kuwait, and Qatar.

"Even the International Monetary Fund, IMF, which is headquartered in Washington, DC, has proposed replacing the US dollar with something called 'Special Drawing Rights', or SDRS."

I'm afraid most Americans simply aren't aware of what's being done and said around the world," said Mary. "I still don't believe we can have a complete currency collapse here in the United States."

"Do you know that there are now approximately fifty million Americans on food stamps? Can a country really be in good shape when one out of every six citizens can't even afford to buy food? Essentially, forty-three per cent of American families are broke! The country will face both a currency crisis and a sovereign debt crisis. It's going to be the same thing that is happening in Greece, but it's going to be a lot worse.

"The United States faces higher unemployment, higher food and energy prices, and sharply higher interest rates. What America experienced in 2008 was not the real crash. The real crash is coming. The data is clear. There will be fifty per cent unemployment, a ninety per cent stock market drop, and one hundred per cent annual inflation."

"So how in the world can we possibly find our way out of the current crisis? We certainly can't do it with savings or increased earnings."

"The only answer for the Rosh administration is to print more money, which will hasten the fall of the US dollar as the world's reserve currency."

"Then in what can Americans invest their money?"

Omar replied, "By buying as much gold and silver as they can reasonably afford."

"But gold has had a huge run, jumping more than three hundred per cent in the past decade!"

"The smartest money managers in the world have all recently taken huge positions in gold. They all recommend buying gold."

Mary addressed the audience: "As it seems, the United states is facing economic disaster on a scale few nations have ever experienced. Most people are unaware of the obscene signs of this crisis, where it came from and how to stop it. While we persist in our superpower mentality, we have quietly become a second-class country in many respects. We no longer produce what we need to sustain ourselves, we import much more than we export, and we are selling off our assets and taking on massive debts to sustain a standard of living we can no longer afford. We are failing even to acknowledge predatory foreign trade practices undermining US industry. Instead, we encourage US manufacturers to design, engineer, and produce in Third World markets like Mexico and China. What common-sense steps should we take to reverse the trend? Do you have an answer?"

With this remark, Mary ended the interview with Omar.

CHAPTER 42

The impact of Omar's interviews with Mary Mackenzie was quite effective. Omar's answers to Mary's questions about politics, economy, and religion had exposed the American biased and ruthless foreign policy in the Middle East. The plots and secrets behind the American foreign policy in the Middle East were now laid bare before the American citizens.

Human right groups demonstrated in several states, calling for just and rational American foreign policies in the Middle East.

Omar's statement that the American economy was wasted on unnecessary wars instead of the welfare of the American people had sparked violent unrest in the streets of many states. Massive strikes took place as teachers, television employees, postal workers, students, and masses of other public sector workers expressed discontent with the handling of the economic crisis. The lower class and the middle class felt that they would lose their social, political, and economic foundations. The protesters called for restructuring the economy to benefit everyone rather than a small elite.

Omar's interview with Mary about the war in Iraq also resulted in large-scale protests against the war in several states.

Thousands of American Muslims also marched in several states, venting their fury against the attack on the Muslim religion, blaming President

Rosh for not interfering to stop Islamophobe hate mongers from slandering the prophet, belying the Koran, and humiliating Allah, the Creator.

The unrest continued for weeks with the realization that the nation's debt soared on an unsustainable path according to most projections.

The widespread civil violence that led to massive civil unrest had forced the defense establishment to reorient priorities to defend basic domestic order and human security. The Pentagon released information that as many as twenty thousand soldiers under the US Northern Command would be trained within the next three years to work with civilian law enforcement in Homeland Security.

President Rosh was furious to see large segments of the American people demonstrating against him. This rebellious attitude from the American citizens would certainly threaten his career. He might lose the presidential election for a second term.

The president summoned the secretary of state to seek his advice on the matter.

"The Egyptian Ambassador is an intolerable nuisance and has started a whole heap of trouble," the president said to him.

The secretary of state said, "Yes, sir, he has violated his diplomatic duties by interfering in the host country's political affairs."

"His interviews have turned the people against me. Community mobilization of hostile groups combined with mass media might affect my second presidential election."

"He has become a headache to our administration. We must do something about it."

"The Egyptian ambassador is causing trouble to my command and order," stressed the president. "His interviews with Mary have led to demonstrations in several states.

"There is also another delicate matter. Whenever the ambassador and my daughter meet, the media releases rumours about their love affair, which doesn't exist in the first place. Elizabeth is married to Senator Hudson, and these rumours annoy him tremendously, as they do the other members of the Republican Party. I seek your advice."

The secretary of state said, "Article two of the Vienna Convention on Diplomatic Relations in nineteen sixty-one stipulates that the establishment of diplomatic relations between states has to take place by mutual consent of the states concerned. According to the Vienna Convention, the ambassador is required to respect the laws and regulations of the receiving state and not to interfere in its international affairs. The ambassador abused his privileges by participating in such interviews."

The president replied, "We will consider him a persona non grata and ask Egypt to replace him with another."

"Yes, this could be a sound solution to such an awkward situation."

"Egypt is the key to peace and stability in the Middle East, and a strong United States-Egyptian relationship is essential to securing American presence in the region. Since September eleventh, however, ties between our two countries have temporarily soured. Asking Egypt to appoint a new ambassador to the United States in succession to the present ambassador can worsen our relationship with Egypt further. We will therefore delay our request until the time is ripe. In the meantime, let the media deal with the ambassador as well as release news about the possibility of such a replacement in the future."

"As you wish, sir."

After that meeting, the whole world turned against Omar. The media called him a terrorist, and Senator Hudson and the Zionist Christian Right and televangelists whipped people upon him like a pack of wild dogs.

The Republicans, the Christian Right, and their coalition with the American Zionists mobilized their biased Islamophobe media to scandalize and attack Omar. The media attacked Omar vigorously, belying his claims about the debt crisis of the United States and the American plot against the Muslim world. The media also pushed that Omar breached the Vienna Convention on Diplomatic Relations when he interfered in the internal and international affairs of the United States.

The attack was so vicious that it caused Mary Mackenzie to take advantage of this opportunity and have a short interview with Omar in his office at the embassy.

Mary said, "Mr. Ambassador, it seems that my interviews with you have evoked resentment and fear throughout the mass media. The media bombarded you with serious accusations that need to be clarified."

"This is the usual ploy of the Islamophobes. No matter what the particular issue at hand, rather than dealing with facts, they throw in every negative aspersion they can to demonize the religion of Islam and Muslims in general. What I mentioned in my three interviews with you were facts that can't be denied. Islamophobia is spreading like cancer to destroy the social fabric of your nation. Your religious leaders and politicians are lying to their followers about the truth of Islam. And there is no doubt that your country is facing an alarming financial crisis. Who would deny this except a hate-mongering media against Muslims?"

"The media consider every new Muslim immigrant as a potential threat to the safety and security of the United States," said Mary. "The media called for treating Muslims citizens like traitors. It also called for purging all American Muslims from the United States!"

"As Muslims, our interests are our values. We cannot accept a violation of these principles by any society. Bad treatment and dehumanizing of Muslims is unacceptable."

Mary said, "The government hasn't interfered to stop the media attack on Muslims. Do you think that's wise?"

"Your administration is influenced by certain political groups governing the internal and foreign policy of this country. These groups are misleading the public through their biased media with distortions, exaggerations, inaccuracies, and fabrications. I consider this an erosion of freedom of expression."

"Are American Muslims really terrorists, as the media claims?" asked Mary.

Omar said, "The media calls us terrorists and wants us dead. Islamophobia has become a social cancer in American society, a threat to the fabric of your democratic way of life. We Muslims assert our faith and rights as citizens, affirming freedom of expression while rejecting those who abuse this right by using it as a cover for their religious prejudice or political gain."

"What was the impact of such a vicious attack on you?"

"Nothing whatsoever. I was trained to stand the heat."

"We hear rumours that you will be replaced by another."

Omar laughed. "I long for my country's bread. My country's coffee."

CHAPTER 43

When Omar started his first TV interview with Mary, Elizabeth got mad. She couldn't deal with the idea that Omar could have an intimate relationship with Mary. She shouted, outraged, "She ruined my life before, and now she is ruining it again!"

Elizabeth called her private detective and asked him to find out everything about Omar and Mary, down to the smallest detail.

After she received pictures revealing Omar and Mary dining together, and others showing Omar visiting Mary in her apartment or she visiting him in his, as well as the pictures showing her onslaught on him, she felt a raging ball of anger within herself.

At dinner, Elizabeth sat mindlessly eating. Omar's relationship with Mary maddened her. She talked nervously to herself while eating: "This woman is a demon. She ruined my life before, and now she is trying to seduce Omar into violating his fundamental faith."

Although it was midnight in Manhattan, Elizabeth couldn't help but pick up the phone and call Omar.

"I knew you were in New York. I am in my house in Manhattan. Hudson is in Washington for a couple of days. I want to see you," she ordered.

"It's too late. You didn't even say hello. Are you all right?"

"Come now and don't be late," she snapped at him.

The butler showed Omar to the living room. Elizabeth was leaning on the mantelpiece. She was wearing a fabulous black deep V-neck Tiffany dress. The sight of her delighted Omar's eye. His heartbeat quickened in his chest. He wanted to touch her.

As he approached her, she stopped him with a sign of her hand. He stopped, staring at her in shock. She took the pictures she had of him with Mary from the mantelpiece and threw them at his face. He looked at the pictures scattered around his feet and understood what made her furious.

She shot at him, "You know, of course, that Mary Mackenzie ruined my life before and put me in shame."

"Yes."

"You flirt with her and thought I wouldn't know, but I knew everything in the end."

"Are you spying on me? I don't like being spied on."

"The nerve you've got." She was wild with anger. She simply went mad. "You are callous and unfeeling." Her heart was thumping madly.

"You scorned my loyalty; you mocked me. You have wounded me. You have insulted my love. I do not love you. You are unworthy of me."

"Give me a chance to breathe, please."

She burst into tears, unable to restrain a fit of sobbing. "I never expected such a thing of you. You, of all people, Omar."

"What have I done to deserve all this?"

"What have you done? I find you very rude. I have watched and waited. I have been jealous and desperate. Do you know how much I hated seeing you with her? Mary is a stunning woman. She crossed your path and threw her net over you."

"Please come to your senses. I meant well."

"How dare you love her! She is a scandalous whore. I feel I don't know you anymore."

"Elizabeth, you became moody and suspicious."

"Why you are doing this to me? How could you have changed so much? How could I think you loved me after putting me through such torture? You have burned me to the core. Are you really that heartless? "Of course, Mr. Romeo, women throw themselves at you right and left and—"

Omar interrupted: "I managed to keep myself from getting involved with her. Mary was making advances, but my defences were in place."

Her face was instantly red, and her mouth flew open. She stared at him in disbelief. His words made her even madder. "Did you sleep with Mary behind my back? That woman is a major screw-up."

"How could that be when I love you so much?"

"Don't you dare say you love me. You blatantly flirt with her."

Her words seemed so unfair that he felt as if someone had twisted a knife in his gut. Omar glanced at Elizabeth. Her eyes were blazing with anger.

"Give yourself a break, Liz, and please listen to me. I was left with no choice. It was strictly business. We just shared conversations and coffee."

"Coffee! The voluptuous Mary could tempt even a saint into sinning."

"From the moment I set foot in your country, I have seen hatred and arrogant hostilities against Muslims and Islam. Afghanistan and Iraq were invaded without plausible reasons. Blindly siding with Israel at the expense of the Palestinians is a matter of fact.

"There has been a persistent push in America by the Christian Right, conservatives, and religious leaders to demean the Muslim faith. They use in their attack deception, lies, and falsehood. All these lies are spewed by a biased media, and your people believe them without even thinking.

"In your country, the Koran was defiled, belied, and burned. The prophet of Islam was slandered, and Allah, the God of the universe, was humiliated. All that happened, and your government hasn't lifted a finger to stop this impudence.

"Muslims are badly treated in your country and are portrayed as underdeveloped terrorists and illiterate savages. Anti-Arab and anti-Muslim bigotry has become an entrenched feature of America's political and social landscape."

"We are fighting political Islam; we are fighting Muslim terrorists. Don't you understand?" she yelled at him.

"Political Islam is not the threat. It is political Christianity that you should fight against."

"Christianity is the religion of love and peace. It has nothing to do with terrorism."

"The Religious Right started all this hatred against Muslims and Islam. The Christian Right sowed the seeds of hatred between non-Muslim and Muslim Americans without any logical reason. The falsehood they disseminated among the people tore the society apart.

"The Christian Right aims to implement an evil and an imperialistic agenda against the Muslim world by tarnishing the religion of Islam and convincing people that Islam is a wicked religion and Muslims are terrorists and heretics. The Christian Right is working hard to picture Islam as an evil religion and its adherents as savages and bloodthirsty.

"Now we can see Republican senators using the issue of Islam phobia in their electoral campaigns. Others in Congress demand restricting the movement of American Muslims and putting them under siege! Others claim that American Muslims are unpatriotic citizens and must not join the army or penetrate Congress. They must instead be deported. They even went to the extent of doubting the honesty and patriotism of the two Muslim senators in Congress!

"Neoconservatives and members of the Tea Party also joined the comedy, and their irresponsible and silly statements about Islam showed their hatred and bigotry.

"The objective is to prepare the ground for a vicious war against Muslim countries in order to divide the Arab world into small entities based on religious differences, ethnicity, and racism."

"Wait a minute here. The Christian Right brought my father to power. My husband, Senator Robert Hudson, grew in an apocalyptic Christian cult."

"This tremendous influence of the Christian right in the American political life explains the attempts of presidential and congressional candidates to seek its consent and to submit willingly to its embezzlements. This is why we often see Senator Hudson and his colleagues barking out their malice against everything Islamic.

"The Christian Right, with its distorted reading of the Bible and its false apocalyptic and dispensationalist beliefs, has destroyed our countries."

"I am afraid you are mixing things up. What does the Christian Right have to do with your countries?" she demanded angrily.

"The Christian Right considers all Palestine a conclusive home for Israel and to hell with the Palestinians, the original inhabitants of the land. The Christian Right should have realized that by blindly supporting the Israeli aggression in Palestine, it had entered into the circle of injustice. Its hands became stained with Palestinian blood, and its conscious became burdened with the crimes of murder and expulsion. In the sight of Allah, supporters of criminals are equally guilty as criminals themselves. These crimes are the product of the Christian Right's unconditional support for Israel without considering the simple right of the Palestinians to live as human beings in their modest homes. They think that by killing Palestinian Muslims, they are clearing the universe from the enemies of God. They must not play God, for God is just to his servants and is against tyranny and aggression. Had they confined themselves to the real Christian teachings aiming at piety, righteousness, and peace, their relationship with God and the world would have been different and better.

"The Christian Right is behind the division we see now in the Arab world. The only country that will benefit from this division is Israel, of course. The Christian Right and affiliated think tanks, and your father and his administration as well as Tony Blair, are all responsible for the chaos and mischief they have caused in our countries.

"The Christian Right is threatening world peace because it is interfering in America's foreign policy, thus directing it to side blindly with Israel. The Christian Right is unwilling to see any peace settlement in the Middle East.

"The Christian Right adjured American policymakers to adopt situations in the Middle East more harmonious to the Torah prophecies and to declare the right of the Jewish people to live on the land that was given to them by God, including the West Bank, Gaza, and Golan Heights. The leader of the Christian ethical majority claimed that as mentioned in the book of Genesis, the borders of Israel stretch east to the Euphrates River and west to the west of Egypt. He also added that the borders of the Promised Land enjoin parts from Iraq, Syria, Turkey, Saudi Arabia, Egypt, Sudan, all Lebanon, Jordan, and Kuwait!

"This is how the evangelical mind thinks. God chose the Israelis, while the evil infidel Arabs were not blessed by God. The Christian Right believes that since it was God's wish that Israel be established, any Arab or Palestinian claims in Jerusalem or in Palestine land are false pretenses.

"They even think that the Arabs are but pieces of chess in a holy cosmetic game, a hysteric power unfit to perform any reformatory or positive role in history. The Arabs are the enemies of God because their conflict with Israel is a challenge to His will. And as history is heading towards its end, the Arabs become the focus of evil, uniting with the disfigured imposter against God!

"The Old Testament heritage made several American Christians look at the Arab-Israeli conflict as a reflection to the events depicted in the

Old Testament. They consider the Israelis of the twenty-first century as the children of Israel mentioned in the Torah, and the Palestinians are the Philistines, whose hero Goliath fought David. It seems, therefore, that for the sake of Israel, the Christian Right is ready to inflame a nuclear war to ascertain the sacred prophecies.

"The American administration, surrendering to the evil desires of the Christian Right, will be responsible before God for the hundreds of thousands killed in Syria, Iraq, and Afghanistan. Allah will charge them for the women, elderly, and children who faced collateral damage and fled armed conflicts.

"The Christian Right, in collaboration with the Zionists, are surely taking America to its demise."

"What else don't you like about America, Mr. Know-It-All?" Elizabeth said mockingly.

"The United States has been trying for years to establish the so-called Greater Middle East, or the New Middle East, as they call it now. It is an Anglo-American-Israeli military road map in the Middle East. This project, which has been in the planning stages for several years, consists of creating an arc of instability, chaos, and violence extending from Lebanon, Palestine, and Syria to Iraq, the Persian Gulf, Iran, and Afghanistan.

"The New Middle East project was introduced publicly by Washington and Tel Aviv with the expectation that Lebanon would be the pressure point for realigning the whole Middle East and thereby unleashing the forces of constructive chaos. This constructive chaos, which generates conditions of violence and warfare throughout the region, would in turn be used so that the United States, Britain, and Israel could redraw the map of the Middle East in accordance with their geostrategic needs and objectives.

"There will be no peace in the Middle East. At any given moment for the rest of our lifetimes, there will be multiple conflicts in mutating forms around the globe. The de facto role of the US armed forces would be to keep the world safe for her economy and open to her cultural assault. To those ends, the United States would do a fair amount of killing.

"The massacre began when Afghanistan and Iraq were invaded under the false pretext of terrorism, weapons of mass destruction, or establishing democracy. The slaughter began when creative chaos was enforced on Yemen, Syria, Libya, Tunisia, and Egypt. These countries are now being torn apart in order to be divided into small insignificant pieces with no borders. Egypt, however, was able to stand against the American plot, and the Egyptians stood as one man, supporting their new elected president.

"And what was the result of such an evil policy of yours? There are seven point four million Afghan men, women, and children now living in hunger and on the brink of death from occupation-induced starvation.

"Six million Iraqis are now refugees, two million of which are displaced internally; two million Iraqi women are now widows; five million Iraqi children are now orphans; and eighty per cent of Iraqis have witnessed shootings, kidnappings, rapes, killings, and other atrocities.

"Palestine, a holy and historic land that has been called home by prophets and saints, heroes and revolutionaries, has been occupied by a usurping entity for sixty-three years. This entity that calls itself Israel also calls itself the 'only democracy in the Middle East'.

"Palestinians scream at the world day and night, at the tops of their lungs, that this democracy is farcical. In Israel, there are at least thirty laws that discriminate viciously against non-Jews.

"There are now over two point fourteen million Syrian refugees in Jordan, Lebanon, Turkey, Iraq, Egypt, and North Africa. These refugees lack basic services, there is a rising number of attacks on vulnerable young women and children, and there is a marked increase in diseases that were eradicated decades ago.

"Tell me, Elizabeth, who is going to pay for all this? You might ask who would dare make us pay, who is stronger than we are. And I would answer you, 'Do you not see that Allah, who created you, is stronger than you in might? Allah destroyed many a city that was mightier than yours, and there was no help for them.

"I had to fight back these lies and plots, Liz. I had to explain to the American people the bare truth. They had to know the suffering we are facing in our land due to your injustice and hatred. I contacted several TV stations to ask for space on their programs, but they refused. I was not surprised about their attitude because they were all biased. Mary Mackenzie gave me this space, and for that I am grateful."

"She gave you this space just to have you for herself."

"Maybe. But you must understand that I've loved you for years, and I swear to God that never, even in my thoughts, was I untrue to you."

"You never stop fighting. Your ardent fighting spirit will put you in jeopardy. You fight with guns and now with words. Sometimes words are sharper than weapons. Your words on TV incited the grudge of the president and his administration. You laid bare their secret plots before the American people. The media pictured you as a person who uses political beliefs as a platform to express racism, hatred, and intolerance of the American people."

"Truth is not racist. Facts are not hate. Allah is just, and He loves justice. Injustice brings His painful chastisement of wrath upon the evildoers. Who is going to protect you against Allah's wrath when it befalls you? Is it your superpower, your atomic bombs!

"What happened to you people? Do you not know that Allah has knowledge of everything? He knows the treachery of the eyes and what the breasts concealed. What happened to you people? Do you not think that you shall be raised up unto a mighty day? A day when mankind shall stand before the Lord of all being? On that day, all mankind shall be exposed, not one secret of theirs concealed."

Elizabeth was shaken by his words. He was fighting alone in a den of snakes. The Arab ambassadors wouldn't dare confront the American administration or the Christian Right and its allies as he did. They didn't have his daring fighting spirit. They were only diplomats dealing with matters in a sensitive and tactful way. But he was different — he was a warrior.

She knew that every word he uttered was true. She knew he was right about the hostile religious and political fabric of her country towards the Arabs and Islam. She knew about the Great Middle East plot and the displacement of the innocents.

She stood staring at his picturesque figure in his neat suit and with his dense black hair. She saw him standing so alone, so disappointed, carrying all the worries of his world on his shoulder. She felt his agonizing loneliness. She hated herself for the pain she'd put him through.

She said with agonizing tears in her eyes, "You fool. You became a public nuisance. The media says you will be replaced with another."

"Do you think I care? In the depths of my heart, I long for this feeling of homecoming. And I won't find rest until I live in its peace."

Her eyes misted, and she started to hear her heart beating quickly. She wanted to ask him forgiveness for enveloping him in her cloud of anger and revenge. Unable to stop the tears that were starting to form in her eyes, she said with a broken voice, "It's late. I am tired, and I want to get some sleep."

"I know my way out," he said, heading to the door. But he stopped at the door and turned back to face her. "I live a barren life searching for you. I'll walk over hot coals to be anywhere with you. And I will always find you, be it in this life or the next."

He opened the door, walked out, and closed the door behind him. She stared at the closed door with tears rolling down her face. An awful emptiness engulfed her. She felt his agony and desolation as well as the misery of her lonely life. How could she have dared blame him with such cruelty? He was not her husband, and she had no right over him. She didn't have the right to blame him at all. But she knew as well as he that there was always this powerful bond of love that strongly attached them together — a love bond that was bigger than life itself.

Suddenly, all her anger disappeared and she wished to spend the night in his arms. This night, alone in her bed, she would hold her pillow and nestle in his protective arms. She would ease his pain and love him all night long.

CHAPTER 44

In her apartment in Washington, Elizabeth was drowning in tears of boredom. She complained to her mother during phone calls that she was bored and just wanted to go shopping. Hudson had planned an outing that included a visit to Madame Tussauds, but Elizabeth refused. The idea of going to old museums would have just bored her to death. All she wanted to do was shop. Elizabeth went shopping at Simon Mall.

It was by mere chance that she saw Omar standing in the men's section looking at long-sleeved shirts and neckties. She kept looking at him from a distance, feeling the quickening of her heart. After a long moment of watching him, she decided to avoid him and go her way, but their eyes met.

He was about to go to her, but something terrible happened. Twelve gunmen rushed into the mall, hurling grenades and spraying bullets just yards from her. Omar ran and threw himself on Elizabeth to protect her from the bullets and the splinters of the grenades that were flying in every direction.

Elizabeth could see the bullets hitting above the display stands and hear the screaming all around her. She heard the gunmen talking to people, telling them to stand up, followed by gunshots. She raised her head a little and saw many dead people, from young people to old women. She glanced at Omar and saw the blood oozing from his back.

"Omar, you're wounded," she whispered, terrified.

"Don't worry. Just superficial wounds of no concern. "Elizabeth," Omar whispered, "Don't move. I'll deal with them with my personal gun. It won't take long, I promise."

The first man he encountered had a machine gun and was guarding one of the mall entrances. Omar shot him down with a bullet in the head and took the machine gun. The man had a small bag full of grenades. Omar took possession of the bag also.

Six of the gunmen heard the gunfire. They came quickly to see what had happened, but they were confronted with a grenade thrown at them by Omar. Trying to avoid the grenade splinters, the gunmen threw themselves on the ground. The grenade exploded; three of them died, and the rest Omar cut down with the machine gun one by one.

The situation was calmer now, and the FBI swarmed into the mall to take down the rest of the intruders. Omar went back to Elizabeth to see her weeping and shaking all over.

"Liz, please don't cry. It's over."

The harder she tried to stop crying, the greater the sobs shook her body.

She was crying about the massacre of the innocents, she was mourning her failing marriage, and she was upset about the emptiness draining at the realization of how far away Omar was.

Omar held her hand and patted it tenderly. "There are moments when troubles enter our lives and we can do nothing to avoid them. And this too shall pass away. Breathe. Let go," he said soothingly.

"Don't touch me. I hate you. Stop saving me. I don't want your help." She snatched her hand away from his.

Whenever she seemed to be getting herself under control, a fresh bout of sobs would begin. She buried her face in her hands as agonizing sobs wracked her body to the core.

"I always remind myself that you are not mine to keep. Just when I think that it is impossible to love you any more, you prove me wrong," she said consumed with sobs.

"I want you because there's no one else like you. In my heart, we are wed. In my soul, you are mine. In your arms, I feel like I am home. Take me in your arms and never let me go." She opened her arms to him.

Broken yet full of love of her, he took her In his arms, wrapping his soul around her heart. She continued to cry in muffled sobs against his chest.

"Liz, please have mercy on a man who never stopped loving you. My life started when I met you. The first time I touched you, I knew I was born to be yours. I never thought I would be able to love anyone as much as I love you."

She disengaged herself from his arms and gazed into his eyes. She said through abundant tears covering her face, "I know that my love for you is wrong. It is dangerous; it will cause you trouble."

"If loving you is wrong, I never want to be right again. Come now — I will take you home." He helped her to her feet.

"My knees are weak and numb. I can't feel them."

"Can you walk leaning on me?"

"I am afraid I can't. Carry me to your car, please."

"The eye of the nation is on us right now."

"I don't care. Do you?"

"I don't care either."

He knew that he was the only one who could pick up her bleeding heart and take her somewhere safe and warm. He lifted her in his arms and headed to the entrance. Her head was on his chest, her luxurious hair falling in waves across his face and shoulders.

The moment was captured by an Associated Press photographer in a dramatic image that was beamed around the world.

The *Washington Post* would later write, "Elizabeth Rosh, the daughter of the president of the United States, was rescued by the ambassador of Egypt after an attack on Simon Mall. The ambassador cut seven gunmen down. He is hailed by the press as a hero."

The *Washington Post* continued: "The bombing and shooting of the Simon Mall resulted in 10 killed and 15 wounded. The attackers of the Simon Mall were from a local terrorist organization."

When Elizabeth arrived home, she found Hudson watching the TV and fuming with anger. He shouted at her, "How could you sympathize with an infidel, hijacker, kidnapper, bomber, terrorist, and non-believer?

Elizabeth was astounded to see such heartless remarks and false accusations.

"Is this very difficult for you to stomach?" Hudson said with animosity glaring from his eyes.

Elizabeth looked at him angrily and shouted at him, "Are you done?"

"Yes, I'm done."

"Shut up, big mouth. I'll make you pay for what you said." She shot him an indignant look and walked away.

CHAPTER 45

The financial crisis of 2007–2008 began with disastrous worldwide effects, first in America, then the rest of the world. Companies went bankrupt, banks failed, and people instantly lost their life savings. Poverty and starvation became real possibilities for everyone. The people panicked. Fear ruled. Governments seemed powerless against the worldwide economic collapse. The Great Depression had begun.

Hudson was always keen to make a little money on the side, so he invested a big deal of money in Enron Corporation, a huge American energy company based in Houston, Texas. Enron's staff of executives, however, used accounting loopholes and poor financial reporting to hide billions of dollars in debt from failed deals and projects. Enron shareholders filed a $40 billion lawsuit after the company's stock price, which achieved a high of $90.75 per share in mid-2000, plummeted to less than $1 by the end of November 2001. Enron filed for bankruptcy, and Senator Hudson lost most of his savings. Hudson had to get big loans from banks to continue Elizabeth's luxurious lifestyle and maintain the high expenses of his appearance; and he had to cover the high costs of his farm. But Hudson was soon unable to pay his huge debts to the banks. The banks were now closing in for the kill, and his only chance to save himself was to find someone who would buy his farm, pay off his creditors, and leave him with a little profit. Thank God he still has some shares in Cameron Matthew Corporation.

Hudson worked with his lawyer to identify which ones were priority debts. The lawyer made a list of all Hudson's creditors, and after days of thorough calculations, the lawyer concluded that three million dollars was now needed to cover the most urgent debts, which, if went unpaid, would possibly cause the creditors to take Hudson to court.

To Hudson, Elizabeth was a golden goose. He married her to become richer, more famous, and more powerful. He would ask her to help him out of debt.

At dinner one night, he asked her shyly, "Elizabeth, can you please lend me three million dollars?"

"What for?" Elizabeth said coldly, without lifting her eyes from her plate.

"I lost all my shares in Enron. I am in serious debt."

She remembered what he said to her when Omar saved her life at the mall. Hudson, her husband, didn't even care to welcome her safe return home but was rather furious and shouted at her, "How could you sympathise with an infidel, hijacker, kidnapper, bomber, terrorist, and non-believer?" She remembered how he'd mistreated Omar when she invited him to dinner.

She lifted her eyes from her plate and looked at him squarely. "What do you think I am, a gold mine?"

Senator Robert Hudson received a call in his office from his broker trading in Cameron Matthew Corporation stock.

"Senator Hudson?"

"Yes?"

"The founder of Cameron Matthew Corporation is frantically trying to sell all his shares because the corporation is going down. The corporation will file for chapter eleven bankruptcy very soon. I advise you to sell all your shares now."

"Okay, sell them now."

"Don't forget my commission."

Hudson said, "Of course. Just finish your job."

One week before the share price of the corporation collapsed, Hudson was able to sell all his shares. The stock tumbled in the following days, and Hudson saved two hundred thousand dollars on the sale.

It was the irony of fate that Mary Mackenzie also had shares in Cameron Matthew Corporation and that the same broker called her at her office.

"Miss Mary Mackenzie?"

"Yes."

"The Cameron Matthew Corporation is going down and will file for bankruptcy soon. I advise you to sell your shares now."

"Oh! Are you sure?

"All the shareholders I contacted during the past five days followed my advice and sold all their shares."

"Can you provide me with the names of those who sold their shares?"

The broker said, "I'm afraid I can't do that. The ethics of my profession prevents me from revealing my clients' names."

"You want me to sell all my shares yet you refuse to give me some names? I just want to be sure that the shareholders have truly sold their shares so I can follow suit."

"Well, two days ago I phoned Senator Robert Hudson to sell his shares. He saved two hundred thousand dollars on the sale."

"Ohio Republican Robert Hudson?" Mary exclaimed.

"Yes."

Mary said, "Thank you for the information. I refuse such cheating. Do not sell."

With a broad smile on her face, Mary put down the receiver. Many congressmen were corrupt and lobbyists. She knew already the names of twelve corrupted senators who were convicted during the last fifteen years. She had even exposed four of them. Hudson may have been an effective congressman, but he was not above the law. Mary muttered to herself, "Will Hudson be number thirteen? I should start digging on Hudson."

How could Hudson pay the three million debt that was due after a few months? If there had been an easy way out, he would have taken it, but there was none. He must come up with something.

Hudson spent weeks with his lawyer, plotting and scheming, but they came up with nothing. The debt was huge, and it was impossible for Hudson to repay the debt to the banks in due time.

There was one way for Hudson to collect cash. He would use his power as a congressman to collect cash, goods, and favours from businesspeople in return for his help. His loyalty could be bought for hard cash. Hudson sold his soul to the devil.

Alexandria County millionaire Harris Wilson visited Hudson in his office.

Wilson said, "As we agreed upon earlier, my company is to spend thousands of dollars to fix your leaky boat so you can sell it, and in return you help keep my company afloat."

"What was the favour you wanted from me?"

Wilson was amazed. "Have you forgotten our request so quickly? We developed Slowed-Rotor/Compound Technology, and we need the Federal Aviation Administration's approval. We needed a champion for our product line, and you stepped out to do it, remember!"

Hudson said, "Of course, of course. I will see to it."

Senator Hudson became an avid supporter of the technology which Wilson's company developed. He introduced legislation aimed at giving government contracts to the company and persuaded the administrator of the Federal Aviation Administration to attend a demonstration of the Slowed-Rotor/Compound Technology at an airport in Manassas.

When the son of contractor David Hanks faced a year in prison for drunken driving, Hanks turned to Senator Hudson, an old family friend. Hanks asked the senator if he would intercede to get his son moved from the county jail to a facility closer to his father's business so his son could get work release privileges.

Over breakfast at a restaurant, Hudson agreed to help. Hudson suggested, however, that they drive to his farm and look at some work he needed done. Over the next few months, Hanks would do at least thirty thousand dollars' worth of work for Hudson.

After a series of letters and phone calls from Hudson, Hanks son was transferred to a halfway house and allowed to spend his days working for the family company. In return, Hanks's company delivered tons of material to Hudson's farm and provided hundreds of hours of labour.

Hudson used his influence to steer almost five million dollars' worth of contracts to Green North America, a lobbying firm owned by his cousin Catherine Hudson and her associates. Hudson accepted bribery to pass laws, special tax cuts, and earmarks that benefited his cousin's firm, with no accountability to the public.

Hudson accepted a bribe of two hundred thousand dollars in gifts and loans in hopes of getting help for Moon Scientific Inc., a nutritional supplement maker. The company's owner gave Hudson an expensive Rolex watch and took him on a thirty-thousand-dollar shopping spree in New York, all in an effort to persuade him to help promote his products. Hudson accepted the loans and gifts as a sort of business arrangement.

The money Hudson collected from his customers, however, was not enough to cover the substantial amount of debt. He then thought of selling his farm. Hudson drove to the farm and met with Carlos, the farm manager.

"Carlos, I want to sell the farm. Find a buyer." Hudson demanded.

"Why do you want to sell the farm?"

"I'm facing a heavy debt, and I want to pay it on time."

Carlos said, "You don't have to. I can help you through my friends in Mexico. I have good connections there.

"How?"

Carlos said, "Mexico harbours violent organized criminal gangs. They traffic in illegal drugs, contraband, and arms. They murder people and launder their profits through regional money changers, banks, and local economic projects."

"What does that have to do with my farm?"

"They can take your farm as a good local economic project. Your farm can be used as a front to launder millions of dollars of the cartel's illicit profits. Your share will be in the millions, of course."

Hudson was amazed. "Explain further, please."

"We will turn your farm into a horse farm. We will buy American quarter horses to train, breed, and race as a disguise. But actually the farm will be used as a front for money laundering."

"And what about the costs needed?"

Carlos said, "The organization will be responsible for all the costs. Outward appearances. That's what we need from you."

After a few months, Hudson's horse farm was booming with business. Hudson was making waves with his million-dollar prize winnings and record-breaking bids at auction houses. But what seemed like a ranch filled with top mares was actually a front for a multimillion-dollar money-laundering scheme, orchestrated by Senator Hudson and one of the most dangerous Mexican drug cartels — Emmanuel Guerrera.

After this flourishing investment, Hudson was able to repay his debt to his creditors, and he still had some millions to play with.

CHAPTER 46

Mary was in a black mood because Omar had rejected her love. She sat in her office feeling the urge to pour out the vials of wrath on anyone who might dare provoke her to anger.

Mary found on her desk a memo from her secretary, reminding her of her daily appointments and the important events that would take place during the day. One of these events was the speech Senator Robert Hudson was going to deliver at the American Public Sector Anti-Corruption Conference. The speech was about credibility, transparency, and accountability.

"Oh, that's interesting," Mary said, turning on the TV.

Senator Robert Hudson opened his speech by saying, "I am honoured to have been invited to take part in this conference and to speak about the importance of ethical leadership in preventing misconduct and corruption.

"Most people are sick of the deception, cheating, and corruption. People don't know who or what to trust. There's clear evidence that congressional representatives and legislators everywhere are held in low esteem and are being criticized for failing to meet appropriate standards of conduct.

"People in Congress are expected to conduct themselves with integrity and transparency in all areas so the public can hold them accountable for their behaviour while holding office.

"Taking my office as an example, I am accountable to the Senate for the financial operations of the office. The Senate may review my budget as part of the annual review of the estimates of the government. An external auditor also audits the office's financial statements every year, and the results are tabled in the Senate as part of my annual report. I consider myself accountable to the public as well. To this end, I submit an annual report on the office's activities to the Speaker of the Senate for tabling in the Senate."

Mary was listening to Hudson's speech with amazement. The man was downright deceitful and misleading, yet he talked about integrity transparency, and accountability!

"Let today be the day I stop this imposter," she said, picking up the receiver.

"Senator Robert Hudson?"

Hudson said, "Yes."

"This is Mary Mackenzie. Do you have time for me?"

Uneasiness curdled his stomach. There was a moment of silence before he said, "Sorry, I'm quite busy … I can't talk to you. Sorry."

"I think you should do what I want. I get nasty when I am neglected."

"Are you threatening me?"

"You're buying yourself a piece of trouble, mister."

"I don't know what you're talking about."

"What I am talking about is a sentence of thirty years."

"Come to my office tomorrow at ten in the morning," he said after a moment's hesitation.

"No. It's you who will come to my office at ten tomorrow."

Hudson felt danger. He had to see Mary to know what she had in store for him.

When he went to see her, he sat in a chair facing her desk. Her glances at him were cruel and sharp. She looked at him like a wildcat wanting to scratch his face.

"What is this all about?" Hudson snarled.

"I admired your speech about integrity, transparency, and accountability. Did you really mean it about those moral issues or were you just misleading the people?"

Hudson stared at Mary with hatred livid in his eyes. "You have gone too far!" he said viciously.

"I sent a report to the Department of Justice and the FBI about your conspiracy, obstruction of justice, and securities fraud arising from your controversial sale of Cameron Matthew Corporation. You will be indicted on these charges, and the broker will be also indicted."

"I'm in the clear. You are nothing but a whore destroying other people's lives. You destroyed Elizabeth's marriage once, and now you are destroying it again." His face flashed with anger.

"I destroyed nobody's life," she said. "I am seeking the truth, and Roy betrayed Elizabeth when he got himself involved in money laundering."

"Get the fuck out of my way or else I'll—"

Mary interrupted. "When I learned that you sold your shares in Cameron Matthew Corporation, I probed further and discovered that you became a money launderer too, Senator Hudson. This is another charge you're going to pay for."

Hudson glared at Mary. Within a few minutes, he had been destroyed. This story would circulate. Before nightfall, everyone in the city would know about it.

"Stupid whore. Don't fuck with me. Mind your fucking business," he said, outraged.

"You can't use your public office as a trough to feed your personal appetite," Mary continued in cold anger. "I'm running a program in four days about your involvement in money laundry, conspiracy, and obstruction of justice."

"That will be the mistake of your life. I'll sue your ass for the next ten years." He looked like a wounded dog backed into a corner. "You don't mind ruining people, do you?" he said, feeling that fate was kicking him in the balls.

"The nation will be glad to get rid of an asshole like you," Mary said with a wicked smile.

"Fuck you. I can't stand your face." He rose from his chair and headed to the door.

Senator Hudson sat at the head of the long dining table, and Elizabeth sat at the other end of the table. They finished their dinner in silence, and then both went to bed. Elizabeth crawled onto the bed while Hudson sat down on the edge of the bed and stared at the floor.

Elizabeth slept for an hour. As usual, she had trouble sleeping. She tossed and turned in the bed, her sleep interrupted by memories of her moments with Omar. When she woke, she was startled to see Hudson still sitting on the edge of the bed and staring at the floor.

"What's up?" she said, feeling a sudden worry.

Hudson had to concentrate to focus his senses. But everything seemed blurred and distorted. He said after a short while, "The bastards are watching me real close. They launched a bunch of stupid allegations against me, none based on solid foundations."

"What allegations?"

"That I treaded my official office repeatedly for money, unlawfully sold my shares in Cameron Matthew Corporation, and used my horse farm as a front for money laundering."

"Who's after you, Hudson?"

"Mary Mackenzie."

"Mary Mackenzie! Mary Mackenzie again. I've been hurt before, and I don't want to be hurt again."

"Don't worry, darling. I'll stand and fight."

"Are you in the clear, Hudson?"

"Of course I am. Don't fear anything, sweetie."

Elizabeth remembered Roy and what happened to him as well as the misery he caused her. "Are these accusations, facts, or just rumours?" Elizabeth asked irritably.

"Just rumours, just rumours," he said with lying eyes.

"You must understand that Mary has access to federal investigators and to the Organized Drug Enforcement Task Force Program. They feed her with the results of their investigations and she disseminates the knowledge in her program. This is what makes her TV program a success."

Elizabeth sensed danger. Mary wouldn't have confronted Hudson if she had no solid evidences against him.

"She put a nail in the coffin of your career, Hudson. Your reputation is on the line now."

"Darling, don't say that, please. I assure you I am innocent."

"If Mary was right, Hudson, and you were lying to me, I'll never forgive you. I will file for a divorce on the grounds of lying and deception."

Hudson hadn't thought about divorce before, but now she had put it in his mind.

"Divorce. A word I won't permit — can't even take it seriously. You shouldn't take that step until the suspicion around me is cleared up." Sweat was trickling down his face.

Elizabeth could see the end of her second marriage. It was true that she didn't love Hudson and sexual resentment on her part had seriously threatened their marriage, but she insisted on keeping up appearances. She and Hudson were living a fake marriage for the cameras while growing increasingly distant in real life. The failure of her first marriage was a big scandal that rocked the nation and embarrassed her father and mother. And now she was going to face the same situation, with more embarrassment and more disappointment.

Hudson's future looked increasingly grim as evidence continued to mount against him every day. The newspapers were already releasing news about his using his horse farm as a front for money laundering and the illegal sale of his shares in Cameron Matthew Corporation.

After breakfast one morning, Elizabeth went to the living room to have tea and read the morning papers. She found herself fighting a mounting sense of panic when she read the following: "Hudson, a Republican close to the president and his son in law, faces a twelve-count indictment on charges of conspiracy, obstruction of justice, and securities fraud. The indictment depicted Senator Hudson as going out of his way to conceal the circumstances of the sale of all his shares in Cameron Matthew Corporation, a transaction that investigators say he made after learning that the corporation's founder was selling his own stock. The broker who provided Hudson with the information was also indicted. Senator Hudson was also indicted for fraud. He was using his horse farm as a front to launder millions of dollars of the cartel's illicit profits ..."

Elizabeth got mad. She was living with an imposter, a man who betrayed her trust. This marriage would destroy her image before the people and would threaten the political career of her father. Hudson had lied to her when he said that he was innocent and the accusations were only rumours. Roy, her first husband, cheated on her and was indicted for money laundering, but he killed himself to avoid the scandal. Hudson was indicted for money laundering and for fraudulent sale of stocks.

She was faithful to Roy and loved him, but he deceived her, humiliated her, and destroyed their marriage. She didn't love Hudson, but she had to marry him in order to have a meaningful life and have kids of her own. But sexual incompatibility was always there to make her life with Hudson feel cold and dry. And that was not his fault but hers. Her heart was captivated by another man she'd loved deeply from the first moment she saw him.

But still, Hudson owed her a lot because she kept her marriage working in spite of this emotional rejection between them. This was a sacrifice on her part because she could have asked for a divorce since the beginning, but she accepted this dry life in order not to embarrass her father. The price, however, was too high: fraud, deception, and betrayal of her trust in him.

Her marriage to Hudson was like a business arrangement that would wind down after the business was finished. Well, the business was over!

Elizabeth remembered that this was the time Mary's program aired. She quickly turned on the TV to see if Mary had anything to say about Hudson.

Mary was reporting all right: "Senator Hudson, the owner of a Virginia farm for breeding horses for racing, was found using the farm as a front to launder millions of dollars of the cartel's illicit profits. Using his economic smarts, Hudson moved the farm profits in an effort to make them seem like legitimate earnings. He hid the root of money gained through illegal means in order to avoid the law. He siphoned off around one hundred million dollars from the profits of his farm into a Monaco bank and several other small American banks. The collapse of the Monaco bank and the small American banks highlighted Hudson's connection to several accounts. Senator Robert

Hudson was also indicted for his illegal sale of his shares of Cameron Matthew Corporation stock."

The news caused a sharp twist in Elizabeth's heart. She was furious. She searched for Hudson and found him in the study, leaning on the fireplace and holding his head in his hands. She said, fuming, "You lied to me. You said that all these accusations were untrue."

"I know you are sad and hurt. I have done you an injury, but one soon forgives a grievance if he loves. And you do love me."

"No, I don't love you, and you know it."

"Love is happiness given back and forth. You didn't give me love. I was patient with you, dear, so please be patient with me in this bad situation. I need your help."

"Our love was fake and for keeping up appearances, nothing more. I felt nothing toward you. You have really hurt me. You are heartless and uncaring. I must take a decision." She blushed furiously.

"I am not a saint; I am not perfect. I have flaws. But please calm down. They have nothing against me."

"You live ankle deep in shit. I was crazy ever to get involved with you. You are so low. I should have known you were trouble. You are better off without me."

"Hey, don't be so hard on me. You ought to stand by me in such an awkward situation." He swallowed hard.

Maddened by despair and grief, she retorted, "Your heart is deceitful and sick. I knew that I married the wrong person. A man with no conscious who only looks after wealth, fame, and power, regardless of what morals and ethics imply. You humiliated my father and me before the people. It's not fair that I made a life with a man who is deceitful and betrayed my trust in him. How can I move past this? File for divorce, of course."

Hudson said, "You're splitting up with me?"

"You are not good enough. I can't live with an imposter."

"Don't be so mean. Stand by me instead of blaming me. I'm trying to respond to the bad situation and come to a conclusion as to what needs to be done."

His deceit maddened her. Elizabeth took a pace towards him and slapped him so hard that her own palm stung. "It's more than I can handle. I have no need for you. Take your ugly self away. I'll divorce you. Get out of my home. You defile my house."

Hudson could see in Elizabeth's face the growing realization of how he had lied, how he had betrayed her. Veins swelled in his forehead and throat.

Elizabeth called her butler. "Peter, take out this garbage. It smells bad."

Peter escorted Hudson to the door and slammed it in his face.

CHAPTER 47

Senator Hudson moved to his old house and waited for a resolution to materialize out of nothing. In the spacious living room, he paced back and forth, his mind in turmoil. For a moment, he couldn't think, breathe, feel, or hear. When he could breathe again, he also started sweating, and the numbness wore off enough for a sharp pain to knife through his stomach.

Hudson sat in his study contemplating the gloomy future. His job was on the line now. He must handle the situation delicately. The last thing he wanted was a public scandal.

Mary Mackenzie had exposed him to the public through her program, *Corruption in the Nation*. She talked about his money laundering and about his conspiracy, obstruction of justice and securities fraud, all linked to his sale of shares of the Cameron Matthews Corporation.

The vicious media followed suit and tore him to pieces. His name was already in the papers, *Time*, and the *Washington Post*. This would surely get him arrested. People would watch as they led him away in shackles.

Hudson called his lawyer. "You're the professional — how does the case shape up in your eyes?"

"You are facing serious charges. Many legal documents need to be drafted before going to court. I am determining now which legal tactics and strategy will be employed and the overall goal of the case."

Now the president was mad. The Republicans were embarrassed and felt betrayed. The Democrats smelled blood.

A serious question arose in his mind: how would his conviction, if it occurred, affect his standing in the House? The House Ethics Committee could recommend reprimand, censure, or expulsion!

"Oh God!" he muttered. "I would be required to come forward to the well of the House and be denounced before the entire nation."

After two nights of thinking, Hudson was drained and weakened. Things were getting out of hand. Things were hopeless.

Long hours had passed, and Hudson had no idea what time it was when the doorbell rang. He looked up, startled. When he opened the door, two police officers entered. One of them addressed Senator Hudson: "I am placing you under arrest, Senator Hudson, for charges of bribery, tax evasion, and racketeering." Hudson's face turned ashen with disbelief.

Hudson was arrested by warrant and taken into custody. The amount of bail was ascertained and a court date set. In the district court, Hudson was charged with criminal offences but was released on bail until he next appeared in court.

While on bail, Hudson thought a lot about Mary and Omar. Elizabeth's love for Omar ruined his sexual relations with her and wounded his pride without repair. As for Mary, she'd ruined his political life. He would be thrown in jail for decades.

His body was numb and in pain. He said a prayer, the first in decades. Then he resumed his non-stop cursing of Omar and Mary.

Hudson swallowed a half bottle of whiskey. The alcohol calmed him for a while, but a wave of nausea rippled through his chest. He quickly lay still on the floor. He breathed deeply, and the pounding started at the top of his head. He thought of Omar and Mary and the pounding intensified. He cursed Omar and Mary incessantly, also cursing himself for his lack of self-control.

"Hellfire is more torturing! The damage I did to myself is irreparable!" he shouted in agony.

Everything was an open game but his integrity. His ass was on the line, but he would walk away from this cleanly. A thought that had been in the back of his mind suddenly came into focus.

"Damn it!" he uttered under his breath. "A bullet could have ended it all. A bullet now could settle the whole thing, quiet the gossip, remove the doubts, and my whole business could go forward."

He had no choice. Omar and Mary had been the cause of it all. He would kill Omar and Mary, and his neck would be protected.

Hudson reached for the telephone and dialed Carlos's number.

"Can your organization help us find a hitman?"

Carlos said, "Of course. Our cartel has its own hitmen. They are the best in their field."

"Omar is dangerous and has to be disposed of quickly. We must get him out of the way. We have to get this settled before it gets out of hand. Put Omar's and Mary's names on the hit list. Take them down."

The Mexican cartel hired a hit man by the name of Orlando Martini. He was ruthless and crazy. He killed just to see if his gun worked. Orlando Martini was a man of many names, faces, and languages, an assassin who struck quickly and left no trail, a fastidious killer who roamed the world but could never be found.

Orlando was tall and broad of shoulder. He was sullen, hard eyed, and surly. He had little to say to anyone, and was more inclined to settle matters with a gun than with words. He was utterly cold-blooded, and would kill a man quickly and with little excitement.

Orlando was a superlative shot. At one hundred yards, without a scope, using just the iron sight, he could consistently hit objects that others could barely see with the naked eye. He boasted that he had more than one hundred confirmed kills. Orlando was also an expert in car bombing.

Hudson attended twelve sessions in court, during which he tried to argue along the way. He mounted a loud, sometimes comic, and frequently vulgar defense. He continually argued that he was the victim of a government vendetta. He argued that witnesses had lied under pressure from prosecutors.

The House later voted 420 to 1 to strip Hudson of his seat.

After a raucous trial lasting about four months, Hudson was convicted on twelve counts. In handing out the sentence, the judge said that Hudson seemed to believe that he was above the law and that he had no respect for government and lied in order to save himself. Hudson was convicted and sentenced to fifteen years in jail and a one-million-dollar fine.

His stockbroker was found guilty too, of perjury, obstruction, and conspiracy.

Elizabeth began divorce proceedings before Hudson was sentenced to prison.

CHAPTER 48

Hudson was serving fifteen years in jail for his crimes. Elizabeth was a free woman after her divorce was finalized, and it was her right to start anew. She needed to organize her thoughts and determine the features of her new life, a life devoid of loss and regrets.

Elizabeth felt a terrible need to see Omar. He was a part of her thoughts for the future and could help her design a future of comfort and love.

It was an autumn day in New York when Elizabeth called Omar.

The sound of her voice did to him what it always did. He took a shaky breath. "Hello, Liz."

"Are you all right?"

"I'm fine, thank you."

"I want to see you."

"Okay."

We must talk. Meet me at the park.

"Sure."

The park was shady with many tall trees. The trees were a magnificent display of yellow, orange, and red. The leaves fell gently in the breeze. It was a sight so touching in its majesty.

The driver's door swung open. Omar's breath jammed in his lungs as Liz got out of the car. Her legs were long and lovely beneath a mid-length skirt, her glossy blonde hair pushed back by sunglasses. She looked stunning and gorgeous.

He was wearing grey slacks, a blue shirt, and a blazer. His hair was longer than it had been before, he had a tan, and he was more handsome than ever.

"Please, my love, allow me to take you in my arms. I want to feel that you are alive and safe." He smiled and held out his arms to her.

She moved into his arms smoothly, and he took her in his arms gently, enfolding her against him. She pressed her head against his shoulder and settled into his warm, safe embrace, trying to block out all her fears. They stayed that way for several minutes, listening to each other's breathing.

Her face lit up. Her soul floated high above earth. She could feel the quickening of his heartbeat merging with her own, and inhaled the strong masculine smell of him. She knew that he was the only man who could fly her away to a place where nothing bad could ever happen.

She whispered, "Take away my sadness."

"I want to spend the rest of my life with you. I want you to bring up my children." He kissed her hair.

It was difficult for her to breathe after she heard his marriage proposal.

"Is that a proposal?" She smiled demurely.

He held her tighter. "You bet it is. Will you marry me? I don't want to live with you in sin."

She didn't want to lose him, but she couldn't bring herself to say yes.

She laughed and tried to change the subject. "In your religion, kissing a strange woman is forbidden, isn't it?"

"Taking you in my arms like that is a sin unless we are married. But I just can't help it. May Allah forgive me. Your love runs in my veins. What I am to do without you, I cannot imagine." He again kissed her hair.

There were things she wanted to tell him, but she knew they would hurt him. Would he be sensible enough to understand?

"Even as I hold you, I am letting you go," she said, shaking in his arms.

Omar cupped her face in his hands and looked her in the eyes.

"I'm not feeling precisely myself lately. I need some time to get my soul a rest. Would you be kind enough to understand?" Her eyes filled with tears. She buried her face in his chest and said softly, "I will make it easier for you to leave by making you hate me a little."

"You play heavy on my heart," he said, feeling a lump forming in his throat.

"I'm afraid you don't understand."

"What Is it that I don't understand? Is there any hope for us, you and me?"

She closed her eyes and breathed deeply in his arms. Minutes passed without a word.

"It was wonderful knowing you. Thank you for these moments," she said as if apologizing.

"I know what you have been through. I understand," he said tenderly.

"Hold me as close as you possibly can." She knew the severe impact of her next words on him.

Thoughts were struggling in her mind. Wasn't it ironic that she found herself running from the thing that she desired the most? Why did she run from love? Maybe she was afraid she couldn't keep it or didn't deserve it.

Dare she risk her heart on a man whose religion was condemned of terrorism! Omar's love was dangerous because it represented the unknown. She was afraid of sailing into the unknown.

Being in love with a Muslim was putting her future in jeopardy. She didn't want to be dominated by imposing barriers on her under the cover of Islam.

He sensed disappointment and frustration coming. He held her tightly, trying to escape from the worries clouding his mind.

"Elizabeth, what happened? Talk to me."

She took a deep breath and said the most difficult words she'd ever had to speak. "I can't marry you now. I'm just not ready."

"And when might you be ready?" he asked, scared.

"Omar my love, don't push me too far, please."

She was scared to accept the idea of marrying him, especially after the failed marriages she had been through. She looked up into his eyes and saw the hurt and pain written on his face. She would have given anything to take away that expression. She quickly looked away, unable to meet his gaze.

"I want to live happily with you, have many children with you, and grow old with you. To tell you every day how much I love you. I love you, Liz. When I love, I love forever." He felt that he was losing her.

"I was foolish to think we were made for each other," he continued. "Maybe I am not good enough for you. I know that this is your world and I have no place in it. You are a real part of the Rosh family — way out of my reach." He felt as if he'd been trodden into mud by the feet of men and horses.

"Oh, please don't say that. You know how much you mean to me. I am backing off because I love you. Your love causes much pain, so much heartache. I don't know if I can take much more," she said after a moment of silence.

"So where does that leave us?" he asked, disappointed.

"Omar, you are a very religious man. I know what it means for a modern woman to marry a Muslim man. I am afraid of the limits, chains, and strict instructions that you may impose upon me. Islam has its own morals and value system, an abyss in which I will be kept away from society. I don't want any chains that might disturb my future. There are sacrifices to be made in being a Muslim in America. Islam would complicate my life because it is not like Judaism and Christianity, part of the American scene. It would alienate me from my family and isolate me from the community. My faith is not sufficiently strong to withstand these pressures. I am sorry, darling. I was just trying to explain the worries I feel about the love we have for each other."

But she knew what she felt. The only thing she wanted was to see her love intact.

"Come to my world. Come to the world of real freedom," he said firmly.

"Freedom?"

"Revelations support man along his earthly journey. They direct his attention to the heavenly origin of everything, the Supreme Power. They help him uncover the divine part within himself because it is that part of man that is capable of freeing him from illusions. Muslims consider themselves free when they live according to the divine law of the Koran. Allah is life, and only through Him does man live. If people abide by the Koran and the teachings of the Prophet, they will undergo a spiritual transformation and become close to Allah. This is the real freedom. Allah is the way, the order, and the supreme. Through devotion in worshipping Allah, they become in Him and He becomes in them."

"I'm not sure about that," she said, puzzled.

"If you read the Koran, you will be free from illusions and will realize the real meaning of life."

He continued, feeling sorry for himself. "I think you still love me, but we can't escape the fact that I'm not enough for you. I knew this was going to happen. So I'm not blaming you for your worries. I'm not angry either. I should be, but I'm not. I just feel pain. A lot of pain."

He took her hands in his, lifted them to his lips, and kissed them.   He looked intently into her eyes and said, "If you have the guts to do something, then you'd better be strong enough to face the consequences. Our love is commitment, loyalty, patience, persistence. To refrain from such strong bonds is weakness and a breach of trust. That's all I got to say to you."

"I understand that Egyptian diplomats and men of the army do not marry foreigners," she said, as if finding an excuse for rejecting him.

"I'll quit my job in a year or two. I'm not really rich as you are. I'm just well off. I can afford a good life for you. I own a large farm planted with orchards and vegetables. I raise Arabian horses and sell them in auctions. The farm and its grand villa overlook the Mediterranean Sea. I am sure you will love the place."

Silence reigned between them for a moment. Then he said sadly, "Can it really mean that we shall never meet again. Is this all there is to be?"

"Nothing remains as it was. If you know this, you can begin again." She was pitying him and herself.

"You do not know what it's like. Loving you is like ripping out my heart. I deserve the pain I feel," he said with a broken heart.

"Omar my love, please try to understand. There is love in holding and there is love in letting go."

He wanted to convince her that he was the right choice, her destiny, but if he truly were to have a future with her, it had to be her decision.

"When I give you my heart, I want you to be willing to accept it," he said, kissing her forehead.

"I just want to be sure marriage is the right thing. I just need a little more time."

He pulled her into his arms. She buried her face in his shoulder and tried to control her emotions. He rubbed her back gently.

"Take all the time you need. I can wait. My love feeds on your love. Everything carries me to you, and as long as we live, my love for you will never fade away."

She started sobbing. His arms tightened, and he touched her lips with his fingers. Tears dripped down her cheeks. His fingers reached up, catching them.

"I still wake with your name on my lips every morning. There was nowhere I could go that wouldn't be you." He kissed her tears away.

"I must go," she said disengaging herself from his arms.

"I will marry you if it is the will of God." He started walking her to her car.

"I don't know what to believe or not to believe. I don't know what the truth is anymore." She said wiping out her tears.

"Seek truth by the light of your inner conscious. Don't give up; something may yet arise to make you see the light. Put your trust in God."

"Yes, we'll leave it all to God."

"Everything that you see happening in yourself and in the world certainly has a reason, but the reason is not to be understood by human logic, as it is based on divine wisdom. We must believe in Allah's absolute wisdom."

He hesitated a second and then said, "Liz, the time has come to tell you that I shall be returning to Egypt."

"Why?" she said, stunned. "How can it be that you are going away? If you leave me, my heart will die. I need you here. While thinking about my future with you, I want you to be near me and keep me close. Oh God, why is all this happening to me?" She began sobbing again.

"It is better this way. I have washed my hands of America. I must leave. I don't want to live in a war zone. I'm tired of fighting, explaining, defending. I long for my house on the deserted beach, with no phones and no people."

"It is torture without you. Miles between us will keep our love apart." She realized that she couldn't live without him.

"Please don't say that. If there is distance between us, just listen closely and you will hear the beating of my heart."

He took a deep breath and then said while looking at the trees and greenery before him, "I want to retire so I can meditate on my farm. My connection with Allah through prayer and meditation always dispels feelings of loneliness and isolation. It makes me feel painfully alive. I want to breathe in the fresh air, not the stale air in that horrible atmosphere. On my farm, I will shut out all external objects. I will cast away desire, fear, and anger. I will purify my heart from the passions of worldly life. I will focus on Allah by reciting His name day and night."

"Liz! There is something I want to give you." He took a cell phone from his pocket. "This is a special cell phone. It is a new technology that can record my every movement. You can reach me on this number in troubled time."

"Do you expect troubles?" she asked worriedly.

"Life throws us unexpected circumstances. Under dire circumstances, I may need to call you. Consider this matter a top secret. Don't disclose it to anybody. You can also find my farm address in the phone memory.

"Now you go," he said. "My heart is filled with hope that one day you will be mine. It is only in my world that you can breathe." He opened the car door for her.

Suddenly, they heard the sound of a gunshot. Omar saw a bullet hitting the car's roof and then changing direction to rip through Elizabeth's arm. Elizabeth fell unconscious to the ground. Omar dropped to his knees and put a hand on Elizabeth's heart. It was still beating! Around the bullet hole in the arm, the cloth of the blouse was smouldering. Omar watched the blood spurt out of Elizabeth's arm. Within a minute, two of his bodyguards, who had been hiding behind the trees guarding him, arrived quickly and called an ambulance. Within several minutes, Elizabeth was in a hospital to receive the appropriate treatment.

Amanda Rosh was in New York at that time. She rushed to see her daughter as soon as she heard the news. There was no mistaking that Elizabeth was badly shot in her right arm and weak from loss of blood. On the bed, Elizabeth looked like a pale shadow lying on white sheets. The doctors, however, reassured Amanda that Elizabeth would regain consciousness soon and be all right.

Amanda found Omar sitting by Elizabeth's bed, burying his head in her palm. His whole body was shaking and couldn't control his tears. Amanda sat silently on a chair behind Omar, waiting for her daughter to regain consciousness.

Omar begged softly, "Liz, answer me. Liz – please Liz."

Her eyelids fluttered but did not open. He leaned over her and stroked her face gently, whispering, "Liz."

Her eyes opened, and she sighed, "Omar! I'm happy to see you. Oh, darling, I love you so much. Why does love seem to hurt so much?"

"Rise and shine, my love." Abundant tears rolled down his face.

She opened her arms for him; he embraced her gently so as not to hurt her. His body was shaking uncontrollably. He was weeping.

"Let your tears come. Let them water your soul. I love you so much." She was weeping with him.

"I would rather die than see you hurt." He burst into tears. "I'm sorry. It's all my fault. You got hurt because you were near me. My love for you is dangerous. We must stay apart."

"Don't walk out of my life, please."

"You deserve a chance to be happy. I don't want to hurt you so please forget about me. I should suffer my pain alone."

"Torture me no longer. It is for you alone that I am living."

"Just get well, my love. I loved you as the very light of God. I loved everything in you; I have lived for you alone." He was weeping in her arms. He held her closely as they both cried.

"The pain I put you through. I did you wrong by loving you," he said through his sobs. "I never meant to hurt you. I will never be the one who hurt you. Show me where it hurts. I can kiss away the pain.

"Am I the right person for you, Liz? My love is dangerous; it has caused you so much pain. What am I to you except pain?"

"You are my love, my hope, my hero. It's hard not having you around and knowing you aren't next to me. Save me the torture of waking up day after day, knowing I can never have you."

"I would die for you. I would kill for you. I would give my life for you."

She held him close and whispered, "Pray for me."

He said through his tears, "I seek forgiveness from Allah, who is there is no god save He, the knower of the unknown and the known, the mighty, the wise, the oft-forgiving, the merciful, the owner of glory and grace; and I turn repentant unto Him. May Allah facilitate for you, Elizabeth Rosh, the doing of good, wherever you may stay. May your days be blessed with happiness and hope."

Tears of worry and joy sprang to Amanda's eyes. Tears of worry because of her daughter's disappointment in her two previous marriages. And tears of joy to see how a dead heart can be reborn. She could see clearly how much Omar's love had taken Elizabeth's heart to lofty peaks. Amanda was seeing, feeling, and experiencing the power of love. Now she was confident that the dead heart of Elizabeth could live again.

The strong love bond she witnessed between Elizabeth and Omar helped her understand how deep love can amend and reform. She deciphered that the power of love was stronger than anything else that existed. Without love, the earth is a tomb. The love she saw in the hearts of Elizabeth and Omar could enlighten the whole world. The way of peace was the way of love. Love was the greatest power on the planet. It conquered all things.

"I am afraid I have to go." Omar said, disengaging himself tenderly from Elizabeth's arms.

"Omar, please be careful." She was extremely worried.

"Don't worry — I'm a survivor, remember? Now relax and get some sleep. I'll see you soon." He kissed her hair and forehead.

On his way to the door, he saw Amanda sitting in a chair. Omar nodded a salute as he neared Amanda. She nodded back.

Amanda stood and took Omar aside. "Omar, can I have a word with you?"

"Of course." Tears were still covering his face.

"Why can't you love the right woman? What is so wrong with you that you rush into situations to which you are manifestly unsuited, which will hurt you and others?"

"I'm loyal to the love of my life. The only love my heart knew. My destinies are guided by my loyalties. Those loyalties are my life, my religion, my reason for living."

"I simply don't want you to get involved with her. You will both be hurt."

"We are bound together with the love of God. You don't know what it's like! You have no idea what I'm going through. You don't have a clue how much this hurts. I know it's hard for us to be together, but I just want to tell you that even though we cannot be together, we will never ever be apart, for the love that I have for her will always grow stronger, as long as I live." Sobs were rocking his body.

Amanda kept looking at him with eyes filled with tears. She felt sincerity in his words and a loyalty to his beloved that deeply touched her heart.

Omar felt something mount and swell within him, a tide of fierce, uncontrollable anger. "She took a bullet meant for me. How can I accept that?" I am here to protect her, not to see her hurt. Someone is after me." He spoke with anguish. "I will kill the assassin. He is my meat. But first I'll beat him and smash his bones with my own hands. And I'm going to like doing of it." Omar's eyes were red and inflamed. "I'll get him now – right now!" Omar shouted while leaving the room.

Elizabeth called to her mother, "Mother, has Omar left?"

"Yes, darling."

"I feel so sad and lonely. I feel a world of gloom upon my heart, a solitude, a chill." Elizabeth felt crushed and defeated.

Amanda's cell phone rang. It was the president. "Amanda, the hospital told me that Elizabeth is going to be okay. Has she regained consciousness?"

"Yes."

"Can she talk now?"

"Not now, they gave her a strong sedative."

"This man is evil. He is taking Elizabeth to a dangerous road that has no end. He has ruined her life with Hudson."

Amanda's reply to her husband was amazing, "John, overcome evil with good, falsehood with truth, and hatred with love. This is the way of peace. Love is the truth that sets us free. All works of love are works of peace. We don't need bombs and guns to destroy, to bring peace – just to get together, to love one another, and we will be able to overcome all the evil that is in the world. Yes, John, the basis of world peace is the teaching that runs through almost all the great religions of the world. "Love thy neighbour as thyself."

"Amanda, are you all right?" the present asked, amazed.

Amanda turned off her cell phone without answering and headed towards Elizabeth's bed. She sat by the bed caressing Elizabeth's hair, waiting for her to wake up.

Omar stepped down onto the street. His cell phone rang. It was one of his bodyguards. "I think they are after you, sir," the man said.

"How do you know that?"

"Two hours ago, we spotted through binocular from another building a massive stranger standing in the middle of your room with a Mauser equipped with a silencer. We have pictures of him, sir."

"Do you know his identity?"

"Yes, sir. He's Hispanic. We traced him and know where he lives."

"Is he the one who tried to shoot me down in the park?"

"Yes, sir."

"Have you got his name?"

"Orlando Martini."

"I want all the information about him on my desk tomorrow."

"Yes, sir."

Mary Mackenzie received death threats through e-mails, letters, and telephone calls. Mary called 911 to report the death threats. The police investigated the death threats but were unable to discover the criminal. However, the investigation remained open and ongoing.

There had been more threats during the day, promising a mass shooting if Mary didn't cancel her program defaming Senator Hudson. Mary was forced to cancel the program because of security fears.

There appeared to be no suspects and no leads at the moment. The reporters buzzed around Mary's apartment and around the TV building like a swarm of bees.

Mary spent long hours in the police station, discussing how to protect herself at home and at work.

"We expect to be notified in advance of all travel plans so that we can arrange security," the police officer demanded.

"You mean you plan to escort me each time I leave the city?"

"Yes, that's my plan. I will assign two more cops as bodyguards, and I want access to your apartment."

It was dark now, almost time to escort Mary home. She had two agents as bodyguards following her in a police car.

Mary got into her car and inserted the key into the ignition. The engine started and roared as she gunned it. Suddenly, the car flipped in a violent somersault and landed upside down. The car was a fireball, roaring away with flames devouring it. Thick, heavy smoke billowed from the fireball, and spread to devour the police car. Mary was blown to bits by a car bomb, as were the police officers.

The news of Mary's death spread like wildfire. Mary Mackenzie was dead. Her death highlighted the failure of officials to respond promptly to death threats.

When the president of the United States learned about her death, he shouted, "Mary Mackenzie is dead! I just can't believe it."

In her room at the hospital, Elizabeth flicked the remote control and saw her father addressing the nation. The president looked sad. He looked deep into the camera and explained to the American people the shocking events of the previous night.

The president launched into the achievements of Mary in her field and called her a towering legend. The president explained that he had ordered an immediate thorough investigation, saying that those responsible would be brought to justice.

"Oh God. She was blown to pieces and killed instantly," Amanda said, sounding terrified.

"She was an embarrassment," Elizabeth retorted.

"The people are shocked," Amanda said.

Elizabeth said with relief, "Yet many of them are happy. Mary is gone."

Omar felt sorry for Mary. In spite of her arrogance, lust, and egoism, she was the one who offered him real help. She introduced him to the American people, and the result was overwhelming. Now the American people knew the truth.

His consolation was that she was killed instantly. She did not suffer. He knew she did not suffer.

CHAPTER 49

Omar found on his desk at the embassy an envelope containing all the information about the assassin. The assassin lived in a ground-floor apartment overlooking a small garden in a poor neighbourhood.

It was midnight when Omar turned the ignition key of his car. The engine roared, and his feet pressed the accelerator against the floor. He jammed the gearshift into drive; the car bolted forward. He shouted in anger, "I will finish off this Orlando fast. Oh, no. I will beat him to death first and then finish him off with a bullet in the centre of his head."

Omar's cell phone rang. "Sir, the assassin's apartment is empty. He is shopping in a nearby market."

All was silence. Omar put his ear to the door and listened. There was no sound. He turned the knob. The door opened easily, and he let it swing wide, standing well out of line. He stepped inside and closed the door after him. There was no one in the room. There was a table with some dirty dishes, where a hasty meal had clearly been eaten. The floor was dirty, with scraps of food lying around. Omar decided to wait. He hid behind a curtained window watching the road. When Orlando appeared on the road, Omar changed position and hid behind the door.

The hitman opened the door and put the groceries he'd bought on a table. The door slammed shut behind him. He turned back to see Omar standing in the middle of the room staring right at him. The assassin stared at Omar, frozen.

It didn't take Orlando long to see that Omar was a hard character and a fighting man. Death was in the air. The assassin felt that he could reach out and touch it.

"Who are you?" the assassin asked.

"I am the man who will decide your fate. I've come for you, Orlando. I've come to kill a mean murderer who shot a helpless woman. I'll gut you like a fish. I'll pull out your insides and make you eat them. The last sound you hear will be your own scream."

"I will gut you from neck to belly. I will tear you limb from limb," Orlando said, laughing aloud.

Orlando's neck was thick, his chest broad and massive. He did not rush or leap. He walked right to Omar.

Lithe and broad-shouldered, Omar stood tall while waiting for Orlando. His powerful shoulders and powerful hands and arms spoke of years of training in the gym. Omar was built for speed. Omar suddenly punched Orlando in the face, and Orlando felt the bones crush under his skull. Orlando staggered back, moaning with pain. Omar stepped in and threw punches with both hands, left and right blows that cut and chopped like meat cleavers. After the terrible beating, Orlando's brain was singing with a strange noise and his blood seemed to drum in his veins. Orlando tottered and fell back half-conscious on the floor.

After half an hour, Orlando opened his eyes to darkness. He stared around, uncomprehending what had happened to him. After long minutes, he realized that he had brutally beaten to near death. Orlando, however, seemed still to feel that some giant was standing close by, waiting for him to wake up in order to smash his bones again and again.

"Get to your feet," Omar ordered. The man staggered to his feet, leaning heavily on the table.

Omar's left hand shot up suddenly, and his fist caught Orlando's jaw. The blow was vicious, unexpected. Orlando head jerked back and Omar threw a left hook short and hard with his right, then followed through with a severe punch that flattened Orlando's nose and showered him with blood. Omar then struck left and right to the body, then left and right to the chin. Orlando fell to the ground and lay still, his head bleeding profusely.

After a few minutes, Orlando got back on his feet again, feeling terrible pain. The man stared at Omar in agony. However, he had the guts to say," I didn't want to hurt her; I only wanted to kill you."

"Oh! Are you so brave? I have come to break your bones. After I break your bones, I'll blow your head off with my gun."

Omar hooked a left and felt the fist sink into Orlando's body. He then punched Orlando, stabbing left. Then his right went down the line again, and blood streamed from the cut cheek. Omar shoved Orlando back and smashed both hands into his body, then rolled aside and spilled him with a rolling hip lock. Omar continued by stabbing a left to the face, followed by an upper cut that took Orlando to the floor.

Omar looked around and found a massive police stick hanging on the wall. He took it and began smashing Orlando's bones with it. The massive hits were directed to the shoulders, knees, wrists, ribs, and skull.

Orlando realized that he was dying, and he groaned, "Have mercy on me. I don't want to die."

"Were you behind the killing of Mary Mackenzie?" Omar shouted at him.

Orlando said, shaking all over from severe pain, "Yes".

Omar yelled at him, "Who hired you! Who is behind you?"

Orlando said, "I don't betray my friends. I can't tell you more than that."

"Oh yeah? Then take this." A massive blow with the police stick broke the bones of Orlando's shoulder, followed by another one to break his ribs into small pieces.

Orlando yelling in the agony of death, "Okay, okay. I was hired by a Mexican cartel."

"Who is your link here?"

"Carlos."

"Who is Carlos?"

"The manager of Senator Robert Hudson's farm."

Omar stood for moment looking at Orlando and then snatched the gun from the holster at his hip and aimed at Orlando's head, firing several bullets.

The FBI men came late to see Orlando lying on the ground, his shirt darkening with blood. Blood was streaming from every part of his face. His lips were shreds, and a huge blue lump concealed both eyes. His face was scarcely human.

The killing of Orlando in this brutal way was the talk of the nation for weeks.

From his office at the embassy, Omar called his friend Walker, the director of the Office of the Military Affairs at the CIA.

"Walker, this is Omar. There is no need searching for the assassin. I found him, and I killed him."

"Killed him! Are you crazy, Omar? We have laws here. You don't have the right to take the law into your own hands. How could you get yourself into such trouble?"

"The assassin would have stopped at nothing to fulfil his aim. I had to find him at all costs and eliminate him."

"We could have arrested him if you informed us about his hiding place," Walker said. "Taking the law into your hands is a serious charge in the United States."

"He made a terrible mistake. He hit Elizabeth instead of me."

"Oh! A personal Vendetta, eh?"

"That's all I have to say to you, Walker."

As soon as Omar hang up the phone, Walker called the president and told him what Omar had just said to him.

The president answered, "Now the time is ripe to take necessary action."

CHAPTER 50

President Rosh asked the secretary of state to seek from Egypt a waiver so that Omar could be judged by the court of the United States.

Egypt announced, however, that it would not take any steps of waiving diplomatic immunity for its ambassador because the killing was in self-defense. Consequently, the ambassador was not by any means liable to any sort of investigations.

Egypt stressed the fact that Under the Vienna Convention, no nation could force a ranking diplomat to appear in court, either on criminal or civil charges, unless the diplomat's government agreed to waive immunity. The American police should have protected the Egyptian ambassador from any danger. However, the assassin targeted the ambassador on American land. The assassin was still on the loose and had to be stopped. When the Egyptian ambassador killed him, it was legitimate self-defense.

The White House and the State Department hadn't welcomed the announcement and had instructed the attorney for the District of New York to press on with an investigation.

The district attorney had taken no chances. He prepared the case against Omar with meticulous care. He put his assistants to work assembling evidence, cleaning up every loose end, cutting off each legal avenue of escape that Omar's attorney might attempt to explore. The district attorney informed the State Department that there was ample evidence to charge Omar. Possible charges included first-degree murder and deliberate manslaughter.

They were on to Omar now. They aimed at prosecuting him. They would put him behind bars for killing a killer. Omar's mind was racing, desperately exploring every possible avenue of escape. There was no room for error. One mistake and the whole plan would fall apart.

Omar contacted the Egyptian authorities and discussed with them all the possibilities that might happen to him in the future. He then summoned his assistants and ordered them to undertake important secret tasks. The trial would be held in New York City Justice Court. There was a public garage one mile away from the court. He gave instructions to his associates to park his car there with a bag in its trunk, containing a military uniform, a ballistic bulletproof vest, a sniper rifle, a machine gun, a machine pistol, a battle knife, and a climbing rope. Omar would fit the parts of the unassembled weapons together when needed. His assistants were also given the task of facilitating shore leave.

After a day's work at the consulate, Omar got into his car and drove towards his home. Suddenly, a black four-wheel drive zipped into the driveway, ducked in front of his car, braked fiercely, and came to a gravel-spitting halt. Walker, whom Omar rescued in operation Bright Star operations years ago, got out of the car and came up to Omar.

Walker said, "Omar, I have a warrant for your arrest."

"On what charge?" Omar demanded.

"For killing Orlando."

"Orlando?" Omar laughed. "You mean for defending myself. Orlando started all this, and he was about to kill Elizabeth and me."

"You'd better not resist. Surrender without condition," Walker said calmly.

Omar said, "I enjoy diplomatic immunity. I am not susceptible to lawsuit or prosecution."

"You have committed a serious crime unconnected with your diplomatic role. The strained expression on your victim's face was like that of a man who had been shocked beyond reason. The method of killing was vicious and brutal."

"Arresting me would be legal if my country waived my immunity, but it hasn't. I have diplomatic immunity to your laws."

"This is just a formality," Walker said smoothly. "If you are innocent, you'll be freed."

"Arresting me is a violation of the diplomatic law and a disrespect to my country. Let go of me."

"Think what you think. I believe in law and order. We have a peaceful country, and we want to keep it that way."

"How ungrateful you are, Walker. Is this a way to repay help and friendship? I've been a devoted friend to you and now you knife me in the back!" Omar said this with a smile.

"Sorry, pal, It's a legal obligation."

Walker led Omar to one of the squad cars and pushed him into the backseat, getting in beside him.

Omar was put into solitary confinement in a small room barely furnished.

When Elizabeth read the news, her stomach churned. She got a permit to visit Omar in prison and rushed out to visit him.

"Elizabeth! What in the world are you doing here?" Omar said, surprised.

"I'm here for you. Are they treating you all right?"

"I'm fine, thank you."

"I'll talk to father. I'll see that the accusation is officially dropped."

"Don't bother. Everything has been settled beforehand."

"What do you mean by that?" she said, frightened.

"I caused your father a lot of embarrassment, but if they don't release me, I'll dig my way out of here."

"Omar, are you crazy? Are you going to fight a whole nation?"

"I have never been humiliated in my life. They treated me like dirt. They must pay," he said furiously.

"Omar, calm down, please. Everything will turn out all right."

"Liz, stay out of this. It's my battle, not yours. I caused you enough troubles already because of my love for you."

"There must be something to be done. I'll do whatever it takes to set you free." With a heart bleeding anger and sadness, Elizabeth left Omar to see her father.

The president was sitting at his desk reading some papers. The moment he saw Elizabeth entering the oval office, he said, "Don't waste any pity on him."

"You are not being fair, Father. He didn't kill an ordinary man; he killed a killer sent here to kill him. He couldn't stand to see me hurting."

"This stranger you got yourself involved with defied my policies and turned the people against me."

"What has he done to deserve all this?"

"He took the law into his own hands and killed a free soul. Before that, he killed seven souls in the mall and we didn't charge him. We have laws here, darling. We have laws."

"Killed a free soul? The investigations revealed that the free soul you were talking about was an international assassin hired to kill people."

"A loving woman will idolize the vices of the man she loves. He himself would never think of such excuses for his crimes as you will find for him. I'm afraid you don't quite realize what you're letting yourself in for."

"You're not being fair to Omar. Don't say there's nothing you could do to stop it."

"Nothing is fair. That's life."

"It's perfectly in order to search him and question him, but there is no reason to threaten and abuse him. He is a diplomat and has immunity."

"He's guilty of murder, plain and simple. There's a dead body, and your boy is going to burn for it."

"You are doing a big mistake detaining him. He is a law unto himself. He's no man to pick a quarrel with."

"God rot him to hell. I will limit him to his proper size. Some things were meant to be, Elizabeth. And that's the end of it. Nothing will help."

"You've burned your bridges with me, father. I can't stay here and let him go to pieces. I have to do something. I will help him get over this."

"Instead of helping him, let him get a lawyer. A good one."

"I will do whatever it takes to free the man I love."

Elizabeth left her father's office extremely worried about what might happen to Omar.

Omar was taken in a police car to the federal courthouse. At this early stage of the court procedure, the Egyptian authorities announced, "The American administration should immediately end the trial of Ambassador Omar. The ambassador's detainment constitutes a violation of the Vienna Convention on Diplomatic Relations, which specifies the privileges of a diplomatic mission that enables diplomats to perform their function without fear of coercion or harassment by the host country." But the Egyptian's request was ignored.

The court was filled to overflowing. Inside the court was an extraordinary gathering. The media was out in full force. Elizabeth sat there fuming.

A special grand jury was seated in chairs against the wall. Across from them sat Omar and his lawyer at a long table. As Omar sat their eyes blazing, the eyes of the whole world were watching him.

A court officer said, "All rise," and the judge entered from the judge's robing room.

The judge took his place on the bench. The spectators resumed their seats. The court clerk handed a court calendar to the judge. "The people of the state of New York versus Omar Abdel Aziz, charged with the murder of Orlando Martini."

Omar's name was called. The judge asked him, "Do you plead guilty?"

Omar stood tall and proud, his head up. He answered the judge: "I killed the assassin, but I am not guilty."

"Why do you think the victim was an assassin?"

"He admitted to me that he was hired to kill me and Mary Mackenzie. Carlos, the manager of Senator Hudson's farm, hired him to do the job. Senator Hudson was the man behind all this."

The trial continued for an hour, but Omar was not listening to the judge or to what his lawyer and the district attorney were saying. He seemed so lost in solitary thought, as if unaware of his surroundings.

Elizabeth was watching him. She knew it was the calm before the storm.

Omar felt a familiar protective surge in his gut, the same chivalrous impulse that had always driven him to defend the rights of the oppressed. A flow of anger coursed through him.

Unexpectedly, Omar rose from his seat and addressed the judge. He talked as if he were in a state of meditation. His words seemed unrelated to the subject of the case.

"Praise belongs to Allah, to whom belongs whatsoever is in the heavens and whatsoever is on the earth, and praise be to Him in the life to come. He is the All-Wise, the All-Aware. He knows all that goes into the earth and all that comes out of it; He knows all that comes down from the heavens and all that goes up to them. He is the Merciful, the Forgiving. All that dwells upon the earth is perishing, yet still abides the face of our Lord, majestic, splendid.

"Enough of this theatre play you call trial. What are you trying to prove against me? I have already admitted that I have killed the assassin as self-defense. I was the man who was attacked by a hired assassin. Host countries have an obligation to protect diplomatic property and personnel. As a diplomat, I should have been protected by your police, but that didn't happen.

"I rose out of the long traditions of the East, where religion runs deep in the marrow of man. The East enfolded me in a culture that was thousands of years in the making. America is still in diapers.

"Since I set foot in your country, I have seen contempt, disgust, and animosity against Muslims and their religion. Your newspapers, TV stations, and news media and publishing platforms excelled in slandering the prophet of Islam, belied and stultified the last divine revelation to mankind – the Koran – and humiliated Allah, the God of creation!

"Your administration hasn't lifted a finger to stop this despicable act. You insolently wounded the feelings of one and a half billion Muslims living in the four corners of the world.

"The Koran you humiliated is a glorious book in a guarded Tablet. It is a decisive Word; it is no merriment. It is a book of exalted power. No false can approach it from before or behind it. The Koran is sent down by One full of wisdom, worthy of all praise.

"Muslims are controlled only by the words of Allah. We Muslims live by our faith. We live by the Koran and die for it. The Koran is the word of God, the final revelation to mankind. The Koran is all about truthfulness, sincerity, honesty, unselfishness, humility, patience, forgiveness, purity, and cleanliness. The Koran shapes our everyday lives, anchors us to a unique system of laws, and inspires us with its guiding principles. Yet you people belied it, defiled it, and even burned it.

"Perish the conjecturers who are dazed in perplexity. You belie the Koran? By the Lord of heaven and earth, it is a surely true as that you have speech. Will you not contemplate the Koran — or do you have locks on your hearts?

"Perish the liars, those steeped in error. What, did you think that God created you for sport, and that you would not be returned to Him? How ill you judge! Your reckoning is with God; surely you shall not prosper.

"Muslims do not live the American dream — to amass fame and fortune! Muslims live for only one reason: to serve and worship Allah the Creator.

"The Muslim life is an act of worshipping the Creator, doing good, and refraining from evil. Allah says in the Koran: 'And I did not create the jinn and humankind except to worship Me.'

"Do those who humiliated the Koran not think that they shall be raised up unto a mighty day, a day when mankind shall stand before the Lord of all being? Surely, the Lord's punishment is terrible.

"Allah gave you guidance, but you preferred blindness to guidance. You are nothing but arrogant people deceived by wealth. You have shed human blood, oppressed countries, destroyed cities. People are doomed if they established their kingdom on bloodshed.

"Listen to me, people, you who are far from justice. Your destructive civilization produces nothing but victims. You showed the Palestinians no mercy. You made them refugees living in camps. You destroyed Iraq and dispersed and frightened away millions of Iraqis. You did the same to Syria, Libya, and Yemen. You vanquished the innocents with your tyrannical power.

"You destroyed the earth through your greed. You have trusted in your wickedness. You are led by arrogance to more crime.

"You are insolent on this earth in defiance of right, but your insolence is only against yourselves. You forget that in the end, unto Allah you shall return, and then He shall tell you what you were doing.

"You hasten about the earth to do corruption in the land, and Allah loves not corruption. You behave arrogantly through the land against all truth and reason, saying, "Who is more superior than us in strength?" Do you not see that Allah who created you is mightier than you in power?

"What is the recompense of the criminals who displaced people, destroyed their cities, and shed the blood of the innocents, except disgrace in the life of this world and the next?

"Now listen, you lovers of pleasure, lounging in your security and thinking there is nobody else like you. The Lord has spoken His Word. You are already set to receive your Lord's loathing and anger. Allah's wrath will come upon you in full measure, in spite of all the might backing you. Yes, a calamity will fall upon you. The calamity awaits its appointed time. Wait for it; it will certainly come and will not delay.

"Yes, remember this and be amazed. Take it to heart, you wrongdoers. Divine punishment is on its way; disgrace will cover your glory."

"Allah destroyed evil nations before you. This is the way of Allah with evil nations, and you are no exception."

"Allah is just and does not love oppression. Allah does not love the transgressors. Allah does not love treachery, betrayal, and falsehood. Allah does not love those who spread corruption in his earthly kingdom.

"Do you think that the universe is yours? Evil is that you judge! The universe belongs to Allah the Creator. Whosoever desires glory, the glory altogether belongs to Allah. Allah is the master of the kingdom, not America. He gives the kingdom to whom He will, and He seizes the kingdom from whom He will. He exalts whom He will, and He abases whom He will; in His hand is the good; He is powerful over everything.

"Today the power is yours, but who will help you against the might of Allah when it befalls you. You have been ungrateful to what Allah has given you. Take your enjoyment – certainly you will soon know.

"Allah is deferring you to a term stated; and when your term is come, you shall not put it back by a single hour nor put it forward. So where are you people going? You cannot escape Allah's punishment. There is none to put Allah's judgement back, and He is swift at reckoning. You are not able to frustrate Him either in the earth or in heaven; and you have not, apart from Allah, neither protector nor helper.

"I have sold the present life for the world to come; and whoever fights in the way of Allah and is slain or conquers, Allah shall bring him a mighty wage. Allah will not let the deeds of those who are killed for his cause come to nothing; He will guide them and put their hearts at rest. He will admit them into the Garden He had already made known to them. Do not think of those who have been killed in Allah's way as dead. They are alive with their Lord, well provided for, happy with what Allah has given them of His favour. All that dwells upon the earth is perishing, yet the Face of your Lord still abides, majestic and splendid.

"I am going back to my world – the source of light and guidance and the shine of inspiration."

Something terrible was going to happen. Elizabeth could feel it in her bones. *Oh God!* she shouted within herself. She understood from Omar's words that he had launched jihad against his enemies. Her heart sank because she knew him. He was not going to surrender. He was going to fight until the end. He was going to fight until the last drop of blood in his veins. He wanted to die as a martyr. She knew that Omar, once roused, would be capable of destroying anything that lay in his path.

Elizabeth had read about jihad, and she knew that there were two types of jihad: the first was small jihad, which was fighting back armed aggression; and the second was resisting evil drives and desires in one's self.

Elizabeth shouted furiously at Omar, "What do you think you are doing! Do you expect a miracle?"

The moment he heard her voice, tears welled up in his eyes.

"I've prayed for one, yes. I hope for one, yes." He felt an overwhelming longing for her.

"You are the only woman I ever loved. All I ever wanted was you. Without you, life is nothing but ashes." He said this with tearful eyes.

"Have you taken leave of your senses? You are in no state to fight. You're going to be killed. If you truly love me, then save your life for me." She was now weeping.

"Each person has to die his own death. I would rather die a martyr than a quitter. Man is born to die."

Elizabeth pleaded through her tears, "Please don't throw your life into perdition."

"It's too late Elizabeth. They have wounded my pride beyond repair. They must pay. I am a man who has come to terms with death. I'll fight this oppression until the end. This is a war I have been trained for."

"Omar, please reconsider. It's your life I'm talking about."

He shouted at the judge and the people present in court as if he hadn't heard her, "You wallow like hogs in the false security of your golden sovereigns, but in reality you are weak and decaying. You suck the world dry. You feed off poor nations and give nothing in return. Cash rules everything around you. Money and power are all that matter to you. You are bleeding our lives away and sucking our blood. You corrupted the world around you. Your world is full of shit and hypocrites. My people will die no more to water your greed. You will kill no more. You who love money and deceit more than right die where you stand.

"What gives you the right to rule the world? No power on earth can protect you from Allah's wrath for long. I see it coming."

President Rosh was watching the trial on TV. He said mockingly, "He is acting like a Baptist preacher predicting doom and hellfire for sinners."

Signs of content on Rosh's face changed when Omar said, "War profiteers. I do not fit in your ugly world. I will fight your oppression to the death. I will show you what war is. I exist according to my own rules, living by my own freely made decisions. And I've decided to dig my way out of here. I'll kill any man who stands in my way."

Omar then walked swiftly to the court's door, where three cops guarding the court obstructed him. The first tried to stop him from reaching the door. Omar, in a fraction of a second, punched him in the nose. The punch was like a thunderbolt. The cop fell unconscious to the ground. Omar leaned down and picked up his gun. The two other cups came swiftly to obstruct Omar's way, but he crippled them by shooting them in the knees.

Omar ran to the staircase, taking the steps two at a time. He reached the entrance door and rushed out to the street. Omar mingled with pedestrians and walked quickly to a public garage. A rented car was ready in the corner. He got into the car and shot from the garage like a rocket. Fifteen minutes later, he was parking the car in another public garage. He opened the trunk and took out a leather bag containing the weapons he'd asked his aides to prepare for him. And from there, he vanished with his car.

Omar's escape was shocking to President Rosh and the people. It was as though the earth had suddenly stopped and time was frozen. The nation went crazy. Hell broke loose.

CHAPTER 51

The president of Egypt was watching the trial of Omar on TV. When Omar escaped, the president asked his presidential secretary to get the American president on the phone.

The president of Egypt said, "Hello, Mr. President. I've been watching the TV. It was unwise to put our ambassador on trial."

President Rosh replied, "We asked for his diplomatic immunity to be waived, but you refused. We had to bring him to trial because he killed a free soul on American soil."

"He killed a killer, Mr. President, not a free soul."

"We have laws here, and we respect them."

The president of Egypt said, "Laws tailored according to your own whims."

"I resent such an accusation, sir."

"Our people are mad because of what you have done to Ambassador Omar. They want to see him returned safely back home."

"This is something I can't guarantee, especially after his escape. Don't forget that he also knocked one officer down and shot two others."

"That's what I am afraid of. If you go after him, more of your men will be killed."

"Are you so sure of your man?"

The president of Egypt said, "Definitely. I'm warning you; Omar is a single soul, and he doesn't care about his life. Many of the people he is going to kill have families. The orphaned families will rebel against you. Haven't you thought of that?"

"Life for life, eye for eye, tooth for tooth. Your man might get killed if he doesn't surrender unconditionally."

"Omar belongs to the most elite special forces in Egypt. He alone is capable of harassing an entire battalion for a long period of time."

"He is on the loose now. The hunt began."

"You forced him to escape. A slaughter is about to happen, I am sure."

President Rosh said, "A slaughter to your man, of course."

"No. To your troops. Wait and see."

"How can this crazy man of yours escape from the United States! Is it by train, by airplane, by boat? He has no chance at all."

"He knows what he is doing. He has his orders. Just let him be."

"What do you mean by 'just let him be'?"

"If you let him be, he can return safely to Egypt. If not, he will sacrifice himself in the way of Allah and will take with him dozens of your soldiers."

Silence reigned between the two presidents for a few seconds, and then the president of Egypt continued.

"Talking about ambassadors, your ambassador Anne Patterson has become an example of America's policy failure in Egypt and the Middle East. We regard her as the person responsible for America's close embrace of Islamists in Egypt. She put your country in an increasingly lonely camp, contributing to ongoing instability and hurting America's image and credibility with the Egyptian people. She was telling a lot of people that my rule, which is backed by all Egyptians, was useless and that the Muslim Brotherhood was the only game in town."

President Rosh said, "We will continue to encourage the Muslim Brotherhood to enable them to participate in the process of freedom of speech and democratization."

"And we will continue to eliminate the Islamic militia you implanted in our land. Your ambassador is only clever in implementing your policy of dividing Egypt Into small pieces as part of the New Middle East project, a matter that the Egyptian people totally reject. At every point, your ambassador misread what was happening. Somehow she pictured my rule as if it were the enemy. What is the matter with you people? You want to bring Egypt to its knees as you did in Iraq, Syria, Yemen, and Libya?"

"There is no such thing, Mr. President. Enough conspiracy theories. Ambassador Patterson is a competent woman, and she knows what to do. I hold you responsible for her safety."

"I hold you responsible for the safety of Egypt's ambassador as well. Speaking about the safety of your ambassador, the American embassy is now surrounded by thousands of protestors calling for the safe return of the Egyptian Ambassador. The demonstrators climbed the walls and tore down the American flag."

President Rosh said, "I am confident that you will protect our ambassador from the mobs."

"We want Patterson out of Egypt. We consider her a persona non grata. She implemented your policy of dividing Egypt into small entities by encouraging Muslim Brotherhood to acquire power. She stood against the will of the Egyptians who rejected a divided nation. She ardently supported your plan to force great changes in the Middle East. Hundreds of millions of lives were lost due to your sponsored wars to divide the Arab world. I have to tell you that your administration's policy towards the largest and most important nation in the Arab world is a big failure. Egypt's bloodbath is America's failure. We are not a small country in the region. We have a strong army that can fight non-stop on land and sea for a whole year. We have a strong arm that can reach your boats and prevent them from launching cruise missiles against defenseless Arab countries. We have no fear of your atomic weapons because other superpowers reject your ugly policies and are willing to stand against you."

President Rosh said, "All right. We will replace Ambassador Patterson with an ambassador who served in Syria."

"No. We don't want ambassadors who worked as FBI agents to divide and ruin our nations. If you send them here, they will encounter shoe hurling."

"Why all this hostility, Mr. President? We are still good allies, aren't we?"

"We were once friends. Our relationship must be revised according to equal footing, according to our weight in the region. We have interests in the region, and our national security must be respected by all."

President Rosh said with a laugh, "Well, back to your man. He escaped, and now the hunt is on. Let's watch the hunt."

"Let's see who will get the last laugh. Start counting your dead. Don't forget that you have been warned."

President Rosh called for Kenny Walker. Walker didn't forget that Omar had saved his life, but he was just doing his job when he arrested Omar because he was charged with murdering the hitman.

The president said, "I am holding you responsible for arresting the killer and bringing him back to rot in jail."

Walker warmed to the task, appreciating the president's confidence in him. He said firmly, "I'll do my best, sir."

The president said, "Radio, press, and TV stations are already in the battleground recording, photographing, and videotaping. A television network asked the opinion of seventy persons about the killer's escape, and it was amazing to see that some of them were sympathetic with him. Women in particular were angry and saw the man who saved Elizabeth's life several times as badly treated."

The president continued: "The whole world is watching the chase. Egypt is waiting to see her hero win the battle. The president of Egypt warned me of heavy human casualties and orphaned families. Some of the foreign ambassadors suggested that it would have been more advisable to send the killer back to Egypt as a persona non grata instead of taking him to trial. My reputation is at stake.

"No mistakes, Walker, no mistakes. Take all the forces you need and bring him back. It will only take a matter of hours to arrest him or rip him apart. He is just a single soul fighting the power of a whole nation alone."

"I understand, sir. He doesn't have a chance."

CHAPTER 52

Omar had learned how to work without the target being aware of him. He had a unique ability to disappear so that he could hit his enemies at their most unguarded moments in which they thought they were unobserved.

Omar parked the car in a deserted lane. He would spend the night in his car. Tomorrow he would settle his account with Carlos, Hudson's farm manager.

Omar called his aides at the embassy and asked them to give him the farm's address and any information about Carlos's habits and whereabouts.

When the morning came, Omar's telephone buzzed. His aides gave him the address of the farm and informed him that at sunset Carlos usually sat on the front porch smoking a cigar, then retired in his bedroom to watch TV until sleep overtook him.

At sunset, Omar pressed the accelerator and the car shot forward. Through the car's GPS, he was able to locate the farm. With the military bag on his back, Omar slipped silently into the farm.

Work had ceased for the day, and the farm workers retired to their rooms. The porch overlooked a large grazing land expanding to a sizeable garden of old fruit trees. Carlos was sitting on the porch smoking a cigar.

Omar hid behind a fruit tree, set down the military bag, knelt, and opened it. Inside were the barrel and stock of a rifle, a telescopic sight clamped to the former, a strap to the latter. Omar took the parts out and attached them.

Omar aimed at Carlos and fired the gun, the explosion echoing through the porch. Carlos flew out of his seat and fell to the floor, blood erupting from his forehead. His eyes were wild and staring.

Omar retreated swiftly to his car, gunned the engine, and sped down the highway. After a few miles, he turned off the highway and onto an unnamed access road that was not paved. He parked the car there. Ten minutes later, his aides arrived with another car. They drove him to a private airport where a small rented aircraft was waiting to fly him to Monterey County, located on the Pacific coast of California. Because Omar's picture was everywhere now, and was familiar to most Americans, the pilot recognized him.

The Ventana Wilderness of Monterey County was characterized by steep-sided, sharp-crested ridges. Thick bushes and dense communities of tall pine trees covered much of the Ventana. The area was a suitable battlefield for operation mobility and was the closest to the Pacific Ocean, his main escape route.

In Monterey County, Omar bought a motorcycle and drove eighty miles to the Ventana Wilderness. He left the motorcycle in a quiet area and entered the wilderness on foot. Apart from being known as an excellent sniper, Omar was particularly skilled at running for great distances and leaping over and across obstacles. With the military bag on his back, he ran for ten miles and stopped at a pine tree that was one hundred feet high.

Omar rested under the tree for a short period, during which he assembled the pieces of the sniper rifle. The sniper rifle could hit a target at a distance of 1.54 miles. Through the sniper optical sight, he could aim precisely at various targets.

With the climbing rope, Omar climbed to the top of the tree and covered himself completely with its leaves. Through his binoculars, he inspected the battlefield below and waited for his enemies to appear. Omar slept until dawn, but his mind was alert.

Walker launched two battalions and airborne troops against Omar. About six hundred soldiers were marching forward on the Ventana land towards Omar, and twenty-four others were in two helicopters hovering over the place and accompanying the dismounted battalions. The helicopters were loaded with combat troops.

With the first rays of the sun, Omar could spot the troops making their way towards his position. The place would be swarming with soldiers in less than an hour. The troops were plainly visible to him. They were in fact easy meat.

Through his binoculars, Omar scanned the troops further, watching their gatherings and formations. Suddenly, he took the binoculars from his eyes and let out a shout of surprise. What a mockery of fate! Kenny Walker was the commander of the troops!

It was an unfair war. The whole nation was against one man, and he will fight them all without mercy; Kenny Walker was no exception. The wolf sprang into Omar's eyes.

His simple strategy was to strike the first blow from a high altitude before anyone had time to attack against him. The more vulnerable he felt, the fiercer the attack.

A shiver of rage went through him. He smiled; the battle had begun. He would cut them down one by one. Omar raised his rifle and fired. The first soldier was lifted off his feet and thrown backwards, hitting the rocky ground with his shoulder blades.

Another soldier appeared in the gun sight, and Omar squeezed the trigger. The face erupted into a mass of blood and shattered flesh. Omar fired again, and the third soldier fell to the ground, blood streaming out of his forehead.

Firing continued. The bullet shattered the bridge of the fourth soldier's nose, and another bullet put out the left eye of the fifth.

Walker gave orders to the helicopters to scan the area, searching for the direction of the bullets. The helicopters swooped back and forth in random patterns searching the area. But there was no sign of Omar, for he was adequately covered by the dense leaves of the pine tree and at an altitude quite close to that of the choppers.

From overhead came the roar of the two helicopters. Omar looked skyward and saw that one of the helicopters was very close.

Omar pointed his rifle at the main rotor above the cabin and pulled the trigger. He then aimed at the tail rotor. The helicopter went down into a spin and crashed against the ground with fourteen soldiers in it.

Walker ordered his troops to hide in the bushes and behind the rocks. But at an altitude of forty feet, Omar was able to locate the soldiers in their hiding places. He started shooting them one by one, thus increasing human casualties to dramatic levels.

Just before sunset, Walker hitched a ride on the second helicopter that was surveying the battlefield. He could see dead bodies down below, lying on the rocks and floating in the small rivers and thermal springs. It was a helicopter massacre and a crushing defeat for the American military.

Walker got off the helicopter and got mad. He was facing multiple casualties. He ran forward leaving his troops behind and shouting, "Come out of your rat hole and face me; I'll kill you now, Omar!"

It was nearly dark when Omar appeared from his hiding place and blocked Walker's way. At last, the two men confronted each other.

"You see me as a rat hiding in a hole, Walker?" Omar said scornfully.

"You killed my men in cold blood. They didn't even start a fight. You ruined my career!"

"Your career! How about my life? It's my life that you were after."

"To hell with your life. I'll take you dead to the president."

"Are you so sure of yourself, Walker? Let's see. Show me what you've got."

Omar's muscles were quivering with the anxiety to begin. In a fury of rage, Omar rushed at him, delivering strong blows to Walker's head. Walker lunged forward and struck out, but Omar slapped the fist away with one hand and then, with a lightning-fast change step, hit Walker on his face with the other hand, hard enough to make his teeth click.

Walker continued to advance, angry and frustrated about not being able to touch Omar with a blow, but Omar gave him a quick kick to the stomach that made him grunt. With a shout of desperation, Walker rushed at Omar, who tugged away and delivered another quick kick to the stomach that doubled Walker up with a snort. Then Omar spun and kicked the side of Walker's head with all his force. Walker rolled over the small rocks and lay nearly unconscious.

"I'll not finish you off, Walker. I'll spare your life for Jennifer and the kids." Omar turned back to disappear into the shadows of the night.

The full dimension of the disaster became clearer the next day, when the press and TV stations reported on the massacre. The news of the massacre was on the first page of the newspapers and became the main subject of TV news. The president was furious that the media was targeting his unreasonable decision for arresting Omar. He spoke to the nation to justify his decision, rebuked the press, and called for an end to idle criticism.

CHAPTER 53

Walker was summoned to the White House. He entered the Oval Office to see the president looking older and smaller, as though the terrible events had aged and shrunken him.

While Walker was still at the door, the president screamed at him: "Can't you be trusted to do a goddam thing!"

"I did my best, sir, but things did not turn out the way they were supposed to."

"What's happening out there? How long does Omar intend this masquerade to go on?"

With a bruised and bloody face, Walker replied, "He is not human. He's like a piece of iron. He's winning. Whatever he hits, he destroys."

"Maybe he worshiped the devil in secret, and in return the devil has given him power on earth," the president said scornfully.

"He is a man of God. He is dying for a cause he believes in."

"How dare you take his side, Walker?"

"His strength was that he wanted nothing for himself."

"An avenger. That's what he has become. But I assure you he will be neutralized. He is a dead man!" the president shouted.

"He is a man carrying the weight of his world on his shoulders."

"He is a killer, Walker, a killer."

"He's a professional fighter sir, not a killer."

"I want him arrested. I want him in prison. You hear me!"

"I doubt if we ever will. He is willing to lay down his life for his belief. What he says, he does. He will never be caught. He will sacrifice himself. He has launched jihad against us. He will die as a martyr."

"What sort of a damn fool do you take me for? A million to one chance and you say you doubt if we ever will?"

"He's winning. Whatever he hits, he destroys. It's going to be worse and worse, with no end in sight."

"He's just an ordinary man, Walker. He is not a supernatural creature."

"He is a man of action. He can think clearly under pressure. He is not human. He's like a piece of iron. He is immortal. Nothing he ever did made him seem less eternal. Maybe because he is God-besotted and extreme in his belief."

"You became too soft to deal with him. I know he covered you with favours, but you had a job to do."

"I encountered him in a fight yesterday, but he knocked me down, and instead of killing me, he spared my life. He did that for the sake of my wife, Jennifer, and my kids."

"He knew Jennifer?"

"They're close friends. He was the one who persuaded me to marry her. He walked her down the aisle on our wedding day. He saved my life years ago and spared my life yesterday. And I'm supposed to be the one who arrests him dead or alive. What a mocking fate!"

The president stopped talking for a while. He looked at the void before him as if contemplating the critical situation and trying to find a solution to the problem.

"Well, Walker. Let's get to the heart of the matter. The operation went terribly wrong. One helicopter with twelve men in it was hit, and thirteen more were killed. Now that Omar's actions have escalated to a dangerous level, I have no choice but to replace you with Major Thomas Lewis.

"Thomas is a good soldier, sir."

"Thomas was awarded the Silver Star for displaying exceptional valour while engaging in military combat operations against the Taliban in Afghanistan. He is brave, focused, tenacious, and has formidable physical strength." The president pointed at a file on his desk. "That's all, Walker. Back to headquarters." The president pointed to the door.

Two hours later, Elizabeth came to see her father in his office. "Daddy, you must stop this massacre. I have an idea. You can issue a call for surrender accompanied by assurance to Omar that we guarantee his safe return home."

"Isn't it a little late to ask? His hands are already stained with the blood of our brave men."

"Brave men? Two battalions and airborne troops against one man and you say brave men!"

"I want none of your advice. This man is the devil in human disguise. He can kill without turning a hair. There was no stopping him. He is nothing but a terrorist." The President said withering.

"That's not fair! That's a terrible accusation. He's not a terrorist. He is just defending himself. He fights and kills to stay alive. He is a man carrying the weight of the world on his shoulders." Elizabeth shouted.

"What the devil is he up to? He doesn't have a chance. He managed to escape this time because he was lucky."

"Lucky! What you have seen was the spirit of God moving on earth, challenging the whole nation with His power. Omar's words in court were the words of God uttered through Omar's tongue to warn our unjust nation of a severe wrath if she doesn't follow God's guidance. He was the spirit of God moving on our land to teach, warn, and set examples. It was a lesson to be learned. Haven't you realized that yet, Father?

"Omar is special, very special. Everything he is, everything he does, and everything he believes in is special. He is my rock, my saviour, a man of belief. God is his refuge and strength. The Lord is his light and his salvation. The Lord is the stronghold of his life. We must let him leave to his place of shelter and be at rest." Elizabeth was now pleading.

"Stop this nonsense and leave me to do my work."

"He'll fight with a fury. He will take down tens of soldiers with him. The families and wives of the dead are accusing you of murdering their husbands and sons for no good reason."

"That's his downfall Elizabeth. He could have surrendered peacefully, but he chose the way of violence and destruction. I'll show him what violence is."

"Don't underestimate the power of a great warrior, Dad. He is a man of action. What he wants, he will have. He's made up his mind, and that – with Omar – is that."

Elizabeth said with tears in her eyes, "When I look at my life and see my frustrations, my failed marriages, the agony of vanquishing on the faces of the innocents, and when I see the arrogance and the destruction we impose on weak nations, I feel that I want to stand by Omar and fight. Fight to stay alive long enough to live out my life next to him.

"Somehow I feel he is struggling to win me. He is struggling to stay alive in order to spend the rest of his life with me. Oh dear God! I will not give up on that man. I love him." Elizabeth's words were broken with tears.

CHAPTER 54

Omar ran in the Ventana Wilderness for another ten miles, heading towards the Pacific Ocean. He reached an area full of giant sequoias. He opened his military bag and took out his powerful L86 LSW machine gun. He assembled the pieces together and climbed a sequoia that was eighty metres high.

Major Thomas Lewis rearranged his troops to attack with new tactics. The main goal was to advance by means of fire and movement with minimal casualties while maintaining unit effectiveness and control.

Thomas took the lead while moving on the battlefield, followed by machine gunners armed with hand grenades. If the troops were not confronted by enemy fire, they gained ground by running out into the open, which Omar left behind. The purpose was to move rapidly to keep Omar off balance.

Thomas gained control of the ground Omar left behind. He distributed his troops at proper distances along the fighting area. Omar would not have the chance to maneuver back and forth; his only option was to advance towards the ocean. And there on the shore, he would not find a place to hide. He would be uncovered, exposed, dead meat.

Through his binoculars, Omar was able to see the formation and the distribution of Thomas's troops. He instantly realized that a more skillful commander had replaced Walker. Omar sensed danger because the troops were more organized and hot on his trail.

Thomas evaluated the situation while scanning the trees ahead of him. As he'd read in Walker's report, Walker couldn't determine from what direction the bullets came. The anatomy of the dead soldiers revealed that they were hit from a high altitude. Omar might be hiding on top of one of the trees. The next step, then, was to get Omar out of his hiding place.

In addition to his troops, Thomas also had two support helicopters. The two helicopters were initially armed with two .30-calibre machine guns and sixteen 2.75-inch rockets, and they accompanied the troops into battle, spraying the battle zone with heavy fire. The gunners leaned out the open sides of the chopper with their eyes on the ground below and their fingers on the triggers.

Thomas gave orders to the helicopters to pour machine gun fire into the top of the trees. The trees were set on fire. The burning trees were tall, and there was wind. The flames jumped from treetop to treetop and burned from top to bottom.

Omar had to climb down fast to avoid the terrible heat. The fire had already burned his arms and face, and he suffered a terrible pain. Thank god, the burn was minor and first degree. He brought out from the military bag a water bottle and cooled the burns by pouring water on the burned parts.

There was a storm raging in his mind. Military training had taught him that in order for things to get better, they often had to get worse. His strategy now was not to show his enemies any weakness or signs of defeat. He must keep moving, stressing his enemies to attack.

Having pushed Omar back, Thomas assumed that since he had not encountered counter-attacks, Omar had retreated. He therefore pushed his troops to advance forward.

Omar placed the slings of his rifle and machine gun over his head and around his chest, leaving them hanging from his back. Omar wiggled his way into the wilderness to where several large trees that were not on fire gave cover. He quickly climbed one of them and managed to reach a branch about thirty feet from the ground. He saw from his position a small party of soldiers passing out boxes of ammunition. He took careful aim at one of them and fired. Not waiting to observe the damage, he continued to fire at the others. He shot down five of them.

One of the helicopters detected the lightning of Omar's bullets, and it poured its machine gun fire into Omar's tree. Omar was not hit, but he fell fifteen feet to the branches below. The top of the tree was set on fire, but the middle part was still safe. The helicopter was so close that Omar had the opportunity to aim his rifle at the pilot. After a few seconds, the chopper spun out of control towards the valley, crashing and burning, killing the pilot and all troops on board.

Omar was terribly exhausted. His flesh was inflamed from the fire. He was oozing blood on his leg, chest, and back due to the fall on the huge sharp branches. His bones were fractured, causing tremendous pain. The bulletproof vest added more heat to his body, so he took it off.

Omar knew that his enemies were closing in for the kill, but he didn't fear death. He had made up his mind to die as a martyr. He would sacrifice his soul to defend his religion. He would fight his enemies because of the foul epithets they said about Islam. They should have known that the prophet of Islam was the seal of the prophets and brought to the world the last divine book – the Koran. Yet they slandered him, called him bad names, and belied, defiled, and burned the Koran. They didn't have an atom of decency when they falsely claimed to their people that Allah the Lord of the universe was a moon god, a monkey god, and a demon god.

He would fight until the end in order to defend the right of his people to live in peace on their land instead of living homelessly in tents scattered on the borders of foreign countries. He would continue fighting to establish the commands of Allah, to spread peace, equality, and love in His earthly kingdom.

Allah did not love the arrogant. Allah didn't love those that waxed proud. Allah did not love the transgressors. He would fight against the unjust detention of the innocents and the torture and persecution of Muslims in the prisons of Guantanamo and Abo Gharib.

His religion had taught him that martyrs do not die because they are alive with their Lord. There was nothing more beloved to Allah than two things: a teardrop that fell from a believer for the fear of Allah and bloodshed in His path. Omar's eyes overflowed with tears when he remembered Allah, the One deserving of all praise. And now his body was covered with blood because he was struggling in the way of Allah. Martyrdom made Allah forgive sins. Martyrs were the first ones to enter paradise, and everyone envied their position. Martyrdom meant dying in order to reach the source of light and seek closeness to the Creator. How dared he to expect anything more than what Allah had decreed to his fate – dying in Allah's cause? What a beautiful and honoured death.

A tremor of valour passed through him. He shouted at the enemies from his hiding place, "Wherever you bury one of us, a thousand warriors will spring up! Before I die, I'll walk you through the gates of hell. We are the knights of Allah on earth. None can defeat us.

We serve Him and defend his religion. Our trait is bravery, and Allah is our guardian." Omar roared like a lion a verse from the Koran: "Those to whom the people said: 'The people have gathered against you, therefore fear them, but it increased them in faith, and they said, "Allah is sufficient for us; an excellent Guardian is He."' So they returned with blessing and bounty from Allah, untouched by evil; they followed the good pleasure of Allah; and Allah is of bounty abounding."

Omar then raised his hands to Allah and supplicated: "My Lord! Judge between me and these evildoers in truth, for you are the best of those who give judgement."

All he could think of now was to kill for his life. He knew that he must fight and kill to stay alive.

Omar quickly descended from the tree to hide in the adjacent bushes, but he had been discovered. He heard Thomas's voice saying, "We have you spotted. You don't stand a chance. So just come out with your hands up and we will settle everything peacefully. Nobody will get hurt."

Omar appeared from the bushes with a gun in his hand. He looked dusty, exhausted, and tired. Thomas had a machine gun in his hand. He looked warlike, strong, and fresh. They stood pointing their guns at each other.

Thomas pointed to his troops shouting, "This is between me and him. Do not interfere."

"Do you think you are made of different clay from other men? You're too much of a fucking pussy to shoot me," Thomas said, smiling.

"What do you want?"

"Your life, Omar."

"Come and get it, you piece of shit."

"Do you have anything to say before I kill you?"

"Yes. Life is short and hard, and the grave is cold and lonely."

Omar stuck his gun behind his back and stretched forth his hands, inviting Thomas to fight. Seeing Omar covered with blood, so exhausted and so dusty, Thomas welcomed the fight. Omar could see the lust for blood in the eyes of Thomas as he approached.

Thomas rushed upon Omar and hit him with both fists, one after the other. The blows came down heavily and rapidly all over Omar's face and head. Omar tried to avoid the blows as Thomas kept hitting mercilessly. Thomas punched Omar's nose. Omar staggered back, and blood began to flow. It was a hand-to-hand combat, and Omar knew the best places to strike and kill an enemy. Mad with rage, Omar made a rush at Thomas and rained down blows all over his nose, eyes, and mouth. Thomas recoiled at the sudden violence of the onslaught.

Omar attacked with all his strength. He used his fingers in a V shape and attacked Thomas's eyes with a gouging motion. He then delivered blows along the bridge of his nose, which caused breakage, sharp pain, and temporary blindness. Omar delivered a blow with the heel of his hand in an upward motion that shoved the bone up into the brain. Thomas was still on his feet but staggering. Omar delivered a punch to Thomas's Adam's apple that severed the windpipe and knocked Thomas unconscious to the ground. Thomas was still breathing. Omar was extremely exhausted and had to strike while Thomas was still unconscious. Omar pulled out his gun and put a bullet in Thomas's head.

Omar ran to the thick bushes to hide, but he was cornered by multiple soldiers. They sprayed him with their machine guns. He felt a bullet tear into him and then another. He felt the hammer blow of another bullet. There was a sudden burning sensation in his mouth that seemed to shoot through his all body. He felt as though a fire were burning in his belly. He began gasping for air, feeling an unbearable agony.

He tried to ignore the waves of pain that wracked his body. With each draw of breath, a new wave of pain would sweep through him. The muscles of his legs and arms quivered with the stress and fatigue of his struggle to survive.

Omar fell to the ground, and blood flowed freely from the wounds of his chest, arms, and back. He crawled to the bushes where his machine gun was lying beside the military bag. Covered with the bushes and moving from one place to another, he harvested five soldiers with his machine gun. He further delayed their advance by shooting right and left while retreating to the ocean.

The raging fire devoured the giant trees and blocked Omar's way to the ocean. It was as if the whole wilderness were set on fire. In such terrible circumstances, Omar struggled to reach the shore, though all strength was gone from him.

In the thick of things, large demonstrations erupted against President Rosh. The demonstrations rejected the high human casualties and the destruction of the natural habitat of the Ventana Wilderness.

The troops received orders to stand down until Major Thomas was replaced by another and until the fire was extinguished by aerial firefighting.

Omar could hear the ocean whispering in the distance. He was racing against time, but he had to stop several times because he was breathless and gasping.

The clouds had completely obscured the stars, and darkness fell swiftly. Omar crawled to the shore and lay nearly dead behind a seal rock. He knew that he was helpless and unable to move. He thought he would die, so He prayed to his Lord: "My Lord! You have indeed bestowed on me your blessings. Creator of the heavens and the earth, you are my guardian in this world and the hereafter. Cause me to die in true submission and join me with the righteous."

After praying, he felt as though he was suddenly released from his body. He closed his eyes and fell into a deep coma.

At midnight, Omar slightly recovered and felt an ardent longing to see Elizabeth. He took the phone from his pocket and dialed. The telephone Omar had given to Elizabeth buzzed. Elizabeth snapped it open.

"Peace be with you," he whispered through his suffering.

"Omar! Are you safe? are you okay?"

"I'm just hoping I'll die."

She knew that he was dying. She'd watched on TV how he was sprayed with machine guns and how he fell to the ground before disappearing in the bushes. His weakness crippled her. She began to scream, but no sound came from her throat. The scream was deep down in her soul.

"Are you badly wounded?" She began crying and shaking uncontrollably.

"I'm trying hard to survive."

"Run for your life, Omar. You're going to get yourself killed."

"Will I live to love you again? I want to see you before I go." His voice faltered, interrupted by sobs and tears.

He was hurting and needing her. His suffocating voice showed clearly that he was weeping, but he was trying hard not to reveal his weakness.

Deep uncontrollable sobs squeezed Elizabeth's breath from her lungs.

"They will not deprive me of my love," he said, feeling dead inside. "I am fighting to win you. I want to live the rest of my life with you. Liz. My love. Come and hold me close and make me strong."

"You are the man I love. I owe you my life. I'll stand by you. Just tell me what to do." Her voice was trembling.

"I am hiding behind a seal rock in Monterey County, the central cost of California." Omar dropped the phone and entered another deep coma.

Elizabeth went to Auburn Municipal Airport and flew her single-engine aircraft. She landed in the private Sanborn Airport in California, and from there she headed to the beach. The beach was safe because the authorities thought that Omar was devoured by the fire and hadn't reached the shore.

It was late in the afternoon when Elizabeth found Omar lying nearly dead behind the seal rock. His face was bloodied. Along the forehead and from the back of the head, blood oozed from his hair. His left leg and left arm were covered with blood. because the water beneath him was stained with blood, she knew that his back was also wounded.

Falling to her knees beside him, she tore off her blouse and ripped it into pieces, pressing them against Omar's wounds. She wiped away much of the blood covering his face and chest. Omar needed help, more help than she could give him. She rested his head in her lap and gently stroked his hair.

He felt her compassionate hand stroking his hair. He opened his eyes for a few seconds, looking at her with amazement.

"Shh, sweetheart. It's Liz. I've got you."

His lips quivered, his tears swam to his cheeks, and then he closed his eyes and went into a deep sleep.

She stretched her body beside him and held him close until dawn. She woke up at dawn to see him looking at her.

"You give me love. You give me hope. You give me strength." He was smiling.

"I believe in you. I believe in your strength. I'm confident that you will win against all odds." She helped him sit up and lean back against the rock.

She brought from her pocket a small bottle of fresh water, honey, and dates. She put the bottle to his lips, and he drank profusely. With a teaspoon, she fed him honey and then offered him a date. Energy ran through him like an injection spreading through his veins.

"Don't be sad, my love. They will remove the bullets, and I'll be whole again," he said, seeming as if he didn't feel his wounds anymore amid all the other torments.

She put her arm around his shoulder and gently drew him close. She kissed his forehead, eyes, and cheeks. She waited for him to start speaking. He shook his head, his face a mask of agony.

"Let the myth shatter and the filth spill over. They made the world plunge into darkness. Symbols of freedom are being destroyed. This nation is going down into the darkest depths of evil and decay. The beginning of the end has come. You are in great danger of invoking Allah's wrath. Allah is All-Mighty and vengeful."

"Yes, we are living in a turbulent world," she said, confirming his words. A sad smile was on her face. She took his hand, lifted it to her lips, and kissed it.

He turned his head and looked at her with tired eyes. "Whatever happens, I want you to know that you're the only woman I've ever loved. Come and share my world with me. Beauty shall rise from the East."

"Who knows — I might do that. We cannot see what the future holds for us. Omar, I am worried about you," she said suddenly. "How are you going to escape? I just don't get it."

"Via the ocean."

"That's crazy, Omar. Are you going to swim from here to Egypt?"

"Everything has been settled. My aides executed the plan I made for my escape, and I had to do the hard part of it — the struggle. In this groove, there is a powerful submerge scooter, a diving cylinder, and a dive light." He pointed at a groove cut into the rock.

"Don't tell me that you will swim to Egypt with a scooter?"

"A Russian submarine will be waiting for me five miles from here."

"Five miles from here? The submarine could be easily spotted by our navy."

"It is a new class of submarines that can freely approach the coastlines of the Unites States without the fear of being detected."

"So the Russians are involved in your escape?"

"This matter had been settled between the president of Russia and our president."

"Oh, Omar! Wading in the ocean in your condition and for such a long distance is dangerous. The clouds are dark. The winds are strong. The night is falling."

"Help comes only from Allah, the Mighty, the Wise. Nothing matters when you are with Allah."

"When will you leave?"

"At sunset."

"That's only six hours from now."

"I'm sorry to have put you to all this trouble. I guess it's you and me against the world, Elizabeth," he said sadly.

"I guess so. All I care about is being with you. I love you so much, Omar." She pulled him close with her left arm and kissed his cheek and hair.

"I've to grab whatever time I can get, but I'm weak. Could you please help me?"

"Of course, darling. I will do anything to help you."

She paused for a long time, looking down at their entwined hands. One by one, drops fell from her eyes. His whole body trembled. Elizabeth felt a tremor, and she realized that he was weeping silently with her. She held him closer to stop the shivering.

"I survive because I still have you. You have been my will to live. Do not cry for me, for I know the path I ought to go. I will go to the land of peace, where Allah's worshippers dwell."

"Do not leave me to grieve. I'll be lost without you. Talk to me before you leave. Tell me words that will live in my heart forever." She was consumed with sobs.

"When you get into a tight place and everything goes against you, you never give up, for that is just the place and time that the tide will turn.

"If you want to change who you are, you will have to change what you think.

"Ask the Lord to guide you to the truth. If you truly love Him, then He already knows it and will deal with you according to the love you carry for Him in your heart.

"Remember, the greatest love is that of Allah. To love otherwise is mere imperfection. Life on earth is a path to the other life. What you sow here on earth, you will reap in the afterlife. The eternal life is what is worth seeking.

"Prophet Muhammad quoted Allah as saying, 'Heaven and earth contain me not, but the heart of My faithful servant contains Me.' The prophet also said, 'The heart is where the Lord resides.'

"The purpose of life is not to amass fame and fortune but to serve Allah. Allah said in the Koran, 'And I did not create the jinn and humankind except to worship Me.' Allah further said that He made this life in order to test man so that every person may be recompensed after death for what he has earned. Allah said in the Koran, 'Blessed be He in whose hand is the kingdom – He is powerful over everything – who created death and life, that He might try you which of you is fairest in works.'

"Man tends to forget the mission for which he came to the earth. He is given life through a physical body in order to use it for sublime goals. Instead, he lets the body's needs dominate and control his direction."

Omar's words made Elizabeth feel as if Allah were speaking to her heart. She felt as if the heavens were opened and Allah was staring right at her. Tears streamed down her face.

"Pray for me, Omar," she said, tears streaming down her face.

"May Allah hold you in the hollow of his hand. May Allah guide you on your journey to all truth. And may He open your mind to the reality of this world and the purpose of this life. May Allah join you with the righteous. May peace, mercy, and the blessings of Allah be upon you. Ameen."

The sun had already set behind the horizon, and the sky was drained of colour. The high waves of the ocean were covered with shadows, promising a light storm with heavy rain.

It was time for Omar to leave. But suddenly they heard a helicopter buzzing in the distance, coming their way. The helicopter flew low over the rock and spotted them.

"Let's move while we have the chance," Elizabeth begged.

Thunder roared, and raindrops began to flood the area. His shaking limbs betrayed him as he struggled to rise. He shifted to his knees with difficulty, and then Elizabeth helped him to get to his feet.

"Allah will deliver me to the land which he had blessed, the land where many divine messages were revealed for all," he said, trusting in Allah.

He supplicated to his Lord: "Our Lord, bring us forth from this country whose people are evildoers and appoint to us a protector from Thee, and appoint to us from Thee a helper. The door is open, and the path is ready to walk on. I'll go where the Nile flows and the trees smile." His eyes were overflowing with tears.

The winds roared. The rain hurt their cheeks and eyes as they struggled to get the scooter out of the groove. With painful effort, Omar walked with Elizabeth towards the sea. He wore the diving cylinder and stood looking at Elizabeth.

"I've got to get moving, Liz." He could feel the agony in her heart.

Elizabeth gazed at him, paralyzed, every pulse of her heart beating out the words "Please stay", but she could not help but saying, "I will always be true to only you. Farewell, my love. Go in peace. Go with God."

He said his last words before leaving: "I see you're beautiful. I hope to see the day you become my wife."

Omar disappeared into the ocean with the scooter. Elizabeth turned away from the ocean, Omar's last words still echoing in her head. He thought her beautiful and hoped to see the day she became his wife. He suffered the insufferable not only for his principles but also to win her. He wanted to take her away to his world and live with her in love and peace. He went through all this hell to be with her. Just to have a life with her, he fought like a wounded lion to escape death.

He had loved her for so long and thought of her all the time, yet she married a man she didn't love. Marrying Hudson was easier and safer, a marriage that would be compatible with the American modern lifestyle. She was afraid of going into the strict life of Islam. But what did she get from her two husbands but corruption and infidelity?

She felt guilty because she was part of Omar's unbearable suffering. She wanted to reassure him that she would live with him for the rest of her life, but she was being a coward. She saw him so broken, so wounded, so dead. He struggled to stay alive in order to have a life with her. What was she waiting for to admit to him that he was the man she always longed for and wanted to have him as a husband and the father of her children? Yes, she really loved him, but she just gave him encouraging words instead of being positive. She was afraid of establishing a serious relationship with him because he was a Muslim and belonged to a different culture. She just loved him from afar. Seized by overpowering grief, she knelt to the ground, weeping hysterically.

Armed police swarmed the place. A military man approached her and asked her where Omar was.

She burst into uncontrollable crying. She screamed at the man, "You bastards. You want to kill my love. He is a victor! He will outlive you all. He will live long enough to spit on you graves."

The scooter tore through the waves and sliced through the water. Omar went flat out for one hour at full speed. There was a submarine scurrying over the waves. Surfacing about twenty yards from the submarine, he proceeded the rest of the way on the surface.

The submarine crew helped him climb to the surface on a metal ladder. The captain of the submarine and his crew stood in two lines in the passageway and saluted him. He saluted back and then collapsed to the ground. They put him under the care of the submarine doctor to bring him back to consciousness, remove the bullets from his body, and tend to his battle wounds.

American navy ships and planes searched the area for fifteen days. They found nothing. Omar was officially declared lost at sea.

The Russian submarine reached Alexandria. Omar, a total wreck, was taken from the submarine to the military hospital. His wounds took a whole month to heal. Thousands gathered around the hospital, waiting for Omar to come out. When he appeared at the front door, people received him and hailed him as they would a hero. A car from the presidential palace was waiting to take him to the president. Omar was cheered as his car passed by the people who'd assembled to greet him. In the presidential palace, the president of Egypt received him with a handshake and a big hug, awarding him Egypt's highest state honour, the Order of the Nile.

Elizabeth was watching the celebration on TV and was glad to see that Omar had regained his health and become whole again.

CHAPTER 55

Elizabeth was all alone in the world now. She felt torn. A wave of sadness hit her. She missed Omar more than she had thought possible. Her feelings for him were as strong as ever. Every time she thought of him, her heart broke all over again.

Depression overtook her in the months following Omar's disappearance from her life. She felt so numb inside. Her knees were jelly and about to give out. A sharp pain rippled through her stomach. She had been unable to eat or go out of the house for weeks now.

Her friends appeared allen to her. She felt as if she didn't have a friend in the world.

It was the crying that was so awful. She couldn't stop. She would be walking down the street and break down. Depression drained and exhausted her.

Elizabeth felt her whole world caving in on her, sending her spinning into a bottomless void. She lost interest in everything. She buried herself in profound solitude. Silence enfolded her world. With the passing days, she grew sick of life.

The spacious house stretched before her with an agonizing emptiness. She wandered forlornly from room to room. The house, while beautiful and luxurious, suddenly seemed a cold, sterile prison. She walked among her walls. She felt the walls closing in like a swollen river.

She was alone, nowhere to turn, no one to go to. She had no one to talk to except her mother. She phoned her mother.

"Mother, I need you, Mother," she said, weeping.

Amanda said, "Are you still hurting, my baby?"

"There is a pain in my stomach, and I can hardly breathe."

"Oh, darling! What you need is …"

"What, Mother, another romance, a third marriage?" Elizabeth sobbed harder.

"Don't cry, Liz. I'll see this through with you."

"It's been almost four months now that he's been gone, and I'm still hurting. I can't sleep, I can't eat, I can't think. My life has turned into a living hell."

"Don't worry, baby. I'll be with you in an hour or so."

"Hurry up, Mother. I feel the world is closing in on me."

A frown of sadness wrinkled Amanda's face when she saw her daughter. Elizabeth was so emaciated that she could hardly stand. She was restless and persistently sad.

When Amanda took Elizabeth in her arms, Elizabeth burst into tears.

"If you'd just try, you could pull yourself out of this misery," Amanda said, patting Elizabeth's back.

"I have lost interest in life. I feel dead inside."

"You have to be strong and carry on with life."

"Omar has gone and left me alone. I can't live without him. I feel empty and defeated. I feel like there is no future for me."

"I can feel how much you are hurting. You have so much to be thankful for. Lots of people have more problems than you do."

Elizabeth sighed, resting her head on her mother's shoulder. "Oh my God, I am so happy you are here, Mother. I love you." Tears rolled down her cheeks.

"I will not leave you my child. I will stay with you until you become whole again." Amanda was also weeping by now.

Amanda spent her nights and days with Elizabeth. She slept next to her in bed, holding her hand until she fell asleep. But Elizabeth wouldn't stop crying and waking up in the middle of the night. These wailing episodes continued on a regular basis. Elizabeth lacked self-control and the ability to calm herself.

During several nights, Elizabeth sat up screaming, "Omar, are you all right!"

Amanda woke up abruptly to her screams. She took her daughter in her arms. "Elizabeth, I'm here. You've been saved. Now it's time for you to heal."

Other nights Elizabeth woke up screaming, "The bastards were trying to slaughter my love, my hope."

Amanda realized that Elizabeth was living in a black hole or having a feeling of impending doom. Elizabeth felt sad all the time and lifeless. These symptoms engulfed her day-to-day life, interfering with her ability to work, eat, sleep, and have fun. The feelings of helplessness, hopelessness, and worthlessness were intense and unrelenting, with little, if any, relief.

Amanda took Elizabeth to a renowned psychiatrist who pointed out that Elizabeth was going through a period of mental distress resulting from severe stress. She was suffering from separation anxiety disorder because she was separated from an individual to whom she had a strong emotional attachment. Now she was on the verge of a nervous breakdown. There was a need for Elizabeth to pause, and relax.

Elizabeth hadn't talked to the psychiatrist in all her sessions. Her mental condition was so debilitating that it prevented her from getting the help she really needed. Her illness became worse because it progressed.

The psychiatrist's prescription was that Elizabeth must indulge in activities that suited her best, like reading a book with a motivational theme, going shopping, and listening to good music. But all this was to no avail.

"Your doctor says that you will get over this and be well. And I believe your doctor," Amanda said, reassuring her daughter.

In the spacious garden of Elizabeth's house, Amanda and Elizabeth sat on a wooden bench enjoying the warmth of the morning sun. Elizabeth was half asleep, leaning her head on her mother's shoulder. Amanda was holding Elizabeth with her left arm, relaxing her chin on her daughter's head.

"You've got to keep your strength up, my child." Amanda said, kissing Elizabeth's hair."

Strength! Omar was her greater strength. His incredible strength, heat, and scent always calmed her fear as much as they excited the woman within her. His strength was the kind she could almost imagine herself melting into.

"Listen to the voice of your soul, my child," Amanda said, rubbing Elizabeth's shoulder tenderly. "It's trying to guide you. The voice lives in the recesses and can only be accessed when you are ready to hear what it has to say."

Cursing herself for her weakness, Elizabeth tried to set her brain travelling backward in order to understand the points of Omar's strength. Why he was so powerful and so strong? It was because of his deep faith in God and his conviction that whatever happened in the universe and whatever befell him only happened through the will and the decree of God. Omar's faith was pure and clear, uncontaminated by any stain of ignorance, superstition, or illusion. He always felt that he was in constant need of the help and support of God. He had no choice in his life but to submit to the will of God, worship Him, strive towards the right path, and do good deeds.

Omar was the one constant truth in her life. She needed him to love her as much as she loved him. It was terrifying to love him so much. She belonged to Omar. She would not allow her life to go waste.

She didn't want to live in doubt and uncertainty. She must step out of the frame and see with a different lens what she couldn't already see.

A battle raged inside her broken spirit. If she didn't find out exactly who she was, and how she could fit into her world, there wasn't going to be a world for her to come back to at all.

Omar taught her to act without fear, to stand tall and fight for justice. His footprints had left behind an open road for her guide. He taught her the beauty to be fearless, the courage to have faith.

Yes, she must have faith in God. She must put her trust in Him and ask him to relieve her from the agony of loss and weakness. She would go to God and ask Him to guide her to the right path.

In her mother's arms, Elizabeth felt her numb body beginning to tingle and her strength returning. She felt a new breath, a new strength, as if she were just beginning her ride in a young and fit body.

Omar may be gone, but he lived on in her heart, and that love gave her strength.

Omar's words rang in her ears: "If you want to change who you are, you will have to change what you think."

Still in her mother's arms, she whispered to herself, "Why doesn't God help me?"

A voice came to her ear: "You didn't ask."

She whispered again: "God, I want to come to your door to seek help."

A voice came to her ear: "You didn't knock."

As the days passed, Elizabeth slightly regained her health. Amanda had time now to stay with the president in the White House for several days, during which she regularly called Elizabeth to make sure that her health was improving. Elizabeth had the time to live a life of seclusion, searching for the truth, the purpose of her existence.

No, she was not enclosed within her body or confined to a hidden and lonely place. She was not a woman who dug holes into the darkness for safety but a free spirit that enveloped the earth and moved in the ether. She would rebel against her wary existence. Elizabeth seemed like she was walking asleep in the darkness, searching for her own awakening.

Now came the time to ask herself, "Why am I here, and what is my purpose in life?" She was a woman of social distinction and high repute, but there must be a more important reason for her existence on this planet. There had to be a purpose for her to live for. She came to this world as many others did. She saw a pathway in front of her so she walked. How did she see her pathway? Was she free and unrestrained or did she walk in chains? Was she free to lead her life or was she being led? Was she walking on the road or was it the road that was moving? She didn't know!

She prayed for strength and light so that she might be able to walk with Omar side by side, in the way of the Lord.

The heroic battles of Omar in Kosovo and the martyrdom of Khadija in Palestine showed their willingness to die for the cause of Allah, the one and only God they believe in.

Believing in one God was the source of Muslims power and unity. God, known as Allah in Arabic, was the only one deserving of any worship, and the ultimate purpose of all creation was to submit to Him.

Elizabeth was going through a spiritual void that must be filled. Several questions were struggling in her head. Perhaps by attending Sunday prayers, she might be able to defeat this feeling of emptiness.

When she visited several Catholic churches, she discovered that things had changed from that to which she was accustomed. Women wore clothing that she thought was shameful. They were dressed to attract attention, usually from the opposite sex.

Despite its beautiful outward appearance, there were evils taking place that she never thought were possible in the church. Cases of adultery and fornication went unpunished. Some priests were hooked on drugs and had destroyed their lives and the lives of their families. Leaders of some churches were found to be homosexuals. There were priests even guilty of committing adultery with the young daughters of the church members.

Elizabeth visited a Catholic church. The priests were nice people and very welcoming. She met a priest and asked him, "What do you think of Islam as a religion?"

"Islam is a man-made religion and filled with contradictions."

"What do you think of Muslims?"

"Muslims will go to hell," he replied.

Elizabeth said, "What do you think of the Koran?"

"The Koran is similar to the Bible because it is Satan's trickery, and something that appears close to the Bible is a better trick."

"What did the Koran say about Jesus?"

"I have never read the Koran, for when I tried to, it made me sick."

Elizabeth was astounded and got out of the room as fast as she could. How could he tell her that the Koran was Satan's trickery when he himself had not read it? He was only repeating what he had been told — or he was making it up as he went along. She was so angry with him and at all the church leaders who had treated Islam as an absolute evil yet they were ignorant of Islam. The priest made her feel as if she were a hypocrite living what she did not believe.

Now she was afraid. She was afraid because she could not trust these people anymore. It was up to her, and only her, to decide what she found to be true and what she found to be falsehood.

Elizabeth visited another Catholic church. She asked to see the priest, but they told her that she had to wait a little longer. She waited for a whole hour before the priest appeared. He apologized, saying, "Excuse me, my child, but the church is in a state of chaos because of a major division among the national leaders. It is splitting into two churches, one group cleaving off because they feel the original church has become corrupt."

Elizabeth first question was, "How do you see Muslims?"

"Islam is exotic, backward, and evil. Muslims are uneducated, governed by tyrant rulers, and are cruel. Some of them think it's good to blow up babies and to beat women and treat them like property."

Elizabeth debated with the priest about questions in her mind: What happened to the people who lived before Jesus came – did they go to heaven or hell? Why did some righteous people automatically go to hell just because they did not believe in Jesus? Why did some rather horrible people get rewarded with heaven just because they were Christians. Why did a loving and merciful God require a blood sacrifice to forgive people's sins? Why were we guilty of Adam's original sin? Why did the Word of God disagree with scientific facts? How could Jesus be God, and how could one God be three different things?

The priest never came up with convincing answers. He only told her to "have faith and to leave reason behind when contemplating God".

Elizabeth said angrily, "I believe that God gave us brains so that we might use them. And I believe that a message of God, when it is questioned, has to offer more answers than that."

Elizabeth visited an Evangelical church for a change. There were rock bands with electric guitars, and people were waving their hands in the air and singing "Hallelujah". She was disturbed. The atmosphere seemed so far removed from the worship of God. Church was not a fashion show. A relationship to God was a matter of the heart, mind, and soul, not the way people dressed or the music they liked.

The sex abuse prevailing in the Catholic churches, coupled with a failure to receive answers, in addition to those having rock music that disrupted worship, were enough to make her seek a change. Thus Elizabeth became hungry for a more straightforward and lucid approach to religion that could provide her life with true guidance, not just dogma that was void of knowledge based on reason.

Before she started her search for the truth, she was living the American dream through worshipping false deities like wealth, material gain, hopes, and desires. Surrendering to the true God would certainly purify her heart from worldly dust and darkness.

Attachment to God would liberate her from her own limitations and make her free. She wanted to be a divine channel through which divine love can flow and reach others. The act of giving was at the same time the act of receiving the grace of God. By giving to others, she would be addressing God.

She wondered how she knew that the Bible was right and the Koran was wrong. She must find for herself. She bought an English translation of the Koran and started reading it. Before she knew it, tears were flowing from her eyes. Her heart overflowed with satisfaction and pain at the same time.

She was awestruck by the mercy and grace of Allah. It was as if a ray of eternal truth shone down with blessedness upon her.

She read as much of the Koran as she could in order to understand the truth. One of the first things that struck her was this statement: "There is no god but Allah; He has no associates, and all prayers and worship are directed to Him alone." This seemed so simple, so powerful, so direct, and made so much sense. From that instant, she started reading everything she could about Islam.

Everything she read made so much sense to her. It was as if suddenly all the pieces of the puzzle were fitting perfectly and a clear picture was emerging. She felt as if all along she had been a Muslim but did not know it until now.

Muslims did not believe in a moon god, a monkey god, or a demon god, as the biased media and some Christian leaders and politicians promulgated. As the Koran explained, Muslims believe in the universal god, Allah, and in the Koran He descended upon Muhammad and in all that was imparted to Abraham and Ishmael, to Isaak and Jacob, and to the tribes of his twelve sons, and in what was imparted to Moses and Jesus. Muslims also believed in all that was imparted to all other prophets from God; they did not discriminate one of them from another.

The Koran says, "We believe in God, and in that which has been sent down on us and sent down on Abraham, Ishmael, Isaac and Jacob, and the Tribes, and that which was given to Moses and Jesus and the prophets, of their Lord; we make no division between any of them, and to Him we surrender.

Elizabeth learned that salvation in Islam was not required because of the stain of original sin. Salvation is required because humankind is imperfect and in need of God's forgiveness and love. Allah's servants are not punished for Adam's original sin. Adam asked Allah for forgiveness, and Allah forgave him. Allah did not require a blood sacrifice in payment for sin. Jesus was not God; he was a prophet like all of the other prophets, who all taught the same message: believe in the one true God; worship and submit to Him alone; and live a righteous life according to the guidance He has sent. Allah was a perfect and fair judge who would reward or punish His servants based on their faith and righteousness.

Islam rejected the Christian doctrine of vicarious atonement. Jesus would not atone for the sins of mankind. Every person was responsible for his own deeds. Jesus was not crucified, but God honoured him by lifting him up to Him.

Whenever a person committed a sin, he alone was responsible for that sin. Every person was responsible for his or her own actions. Jesus would not be there to carry the sins of the sinners.

God says in the Koran, "And no bearer of burdens shall bear another's burden."

The Koran teaches the necessity of both faith and good works for salvation. Salvation is attainable through the worship of God alone. A person must believe in God and follow His commandments. This is the same message taught by all the prophets, including Abraham, Moses and Jesus. There is only one worthy of worship. One God alone, without partners, sons, or daughters. Salvation and thus eternal happiness can be achieved by sincere worship.

The Koran says, "Those who remember God standing, sitting, and lying down on their sides, and think deeply about the creation of the heavens and the earth, (saying), 'Our Lord! You have not created (all) this without purpose, glory to You! Exalted are You above all that they associate. Give us salvation from the torment of the Fire."

Throughout the Koran, God continually asked His servants to turn to Him in repentance and ask for His forgiveness. This is the road to salvation. This is the rescue from destruction.

As she read in the Koran, "And whoever does evil or wrongs himself but afterwards seeks God's forgiveness, he will find God Oft Forgiving, Most Merciful" (An-Nisa',10).

The prophet said, "When Allah completed the creation, He wrote in His Book which is with Him on His Throne, 'My Mercy overpowers My Anger.'"

Islam Is the religion of peace. Islam invites all people to peace and does not follow the footsteps of Satan. The Koran says, "O believers, enter the peace, all of you, and follow not the steps of Satan; he is a manifest foe to you" (Al-Baqarah, 208).

God instructed the prophet to address the believers with the expression "Peace be upon you" and to proclaim to them what it would please them to hear: "And when those who believe in Our signs come to thee, say, 'Peace be upon you. Your Lord has prescribed for Himself mercy. Whosoever of you does evil in ignorance, and thereafter repents and makes amends, He is All-forgiving, All-compassionate" (Al-An'am, 54).

The dwellers of paradise would live in a world of peace in the august presence of God.

Theirs was the abode of peace with their Lord, and He was their Protector for what they were doing (Al-An'am, 127).

The believers shall be recipients of God's mercy and grace in heaven. In that state of happiness, they will call out, "Glory be to You, O God", while their greeting in it will be, "Peace". And the close of their call will be, "All praise is due to God, the Lord of the Universe".

The Koran says, "Their cry therein, 'Glory to Thee, O God,' their greeting, 'Peace,' and their cry ends, 'Praise belongs to God, the Lord of all Being'" (Yunus, 10).

The Koran stated that Jesus, the son of Mary, was sent to guide the children of Israel with a new scripture, the Injîl or Gospel. The Koran stated that Jesus was born to Mary as the result of virginal conception, a miraculous event which occurred by the decree of Allah. To aid in his ministry to the Jewish people, Jesus was given the ability to perform miracles with the permission of God rather than of his own power. According to the Koran, Jesus, although appearing to have been crucified, was not killed by crucifixion or by any other means; instead, Allah raised him unto Himself. Like all prophets in Islam, Jesus was considered a Muslim (i.e., one who submits to the will of Allah), as he preached that his followers should adopt the straight path as commanded by Allah. Islam rejects the Trinitarian Christian view that Jesus was God incarnate or the son of God, that he was ever crucified or resurrected, or that he ever atoned for the sins of mankind. The Koran said that Jesus himself never claimed any of these things, and it furthermore indicated that Jesus would deny having ever claimed divinity at the Last Judgement and God will vindicate him. The Koran emphasized that Jesus was a mortal human being who, like all other prophets, had been divinely chosen to deliver Allah's message. The Koran forbade the association of partners with Allah, emphasizing a strict notion of monotheism (tawheed).

She understood from the Koran that for those who had bartered the hereafter for the life of this world, their torment would not be eased, nor would they receive any help.

The Koran said, "Surely those who look not to encounter Us and are well-pleased with the present life and are at rest in it, and those who are heedless of Our signs, those — their refuge is the Fire, for that they have been earning. Surely those who believe and do deeds of righteousness, their Lord will guide them for their belief; beneath them rivers flowing in gardens of bliss; their cry therein, 'Glory to Thee, O God,' their greeting, 'peace,' and their cry ends, 'Praise belongs to God, the Lord of all Being'" (Yunus 7–10).

Elizabeth was rich; she had a private plane, luxury vehicles, expensive clothes, maids, a butler, a mansion, and several vacation homes. The Koran taught her that the present life was but the joy of delusion. Man was not created to amass fame and fortune but rather to recognize the Creator, to be grateful to Him, to worship Him, to surrender to Him, and to obey the laws that He had determined for His servants.

She read in the Koran, "Know that the present life is but a sport and a diversion, an adornment and a cause for boasting among you, and a rivalry in wealth and children. It is as a rain whose vegetation pleases the unbelievers; then it withers, and thou sees it turning yellow, then it becomes broken orts. And in the world to come there is a terrible chastisement, and forgiveness from God and good pleasure; and the present life is but the joy of delusion."

The Koran taught her that the noblest of men in God's sight were not the wealthiest but the ones who feared God most. People before God were all one, and the most honourable of them in the sight of God was the most God-fearing.

Only now did she understood the purpose of life as the Koran plainly described it: "And I did not create the jinn and humankind except to worship Me. I desire of them no provision, neither do I desire that they feed Me. Surely Allah is the All-Provider, the Possessor of Strength, the Ever-Sure."

The Koran made it perfectly clear that all humans would be questioned about their actions on the Day of Judgement. And in this matter, even prophets would not be spared: "We shall question those unto whom a Message was sent, and We shall question the Messengers, and We shall relate to them with knowledge {their whole story} assuredly We were not absent.

Elizabeth read that the Prophet said, "The feet of a slave will not move on the Day of Judgement until he has been questioned about [four things]: his life – how he spent it, his knowledge – how he acted upon it, his wealth – where he earned it and how he spent it, and his body – how he used it."

The Koran stressed that life is but a short enjoyment. Although short compared to life after death, the present life was decisive because treating it wrongly would bring disgrace forever in the hereafter.

Islam looked at the present life as a test. The second life (the hereafter) was the time when each individual enjoyed or suffered from the outcome of his deeds during the test period. The deeds of each individual would be judged by Allah on the Day of Judgement.

The Muslim knows that his life is a very short one – a hundred years, more or less – whereas the second life is eternal. With this belief in the hereafter and the Day of Judgement, a Muslim's life becomes as purposeful and meaningful as possible. A Muslim's long-standing purpose is to go to paradise by pleasing his Creator.

Success in the sight of God is not by hoarding riches and wealth but rather achieving the ultimate goal – paradise. Every soul shall taste of death. Whosoever is removed from the fire and admitted to paradise, he indeed is triumphant – this in the sight of Allah is the ultimate success.

She read the following in the Koran: "It is not your wealth nor your children that shall bring you nigh in nearness to Us, except for him who believes, and does righteousness; those – there awaits them the double recompense for that they did, and they shall be in the lofty chambers in security."

Allah does not need us. We need Him.

The Koran says, "O men, you are the ones that have need of God; He is the All-sufficient, the All-laudable. Let not the wicked think that it causes Allah any annoyance if they do not worship Him. He is high above all needs. But He turns in His Mercy to all who call on Him. For those who arrogantly reject Him, their disbelief shall be laid to their charge and they shall have much to answer for. The punishment is bound to overtake them."

The Koran also says, "Say {O Muhammad, unto the disbelievers}: 'My Lord would not concern Himself with you but for your prayer. But now you have denied {the truth}. Therefore, the torment will be yours.'"

She also read from among the sayings of the prophet that the Lord said, "O My servants, I have forbidden oppression for Myself and have made it forbidden amongst you, so do not oppress one another."

The Lord also said, "O My servants, all of you are astray except for those I have guided, so seek guidance of Me and I shall guide you. O My servants, all of you are hungry except for those I have fed, so seek food of Me and I shall feed you. O My servants, all of you are naked except for those I have clothed, so seek clothing of Me and

I shall clothe you. O My servants, you sin by night and by day, and I forgive all sins, so seek forgiveness of Me and I shall forgive you."

The Lord has also said, "O My servants, you will not attain harming Me so as to harm Me, and you will not attabenefit Me. O my servants, were the first of you and the last of you, the human of you and the jinn of you to become as pious as the most pious heart of any one man of you, that would not increase My kingdom in anything. O My servants, were the first of you and the last of you, the human of you and the jinn of you to be as wicked as the most wicked heart of any one man of you, that would not decrease My kingdom in anything. O My servants, were the first of you and the last of you, the human of you and the jinn of you to rise up in one place and make a request of Me, and were I to give everyone what he requested, that would not decrease what I have, any more than a needle decreases the sea if put into it."

"O My servants, it is but your deeds that I reckon up for you and then recompense you for, so let him who finds good praise Allah, and let him who finds other than that blame no one but himself."

It had always frustrated her that the Bible had been written down long after the events had happened, that it was written by many different authors, and that she could never see the original Message of God in the language in which it had been spoken. She was excited to know that the Koran had not been tampered with.

Her soul unfolded itself like a rose of countless petals. She found comfort in Islam, a religion professing peace, equality, freedom, and hope – things she believed in and felt they were worth fighting for – a religion that put everything in its proper perspective and appealed to her heart and intellect. At last, she had found the truth and the path of the soul. She had found a place to rest her faith.

Elizabeth wept incessantly when she read what God said to the prophet: "I do not fit into the heavens and the earth, but I fit into the heart of my faithful servant. I was a hidden treasure, I willed to be known. I created the creation so that I would be known." He would be known in this material world through His attributes manifested in His creation.

Allah could see deep into one's heart. The faithful sees by the eye of Allah. Her purified heart contained Allah; Allah enlarged her heart and fitted himself into it. Allah felt the yearning of her, and He too longed for her.

Allah's will worked silently in her soul. She felt a gradual perception of monotheism, a realization that Allah was One and above names. She realized that the main purpose of human beings was nothing else but to serve Allah, to be grateful to him, and to worship him alone.

Elizabeth found with Allah a state of peace and serenity. She brought herself to disappear in the essence of Allah. She emptied her heart of everything but Allah's love. The utter need and love of Allah was her strive to reach perfection.

She had seen a light of dazzling beauty. She felt happy amidst all her grief. The veil was lifted from her eyes, and her soul was filled with divine ecstasy. Her soul longed for the supreme. She saw the light by the grace of Allah. There was a peace slowly spreading over her heart.

She would praise Allah for guiding her to the right path. She would drink His remedy gradually and in silence. This harmonious relationship with the Koran would remain a precious secret in her heart.

Elizabeth first let Allah's light shine in her own self and through the darkness around her, then walked with steps firm and sure.

Suddenly, she felt an urgent need to see her father.

CHAPTER 56

Elizabeth decided to see her father. She had a lot to say to him. In the elegant living room of the White House, John Rosh, the president of the United States, and Amanda Rosh, the First Lady, received Elizabeth Rosh, their only daughter, with tenderness and love.

Elizabeth sat with her father and mother. She wasn't exactly crying, but she had tears and seemed very frustrated.

"Dad, I came here because I have a lot to say to you. I just want my voice to be heard."

"Of course, dear. I'm all ears," the president said, aligning his back against the back of his chair.

"For as long as we live, to the day we die and beyond, each of us who does whatever he can to help will be able to face the future with a clear conscience. I want to be counted among those with a human heart."

"You are indeed, darling. You are living a life that is in alignment with your values and the things that you believe in. Your excellent humanitarian work is appreciated by all."

"My conscious is the measure of my honesty and devotion to my country. Wrong does not cease to be wrong because the majority share in it."

"I don't exactly understand what you mean." Elizabeth's remark had left a frown on her father's face.

Elizabeth said, "The American administration has been dishonest to the American people about its wars in the Middle East. Anyone ignoring the fact that America is terrorizing the Middle East either is a fool or plays one. I would be wronging myself if I didn't say that."

The president listened, stunned. Then he said, "The world has changed since September eleventh. We live in a more dangerous world than we did before. There are now people out there who want to kill us. And why would they like to kill us? Because they hate our freedoms." President Rosh was trying to justify his wars in the Middle East

Elizabeth, said, "They hate us not because they hate our freedoms but rather they see us as a threat to their way of life, either through military or corporate intervention or by the influence our loose culture has on them. The world didn't change on September eleventh. It was the same world. It's just that the people who assumed power failed to protect this nation."

"I did a lot of good things in the Middle east. I gave Iraq its freedom."

Elizabeth said, "You were wrong about Iraq's weapons of mass destruction. You have manipulated intelligence and misled the American people."

"I relied on the collective judgement of the intelligence community when I determined that Saddam Hussein had weapons of mass destruction. Those who are claiming that the information had been manipulated are playing politics with the war."

"Iraq had nothing to do with nine-eleven. Iraq was not an imminent threat to us or anyone else. Iraq was being kept in line by UN sanctions already in place to insure that they would not emerge as a threat. But what we did is invade Iraq without any logical reason. We bombed civilian targets. We sent our troops to sustain an immoral occupation. We suppressed the free press in Iraq, and we denied its people their human rights."

"The people of Iraq are better off now," said her father.

"Are they really? They are occupied by a foreign nation. People are interrogated and restrained without cause. Innocent people die. Our forces have destroyed civilian sources of food, power, and clean water. We destroyed home and families."

"Iraq is now better without Saddam Hussein. I dealt with Iraq as I saw fit to my nation."

"We went in to remove one man, but what we really did was to kick the shit out of an entire nation. We've killed civilians and destroyed homes. The weapons of war do not bring freedom but only ruin, destruction, and death. You served up freedom in Iraq, nourished with bombs. Their blood is on your hands. You have planned the crime of the century, Father, and you think you've gotten away with it?"

"We went to Iraq to defend the human rights of Iraqi citizens."

Elizabeth said, "Your speeches about democracy and human rights may deceive your people, but God knows what is in your heart. You are the most contentious enemy to the Arabs. You spread mischief through their land, and God loves not corruption."

"I am not against the Arabs or Islam. I say in my speeches that Islam is a great religion."

"Stop talking about Islam, for you know nothing about it. In your closed meetings, you connect Islam with terrorism, while it is not. Your hatred of Muslims tinges all your judgements.

"And how about the Palestinians? You killed their dream of living peacefully on their land. Their blood is on your hands. Your hands are stained with the Palestinian blood."

"The Palestinians are always the aggressors. They started the suicide bombings and all acts of terrorism."

"That is a bald-faced lie. Precisely the opposite is true. The Israelis are the aggressors. They are backed militarily, politically, and financially by America. They have billions of dollars' worth of weapons, all paid for by the American taxpayers. Not only do the Israelis have many state-of-the-art jet fighters, tanks, and attack helicopters, but they even have three submarines carrying missiles with nuclear warheads."

"Have you heard about the intifadas and how the Palestinians attacked the Israelis without reason?"

"They are desperate people. They see their fathers, mothers, and children being killed before their eyes every day and you don't want them to fight back? They see their land stolen, their houses demolished, and then they are thrown in refugee camps and you don't want them to fight for having decent lives on their own land!"

The president said, "I did all I can to help the Palestinians. I called for two states for two peoples – an independent State of Palestine alongside the State of Israel."

"False announcements that led nowhere for the Arabs. The road map failed, and violence continued. You are to blame for not engaging in the Middle East conflict actively enough — and look where it has gotten us today." .

Suddenly, anger came sweeping through her body. She leapt up shaking all over.

"Just who do you think you are? Barking out deceiving announcements favouring Israel by giving it the green light to attack and assassinate, and at the same time numbing the Arabs by promising a Palestinian state that you know will never be established! Your cunning promises and claims will come back to you. Being a president is more than talk; there is responsibility there."

"In their latest intifada, they used suicide bombing against the Israelis."

"The latest Intifada began when the Israelis first provoked the Palestinians at the Al-Aqsa Mosque and then brutally, massively terrorized them with their powerful military. Suicide bombings are the desperate reactions of despairing individuals to this ongoing Israeli state terrorism."

Elizabeth's anger erupted into full fury. She shouted at her father, "Is it not enough that you supported the Israeli plan about outlining the borders of Israel without consulting the Palestinians! Is it not enough that you gave Israel clear permission to reoccupy the West Bank and the Gaza Strip? You approved that the Israelis destroy the private and public properties of the Palestinians without restrictions during the annihilation of the West Bank. Was it not enough that you supported Israel in its contempt and ignoring the resolution of the International Court of Justice, which compels Israel to pull down the separating wall! Your administration has swallowed its declaration about the date for establishing the Palestinian nation, saying that there are no sacred dates! You sided with Israel when it refused the return of the refugees to their homeland. You gave Israel a license to devour the Palestinian land under the pretence of outlining the borders. You have established the ugly fact that in your time, America stands against the international law and imposes by force her biased views about the Arab-Israeli conflict.

"I was there in Palestine, remember! I have seen horror and terrible oppression. It was just wholesale slaughter. People pulled dead bodies around them for protection. Mothers wrapped their children with blankets and hugged them with their backs towards the entrances. I can still hear their cries, the little kids screaming.

"What would you do if a viciously racist foreign military force assaulted your town and slaughtered your children, your brothers, sisters, mother, your father, grandfather, or grandmother, your husband, wife, or your best friend? What if you saw the soldiers laugh after they blew up your sister, making fun of her bloody disfigured face? What if they raped your brother's wife after murdering her husband or father because he tried to stop them? What if you had to bury your six-month-old baby because an Israeli bullet ripped through its tiny little fragile body? What if they beat and tortured you and your father and brother, sneering insults at you as they urinated on you?

"Can you really imagine what you would feel like? Would you even be strong enough to stay sane? And what if the Israelis got away with it year after year after year and it looked that the whole stinking world didn't give a damn whether you lived or died? And those invaders had tanks and helicopter gunships and F-16 jets while you had nothing but rocks. And they would shoot you if you throw them. They'd shoot you when you were standing by your window or your front door. They'd shoot you when you walked outside to get food at the store, even after they said they had lifted their curfew that had kept you starving inside cramped little rooms for days and days. If you saw a tank when you went out for food, you'd have to run back and hide because the Israeli in that tank would murder you for the crime of being a Palestinian human being."

Amanda said, "That is sad."

"They seemed to me so vanquished, so humbled, and crushed," Elizabeth said, weeping. "You give the Arabs and Muslims promises and satisfaction with your mouth, but your heart is averse to them. Evil indeed is what you have been doing. What makes you treat people so horribly? Speak the truth. Be just. You have killed many in Afghanistan, Iraq, and Palestine."

The president's eyes flashed with indignation. "No, I won't listen to this." He stood up.

"Sit down, Father. It's about time you faced the truth. I'm tired of the lies and cheating and the broken promises that were never meant to be kept. Your lies circulate through the world. The worst of the people are those who are doubled-faced hypocrites. You appear to your people with one face and to the Arabs with another face. Hypocrites are the denizens of hell.

"You ought to be ashamed of yourself. You let yourself be manipulated by the Christian Right and their coalition with the Jews. You implemented their agenda, which was designed to destroy the Arab world."

The president went to his desk and sat there watching her, his face pale. There was a long silence. The president said, "So what else have I done wrong?"

"Are you afraid of the neocons, Christian Right, Right Zionist wing, or the Judeo-Christian coalition? It is evident that you are totally influenced by such political and religious groups. Hostile announcements against Muslims and their religion were issued from these groups. You surrendered to their plot against the Arab world. In your time, Iraq and Afghanistan were invaded and the Israelis were allowed to steal more Palestinian lands, thus oppressing the Palestinians further. In your time, American Muslims were maltreated, the Koran was burned and defiled, Allah was attacked and humiliated, and the prophet of Islam was slandered. The Muslim prisoners were severely tortured in Abo-Gharib and the Guantanamo prison, without fair trials."

"The neocons, the Christian Right, and the Judeo-Christian coalition brought me to power. They represent the political and religious fabric of the United States."

Elizabeth said, "These groups are the cause of such hatred towards Islam and Muslims. Our political system is overwhelmingly influenced by such groups. These groups moved from mere Christianity to political Christianity, which has spread like cancer to all aspects of the American life and then crossed the borders to affect Muslims in their own countries. America must revise its political system, which is dominated by such internal groups."

"This is an outrageous lie. What else do you have against me?"

"God has blessed America with greater power and knowledge; use this for the sake of humanity. Instead of becoming an instrument of destruction, express your gratefulness to the Lord by helping the oppressed. Offer a true example of justice and be a protector of the rights of all. Make sure that all get their due share and no injustice is inflicted on anyone. Respect the international law and see that it is administered justly and fairly."

Elizabeth ceased talking for a few moments to hold her breath, then said in a sad voice, "God will ask you for each drop of Muslims' blood shed in your wars in Afghanistan, Palestine, and Iraq. The cruel crimes against humanity perpetrated by America's rulers will drag this nation down to its inevitable karmic doom." Elizabeth words were covered with sorrow and grief.

"Stop this nonsense, Elizabeth," said the president. "I am sure that your fears are imaginary."

"Evil empires always meet their doom. I can assure you that this country would be in one hell of a lot of trouble. What are you trying to do? To bring this great nation to its knees! Do you realize what terrible trouble America is heading for unless she changes?"

"What do you mean by that?"

"Without family values, this country would be up the creek even worse than it is. I look around me and see gambling, blind racism, homosexuality, same-sex marriages, premarital sex, gay pastors and bishops. Gays are allowed to serve openly in the military. The Justice Department backs gay marriage. All this is spreading like fire to destroy the fabric of our country.

"You have committed a terrible crime against God and against humanity. For what a wretched price has you sold your soul? You have incurred the wrath of God on yourself and on this country."

"You are difficult to get along with."

Elizabeth looked at her father and screamed at him, "Which god are you, John Rosh! Should I fall on my knees to you?" Liz bit her lip to stop the tears from flowing and glanced helplessly at her father.

"The greatest purveyor of violence on earth is my own government. Truth is always offensive to those who live a lie. America is being bullied from within. Republicans and the mischief they spread in the Arab counties are worse than the terrorists."

"Watch your tongue. I don't know how the hell anything like you came from my loins. I am looking after the American interests, and I design policies directed to protect such interests."

"Your motto is to talk smoothly while holding a thick cane in your hand. You are associating your deceiving diplomacy with the democracy of cruise rockets."

"Don't talk to me like that, Elizabeth, and don't try to tell me how to run my country". His voice was quiet but deeply angry.

"You do that at the expense of the poor and downtrodden. You are arrogant in the land without right."

The president said, "We have interests in the whole world to guard and protect. This demands strength and power, and we are a nation of might and power. Who is mightier than us in strength?"

"Do you not see that Allah, who created us, was stronger than us in might? There is no power and no might except in Allah. Stop evaluating things according to power and materialistic gains, according to your might and sovereignty over the world. These are nothing against Allah's wrath when it comes to overthrowing the oppressors and shaking the land beneath them.

"Allah sees all that you do. Allah knows the deceitful eye and what a man's breast conceals. Have you forgotten that to Allah belongs all power, and that Allah is severe in chastisement? Do you not consider that you will stand before Allah, the Lord of the worlds?"

The president was stunned to see his daughter behaving like Muslims. She'd uttered the word "Allah" before him instead of the word "God".

"You were born into a devout Christian family, yet you talk like Muslims! What is the matter with you? Have you read the Koran?"

"Yes, I read the Koran, mainly to be faith literate. I also wanted to understand how Muslims think and behave."

"And how did you find the Koran?"

Elizabeth said, "Immensely instructive and surely divine."

"What you have heard from Elizabeth, John, is a true word at an unjust ruler," interjected Amanda.

Elizabeth said, "Today's empire is tomorrow's ashes. Nothing lasts forever. You exchange Allah's bounties with ungratefulness and cause people to dwell in the abode of ruin. You know what Allah said to His prophet Muhammad: 'Pride is my cloak and greatness is my robe, and he who competes with Me in respect of either of them I shall cast into hell fire.'

"Mom, what is to become of me? I'm afraid to look into the future. I'm troubled by forebodings and am living in a haze." Elizabeth said downhearted.

"Don't be downhearted, my darling. Perhaps everything is for the best."

"Why was I so unlucky in love? Why didn't the world want me to be happy for long?"

Amanda said, "I still see you suffering and hurting, my darling. You are lacking nothing. You are extremely rich and the daughter of the president of the United States of America."

"Just living is not enough, Mother. One must have sunshine, freedom, and even flowers." Elizabeth spoke with difficulty through her tears. "The man I truly loved has gone. I still love him."

"I know, sweetie, I know. He was your true love. It's always the hardest to get over. I love you, and remember that no matter what happens, you will always be my little girl." Amanda's tears were also overflowing.

"People thought that he was fighting the world to save his life. But he was fighting the world for me, to be with me. To make his love survive. It was an unequal hell of a fight, but he won. All that fighting happened because of me."

"You suffered a lot and can get over this pain."

"I am a woman, Mom. I want to make the barren life fruitful."

The president said, "He comes from a different world than yours. I merely want to caution you."

"Omar is all I ever wanted. No word that was not true ever passed his lips. He is magnanimous and merciful."

"You are about to be a woman of ill repute. Without him, you are much better off."

"I can handle myself. I don't think my affection for Omar is anyone's concern."

"Only a woman helplessly in love would trust so blindly and so foolishly."

"I am safer under Omar's eyes than I am in my own bed."

The president said, "Don't follow his path, Elizabeth."

"I follow my own choosing."

"Use your common sense, girl. You will get over him. How did you ever allow him to come into your life?"

"His presence in my life was benediction."

"Stay out of this," said her father. "You worship him — it's written all over your face. He's your big hero. Taught you how to hate your daddy, taught you how to hate your country and your religion. I hope it's some sort of phase you are going through."

"I love Omar very much, and I resent your talking about him like that."

"He is too far to understand the way it is today. He's completely out of touch with our world."

"He's my hero and saviour. There is no one equal to him in honesty on earth. I am talking about love, Father. Without love, there is no mercy. Without mercy, there is no forgiveness. Without forgiveness, there is no hope. Without hope, there is no salvation."

"I intend to undertake a journey. I'll live on Omar's farm, where it's quiet and peaceful all the time. He has a garden with beautiful flowers. I'll have a home in the virgin desert. I'll get married and have children." She said this with a ray of hope showing on her face.

Her father said, "What's the matter with you? Are you out of your mind?"

"Omar leads a life of purity, virtue, and obedience to the laws of Allah. No word ever passed his lips that was not true. That who is pleased to see a man from the inmates of paradise should glance at him."

"You're willing to give up everything, go against your family, and fight to become his wife?"

"He is the light of my life. I'll go to the man whom my spirit has chosen. To the man through whose eyes I see the world. I will cross the Atlantic to be reborn on the other side."

Amanda said, "I am actually beginning to love the name Omar. Be careful, dearest, and look after yourself. Avoid everything dangerous and spare your parents the grief and worry."

"I don't want to be an American who pretends not to approve of such things, yet he looks the other way and remains silent while his evil military and government commit these bloody crimes against humanity all over the world. 'American' Is a word of shame. The world screams in pain, and Americans are deaf, indifferent to everything but their own selfish material comfort."

"This is crushing. Compose yourself. How did you come to such a state? You ought to be ashamed of yourself."

"I fear Allah. We are quite worthless without the fear of Allah. Allah gives every person the place in life he deserves, and my place is with Omar. Allah alone is the Majesty in the heavens and the earth, and He is the All-Mighty, the All-Wise. The prophet of Islam said, "Truth leads to piety, and piety leads to paradise. A man persists in speaking the truth until he is enrolled near Allah as a truthful man. Falsehood leads to vice, and vice leads to the Fire. A person goes on telling a lie until he is recorded a liar in the sight of Allah.

"By searching my heart, I saw that I had been right. I miss Omar so much that I don't think I can stand this. I love him more than I love myself."

"I understand, my baby. I truly understand." Amanda said comforting.

"I don't know where to fit, Mom. I don't know where I find a place. Why does it hurt so much? My life has been stolen from me. I'll never be with a man again who fails to treat me as I deserve. Omar has proven his love through his actions, not his words. He has saved my life several times. He is the best man I have ever met in my life. I love him."

"It hurts me so much to hear this from you," said her father. "My heart is sore. That is what you have come to? Is that what has become of you? You are ruining yourself. You don't know how I suffer on your account."

"Forget about me, Father. I have found my way. Do care about America. Your nation rots from the inside out."

Amanda said, "You will survive, darling. I am sure of that. I know nothing will deter you. If you love him that much, then go for it. Go to him. Don't deny yourself real happiness."

"Amanda, are you out of your mind! Whose side are you on?" the president said, clearly angry and astonished.

"You're a stubborn old fool, John. She had made up her mind, and there was no way to dissuade her. She is doing this out of the goodness of her heart. He is her dream, John, and who am I to kill her dream!" Amanda said angrily.

Confusion and bewilderment reigned the room.

"Allah dwells in my heart. He guides my steps. His light illuminates my soul. I want to kill my ego and direct my face to Allah. I want to have a new birth, a new life, a new resurrection. I want to liberate myself from any attachment except to Allah. I want to be born again by having a new life." Elizabeth said this with her tears overflowing.

"America will perish because wickedness is abundant. I will never set foot on this soil again," she said, getting to her feet. "I will give away all this. I am withdrawing from you all! Oh, I don't care. I no longer mind.

"Mom I was a coward. I was afraid to tell him that I want to spend the rest of my life with him and be the mother of his children. I let him hear the words of love to back off. I will not give up on that man. I will fight to get my love back."

"I love him. I love him." Elizabeth said while heading to the door. She kept saying this until she vanished from sight.

CHAPTER 57

The US Senate wanted to know more about the last hours of Omar on American land before he disappeared into the sea. Elizabeth was spotted on the beach with Omar, and there was the possibility that she might have been spending a vacation on the beach and met Omar by mere chance. They figured that he surely had detained her, maltreated her, and used her as a human shield before escaping via the sea.

A congressional hearing was held in the Russell Senate Office Building in order to hear Elizabeth's oral testimony about her last hours with Omar the terrorist. Members of Congress sat in the tiers of raised chairs, while Elizabeth sat below.

The chairman started the hearing: "Ms. Elizabeth Rosh, the daughter of the president of the United States, attends this hearing today in order to tell us how she endured the unendurable and suffered the insufferable. She was promenading on the beach when she met the terrorist by mere chance. He detained her and used her as a human shield until he managed to escape. She is here to tell us how she showed great courage and fortitude. We applaud her courage and determination. We want to share with her the agony that left her physically and emotionally drained. Ms. Rosh, the floor is yours."

Elizabeth looked before her, unable to focus. She felt as though she were off balance, spinning, whirling. Elizabeth took long moments to pull herself together. When she talked, her words were screams of agony coming out of a tormented heart. Her words had also a spirit of mockery.

"I was not detained or abused in any way. I just stood by the man I loved. I went to him of my own free will, to share with him the struggle against tyranny and oppression. Omar, the man you call a terrorist, is a professional fighter, not a killer. I saw in him loyalty, honour, and a willing heart. We shared a special bond that can never be broken. Nobody has experienced the kind of relationship that we shared. What we shared was so special that it could never be replaced. I just wanted to stand by him in his struggle and be sure that he would leave our unjust land in peace.

"There's a lot I could say about Omar. I guess what matters is what he stands for, what he lives for, and what he wants to die for.

"Omar is an Egyptian military officer whom I met in Kosovo. He was given the mission of escorting me to Prekaz, where the United Nation's refugee camp was situated. The road to Prekaz was extremely dangerous, but he protected me with his soul. An armed Serbian shot at me, but Omar protected me with his body and took the bullet instead of me. I saw acts of valour, self-denial, and sacrifice I never imagined I could see in a man. I saw in him piety stemming from his belief in one god and a tremendous ability to fight bodily temptation. This rock who killed one hundred men during our journey to Prekaz collapsed and cried like an infant when burying a female baby, we found still alive in the arms of her dead mother after a massacre committed by the Serbs.

"This event was very special for me because when he collapsed in my arms weeping, I realized that he had captured my heart forever. Yes, at that moment, I fell deeply in love with him, and I still am.

"The years separated us, and I married another man to whom I felt frigidity and lost all interest in being intimate with him. I don't know why, but maybe because my love for Omar strongly overshadowed any other man I could think of.

"You all know the man I married, of course. He was a senator like you, a colleague you worked with. He is now spending fifteen years in prison for his crimes.

"When Omar arrived in the United States, the old love revived in my heart and I was sure that somehow I was going to spend the rest of my life with him.

"The moment he set foot in the United States, he saw hostility and hatred from the political and religious fabric of our nation towards his religion. As a man believing strongly in his religion and carefully obeying its rules, he horribly witnessed the humiliation of his God, the slandering of the prophet of Islam, and the defiling, belying, and burning of the Koran. Yes, we made Islam our enemy, and we waged war against it.

"This hatred towards Islam is in fact lacerating America and taking it down. The religious fabric of the nation, exemplified by the Evangelicals, the Christian Right, the Judeo-Christian coalition, and the televangelists, has tarnished Islam. Those known as the Christian leaders, without having any knowledge about Islam except from the biased media, are smearing Islam with dirt and are not aware that by doing this, they are bringing God's collective punishment on their heads and on their nation.

"Do these ignorant people think they will be left unpunished? Are they so ignorant as not to know that he who sets himself against God and His prophet shall suffer the fire of hell?

"You should have known that God knows the thoughts in people's breasts. He knows all that is in the heavens and all that is on earth. He knows all that is being said. Do they think that the foul epithets they utter against Islam are just words that will disappear in the air? They must understand that all the words they utter since they were in the cradle and until their deaths are recorded.

"These hate-mongering politicians and Christian leaders are found in every level of American society. You find them in churches, the military, Congress, the Tea Party, the neoconservatives, the Judeo-Christian coalition, the Christian Right, and the Evangelicals. It may seem that the whole country stands now against Islam and Muslims, but in fact they stand against their Creator and His last message directed to them in particular. The perpetrators are in fact turning their country into an evil land vulnerable to God's wrath.

"Omar watched the execution of the Anglo-American-Israeli 'military road map' known as the New Middle East. This project was aimed at serving the American interests in the region by dividing the Muslim countries into sects and factions living without borders through creating an arc of instability, chaos, and violence. The result of this instability was the killing of millions of innocents in Lebanon, Palestine, Syria, Libya, and Iraq as well as the displacement of hundreds of thousands of refugees now scattered on the borders of Egypt, Turkey, and Jordan.

"We didn't care much about the health and lives of these people. To hell with them; they are not Americans. People of the world want to be allowed to work and eat their food in freedom, yet we deprived them of their fundamental right to live in peace.

"We forgot that people were created equal and have the right to live peacefully on their land. America calls for human rights, but she denies the right of her victims to live. This is blind racism. We are bloody racists.

"We are all criminals; we are going to pay dearly for the crimes we committed against humanity there. Their blood is on our hands.

"The government and media were lying to the people and depicting the matter as war on terrorism, claiming that Islam was the enemy. Omar watched all this and decided to raise his voice. He said that what was happening was cruel and not right. It was unfair to keep the people in the dark on this matter. He therefore addressed the people and told them the truth about the American plot against Islam and the Muslim world. He exposed our reckless monetary policy that dried up the American treasury by spending billions on unnecessary wars. He warned about the terrible consequences of a divine wrath that might befall us for our crimes against humanity.

"The response of the American people to Omar's TV interviews was overwhelming. They realized the failure of the government's policies and demanded transparency and reform. This incited the grudge of the administration against Omar.

"I was wrongly shot by a hitman hired by my ex-husband to kill Omar. Omar took revenge by killing the hired assassin. He didn't kill a good soul but a killer, a murderer. Although he enjoyed diplomatic immunity, we considered him a persona non grata, put him on trial, and wounded his pride. When he fought back, we considered him a terrorist and forgot that he was a splendid fighter. He won his fight against a whole nation, and we lost. A man standing alone against a whole nation and winning all his battles is surely an act of God.

"Omar left behind fifty orphaned families, but this was not his fault, for we should have listened to the request of Egypt not to put him on trial and deliver him intact according to the international diplomatic law.

"All I wanted was for Omar to be safe and to be treated fairly. They wanted to eat him alive, but he did not intend to let them have the last laugh. While fighting his opponents, his agonizing cry was worse than any thunder. His voice was a roar. I saw glory in his eyes, strength in his heart. How perfect the composure of his soul was. He was on the side of the angels.

"I don't know what I'll do since he's gone. I'm plunged into a bottomless abyss of grief.

"George Washington said, 'It will be worthy of a free, enlightened great nation to give to mankind the magnanimous and too novel example of a people always guided by an exalted justice and benevolence.'

"I look right and look left and see that deep corruption is eating away at every level of the American society like cancer. We can see this in our families, we can see this in our business, and we can especially see this in our government. We have the highest rate of divorce in the world; we have the highest rate of teen pregnancy in the world; we have the highest rate of obesity in the world; and nobody has higher rates of cancer, heart disease, and diabetes than we do. Shooting in schools has become common, the suicide rate is soaring, and our economy is falling apart. America has led the way in protecting the rights of gays and lesbians. Gays and lesbians may now actively and openly serve in the military. Marriage between two persons of the same sex is legal in some states. America, why did you have to let it happen? The dreams, the ideals, the hopes, shattered beyond repair.

"It seems to me that our government does not understand the fact that the political and religious fabric of our nation is leading America into peril. Our politicians say, 'The United States stands by Israel because the two nations share many values. Their historic development provides a natural and genuine bond. Both nations share Judeo-Christian values. To be Christian is to be Jewish. It is therefore the duty of a Christian to put support for the land of Israel above all else. After all, we worship the same God!

"The term Judeo-Christian is a myth and highly hypocritical because the Jews do not worship the 'Christ-God'. The idea of a single Judeo-Christian tradition is an American invention for political reasons. Theologically and historically, there is no such thing as the Judeo-Christian tradition. It's a secular myth promulgated by people who are driven by political agendas.

"Christianity and Judaism are two distinct religious inheritances, despite all the superficial attempts by modern scholars to manufacture a 'Judeo-Christianity'. Judeo-Christianity should be seen for what it is – another secular twentieth-century fraud, manufactured for narrow political ends.

"The term Christian Zionism is simply that every action taken by Israel, whether good or bad, is divine! Israel's actions should therefore be supported and praised by all people. It is perfectly accepted to give the green light to whatever Israel wants, without exception. Everything Israel does, including lies, theft, and murder, is justified as long as Israel wants it. This includes the invasion of Lebanon, which killed one hundred thousand Lebanese; murdering thousands of Palestinians in cold blood in Sabra and Shatila camps; bombing of a sovereign country such as Iraq; deliberate methodical brutalizing of the Palestinians; breaking bones; shooting the innocents; demolishing houses; steeling the Palestinian land and building Jewish settlements on it; and the expulsion of Christian and Muslin Palestinians from a land they owned for over two thousand years.

"Christian Zionist support for the state of Israel has had a major impact on the Palestinian-Israeli conflict. They advocate for the removal of all Arabs from the West Bank and the destruction of the two mosques that currently reside in the Temple Mount. Many of these Christian Zionists do not believe peace is possible between the Palestinians and the Israelis and have played a role in the demonization of Muslims everywhere.

"The message of the Christian Zionists is always the same – there is no such thing as moderate Islam because Islam is inherently violent, and the only reason there are moderate Muslims is because they are not good Muslims. They also claim that the terrorists are the only 'true' Muslims because they are just doing what the Koran tells them to." This is the same message we hear from so-called 'experts' on Fox News, talk radio, and from fundamentalist preachers.

"Christian Zionism creates several problems for the international committee. It creates a situation in which Israel is judged by a different standard than the rest of the international community, and it plays a major role in demonizing the religion of Islam as well as the Palestinian people.

"There is no denying that there is a direct link between this movement and the rise of Islamophobia in America and the hatred Muslims feel towards America.

"How has America become this nation belligerent to all? How has this nation that was once guided by an exalted justice and benevolence become guided by prejudice, double standards, shameful injustice, and malevolence?

"You, the political leaders of America, appear unable to grasp the magnitude of the dangers the country now faces. Mired in your rancorous culture wars and squabbling among yourselves, you seem oblivious of the fact that American global leadership is fast ebbing away. You have in fact transformed America into an evil land vulnerable to God's wrath. When leaders of your kind dominate a community, it is to be expected that God has made a decision to punish it!

"It's not justice that reigns on the earth; it's force. America, you are a pale shadow. A little sunrise will make you disappear. America, you have lost your allure. America, I fear you the chastisement of an encompassing day. You can't defeat God. God's wrath shall surprise you. Pale and dumb shall you stand, confused and unable to avert it, nor shall you be granted respite. God's wrath will bring your world to its knees.

"My days with Omar have signposted my road. He is like a shining star leading me from deep misery. When I ask, he gives brilliant responses. When I ask him religious questions, he answers with new perspectives. He sets my mind at rest at all points. He is a man in every way. I trust him. He talked as if he could see into the future. I bow to him, the pious believer.

"Now you understand why I fought with Omar shoulder-to-shoulder in Kosovo. We fought against oppression and tyranny. We fought against racial discrimination. We fought to promote quality and justice. We fought to promote human rights and freedom.

"Now you understand why I went to see him before he left our evil nation. I went to wipe his tears. I went to tell him that I understand his agony and that I stand by him. I am his until the end. My last doubts have vanished. My love will live. I love him.

Elizabeth rose from her chair and walked to the door. The guard opened the door for her. She paused at the door and turned back to face the members of Congress.

"We must have strong minds ready to accept the truth. Omar is dear to me, but dearer still is truth. And I have spoken the truth." She stepped out the door in search of fresh air to breathe.

CHAPTER 58

Great nations do fall. Throughout history, many societies and civilizations have suffered great catastrophes because of their blasphemy, perversion, and oppression. These societies that rebelled against Allah, regarded His messengers as enemies, and transgressed in the land were wiped off the face of the earth. All of them were destroyed, some by volcanic eruptions, some by earthquakes, some by disastrous floods, and some by sandstorms.

The rise and fall of the nations do not happen at random, but rather by the decision of Allah. When Allah blesses a nation with His bounties, He continues his blessing as long as that nation keeps its obedience and loyalty to Him. After losing this loyalty, that nation necessarily loses Allah's grace.

Allah says in the Koran:

Allah changes not what is in the people until they change what is in themselves. But when Allah decrees punishment for a people, there is no turning it back, apart from Him, they have no protector (Al- Ra'd, 11).

Fearing Allah by following His commands and avoiding His prohibitions bring goodness, remove evils and keep Allah's bounties. Disobeying Allah however brings his punishment.

The Koran says:

Yet had the peoples of the cities believed and been god-fearing, we would have opened upon them blessings from heavens and earth; but they cried lies, and so We seized them for what they earned (Al- A'raf, 96).

The Koran particularly draws attention to the fact that the majority of the communities which perished had established high civilizations: "How many a generation We destroyed before them that was stronger in valour than they, and when Our torment came, they ran for a refuge in the land! Could they find any place of refuge for them to save themselves from destruction?"

The people of Lot practiced sodomy by having sexual intercourse with males instead of females. Allah then sent Lot to them, calling them to Allah, enjoining righteousness and forbidding them from evil practices and wickedness. But the people of Lot rejected Allah's warning. Allah sent against them a violent tornado with showers of stones, which destroyed them, with the exception of Lot's household.

In the United States, same sex marriage became legal in Indiana, Oklahoma, Utah, Virginia, and Wisconsin, paving the way for six other states.

There are already more than eight million adults in the United States who are lesbian, gay, or bisexual, comprising 3.5 per cent of the adult population. In total, approximately nine million Americans identify as lesbian, gay, bisexual, and transgender. This distorted behaviour, which Allah had forbidden in all His divine books, may bring His wrath upon the evildoers.

Allah had asserted the importance of honesty in monetary dealings and highlighted its vital role in social stability and peacefulness.

504

Allah forbids all unclean and corrupt means of making money, such as dishonest trading, gambling, and bribery. The Holy Koran has explained and described such practices in many of its verses.

The financial crisis of the United States was due to fraudulent practices such as dubious mortgages portrayed as sound risks and packaged into even more esoteric financial instruments, the fundamental weaknesses of which were intentionally obscured. As result of this monetary cheating, the United States drew upon herself the wrath of Allah, and abasement and poverty were pitched upon the country.

The United States is the nation with the most debt by far in the history of human civilization. The total debt, including personal debt, real estate (mortgage) debt, consumer debt, credit card debt, and government debt totals $47.9 trillion, roughly 2,400 trucks full of money.

The United States borrowed $1229 billion in 2011. The United States runs a mega 35 per cent budget deficit, far above the 3 per cent max limit set by the EU for economic stability standard.

Without a budget in place, the US government has run out of the cash needed to pay thousands of government workers in Washington and keep national parks open. An even more critical issue comes to the fore. The country could be forced to default on its borrowings if it does not secure a rise in the $16.7 trillion debt ceiling.

Riots over the economy flared in towns around the country and posed an immediate challenge to the "fraudonomics" and everything that was built on fraud and manipulation that made the dollar lose its reserve status.

Commodity prices of milk, bread, and gasoline soared. The markets became devoid of food and bread. The banks closed their doors.

People's credit cards stopped working. People were not allowed to buy gold or foreign currency. Food stamps failed, and social security cheques came to a halt.

States with the largest fiscal deficits, with the most excessive debts, and with the largest unfunded worker pension and benefit liabilities were Arizona, California, Nevada, Illinois, Massachusetts, Connecticut, New Jersey, New York, Ohio, Wisconsin, and Alaska.

A wave of civil disturbance swept the United States following the financial disaster. Some of the biggest riots took place in Washington, DC, Baltimore, Louisville, Kansas City, and Chicago.

The White House dispatched some 13,600 federal troops to assist the overwhelmed DC police force. Marines mounted machine guns on the steps of the Capitol, and army troops from the Third Infantry guarded the White House. Rioting reached within two blocks of the White House before rioters retreated.

By the time the cities were considered pacified, thousands had been killed, four thousand injured, and over ten thousand arrested. Additionally, some three thousand buildings had been burned, including over fifteen hundred stores. Damages reached one billion dollars.

With the destruction or closing of businesses, thousands of jobs were lost and insurance rates soared. Made uneasy by the violence, cities' residents of all races accelerated their departure for suburban areas, depressing property values. Crime in the burned-out neighbourhoods rose sharply, further discouraging investment.

The result was a complete breakdown in law and order, riots in the streets, financial collapse, and a repressive government response.

One basic element in the value system of Islam is the principle of equality. The stock of man, the colour of his skin, the amount of wealth he has and the degree of prestige he enjoys have no bearing on the character and personality of the individual as far as Allah is concerned. The only distinction, which Allah recognizes is the distinction in piety, the only criterion which Allah applies, is the criterion of goodness and spiritual excellence.

Allah says in the Koran, "O mankind, indeed We have created you from male and female, and have made you into nations and tribes, that you may know one another. Indeed, the most honoured of you in the sight of Allah is the most righteous. Indeed, Allah is All-Knowing, All-Aware."

Even wealth and clan have no value, as Allah says in the Koran: "It is not your riches nor your children that draw you closer to Allah, except for him who has faith and acts righteously."

Racism is a vicious cycle: racism creates pride, and pride feeds racism. In order for this vicious cycle to end, Allah made pride a severe sin, an atom weight of pride in one's heart would deprive him from entering paradise.

Discrimination permeates all aspects of life in the United States, and extends to all communities of colour.

Michael Brown, an unarmed black teenager, was shot dead by a white police officer in August 2014, a case that inflamed racial tensions in the United States. Largely peaceful protests spread from New York to Los Angeles as demonstrators across the United States demanded justice for Michael Brown. The protests were taking place in 170 cities across thirty-seven states. The demonstrators chanted, "They have given us no justice! We will give them no peace."

Protesters returned to the riot-scarred streets of Ferguson a day after crowds looted businesses and set fire to buildings in a night of rage against a grand jury's decision not to indict the white police officer who killed Michael Brown.

In Cleveland, demonstrators blocked traffic in protest at the death of a twelve-year-old black boy killed by police as he played with a toy gun.

From Lebanon, the United States adopted a new method to protect US interests in the Middle East by creating Islamic religious extremism in order to fight the Arabs with this method rather than with its own soldiers. The wars in Libya, Iraq, Syria, Palestine, and Yemen, and the chaos which failed in Egypt, were planned by the United States under the false pretext of "protecting the American interests".

The United States shifted from War on Terror to the side-lines of foreign policy issues designed to inflict damage on the Arab world without directly costing US lives. The United States is using extremists as human shields fighting on its behalf so that American soldiers will no longer be in danger of returning home in coffins. The Islamic State of Iraq and the Levant (ISIS) Islamic Front and Al-Nusra factions in Iraq and Syria are part of an American plot.

America planned the Arab Spring based on riots, violent demonstrations, civil war, and chaos. The United States also created international frictions with insidious policies of provoking anger and violence, thereby justifying war and destruction, which triggered further acts of terror and violence in the fashion of a vicious cycle.

The evidence is overwhelming and irrefutable that the raging chaos in the Middle East, North Africa, and Eastern Europe is not because of the misguided policies of the United States and its allies. Rather, it is because of premeditated and carefully crafted policies that have been pursued by an unholy alliance of the military-security-industrial complex and the Israel lobby in the post–Cold War world.

Due to the evil and deceitful policy of the United States and her allies, every major Arab Spring state had, to varying degrees, fallen prey to anarchy or authoritarianism.

The wars in Iraq and Afghanistan have devastated the people of those countries. Hundreds of thousands died as the result of the wars.

Due to the unnecessary wars that America created in the Middle East, there are now 2.14 million Syrian refugees in Jordan, Lebanon, Turkey, Iraq, Egypt, and North Africa.

The American administration, proud of its military power, seemed to forget that all kinds of honour and power lie in the hand of Allah. They forgot that there is a God ruling this universe and to Him is the return of all.

America thought that she owned the world, she owned Allah's kingdom on earth. She forgot that to Allah belongs the kingdom of the heavens and the earth. Does America fail to realize what a curse she was heaping on herself by such criminal frivolity?

The Creator warned them in the Koran: "Knowest thou not that to God belongs the kingdom of the heavens and the earth? He chastises whom He will, and forgives whom He will; and God is powerful over everything."

They forgot that Allah hates oppression and mischief in the land. Because Allah was not on their horizon, they didn't realize that by conducting such terrible acts, they had spread mischief and violence in the land. This was a matter that led to millions of deaths, displacements, and refugees that once were decent families living in peaceful homes – now they are scattered on the borders of four countries without food or water, and their women and daughters are being raped before their eyes.

They forgot that the retribution for an evil act is an evil one like it. They forgot that transgression without justification is forbidden. They forgot that Allah is not heedless of the things they do.

They forgot to ask themselves, "Who is going to pay for all these deaths, displacements, and dissensions?" The answer is clear: the perpetrators, of course.

They forgot that their empire could perish in an instant if they disobeyed Allah and transgressed in the land.

We read in the Koran: "Say: 'O God, Master of the Kingdom, Thou givest the Kingdom to whom Thou wilt, and seizest the Kingdom from whom Thou wilt, Thou exaltest whom Thou wilt, and Thou abasest whom Thou wilt; in Thy hand is the good; Thou art powerful over everything.'"

Do they not think that they will be resurrected for reckoning?

California is one of the United States' biggest food producers. It is responsible for almost half the country's production of nuts and 25 per cent of milk and cream. In addition, 80 per cent of the world's almonds come from the state, and the state uses an extraordinary amount of water to produce them: 1.1 gallons per almond.

But this food-rich state is in its third year of drought. California's current drought cost the state $2.2 billion and seventeen thousand jobs.

No wonder abasement and poverty were pitched on the rogue country and she was laden with the burden of Allah's anger. Allah was tormenting her as requital for her ill deeds.

For a society already under severe economic strain, with a high rate of unemployment and the government's spending cuts in social programs having hit the country's poor especially hard, including large numbers of minority youths who were at the forefront of the unrest, the net result was a complete breakdown of trust between the governing and the governed.

After all these distortions, mischiefs, and oppressions, Allah's wrath came upon America while she was unaware. It was justice demanding its payment.

In a day of ill fortune, Allah's wrath came suddenly to overtake several States and cities in America. Allah loosed against New York, Los Angeles, Chicago, and San Francisco, where sodomy was common, a calamitous wind plucking up men as if they were stumps of uprooted palm trees.

Thunderstorms pummeled the States of Iowa, Nebraska, and Wyoming. Huge earthquakes devastated Oklahoma, Santa Fe, and Phoenix. A lightning strike killed hundreds of pedestrians in Colorado.

Allah loosed against Montana, North Dakota, Wisconsin, and Minnesota a barren wind that left nothing it came upon but made it as stuff decayed.

The West Coast was destroyed by devastating earthquakes that tore the earth apart. The devastation was tremendously intensified by the huge waves that covered the roofs of the houses and destroyed urban cities and rural countries. Coastal inhabitants hadn't enough time to flee to higher ground. The death toll amounted to tens of thousands.

Series of earthquakes of the magnitude of 8 on the Richter scale affected more than fifteen million people in eight states – Alabama,

Arkansas, Illinois, Indiana, Kentucky, Mississippi, Missouri, and Tennessee.

The sea level rose to an outstanding level to drown the southern states. The fierce waves covering the States forced the evacuation of thousands of people from towns and cities. At least eighty towns and over 1 million people were affected. The waves killed 1.5 million people. The southern states were declared a disaster zone.

The earthquakes were so powerful that they made the Mississippi River flow backwards.

An undersea earthquake measuring 9 on the Richter scale, with its epicentre about 160 kilometres from the northern portion of California, severely hit the western states of California, Oregon, Nevada, Idaho, Utah, and Arizona. The quake caused a conflagration that raged for the next five days, destroying much of the American West's cities. The fire, along with water damage and other indirect acts, proved more destructive than the earthquake itself.

In Alabama, a tornado peeled the roofs from buildings, toppled trucks, and blew down oak trees.

Allah did not wrong them; they wronged themselves. Their arrogance and might did not protect them from Allah. Such is the seizing of Allah when He seizes the cities that are evildoing; surely His seizing is painful, terrible.

After all these calamities, the states revolted against the federal government. Riots sparked in more than sixty cities. As anger flared, the government used strong-arm tactics to maintain law and order, which brought about repressive political system, which contradicted the tradition of the United States. The government sent riot squads to act against the protesters in the different states. Nationwide damages were well into the millions.

Massive protests by government workers in ten states brought the nation's debt problem sharply into focus. Many states faced bankruptcy. Wisconsin and Ohio were financially in the worst shape in this regard.

The American plot was to divide the Arab countries into small dominions, or entities without borders – entities based on factions and sects struggling among themselves due to differences in religion, ethnicity, and racism. Now the American administration was drinking from the same cup. With riots spreading all over the American states, and the inability of the American administration to put things in order, the states found it wise to separate themselves from the federal government. The states became independent and busy fighting each other, each trying to protect its own natural resources.

Elizabeth crossed the country from east to west, without stopping. She flew over the ruined areas and back. Elizabeth could see from the aeroplane cars and houses submerged by high waters, houses and establishments severely damaged. Thousands of victims were sucked out to sea. Cities and provinces were devastated by waves that reached fifteen feet high.

She was sad to see looting, arson, random attacks on people, and buildings burning, often without police or firefighters in sight.

Elizabeth knew that what happened had devastated her father. She called him from the aeroplane.

"Father, are you okay?"

She heard him weeping. "Everything lies in ruins: my country, my reputation, my ruling, my honour."

CHAPTER 59

It had almost been three years since Elizabeth had last seen Omar. She had managed through these years to start life once more, but she had never been whole again. She had a face looking outwardly serene, yet hidden inside was a woman full of pain and regret.

Elizabeth entered Omar's farm as springtime was leaping upon the hills. The moment she arrived at the farm, the world that seemed so dull and cold came alive once again.

Her days without Omar were like winter, dark and cold. But now the springtime on this bright and sunny day was inviting her with an outstretched arm. She walked through the farm smelling the fresh scent of morning dew combined with the fragrance of blooming flowers. She heard the songs of the delicate birds up in the trees and the rustling of the leaves as the breeze swept through them. Life stood before her like an eternal spring. A smile formed on her face.

In the distance, she could see a grand villa standing on a hill overlooking an enchanting landscape of valleys covered with flowers and orchards. It was Omar's villa. She went on towards the villa, heart racing.

When she reached the house, she stood looking at the valley below. She could see miles of vines, olives, pomegranates, orange, and mango trees under perfect cultivation. Date palm trees surrounded the entire plantation. Horse stables, a riding arena, cattle barns, and pastures were also in sight.

Her heart raced with anticipation to see the man who'd captured her heart – to see her protector, her hero, her rock. She felt as if she was being watched. She turned around to see Omar on a hill riding an Arabian horse. He looked like an Arabian knight of valour and honour against whom none could stand his glorious charge. It was as if the bullets he received during the battles had hardened his body even further. His black hair fell almost to his shoulders. He was wearing traditional Egyptian dress: white *jellabiya*, a black Arabian cloak, and riding boots. He looked beautiful and exotic.

Omar rode down the hill towards Elizabeth. Her heart pounded in her chest and her mouth went dry as he dismounted and stood just few metres away from her. How badly she needed to get into his arms.

"Don't come near me or I'll burst into tears," she said, shaking uncontrollably.

He opened his cloak for her. She ran to him weeping. He gave strength to her shaken senses by wrapping her shivering body in his arms. She wrapped her arms around him as if she were clinging to him for dear life.

His body shivered suddenly. He clutched at her, held her tightly, and she realized he was weeping.

"What are you doing here?" he said through tearful sobs.

"I live here. Your love is my home."

"Yes, my love, you are home."

"I want my heart back," she said, clinging to him.

"It's yours. It's always been yours. I've been waiting for you to say that for so long. I thought you would never come back to me. Please tell me this isn't a dream." He was weeping convulsively.

"Hold me tight. Dry my tears and ease my pain." She was crying bitter tears.

His hold on her tightened. She felt so right in his arms. His arms felt like home. She broke down further and whispered: "Cleanse me and make me anew."

He released her and looked into her eyes. He saw her like a withering rose waiting to be watered by his love.

"I live my life for you. I would do anything to make you happy. I'll make you the queen of my heart. You are mine till the end of eternity." The storm of weeping swelled, and he burst into a new round of crying.

"Take me out of misery. Tell me things I like to hear." She clung to him, seeking safety and protection.

"I have left the army. I'm free now. Marry me."

"I'll walk with you side by side in the way of the Lord. I'll follow you, embrace your faith, be the dust beneath your feet." She nestled in his arms and melted in a marvelous peace.

"Are you willing to live like that?" he said with a foreboding heart.

"I am if you are."

"Come, I want to show you the house." He walked her towards the mansion.

The villa was a three-level house made of old stone and plaster. One level below the house was a garage and a gymnasium. A marble staircase led to upstairs bedrooms, an office, and a tiled-roof terrace. The entire house was furnished with Egyptian antiques and filled with flowers.

This was the place where he now intended to carve out a future for himself and his descendants. She would live here in this remote spot and tune herself to such wonderful beauty. She had found what she was looking for.

At the small mosque on the farm, she converted to Islam and took shahada. With the pronunciation of shahada, all her past sins were forgiven and now she was newly born. She would start a new life of piety and righteousness.

After declaring the shahada, Omar and Elizabeth got married in the same mosque where the workers prayed in congregations, recited the Koran, and sought Islamic knowledge.

Although Elizabeth felt peace inside after marriage, she was terrified of what was yet to come. She was intoxicated with Omar's love, but she was afraid to have sex with him. He was a virgin and knew nothing about sex. Omar was too big for her and might hurt her. She felt a shiver of fear at the thought that she might not be able to satisfy the man she deeply loved. *What if I don't please him?* she wondered.

When she learned that her first husband, Roy, was cheating on her and was involved in money laundering, she deserted his bed and went to another room until he died. Hudson never satisfied her, and with him she experienced vaginal dryness and had to use moisturizing treatments, but to no avail. During these years, she forgot all about sex and had lived with sexual deprivation ever since. Would she experience a sexual awakening with Omar?

It was their first night together. She lay in bed waiting for Omar to come. Omar came like an innocent boy who was about to perform a task he knew nothing about. He lay down beside her, clearly hesitant to take the lead. She wanted to tell him that she was a tiny woman and that he must go slow so as not to hurt her, but she shyly withheld.

"I have been waiting for this day to come for a long time, and my love is still the same as it was when I first saw you." He said trembling all over.

"Please love me slowly." She was having a hard time meeting his eyes as her blush crept up her face.

"You are my first love. I haven't touched a woman before. Show me how to please you."

"Just take me in your arms until my breathing calms," she said tenderly.

He held her steady until her breath calmed down. She had been waiting for this moment and dreading it with equal intensity. His eyes traced her face from her forehead to her chin. Her cheeks were pink. He kissed her cheek; he kissed her lips. He smiled down at her, and her heart burned as she looked at his most arresting eyes. She moaned slightly as his lips tantalized her neck, his jet-black hair tickling her cheek.

"My sweet Liz," he muttered as his lips found her jaw, her brow, her eyes, behind the ear. His lips returned to her lips, moving over them gently. She trembled from his kisses.

He said, looking in her eyes so tenderly that she saw his heart in his eyes, "You're the best thing that's ever happened to me."

Her heart burned at his words, and she lay beneath him, soft, willing, and loving. He kissed her with such love and yearning, happy to have her in his arms.

She got excited when he reached for warm breasts that begged for his touch. He kissed her breasts and upward towards her neck and her lips. When he lifted his head, her lips were soft and her eyes were cloudy. "I am so hungry for you," he said, lured by the soft, creamy texture of her body.

The warmth of his lips made her go soft and liquid inside. Her body quivered for more. She longed to feel his heart deep within her.

His heart pounded, and his blood drummed in his head. He went deep, losing himself in her, and she sucked him in, pulled him to her with those smooth arms and devoured him as he was devouring her. She was lost in him, and he was lost in her.

Her soul rang with sweet and stirring ecstasy. He'd resurrected her heart, and for the first time in several years, she sensed life.

Something in him wanted to cry. Suddenly, his overwhelming ecstasy crumpled into sobs.

"I've dreamt my whole life of this moment. My dream was unreachable. But Allah bestowed his favour upon me by making my dream come true. He sent you to me to keep my soul at rest. Liz, you are a divine blessing that I must treat with reverence."

His words stole her breath away. She loved him as she'd never loved a man before. She felt extremely blessed to have him in her life.

"Liz, you made my love complete. You made my life whole. You have entered deep down in my veins. Loving you is the best thing that's ever happened to me." His sobs increased as if afraid that he might lose her.

She lived a sterile life: no happy marriage and no children. She wanted to feel like a real woman. The strong sent of his masculine body reached deep within her. She wanted him more.

"Oh, my love, touch me, caress me, make love to me," she begged in a husky voice. Her voice felt so delicious as it caressed his heart and soul.

Caressing her soft skin and feeling skin-to skin-contact excited him more and more. "Oh God. I have wanted this so much." He was enjoying the feeling of her body. Her confidence grew as she saw how good she made him feel, and it aroused her beyond words.

"I open all my petals to you. Come into my garden and eat my pleasant fruits." She stretched her body to accommodate him once more.

He held her and loved her as she never could have dreamed. Omar touched her in a way that no man had ever touched her. He drove her wild with ecstasy. He burned her from within.

The night was silent except for their loving gasps.

"Sip of my well and slake your thirst. Split me and tear my heart open," she said with endless pleasure.

Their bodies entwined, becoming as one, and exploded in ultimate pleasure. He was unquenchable and so creative. He made her enjoy the ecstasy of love. She found herself climaxing repeatedly.

Lying beneath the sheet, she felt younger, more beautiful, and more alive than she ever remembered. She had never felt such a deep calm. She lay content in his arms, all her energy spent.

"He is insatiable. I must discipline him. I must orchestrate his lovemaking," she whispered with a large smile on her face.

The birds began their morning song, and she awakened in his arms. This time it was not a dream, for he was there beside her. Being in his arms felt like heaven. She watched his sleeping figure. He was so muscular, so beautiful.

He excited her beyond anything she had ever felt before. She would have wondered who'd taught this virgin man how to truly love a woman, but she knew it was natural inborn love. Love was an inborn skill. No woman was there in his life before her. This is why his love was like a hurricane. She was like a tree bending beneath the weight of his abundant love.

She could hear his soft breathing. She brushed strands of hair from his face. Her love deepened further. The love she was living through him was simply blissful. She felt tears of joy prickle in her eyes. She cradled her head into his chest and whispered, "Life is good. It's beautiful to live."

Now she was in a private world where pain didn't exist. Nothing could hurt her here. In his arms, she felt warm and cozy as a little bird in a nest. Now she knew the meaning of happiness – happiness was being with him.

Omar woke up slowly to see Elizabeth lying awake in his arms. "What did I do to deserve you? What more can there be?" He tightened his arms around her.

"You did a lot. You fought battles with words and sword."

"I never knew how magnificent love could be until I made love to you. God, Liz. That feels so good."

"We're going to grow old together," she said, raining his face and chest with her soft kisses.

"You're the reason I breathe. You're the love of my life. I knew I was born to be yours. What more could a man on earth wish? I love you, Liz."

Now she knew that she owned that man, he belonged to her, to no one else in the world, and he could never been taken away. In his arms, all uncertainty and dread of the future dissolved. All grief, all tension, all bitterness, and all resentment fell away. Nothing would separate her from his love or snatch her from his arms.

They didn't leave the bedroom for a week. They made love, ate, laughed, and cried. Madly in love after so many years of deprivation, they enjoyed the miracle of loving each other. They enjoyed deep intimacy and intense companionship of happy mutual love.

They lay on the chase long her head on his chest. He wrapped his arms around her, stoking her cheek, brushing her hair back. The morning light sprayed into their bedroom, englobing them in its golden rays.

It was a perfect morning when Omar stood on the balcony of the bedroom, gazing at the valley before him. The sun had splashed pink clouds across the horizon, and rivers of silver light ran through the valley, penetrating its hills.

Elizabeth stood behind him, contemplating him. He looked tall, quite robust, and strong. What an amazing man he was. This rock solid man of war was reduced to anguished sobbing in her arms. He was a ferocious warrior yet quite docile and submissive to her.

Omar did not hear Elizabeth as she came up behind him and put her arms around him from behind, holding his abdomen. She stepped in front of him and kissed him deeply. She then stood beside him, holding his hand, her head on his shoulder, his love in her heart. Nothing was spoken. Nothing needed to be said. She loved him.

Elizabeth looked before her to see what Omar was looking at. She saw a valley clad with colourful displays. The valley was filled with a sea of gold, purple, pink, and white flowers. The canna lilies and the oriental poppies were all at their best, showing amazing colours of love. The buds and leaves were all coated with sweet spring dew. The striking beauty of the valley lifted her spirit. Before she came here, she forgot what spring was like. But now life stood before her like an eternal spring.

Omar stared at her. The morning sun shined down upon her beautiful face. Her dazzling hair flowed softly in the gentle breeze. His heart was so full of love that it overflowed.

"I was thinking about you," he said, breaking the silence.

"What were you thinking about me?" she asked eagerly.

"I never thought that love could be so magnificent until I made love to you. The taste of you is like the rivers of paradise, which the God-fearing have been promised. Rivers forever pure, rivers of milk unchanging in flavour, rivers of wine – a delight to the drinkers – and rivers of honey purified."

"Do you love me that much?" She felt that she had been gifted with the riches of the world.

"My heart beats with the rhythm of yours. You are my world, my heart, my pulse. In your heart, I have found my home."

Elizabeth let herself be taken by the rare moment. She could see herself reflected in his eyes, beautiful, desirable, beloved. She looked into his eyes, and there she saw that with this man, she had entered a world in which no more questions were necessary. She had only to follow the lead.

Elizabeth had never been on an operating and working farm before, so Omar gave her a tour. He drove her across miles of mango, orange, lemon, peach, and date palm trees. Gardens of vines, olives, and pomegranates were also in sight.

In the barns, she saw buffaloes and cattle raised for the production of milk and dairy. Milking was done by hand and machine. She was interested in the dairy factor, where milk was processed into a variety of dairy products such as cream, butter, yogurt, and cheese.

She liked the way he was explaining things to her. He was talking in earnest, expressing seriousness and clearly proud of his work.

"Additional dietary supplements are added to the feed to improve milk production," he told her. "We sell the male calves for veal."

Omar showed Elizabeth his poultry farm, where chickens, turkeys, ducks, and geese were raised for producing meat and eggs.

They also went through rows and blocks of vegetables for consumption on the farm, with the excess sold in nearby towns.

Omar took Elizabeth to the stables of the pure Arabian horses. "Our horses are decent. We teach them good manners."

"What do you mean by good manners?"

"Lead quietly in hand; allow every body part to be touched; stand quietly to have feet handled; accept paste wormers; get on a trailer; wait when he is ordered to; be caught; stand tied."

"Why do you raise Arabian horses? Isn't it an expensive hobby?"

"First, they bring joy to my heart. Second, our horses are not ordinary horses but pure Arabian horses. I own one of the most successful Egyptian sires today. He carries the precious blood that is so necessary in most show champions. With this sire, you can count on a beautiful head, fine long neck, extra smooth body with a long flat croup, and the powerful trot and tail carriage that is his trademark. Here are two of his finest daughters." He pointed at two beautiful mares eating in the pasture.

The tour had taken three hours. It was almost noon when they returned to Omar's mansion. After a wonderful lunch in the dining room, they sat in the living room for tea.

"You never said that you were that rich!" Elizabeth said while drinking tea.

"I told you before that I'm well off and I can afford you a decent living."

"But this huge farm is worth millions, and you have clearly invested a lot in it."

"My fathers and grandfathers own vast lands in the Nile valley. I sold my land there and bought the land you see here. In order to make the new land productive, I had to invest heavily in the farm's components you have just seen."

"You never cease to amaze me. How can a man so rich throw himself into danger and leave all this wealth behind?"

"Muslims live for Allah and strictly abide by his rules. Allah has ordained that we perform jihad in the way of Allah with our lives and wealth when necessary. Dying in the way of Allah is far better than all we could amass. Fighting in Allah's cause is better than the world and whatever is in it. We fight to protect our land from invasion. We fight for self-defense. We go as far as it takes to stop aggression, but we do not go beyond that. There is another more important level of jihad: the inner spiritual struggle against sin and temptation. It is a struggle to purify the soul of satanic influence, both subtle and overt. The rich and the poor must share in jihad."

"What do you mean when you said that fighting in Allah's cause is better than the world and whatever is in it?"

"Whatever thing we have been given is the enjoyment of the present life, but with Allah everything is better and more enduring for those who believe and put their trust in their Lord. The martyrs in the cause of Allah are not dead. Death is in fact the true real life, which they have entered through the gateway of death. They enjoy in the new life the ineffable presence and nearness of Allah."

"It is amazing to see that the word jihad in the West is synonymous to terrorism."

"The enemies of Islam have emptied the word jihad from its beautiful meaning in order to deceive their people and incite their grudges against Islam.

"Now, darling, let's move on to another subject. How about you becoming responsible for the agricultural activities you have seen today?"

"What? I don't have the experience, and ..."

"I just want to keep you busy," he interrupted. "Don't fear anything. Each agricultural activity has a manager already. You will supervise their work and report to me."

"And what are you going to keep for yourself. Thoroughbred horses and bloodlines?"

"Yes, darling. I hope you accept."

He saw the flare of worry in her eyes, so he assured her with a reassuring smile. "I will smooth away any problem you might encounter. Now that you have become my wife, my money becomes yours. Manage your money, darling."

This is how Omar helped Elizabeth escape boredom. He filled her life with obligations that made her days busy. She always had something to do during the day. She was torn between orchards, milk and dairy, poultry, transportation, and marketing. The managers of the diverse agricultural activities were looking forward to working closely with her. They greatly valued her sound judgement and leadership, a matter that made things easy for her.

Elizabeth was happy with her new life. She loved being busy, waiting impatiently for the night to fall in order to enjoy sleeping in the arms of her beloved.

Although Elizabeth had daily activities that left her quite busy, she had time to build a small centre for taking care of the workers' children while their parents were busy at work. She was able to deal with the children through some Arabic words she'd learned. She organized daily play with the children, provided them meals, and talked to them about their concerns and worries.

Elizabeth got on well with the children. She had patience and tolerance, and her caring attitude was highly appreciated by their parents.

Omar was watching Elizabeth from a distance. He saw the glow that she had when in the presence of children. She revealed her compassionate motherhood through her love to the children. It was the intimacy of motherhood that she missed. He wished he could give her a child; it would complete the bond and love they had for each other.

At bedtime that night, Elizabeth nestled in Omar's arms. He brushed her hair back from her forehead and kissed her temple, eyes, and lips. She surrendered to his affectionate touches and kissed the hair of his chest. His scent, musky and masculine, aroused her.

"How beautiful you are, Liz. Haven't you thought about having a baby? I want to have a child with you."

She smiled at him. Her smile kind of hugged him.

"Being a mother will make your life complete and fulfilling. A baby would make our lives whole."

"Frankly, I can't shake the thought of having a baby with you."

"Then stop taking the pills."

"I stopped taking the pills a week ago."

"Then I promise you the night of your life."

Her eyes flashed. She raised her hand and softly stroked his cheek. Her soft lips submitted to the pressure of his with a calm, intense passivity, just as the water of a lake accepts the light of the moon.

She gave herself to him as naturally as the sun gives heat or the flowers their perfume.

When she became pregnant, a warmth emanated from deep within her. She was thrilled that she would share a child with the man she was enthralled with. The doctor told her that she was pregnant with twins. With the passing days, the babies grew and leaped in her womb. On her due date, she gave birth to a boy and a girl. They called the boy Mostafa (the chosen) and the girl Aziza (the dearest).

As she held the twins in her arms, she felt something she had never felt before. Her holding them when they took their first breaths was a special moment that only she and Omar could share. When Omar first carried them, his eyes became a fountain of tears.

Elizabeth looked at her babies and saw the tender, fragile skin that invited a finger's touch. She kissed their cheeks, and her lips sank down and seemed never to find bones. The soft scalps and the folds of soft flesh filled her with tenderness and love. The fragile babies melted in her arms as though they might at any time flow back into her body.

Giving birth to her babies made her the proudest and most fulfilled woman in the world. Her life now had a more positive impact. She had found her passion for life.

Whenever Omar entered the bedroom, he saw Elizabeth cuddling and caressing her babies lovingly. Omar kissed them and held them all. He said while holding them closely in his arms, "If I count Allah's blessings on me, never shall I be able to count them. Allah rescued me from tough situations and blessed me with you as my wife. And now He has blessed me with a boy and a girl. The best that Allah can expect from his servants is their gratefulness for his bounties. He accepts gratitude for his blessings upon his servants. May He be glorified and exalted for His many blessings and favours upon me." Sobs seized him.

Elizabeth's tears mingled with Omar's tears, and her sobs echoed his sobs as they spent long moments finding great happiness in appreciating Allah's bounties and favours.

"The one who is most deserving of thanks and praise from people is Allah. Allah increases His blessings on those who give thanks to Him. Allah accepts sacrifice from His servants. I will slaughter two cows and two rams for Allah and distribute their meat to the poor." He was still holding Elizabeth and the babies in his arms, his body wracked by sobs.

"You are my pillar, my stone of strength. You are the man I truly loved," Elizabeth said, clinging her soul to him.

Omar gave all of himself to Allah. His nights passed with little or no sleep in secluded prayer and meditation.

Three years had passed, and the babies had grown into beautiful children. In the spacious garden of the house, you could see Elizabeth having water fights with Mostafa and Aziza, or playing hide-and-seek, or making tents out of sheets. She would take them to the small centre she'd established for the care of the workers' children and have them play with the boys and girls who were their age. The children were the joy of Elizabeth's life. With them, she felt her worries give way to a sort of calm, detached peace.

CHAPTER 60

The White House announced that Amanda Rosh would visit the Middle East. Part of her visit was to enforce Washington's commitment to promoting freedom and supporting women and girls across the Middle East.

After Amanda finished her visit to the Middle East, she decided to visit her daughter in Egypt. Elizabeth hadn't severed ties with her mother, and there had been always contact between them. Elizabeth loved her mother because she was always there for her.

Amanda arrived at the farm with a car from the American Embassy, accompanied by two security guards. The car headed directly to the farm's house.

Elizabeth was sitting on the porch, and her children were playing. When she saw her mother, she cried out in delight and ran over to her and hugged her. She whispered through her tears, "Thank you for coming."

"Oh, my beautiful joy, you are radiating beauty."

"I missed you, Mother. I missed you terribly."

"You are in my heart and always in my thoughts."

They laughed and cried in each other's arms.

Amanda continued to cry silently, the soul-deep weeping of a woman who had been separated from her only daughter. Elizabeth clung to her mother and caressed her; she was anxious to drive the suffering of separation from her face.

"I realized how much I love you after I moved out. I just want to say I love you and miss you a lot." Elizabeth clung to her mother.

Elizabeth moved away from her mother and pointed at her kids, "Mother these are the ones I talked to you about – your grandchildren."

When Amanda first laid eye on them, she bit her quivering lip and started to cry again. She felt an aching love that painfully squeezed her heart. She found herself loving them so very much more than she loved herself.

Amanda knelt down and held her arms out to the twins. They ran to her, and she held them close to her heart. She stroked their hair and kissed the tops of their heads. They were beautiful, the most precious gift ever. She wasn't aware of time passing as she held them.

Omar came out from inside the house, took Amanda by the hand, and gently helped her to her feet.

"Your coming has brought honour to our family. We gladly welcome you with gratitude as the grandmother of our children." He was glad to see her.

Amanda was still crying. Omar soothed her by kissing her hand and rubbing her back gently. "You must be tired. I'll take you to the guest room."

They walked hand in hand to the guest room. Elizabeth and the kids followed at their heels.

"I feel blessed having Elizabeth as my wife," Omar said as they walked. "She is the light of my life, without which I could not exist. I truly hope that I can be a parent to my children just like how you have been to Elizabeth. Madam, you brought Elizabeth to life, so you are the reason for my happiness. I love you. And now I leave you together, for I have a few things to do." Omar left Elizabeth to arrange her mother's things in the guest room.

Amanda spent lovely days on the farm with Elizabeth and her grandchildren. Elizabeth arranged a tour by car for her mother.   It was an exciting opportunity for Amanda to see the diversifying agricultural activities of the farm.

"With Allah's blessing, the farm yields its produce twofold," Elizabeth said while driving her mother back to the house.

The Mediterranean Sea was only a few miles away from the farm. The morning was just starting to unfold when Elizabeth took her mother and the children to the beach. The air was sweet and delicate, appealing to Amanda's gentle senses. The beauty of the scene was pouring like sunlight. The children were happily playing on the beach, where white sand dunes and wild little plants were scattered.

With two chairs and an umbrella on the beach, Amanda and Elizabeth sat talking. Although Amanda could plainly see that her daughter was infatuated with Omar, she couldn't prevent herself from saying, "I don't want you getting the wrong impression, but what do you exactly see in him? I thought you were merely going through some psychological or romantic phase like most young people do."

"Mom, I have become a Muslim. I found that my new religion allowed me a spirituality and understanding of Allah that previously seemed elusive. Islam has brought great peace and beauty into my life. Omar and I are legally married before Allah.

"I would have thought it impossible to love Omar more than when I married him, but every day increases my passion. He is not only a charming lover but also a delightful companion. I simply adore him." Elizabeth spoke with such passionate sincerity that it was impossible not to believe her.

"On our first night of marriage, I never thought it was possible for a man to love a woman as he loved me that night. No woman ever had such a wonderful lover as I had that night. I never knew a woman was capable of such adoration as I was filled with. And he was my husband. Mine, mine. I adore him. What more could anyone ask?"

"Aren't you romanticising?"

"I feel alive again. All the pain is gone. I've never been so happy before. I've never been so complete. I feel safe in his arms. I feel loved and cherished. I feel as if I have the world in my hands. I'm so proud to be his wife and to be so much in love. I think that I have been truly blessed."

"Does he know how lucky he is to have you?"

"Lucky! I'm the one who is lucky to have him. He is the rhythm of my soul, the song of my spirit. He is my every breath beating in my heart. He gave me the world. Omar is my everything. There is not another person I could ever imagine myself with."

"So you are happy with him."

"It's all so dreamlike just being with him. He is so solid and so real that when I am leaning on him, he's like the earth itself. What more could anyone ask?"

"Can I ask you a personal question?"

"Of course."

"As I recall, you were not sexually satisfied with Hudson. What is it like with Omar?"

"What do you mean?"

"Is he ruthless in bed?"

"Oh, Mom. The nerve you've got!"

"During his escape, Omar killed fifty soldiers and shot down two helicopters. Then there are those he killed in the mall as well as Carlos and the hitman. Violence, my dear, is every woman's fear. Knowing about your intimate life with Omar would certainly clear out my doubts."

"Omar was a virgin and I was the first woman he touched. He was insatiable, and it was difficult to slake his passion. He's wild, but our souls take comfort in each other. He brings me to heights I had never achieved before."

"He's not wearing you out?"

"I tried to discipline his lovemaking, but still, his love is so intense. I'm enchanted in his arms. He is my lover, and he pleases me."

"I'm delighted to see you happy. If you're happy, I'm happy. You have found someone with whom you can spend the rest of your life," Amanda said cheerfully."

"We are now bonded in hearts, souls, and bodies. He is deep like an ocean and simple to the point of primitiveness. He is like a big baby. I comb his hair, I cook his meal, and I read him books. I feel such love and ecstasy with him. My love for him overtakes my senses, and all I want to do is to be in his arms forever. I have at last arrived at peace with myself. Now I am ready for all the wonderful things life has to offer."

"I see that he is treating you so nicely."

"You don't know how sweet he is. With me, he's always been angelic. Nature means the world to him. He is drunk with the loveliness of it. I can't tell you how moving it was to see that great hulk of a man uplifted by an emotion so pure and so beautiful that it made me want to cry. He might fall in love with a reflection in the water or a ray of sunshine or a cloud in the sky."

"You will make a wonderful life together, I'm sure."

"How much I wanted to be a mother. I wished to love a child so much that it hurt. I knew in my heart that Omar would be a great father. You don't know how much I wanted a child with him."

"I understand. If I had known how wonderful it would be to have grandchildren, I'd have had them first."

"I was blessed with twins. I was happy to hear their first cries. Every second with them is magical. Watching them grow is wonderful. It is such a blessing to see their faces change every day as they turn into the prettiest babies I've ever seen in my life. And they are mine."

"Life is easier if you hear the steps of grandchildren walking beside you," Amanda said, watching her grandchildren playing on the beach. She heard their squeals of laughter while they played. A garden of love grew in her heart.

"They are so cute. They have your eyes, Elizabeth. Omar is a handsome man, and you are a queen of beauty. No wonder the children are so beautiful." Amanda filled her eyes with her grandchildren's beauty and struggled to hold back her tears.

"Omar is the kind of man I want my children to grow up to be," Elizabeth said, also enjoying the beauty of her children.

Amanda spent beautiful days on the farm. She played with her grandchildren, held them close, and kissed them. She bathed them and read them stories before bed. Being with them was comfort, peace, joy, and delight.

After long and busy days, Amanda watched Omar and Elizabeth strolling into the house hand in hand. It delighted her heart to see them talking, laughing, kissing, and hugging. Their eyes shone with a clear light. Their faces were aglow with wisdom and intelligence matured into serenity; their words and voices rang with childlike joy.

The sun had set. The leaves were wet with dew. The sky was growing dark, bringing into view the twinkling stars. There was no breeze, but it was pleasantly and restfully cool. The front garden glowed in the dark with white flowers and plants.

Amanda and Elizabeth spent the night talking on the front porch.

"Do you miss America?" Amanda asked, hoping to hear encouraging words.

"I miss nothing from the days before I converted to Islam. Islam is enough for me. You don't need anything else once you've found it. I've achieved the fulfilment I was looking for. Islam turned my life around. Embracing Islam has made me see life in a new way. Life is a gift from Allah.

"Islam brought a structure and discipline to my life that led to an inner peace. Islam brought me peace, happiness, direction, and a true understanding of humanity. It was a slow dawning. I continue to grow with it. Praise and thanks be to Allah for guiding me to Islam.

"I came from a people that preferred the present life over the world to come, the day that every soul shall come disputing in its own behalf and every soul shall be paid in full for what it wrought. For those who prefer the present world over the world to come, Allah has set a seal over their hearts, and their hearing, and their eyes. Those are the heedless ones; in the world to come, they will be the losers."

"You mean that America is not a good place to live anymore?"

"I have two children. I am trying hard to raise them properly. But how would I do that in a society opened to deviation and abuse – a society in which the prohibited is allowed and the unlawful is permitted. I want to abide by Allah's law. I want to raise my children in chastity, in a pure environment."

"Yes, dear, but you can raise them decently in America as well. You can take them to the church to be taught the word of God."

"I was raised as a Roman Catholic. You made me go to church every Sunday. I never liked church very much; it always seemed to me like a place for a fashion show. You have to wear your very best outfits and sit and check out everybody else. I would see people nudging each other and gossiping about people as they came through the door or looking at them with their noses in the air. I never liked that atmosphere. Then it came time for the preacher to show up. He would start slow and easy with the preaching and it would build up as he went along. Soon he would grab the Bible and start preaching and jumping up and down, running everywhere."

"Elizabeth, please! It is ridiculous to cry about something so trivial and forget about what the Church teaches. It teaches the word of God."

"The Catholic Church holds that there is one eternal God who exists as three entities: God the Father, God the Son; and God the Holy Spirit, which together are called the Holy Trinity. The Holy Trinity is not mentioned in the Bible. Jesus never said that he is one in three or three in one. The Trinity is a myth, man's invention. In Islam, Allah is only One and not three. Associating Allah with other partners in worship is glaring polytheism. Allah doesn't forgive when He is set up with other partners, but He forgives anything else that pleases him. To set up partners with Allah is to devise a sin most heinous."

"There is no body of ancient literature in the world which enjoys such a wealth of good textual attestation as the New Testament," Amanda commented. "The Bible is the most reliable place to turn to in order to find the key to a life of love and good works."

"The Oneness of Allah, known as tawheed, is the first and paramount constituent of the Islamic concept, as it is the fundamental truth of the Islamic faith. Among all the belief systems and philosophies currently prevailing among human beings, only the Islamic faith can be characterized as having a pure form of monotheism.

"The message of the Oneness of Allah has been the chief constituent and characteristic of all religions brought by the Messengers of Allah since Adam until Muhammad. Religion with Allah is only Islam. Every religion sent from Allah was nothing but Islam, which is submission to Allah alone by following the way prescribed by Him in the divine books He descended on His prophets and messengers. Unfortunately, after these messengers passed away, interpolations and deviations were introduced into the pure religion of Islam, producing many impurities in these religions so that no belief has been left in its correct and pure form apart from the concept brought by Prophet Muhammad. With the Koran, Allah Himself has protected the principles of the Islamic faith so that no deviation has ever touched it nor has any impurity ever entered into its beliefs. This is why the Oneness of Allah has become the distinctive characteristic of the Islamic faith. The relationship between Allah and everything else is that of the Creator to His creation and of the Lord to His servants. This is the first principle of the Islamic concept, and all other principles follow from it. Because the Islamic concept rests on this basic principle, the Oneness of Allah is its most important characteristic.

"Allah says in the Koran, 'We sent no Messenger before you without revealing to him, "There is no god but Me, so worship Me {alone}"'"

"I understand, darling. But still, don't try to protect your kids from our society, the most progressed and freest country in the world."

"Is America a free society and is it the most progressed? In America, our children's heroes are basketball players, fashion models, singers, and movie stars who do nothing important. They teach nothing good in a real sense. They contribute nothing to society. All they do is present an example of a wild and wealthy lifestyle, which makes the children want to duplicate it."

"You are trapped in a prison of morals, I'm afraid."

"In America, two out of every three marriages ends in divorce; violence is becoming an increasingly inherent part of our schools and our roads; self-responsibility is on the wane; self-discipline is being submerged by 'If it feels good, do it'. Various Christian leaders and churches are being swamped by sexual and financial scandals. American culture is becoming a morally bankrupt institution, and I was feeling quite alone in my personal religious vigil."

"I must admit that corruption has appeared in our society for what the hands of the people have earned."

"Anywhere you look in American society, there is a reminder that the female body should be flattered, displayed, and used to attract men. Why do women dress half naked yet they want respect? If I were a man, I do not think I would respect a girl that displays her private parts for the world to see. If women are covered up, men might take them seriously."

"Muslim women are covered from head to toe and are not allowed any freedom of rights. Darling, you are wearing a veil. The veil is an obstacle clouding your mind. The American society is the society of freedom and human rights. The West considers the veil the greatest symbol of women's oppression and servitude."

"The only purpose of the veil in Islam is protection. The Islamic veil is not a sign of man's authority over woman, nor is it a sign of woman's subjection to man. The Islamic veil is only a sign of modesty with the purpose of protecting women. The Islamic philosophy is that it is always better to be safe than sorry. In fact, the Koran is so concerned with protecting women's bodies and women's reputations that a man who dares to falsely accuse a woman of unchaste behaviour will be severely punished.

"The veil is a woman's ticket to liberty. The veil gives me more protection. The veil is a public declaration of commitment. Women regained their dignity as human beings in Islam. For centuries, clergymen held women on an equal footing with the devil, until the gentle breeze of Islamic civilization blew on Europe via Andalusia. Only then did clergymen begin reconsidering their views of women. They kept modifying their views until they eventually came to approve some of women's rights, which Islam had already granted them fourteen centuries ago.

"Nothing in Islam has made me happier than men's support and protection of women. I take pleasure as well as pride in it. I am a woman with a man to take care of me. Confident in his strength, I can face the world, and armed with Islam, we can both defy it."

"Yes, but don't forget that the emancipation of women is one of the glories of Western civilization and one of the great chapters in the history of freedom. Women in the West are already liberal and—"

Elizabeth cut in. "Women in the West rush behind slogans of liberation and therefore put themselves to a lot of trouble. I believe that many American women's societies that uphold slogans of liberation are beginning to change a number of their views and are gradually realizing the falsity of the mottos they supported. The institution of marriage is threatened, not enhanced, by the supposed gains of the feminist movement over the last fifty years. It is a fact that US marriage rates keep declining."

"But, darling, American women enjoy complete freedom and—"

Elizabeth interrupted again. "I reject the freedom that American women claim to have. Women in our society are portrayed as sexy and independent enough so that men have no real responsibility towards them or the children they help create, but dependent enough that they are continually in search of a new man.

"In American society, all the people have beliefs that they live according to. If having sex is someone's belief, the person will do everything to achieve this. If he believes drinking is one way to enjoy life, then he does do it. If making money is someone's belief, he does it. But these are sins forbidden in all religions, leading to nowhere. And in the end, no one is truly satisfied. In a society of equal rights, girls are expected to have boyfriends or they are weird. This is a form of oppression, even though women do not realize it. The American society defined such terms as liberty and freedom, and then women accepted these definitions without even attempting to challenge or question them. Everything seemed to be generating backwards. There is an Almighty God, and we will surely be held accountable for our deeds; therefore, we should live a life that is governed by ethical values. The mere thought of raising my girl in America fills me with dread. My children are my riches. I don't want my children to go through all that.

"In Islam, marriage is an important part of life, the making of the society. Therefore, a woman should not go around showing herself to everybody, only her husband. Allah has commanded Muslim women to cover themselves for their modesty. In Western societies, women are attacked and molested because of how they are dressed. Just because a Muslim wife must obey her husband and cooperate with him does not mean she is oppressed. Where a man goes, the woman follows."

Elizabeth ceased talking. She smiled at her mother and then took her hand and lifted it to her lips, kissing it. She asked her mother, "As the First Lady, you took interest in women's rights. Where have all the good marriageable American men gone?"

"Based on the statistics I have, the number of women in the workforce has surpassed the number of men. The divorce laws increasingly created a dangerously precarious financial prospect for the men cut loose from marriage – men are simply no longer finding any benefit in it. When men are asked why they don't get married, the answer is always the same: women aren't women anymore. Feminism, which teaches women to think of men as the enemy, has made women angry and defensive, though often unknowingly. Men are tired of being told there's something fundamentally wrong with them. Tired of being told that if women aren't happy, it's men's fault. Feminism and the sexual revolution have simply made marriage obsolete."

"It's the women who lose in the end, Mother, right?"

"I am afraid so."

A vast silence reigned over them, then Amanda asked suddenly, "After you married Omar, what is the wish of your life now?"

"That every man and woman must understand that they will be held responsible for their actions by a just but merciful judge – Allah. I have never been so close to Allah as I have been since becoming a Muslim. We pray in our distress and in our need and also in the fullness of our joy and in our days of abundance. I kneel in supplication asking Allah to provide Omar and me with good in this world and good in the hereafter, saving us from the penalty of the fire. I can smell the mercy and sweetness of heaven. I can feel the presence of God in my torn, sick heart. You could not believe the good fortune and the blessings that God has showered upon me. I have finally come home and found peace. The wish of my life is to win paradise.

"In our pilgrimage through life, I feel assured that the only befitting garment we can wear is submission, and upon our heads the headgear of praise, and in our hearts love of the One Supreme."

"What did the Koran teach you?"

"When I read the Koran, I knew this was not the Arab thing I was taught to think was dirty. The Koran was my life wrapped up in a few pages. I was reading my soul, and it felt good but regretful. I have found what I was looking for. There was a peace slowly spreading over my heart. It was as if a ray of eternal truth shone down with blessedness upon me.

"Never did the world, impoverished by its own lusts and greed,need the values of the Koran more than now. I believe the most important contributions that will be made by Islam in America involve racial justice and public morality. Islam offers us guidance in our personal lives as well guidelines for the improvement of human relationships in our communities."

There was a wonderful radiation in Elizabeth face when she said those words.

In the morning the garden of the villa was particularly lovely. The sun came out smiling. The wind was singing in the branches, and the sun was dancing on the leaves. Trees and grass glittered with dew, and the hibiscus and bougainvillea were just beginning to open and show their lovely pink, purple, and orange colours. In such natural beauty, Amanda saw the house a little piece of paradise. The children were running and leaping for joy, and Elizabeth was singing softly. She could see Omar after a long day of work running to Elizabeth and catching her up, swinging her around in a circle. Their laughter rang out through the house. They looked so happy together.

A few hours before Amanda's departure, Omar took her in his arms, grateful for the chance to show her that he could provide Elizabeth with a happy life and show how he loved and cherished her.

The twins were standing at the front door. Amanda knelt down and gave them each a loving hug. "I'm so proud of you. Aziza, you are such a pretty girl. You have such a great smile. Mostafa, you are such a handsome boy." Her voice broke and she stopped to wipe her eyes. "I'm so happy to have you both in my life. I'm so proud of you. You can't even imagine how much I love you. Being your grandma is one of the greatest gifts in my life."

Mostafa said, "Grandma, please come again."

"I'll definitely come again. I love this place. I promise to love you always. You are a part of me." Amanda dissolved into tears.

Amanda then held Elizabeth close to her heart. They wept in each other's arms.

"Well, you and Omar seem pretty cosy. I do like Omar; one can't help it. You know you can always call on your mama, right?"

"Of course, Mom," Elizabeth said tearfully.

With her heart beating quickly, Amanda descended the steps to the car. She waved goodbye to them as she brushed her tears away.

CHAPTER 61

When Amanda entered the president's office for the first time after her return from Egypt, she saw her husband broken, defeated, and frustrated. He was sitting at his desk with his head in his hands. He didn't welcome her by greeting phrases but rather lifted his head to her in pain and said, "The whole country fell into chaos. The uprising escalated into a full-scale national revolt. Chaos ensued, with gunfire, fights, casualties, and burned cars. There are food riots as well. The states separated themselves from the federal government and are now fighting the others to protect their own resources. The army failed to establish order. I am ruling over practically nothing."

Amanda said while sitting on a chair facing his desk, "What you are seeing, John, is the consequence of your bad foreign policy that failed to accomplish its objectives and behaved counterproductively. Force replaced diplomacy. Military solutions trampled negotiations. Counter-insurgency produced insurgents."

"Amanda, don't argue with me, please. Stand by me in such a critical situation, please," President Rosh said, pleading.

"Your bad policies had caused international catastrophes. Interference in internal affairs of nations and direct American military Involvement has not brought peace and stability to the world. Your wars in Afghanistan and Iraq expose a consistent lack of statesmanship, ineffective methods of diplomacy, and a disposition to use military force."

"My wars on terror ended with a decisive victory for the forces of freedom, democracy, and free enterprise. I defended human rights and our national security. I guaranteed political and economic freedom."

"Oh, no, John. Don't live under the illusion that you defended freedom and guarded our national security. My tour in the Middle East taught me a lot. You have but shown the ugly face of America. You demand obedience to your cruel and biased policy in the Middle East or threaten denunciation. You arrogantly announce that we will declare war on any corner of the world, which might be suspect in the war on terrorism. We breach the resolutions of the UN Security Council by adopting instead a radical approach to using our military might. You and your administration must be convicted in war crimes."

"So the only reason you're here now is to reprimand me. Please have mercy on me, Amanda. I'm tired. I actually got reprimanded by the nation several times." President Rosh had watering eyes.

"Whatever affliction may visit you is for what your own hands have earned. You have laid upon yourself calumny and manifested sin. This is an exemplary punishment from God. I have learned and seen a lot during my trip to the Middle East. The Syrians were living happily and peacefully in their beautiful homes. Now they are widely referred to as Syrian refugees. They left their homes to escape the violence and war you started in their country. More than two million Syrian refugees have fled the country to neighbouring Jordan, Lebanon, Turkey, Iraq, and Iraqi Kurdistan, while thousands also ended up in more distant countries of the Caucasus, the Persian Gulf, and North Africa.

"The number of registered Syrian refugees has reached over two hundred thousand. Also, according to the United Nations, six million people inside Syria needed help and about four million Syrians were internally displaced because of the Syrian Civil War you initiated and sponsored.

"The American administration, surrendering to the evil desires of the Christian Right Republicans, will be responsible before God for the hundreds of thousands killed in Syria, Iraq, and Afghanistan. God will charge them for the women, elderly, and children facing collateral damage and fleeing armed conflicts.

"It is clear that God is not on your horizon. If He were, you would not have spread mischief in the Arab world. Through your intelligence, troops, and the evil traitors of Islamic militia that you mobilized and supported, you were able to frighten, disperse, and displace millions of Muslim families. You created deliberate chaos under the pretext of the Arab Spring.

"I heard the cries of the bereaved mothers and suffocated children. The widowed mothers expressed their mourning with their heads held high, declaring the oneness of Allah.

"All your dreams of wiping out Islam have been dashed to the ground. The plan of occupying their world has died its own death and the heinous technology has badly failed.

"I must tell you that now none can stop America from division into fragments. Now she is fighting with herself. The white is fighting the black, and much more will be done. The crime of disgrace of the Holy Koran is not a minor one. This is the fire that has now broken out and has been puffed. You have invited the wrath of God upon us. A horrible wrath of God has befallen us."

"What I did might look politically disastrous, but it was also good for the country."

"Good for the country! You left the US economy in doldrums, affecting the global economy in a similar way. The United States is no longer a rich country. We're borrowing from the Chinese and others. We're up to sixteen trillion dollars in debt."

"You are painting a very ugly picture of where this country is heading."

"The official unemployment rate is sixteen per cent, and some believe that it is high as twenty-one per cent."

"What about Elizabeth? Have you seen her? Is she okay?" The president was trying to escape Amanda's sharp reprimanding.

"Yes, she is okay. She left your ugly world to go to a peaceful and beautiful world. She embraced Islam and married the man she truly loved. She has two cute kids, a boy and a girl. You have two Muslim grandchildren, John!"

"What! She embraced Islam and married this killer? She did everything she could to humiliate me. She is a disgrace to my family."

"Everything happens for a reason, John. God felt her suffering and reached out to her."

Tears streamed down Amanda's face. She retrieved a tissue and cleaned up her tear-stained face before continuing.

"He loves her; she loves him. That's the short version. I am happy that Liz and Omar are married. I have given them my warmest good wishes for their future together. I have had lovely days with Elizabeth I wished they never ended. With her, I could smell the mercy and sweetness of heaven. I could feel the presence of God in her sick heart.

"There, in their forgotten corner of the world, he gave her the world bit by bit. It never matters where they are. It is simply enough that they are together. They bring their own happiness with them, their own special excitement in each other.

"His love for Liz was a delight to see; he adored her and thoughther the most beautiful, brilliant, and fascinating creature in the world.

"I have been watching her, and I have realized that she didn't destroy her life. I see that Islam has brought her happiness, not pain and sorrow. I am proud of her accomplishments, and I can see that she is truly happy and at peace.

"I have seen the glow of happiness on her face. Love gave meaning to her life and directed her to goodness. Love made her awaken the light on the faces surrounding her.

"Their love went through pain and agony, but it was pure and sincere. God saw their suffering and rewarded them by reuniting them in marriage. She submitted her will to the will of God and was pleased for all that came from God. She became like a ray of sunshine."

"I doubt that he will make her happy. He is a murderer, a killer. He killed one hundred men in Kosovo, seven in the mall, and fifty brave soldiers of our troops. With a body torn with bullets, he was able to travel several nautical miles under water to a Russian submarine! I just can't understand how he survived all this."

"Can't you understand, John? Omar obeys God and observe His commands. So God made him a spirit that envelops the earth and moves in the universe to execute His commands through divine help."

CHAPTER 62

It was springtime at the farm. The hand of the Creator had planted the earth. The panorama was vast and awesomely beautiful. The sun was high in the sky, and the tender leaves were budding green. The fruit trees were a green carpet, and far away on the horizon, the sea and the sky melted together in a passion of blue.

Elizabeth saw Omar sitting on a hill watching the beautiful nature before him. She came dressed in white, glittering in the sun, dazzling his eyes. She sat beside him, caressed his hair, and kissed his face. The sun shot gold lights into her hair. Omar circled her back with his left hand and kissed her flying hair.

They kept looking at the tall trees that stood in flowering splendour, welcoming them with their gentle and soothing rustling. The valley was ablaze with bright, fragrant flowers.

Long moments of silence crept over them. The silence was finally broken by Omar's words: "The beautiful creation I see before me makes me cry with the love of Allah. Allah is beautiful and loves beauty. It is for this that the whole of Allah's creation has been designed and created according to the highest heavenly standard of splendour and order, impossible to ever be emulated by anyone. Allah says about this: 'Such is the Creation of Allah. Now show Me what is there that others besides Him have created.' Allah also says, 'He Who created seven heavens one upon another. You will not see any disparity in what the

Lord of mercy creates. Look again! And again! Your sight will return to you weak and defeated.' It is enough to realize Allah's beauty when we know that every beauty in this life is created by Him, so what of the beauty of Allah, the Shaper, the Maker?

"Allah appreciates reaching Him through reflection of His beautiful creation. This type of contemplative remembrance produces joy and happiness in the heart, strengthens the body and mind, and brings Allah's pleasure.

"We read in the Koran, 'Surely, in the creation of the heavens and the earth and the alternation of the night and the day are signs for those of understanding. Who remember Allah while standing or sitting or [lying] on their sides and give thought to the creation of the heavens and the earth, [saying], "Our Lord, You did not create this aimlessly; glory be to Thee. Guard us against the chastisement of the Fire."'

Omar's words touched Elizabeth's heart. They inspired her to contemplate Allah's mercy on her. Despair permeated her heart but Allah the Most Merciful, the Most Gracious, showered her with his mercy and guided her to Islam. Islam taught her that Allah is full of love and kindness to His creation. Islam taught her that Allah is more merciful towards His servants than their own mothers are. How can it be otherwise when some of His glorious names and attributes include the Acceptor of Repentance; the Loving, the Bestower, the Most Generous, the Most Gracious, the Most Merciful?

Elizabeth whispered a verse from the Koran: "Limitless is your Lord in His mercy."

"Yes, darling," Omar muttered. "This limitless mercy is also emphasized when Allah said, 'O son of Adam, were you to come to Me with sins nearly as great as the earth and were you then to face Me, ascribing no partner to Me, I would bring you forgiveness nearly as great as the earth.'"

Omar continued: "Allah tells man of the greatness of His forgiveness and mercy so that no one would despair due to the amount of   sins he may have committed. Allah says: 'O My servants who have transgressed against their own souls, despair not of the mercy of Allah. Indeed, Allah forgives all sins. Truly, He is Most Forgiving, Most Merciful.'"

Omar and Elizabeth sank into a contemplative silence, absorbed in the beauty of the valley stretched before them. Omar broke the silence and murmured a verse from the Koran: 'Behold! In the creation of the heavens and earth; in the alternation of the night and the day; in the sailing of the ships through the ocean for the profit of mankind; in the rain which Allah sends down from the skies, and the life which He gives therewith to an earth that is dead; in the beasts of all kinds that He scatters through the earth; in the change of the winds, and the clouds compelled between heaven and earth – here indeed are Signs for a people that are wise.'

Omar continued, "This verse from the Koran stands out like a hill in a landscape, enhancing the beauty of our view. Allah is One, and among His wondrous Signs is the unity of design in the widest diversity of nature. Everything around and within us points to Allah. Glory be to Allah, in whose hand is the dominion of everything, and unto whom we shall be returned. Praise be to Allah, unto Whom belongs whatsoever is in the heavens and whatsoever is on the earth. His is the praise in the Hereafter, and He is the Wise, the Aware."

Elizabeth saw a trace of tears in Omar's eyes. She took his hand in hers and whispered, "Praise belongs to Allah, who guided us unto this; had Allah not guided us, we had surely never been guided."

"Yes, darling. Allah gives light according to His will and wisdom. The prophet is only a messenger. It is not required of him to set people on the right path, but Allah sets on the right path whom he pleases."

Elizabeth replied with a verse from the Koran: "Whoever Allah guides none can misguide, and whoever He allows to fall astray, none can guide them aright."

Omar responded with another verse from the Koran: "Whosoever is guided is only guided to his own gain, and whosoever goes astray, it is only to his own loss. No soul laden bears the load of another."

"I want to feel peace of mind, tranquility, a sense of well-being, and a relaxed disposition. I want to live a happy life under the realm of Islam," Elizabeth said hopefully.

"Islam teaches that true happiness can only be obtained by living a life full of Allah-consciousness and being satisfied with what He has given us. Happiness is not restricted to material prosperity. The material aspect is merely a means but not an end in itself. Happiness depends totally on the degree of growth and development attained by the soul, both in this world and the eternal hereafter.

"Allah says, 'Whoever does good whether male or female and he is a believer, We will most certainly make him live a happy life, and We will most certainly give them their reward for the best of what they did.'"

"Can you summarize happiness in just a few words?" she said with a laugh, knowing that her question was difficult to answer.

"Live modestly. Love generously. Care deeply. Speak kindly," Omar said simply.

"I remember when we met at the park years ago and you said that Muslims consider themselves free when they live according to the divine law of the Koran."

"People in the modern world consider freedom to be the ability to satisfy all of their desires without control. A direct and clear relationship with Allah, as well as the sense of purpose and belonging that one feels as a Muslim, frees a person from the many worries of everyday life. The Islamic way of life is pure and wholesome. It builds self-discipline and self-control through regular prayer and fasting, and it frees human beings from superstition and all sorts of racial, ethnic, and national prejudices. By accepting to live a conscious life with Allah and realizing that the only thing that distinguishes people in the sight of Allah is their consciousness of Him, a person's true human dignity and freedom are realized."

Elizabeth pressed Omar's hand to her bosom and said, "I thank Allah for all the blessings He showered me with. I long for an eternal life in the Gardens of Bliss. Allah will admit those who believe and work righteous deeds to the gardens beneath which rivers flow. They shall be adorned therein with bracelets of gold and pearls, and their garments there will be of silk."

"The realms of paradise is the prerogative of Allah alone; and the two absolutely inseparable pre-conditions the Lord has conveyed in His message for one's entry into the Eternal Gardens of Paradise are

belief and righteous good deeds in accordance with the Guidance of the Lord, while those who reject Allah will enjoy this world and eat as cattle eat, and the fire will be their abode." Omar went on to say.

"I bear witness that there is none worthy of worship but Allah alone, and I bear witness that Muhammad is His slave-servant and the seal of His messengers," Elizabeth said, confirming the Islamic creed.

Omar drew Elizabeth close to his heart and said, "Elizabeth, Allah stated in the Koran: 'Say: My Lord pays attention to you only because of your invocation to Him.' Let's invoke Allah.'" Omar raised his hands up to the sky; Elizabeth raised her hands too.

Omar supplicated: "Our Lord we have heard the call of Muhammad calling to Faith, and we have believed. Our Lord forgives us our sins and remits from us our evil deeds, and makes us die in the state of Islam. Lord of the Throne, take us not to task if we forget or make a mistake. Our Lord, charge us not with a load such as you did lay upon those before us. Our Lord helps us do what pleases you and safeguard us against what causes your wrath. Our Lord, do not burden us beyond what we have the strength to bear. And pardon us, and forgive us, and have mercy on us; you are our protector. Ameen."

Elizabeth repeated after him: "Ameen."